FRONTIERS OF FIRE

The Paraguayan War Series Book I

Borba de Souza

Table of Contents

Chapter I

1864, Christmas Day.

Luis Caetano Gomes de Carvalho became a lieutenant days before and needed just one more week serving in the Fort of Coimbra to justify his new rank. Then, after the New Year, he would return to the Paraíba Valley to assume a position in the National Guard.

Only eight days separated him from the end of a two-year period with the imperial army in distant Mato Grosso.

Luis crossed the fort's backyard. The breeze hit his olive skin. His imagination flowed, visualizing a welcome back party attended by the most influential names in the region. These distinguished gentlemen, of course, would bring their unmarried daughters.

At least, that's what the lieutenant believed.

Months later, his optimistic plans for December 1864 became a distant memory. Months later, he asked himself how he did not realize that the visit of a high-ranking officer signaled that instead of waltzes and champagne, he would dance to the sound of cannons, the taste of agony, and the sight of splitting bones.

With the confidence of those who do not know their own destiny, on the afternoon of December 25 Luis planned his trip back to São Paulo.

There were no land connections. The way home was through the Paraná river, toward the Atlantic, and from there to Santos. To brighten his sailing days, Luis negotiated to buy two aguardiente bottles from Gaspar, a Guarani smuggler who visited the fort three or four times a year.

The lieutenant's muscular body shape and wavy, short black hair contrasted with the slender merchant. Gaspar had a discreet posture, light steps and a bland voice. Luis, however, occupied twice the necessary space as he walked—not because of his height, for he was not lanky, but because of his wide legs and broad shoulders.

"I offer a thousand réis for the two bottles," the lieutenant said, already holding one flask of the elixir, "it's my last week here, so I deserve a discount."

The Guarani did not concede. "If it is your last week, you should pay more since I lose a client. Let's settle for halfway, twelve hundred réis. It is less than what I charge the sergeants and half of what officers pay me."

"Fine then. I only have eight hundred here. I give you that now and the next time you ask for Simas to pay you the rest. He owes me."

Gaspar agreed.

It amused Luis that the smuggler set prices according to rank. He paid Gaspar and put the bottles in his bag. Seconds later, two superiors approached, coming from a mass at the fort's chapel, and almost saw the alcohol flasks. They were his immediate superior, Captain Benedito De Faria, and Colonel Portocarrero, the military district commander.

"Ensign Gomes!" called Captain De Faria. The captain was shorter than Luis, but with an equally powerful shape. Even officers performed physical work in the fort because of its limited staff. The good access to meat guaranteed that after a few months, they developed the muscles of a bricklayer.

"Lieutenant, sir." Luis dared to correct him

"Well remembered, Second Lieutenant Gomes." Showing no embarrassment after the mistake, Benedito De Faria continued, "The Colonel and I want to ask you something."

Luis's eyes stopped on Colonel Portocarrero.

"Congratulations on the promotion, Lieutenant," the Colonel said. "Although the captain already approved your transfer, we want to know about the possibility of postponing your departure by a week or two, considering the new orders."

Luis Caetano had heard the same request from the captain. "Sir, I already purchased my ticket to Buenos Aires and Santos. If the military district reimburses me, I can stay two weeks more."

The lieutenant knew this was impossible, so he expected Portocarrero's rejection. The colonel thought for a second. "Given the new orders, it may be possible." Portocarrero's first words made Luis widen his eyes. "For now, your departure is still valid. Tomorrow I will confirm the refund and your service extension for another fortnight."

"Sir, what are these new orders?" Luis asked.

Benedito De Faria raised his eyebrows. "I believe the Colonel has a busy agenda," the captain said, "but I can explain everything to you. Come to my office in thirty minutes."

With a journey to plan, Luis spent the time selling what was too heavy to carry during his trip back home. He wondered if the other soldiers knew what the new orders were. *It must be something important*, he thought, *otherwise why would a colonel ask a lieutenant to stay a few weeks more?*

After thirty minutes, Luis entered the Captain's office. "Ensign Gomes, I believe you already know about the imprisonment of the steamboat Marquês de Olinda last month," the captain said.

"I am a lieutenant, not an ensign, sir," Luis said. "The boat confiscated by the Paraguayans in Asunción? I heard rumors of big-name politicians taken as hostages. Is it true?"

4

"Yes, the provincial president." The captain took a deep breath before continuing. "The Guaranis imprisoned him and all other passengers, cargo, and the money on board."

"They attacked a civilian ship?" Luis clenched his teeth. "I just don't call these people pirates because they have no sea."

The captain grinned.

"But how is this related to the fort, sir?" the lieutenant asked. "The capture of the Marquês de Olinda happened far from here."

"Perhaps nothing and the Guaranis will regain their common sense, return the steamboat and release the prisoners, calling it an inspection error." Sitting and holding his chin with flat hands, Benedito de Faria looked at the room ceiling for a few seconds. "But perhaps their *Mariscal* has lost his head, and the capture of the ship is the prelude to war. In this case, we are Mato Grosso's first defensive line."

Luis Caetano, suspicious of the captain's wrinkled forehead and deep gaze, asked, "So are the new orders to prepare for war?"

"War?" The captain smirked, shaking his head to the left and right. "With so many broken cannons, if we work hard, we can prepare the fort for a few hours of battle. What I need from you is to leave trivialities behind and spend all your time handing over the tasks to your substitute, Ensign Coelho."

The lieutenant clicked his boots, saluted the captain, and left the room.

However, the next morning, Luis woke up in a grim mood because he needed to teach Ensign Coelho.

Antônio Coelho came from Santos, from a family with possessions, like many other army officers. Despite coming from similar conditions and from the same state as Luis Caetano, they could not be more different.

While the lieutenant loved games and gambled with even the lowest soldiers, Antonio was quiet. Luis walked with an imposing gait and resolute steps, keeping his legs separated as if his knees hated each other. Coelho dragged his feet on the floor as a person too tired to march. The lieutenant had a straightforward demeanor and spartan taste that allowed him to get along with privates. Coelho behaved with the pride of a colonel but was not even a lieutenant.

Every morning after breakfast, Luis Caetano's first task was to lead a group of horsemen to the hilltop behind the fort. One of them was a Kadiwéu called Nopitena. From a nearby tribe, he had served as Luis's most trusted soldier since the Lieutenant's arrival.

Nopitena was one of many Kadiweus in the army. Their alliance with the Brazilians dated back to the early 19th century. At that time, the natives, under the command of a legendary chief called Nawilo, terrorized Paraguayans who dared to invade Brazilian land. For his services, Niwalo became a general of the National Guard. The cooperation between the Empire and the Indians benefited both since in Paraguay lived the Guaranis, enemies of the Kadiweus since the story of the tribes began to be told from generation to generation.

Coelho rolled his eyes when he realized that his first subordinate was a native, and his main morning duty was to climb a hill to watch the river. A river where, for years, only smugglers and fishermen sailed.

"Nopitena, here is Ensign Antônio Coelho. From next year on, he will inherit my post and be your superior officer," Luis informed the Indian.

Shorter than Luis, the Kadiweu had no beard or mustache but a bowl-shaped haircut. His torso and shoulders were marked by the geometric, white-ink tattoos typical of his tribe. Some native boys received it during their passage rites. Nopitena saluted Coelho, who sweated profusely and had reddened skin because of the December's glaring sun.

"Today, you and the other horsemen patrol the hill alone," the Lieutenant said to Nopitena, "because I have to train this boy before the sun melts him down."

The new junior officer was the only one not amused by the comment. After the laughs faded, Luis and Coelho turned their backs and walked toward the north wall, where the ensign would learn about the Fort's defense batteries.

From the top of the saddle, Nopitena asked what to do if they found any suspicious vessel on the horizon.

"Two years watching, and we found nothing," replied the Lieutenant. "If you see something strange, put a hand on your forehead. Maybe it is fever."

Chapter II

Nopitena and two other natives left the fort via the northern tip. They rode two kilometers on a track skirting the hill, culminating in a yellow Ipê tree. Below its golden blossoms, they tied the horses and marched to the hilltop. A narrow path led them to the top, paved with stones and zigzagging among the trees, thorns, and snake nests. The soldiers, accustomed to the smell of manure and sweat, appreciated the fragrance of the Jenipapo flowers. The path had existed for decades since colonial times. Generations of white officers and Kadiweu soldiers made the same scouting routine to guard the Brazilian border against hostiles.

The morning sun rose over the horizon while the three Kadiweus climbed the steep three-hundred yards ramp in less than half an hour.

Luis Caetano always led the patrol, except that day. His task comprised of watching for any unusual movement on the border with Paraguay. Nopitena spent the first minutes at the hill looking to the opposite way, toward his village, less than a league to the north.

He had arrived at the fort as a soldier, being promoted a couple of years later to anspeçada, an imperial army rank equivalent to a lance corporal. He continued to visit his village on his free days. Thanks to his good relationship with Lieutenant Luis, the Kadiweu took freshly slaughtered meat from the fort each time he visited his tribe. His arrival was synonymous with banquets, especially for Natena, a childhood friend, and Nialigi, a neighbor for whom he felt desires beyond friendship.

The sunshine illuminated the treetops and reflected on the waters of the Paraná River. From the hilltop, the Kadiweu could even see the inhabitants of nearby settlements fishing in their chatas, canoes with a flat bottom commonly used in the region.

He glanced to his village for a moment until he recalled that his task was to observe the Paraguayan side and watch the border. Nopitena turned his neck and saw a gentle cloud of smoke downstream, some two leagues distant, just beyond the river bend. Nobody could notice the smoke from the ground level, but from the hilltop, he saw it, and more. Below the dark cloud, a flotilla of several steamboats and two schooners.

Smugglers or fishermen did not own boats like these, nor did they sail in flotilla formation. Either it was the long-awaited new provincial president of Mato Grosso or something more sinister.

***

"Ensign, here on the right we keep food supplies," Luis, inside the storehouse with his young replacement, pointed to bags of salt, flour, and coffee, "and on the left is the livestock."

Coelho approached a relatively small water tank in the middle of the warehouse. "Isn't this reservoir too small to store water for so many people?" asked the apprentice.

Luis chuckled so hard that the boy blushed.

"Water, Ensign? Look to your right. Why would we store more water when we are at a riverside? Don't be a dimwit."

The three Kadiwéus arrived from the hilltop, sweating, and rushing to leave their horses and report the situation. Still chuckling from Coelho's naiveness, Luis called Nopitena. "Anspeçada, what is the Paraguay River made of? The boy here is afraid of dying of thirst."

"Of water, sir." The Kadiwéu replied. "But I believe something strange is sailing on it."

Luis frowned. This last phrase was not part of the mockery. The lieutenant asked the Indian to elaborate, and the Kadiweu explained what he saw.

"Are you sure?" asked Luis after listening to the report. "Weren't they traders or the usual fishermen? If I warn the captain that we saw an enemy fleet, but we attack a group of peasants, my head will hang on the gallows."

"They were not peasants, chief, because no fishermen have ships of that size. But they could be that governor everyone is telling will visit us."

"It may be." Luis relaxed his shoulders. "I hope it is. I don't need a Guarani invasion right in my last week here. Come with me. We need to inform this to the Captain."

***

Close to ten in the morning, the lieutenant and the Kadiweu approached the Captain's office.

Like most fortresses, the walls and roof were painted white, but the doorframes and windows were turquoise blue. Inside the room, two tables, each with one armchair behind— one for the captain, the other for visiting authorities, like Portocarrero. Shelves with rolled-up books and maps broke the monotony of the undecorated walls. On the side, a door gave access to the captain's quarters.
The office smelled faintly of burnt oil, a result of the Captain's habit of working after sunset by the lamplight.

Both De Faria and Portocarrero worked on their desks, focused on paperwork. Luis thought the Colonel would question why he did not accompany the Indians to the hilltop, even though he was only following the Captain's orders to put everything aside to teach Ensign Coelho.

Good for him that Portocarrero had a friendly demeanor when compared to the other high-ranking officers. Fruit of the colonel's origin, in the northern state of Pernambuco. It contrasted with the combative soul of the southern officers Luis met at the military academy.

"Sir, permission to report!" Luis entered the room. The Colonel, busy reading a letter, didn't answer, but the captain signaled for the lieutenant to proceed.

"This morning, the Anspeçada Nopitena sighted a force of steamboats and a pair of schooners downstream."

The remark attracted Portocarrero's attention. "Steamboats?" the colonel asked. "Were you there to assess their types?"

Luis got ready to answer that he wasn't, but Captain Benedito de Faria intervened, "Sir, the lieutenant was absent under my orders. He handed over this task to his men so he could train his substitute."

Portocarrero stared at the captain but appeared to accept the explanation.

"Soldier, how many boats, and how big they were?" The colonel asked the tattooed Kadiweu.

It was the first time a high-ranking officer had talked to Nopitena. Even the captain rarely spoke to him. His eyes showed confusion about how to address the Colonel. He ended using the pronoun learned for the visit of the provincial president.

"Your Excellency, they were eight steamships, two schooners, and a few more flat canoes."

"I'm not a general, soldier," said Portocarrero. "Therefore, I'm no excellency. You can call me sir. Did you see their flags? Can you describe their shape?"

It was impossible to see any flag from such an enormous distance, but Nopitena's description of one ship alerted Captain De Faria. "Sir, I suspect this vessel is the Marquês de Olinda. Perhaps the Paraguayans have recovered their common sense and released the ship and passengers."

Portocarrero walked around the room. The others remained quiet, waiting for his judgment.
"Either that, or they are using it for a surprise attack." The colonel broke the silence. "As I recall, the entourage sailing with the Marquês de Olinda was just one frigate, not an entire fleet."

The colonel and the captain agreed that a patrol should climb the hill again to collect fresh observations. This time, Luis would lead them. Of everyone in the room, the colonel had the most obscure countenance, even though the thick beard conveyed the tranquility of the wise. If it was an invasion, not only were his men at risk, but also his wife and children, who were at the fort with him. A family that was not expecting a battle.

Luis and Nopitena left the commanding room to pick their horses, leaving only Captain De Faria and the Colonel in the place.

"This Lieutenant is an unusual fellow, captain. Why does he walk like that?" asked Portocarrero, looking toward the courtyard and lighting a pipe.

"He told me once that it is good for the balls, and every man should walk like that," answered De Faria.

"Good for the balls?" The Colonel chuckled, "a peculiar fellow indeed!"

***

Before eleven in the morning, Luis saddled his horse and left with Nopitena and the other two Indians. Ensign Coelho joined them to practice the morning scouting at the hilltop. Clouds formed in the sky, providing some shadow from the scorching heat.

They rode through a narrow and irregular path on the hill skirts. Coelho followed, sweating profusely while trying to keep the group's pace. The ensign lagged even behind the Indians. Halfway, Luis provoked the Ensign's pride. "Having some trouble there, cadet? When we return to the fort, Nopitena will teach you how to horse-ride."

Coelho's face just didn't redden in anger because the sun had already left his skin red enough.

"And since when can Guarani Indians ride better than we...civilized fellows?" said the breathless Coelho.

Nopitena stared with contempt.

The Kadiweu Indians, also called Guaicurus, like him, were no Guaranis. They did not understand the Guarani language. They wanted no contact with the rival tribe that often-invaded Kadiweu territory from time to time to kidnap and enslave them. This led men like Nopitena to enlist in the Brazilian army and take up mounted patrol posts. For the Kadiweus, that killed two birds with one stone: the Brazilian army paid them, and they could protect their own villages. The double incentive stimulated young Kadiweus to perfect their horse-riding skills to a level comparable to trained horsemen of the best cavalries.

"Guaranies can't ride," Nopitena replied, "But there are none of them here. Maybe the heat made the ensign delirious." The laugh burst from Luis and the other troopers confirmed that Nopitena won the mockery dispute.

They tied the horses under the Ipê tree and climbed the stony path to the hilltop. Clouds covered the sky.

"The clouds are getting lower and full of rain. Soon it will be impossible to see the boats." Nopitena's words had the experience of a person born and raised in the region. "We should go faster."

"Are we taking orders from the Indian now?" Coelho said.

Luis intervened, "Ensign, walk faster and speak less, and this is an order."

When they reached the cliff, Nopitena's prediction became a reality. In the same place where they saw boats hours earlier, a cloud dissolved in torrential rain. Droplets that quickly became bullet-sized drops soaked the land, raising a pleasant smell of wet grass. The river bend was almost invisible under the veil of the storm.

***

The rainstorm persisted while they returned, completely wet, to the fort. Luis tried to clean his boots before entering the captain's office, but he still left muddy footprints on the way. During his report to De Faria and Portocarrero, he suggested putting the group on standby and going up again if the weather cleared.

Deep down, the lieutenant felt guilty for leaving Nopitena alone with the men that morning. If he was there, he could identify whether the ships belonged to the Brazilian imperial armada or to Paraguayans. Officers learn these things. By leaving the morning patrol aside to teach the pedantic Coelho, he may have risked the fort where he lived for years. He was, however, only acting on the captain's orders. *But why do I still feel guilty?* Luis wondered while waiting for the captain's decision.

"Well then, keep the guard, lieutenant," the captain agreed. "If the weather clears before dark, go up again.

Regardless of what happens, report to the officers' meeting at 19:00."

Luis informed Coelho that Lieutenant Melo would teach him about the southern wall defense protocols in the afternoon. It was convenient for the ensign to learn it that day, given the possibility of an attack, but it was also satisfying for Luis and Nopitena to get rid of his non-sense.

The lieutenant and the anspeçada stood at the northern gate. Both looked to the sky, hoping for clear weather. If the clouds dissolved and they saw the boats again, Luis could discover what visit would mark his last week: a provincial president or a Paraguayan invasion.

Luis glanced at the firmament and remembered his gambling and brandy nights of the past two years. He recalled he still needed to pay the Kadiweu for a lost bet. "Nopitena, how much I owe you?"

The Indian raised his eyebrows. "For the race bet? Four hundred réis."

It was not much for a lieutenant salary, but enough to afford a soldier's night of revelry. "I'll pay you tomorrow."

Night fell at nineteen o'clock, heralded by the birds flocking back to their trees and by the cicadas screeching to a crescendo with the moon's rise. Luis dismissed Nopitena and headed to the officer's meeting. Among the present were Colonel Portocarrero, Captain Benedito de Faria, Lieutenant

Melo, Lieutenant Balduino—commander of the Anhambaí ship—and the novice Ensign Coelho.

With a dry tone of voice, Luis began his report. "Sir, the clouds did not leave but went even lower, making it impossible to see anything."

Even though Portocarrero had the highest ranking in the room, he attended the meeting only with his ears. Captain De Faria, standing beside the Colonel, addressed the soldiers and, with a wooden pen, pointed out places on a map—a plan of the fort's premises.

"I want two shifts on the night watch, Melo," the captain addressed the officer—also known as Melo *Bravo* because of the ferocity in training his soldiers. "Balduino, cover us by the river using the Anhambaí ship. Any movement upstream, alert us with two rifle shots." After distributing the orders, the captain turned to the Colonel, "Sir, anything you want to add?"

Portocarrero stood up and cracked his neck. His eyes examined the face of each officer in the room. "To those who will watch over us tonight, thank you, and may God protect you. To the others, have a restful night. Tomorrow we will either celebrate a dignitary, or we will enjoy the opportunity to defend our land. Either way, it will be a significant day."

Chapter III

Before the bugler played the reveille call, Luis Caetano woke up and left the room he shared with Melo Bravo. He washed his face using a water pitcher and left to the courtyard. Except for the footsteps of the sentinels and the chirps of the Maritacas, it was a silent dawn.

The silence relieved the lieutenant. If what Nopitena saw was an invading squadron, by daybreak, they would already be in battle preparations. Perhaps it was only the arriving entourage of the provincial president coming one month late. If that case, he could expect a banquet and a goodbye in high style. In two years of service, this would be the first event worth bragging to his half-sister, Joana, and his father, Dom Caetano, when he returns to the 3-Estados farm.

While Luis pondered about life after the Coimbra fort, Nopitena approached.

"Good morning, chief. I think there will be no fight postponing your departure."

Luis chuckled. "Yeah, the closest thing to a combat here will be you slapping Coelho for all the bravado he says."

Nopitena recalled the stupidities said by the ensign the day before, "He is far from ideal, sir."

"Far from ideal? No need to measure words, Nopitena. He is a prick, a rascal."

Nopitena grinned at the unprecedented insults against Coelho.

"But today, he is not coming with us," Luis said. "He will spend the day with Melo Bravo, who should give him a whip if he misbehaves."

Both walked to the stable to saddle the horses and leave for the hilltop morning patrol.

While preparing the animals, one watchman signaled to open the gates, and an Indian-looking boy entered the fort.

"Nopitena, is it one of yours?"

"No chief, he looks like a Guarani."

The guards led the visitor to Luis, as he was the nearest officer. The boy had the same bowl-shaped haircut as Nopitena but was younger and skinnier—the type usually chosen as couriers. Mud and dirt covered his clothes, hiding its colors. Everything in him was brownish, including his teeth and barefoot feet.

"What are you doing here?" Luis asked him.

"I came to deliver a message to the fort commander." The boy's accent denounced a recently learned Portuguese.

He gave Luis a folded, sealed paper, who didn't open it but told Nopitena to feed the horses while he went to the Captain's office.

In the office, Captain De Faria organized morning routines with Colonel Portocarrero and Lieutenant Simas Bitencourt when Luis arrived, carrying the paper. The same morning tranquility that made Luis rule out the chance of enemy invasion also gave the captain a calm semblance. "I believe it is an invitation from the new provincial president to celebrate his arrival." De Faria took the message and handed it to Portocarrero. turned to the colonel, "as you, sir, have the highest rank here, I understand that a message to the commander is a message to you."

Portocarrero unfolded the paper.

The note's handwriting was familiar, but he could not remember from where. While reading it, the colonel's expressionless face told nothing and contrasted with the lieutenant and captain's expectation of good news.

After reading everything, the Colonel took a deep breath, walked closer to the wall, and, turning his sight at the tiny window facing the river, sighed.

"Barrios..."

"Sir?" asked Benedito de Faria, already certain that the message was not so positive.

Ensign Coelho and Lieutenant Melo arrived. "Sir, we lined the soldiers in the patio for the morning inspection." Melo clicked his boots and saluted the Colonel.

"Good that you arrived, Melo," Portocarrero said. "Captain, are all the officers in this room?"

"Yes, except for Lieutenant Balduíno, who is on the Anhambaí."

Portocarrero gave the note to the captain and asked him to read it aloud to all present:

Onboard the Paraguayan steamer Igurey - December 27,
1864

The commanding colonel of the operational division in Alto Paraguay,

By virtue of expressing orders from his Government, we claim the possession of this fortress. As a proof of moderation and humanity, we invite you to surrender within one hour. Otherwise, and once the deadline is expired, we will take it by force, leaving the garrison subject to the laws of war -

Waiting for your prompt reply.

Colonel of the operational division in Alto Paraguay, Vicente Barrios. To the Lord Commander of Coimbra.

After the captain read the letter, each man in the room looked concerned with the inverse proportion of the rank. The colonel, leaning against the wall and lighting a pipe, was the most serene. On the other side, Ensign Coelho raised his hands to head, turning pale.

"Is the messenger who brought this note still here?" Portocarrero asked, breaking the silence that flooded the room.

"Yes, sir. I asked the guards to escort the lad to the courtyard and give him something to eat," replied Luis Caetano.

"Good. Captain, please take a pen and a paper."

De Faria moved to his desk, sat on his brown leather chair, took his pen, and dipped it in the inkwell. The Captain then nodded, signaling to the Colonel that he was ready to write the answer to the subpoena they received.

Military District of Baixo Paraguay, in the Fort of Coimbra, 27 of December 1864.

The undersigned Lieutenant-Colonel of this Military District, responding to the note sent by Your Excellency Mr. Colonel Vicente Barrios, commander of the Division in operations in the Alto Paraguay,

It is my honor to declare that according to the regulation and orders that govern the Brazilian Army, except by superior order (to whom I re-transmit the received note), just for the luck and honor of weapons, you may achieve so. I assert to you, however, that the same feelings of moderation and humanity that nourish your excellency also nourish me.

I look forward to the deliberations of your excellency. May God guide you. - Hermenegildo de Albuquerque Portocarrero, Lieutenant-Colonel.

"Lieutenant Melo, prepare the garrison of the southern wall. I expect the attack to come from there." the Colonel said. It made sense that the Paraguayans would attack from the south. The neighboring hill protected the west, while an attack from the north or east side would only be possible if the ships forced the passage through the river, exposing themselves to the Brazilian cannons.

Portocarrero then ordered Ensign Coelho to take the answer to the messenger, which he reluctantly obeyed, and turned to Luis.

"Lieutenant Gomes, climb the hilltop with your Indians and return before noon with information on the enemy's numbers and condition. Lieutenant Simas, select two men, go to the pier and take a barge with good sails. Paddle to the Anhambaí ship and communicate the situation to Lieutenant Balduíno."

"And what orders should I pass on to Balduíno, sir?" asked Simas.

"Tell him to make available three men with brawny arms to row you to Corumbá to warn the town that we are under attack. Also, instruct Balduíno to get the cannons ready and fire first on these vagabonds."

The last person in the colonel's company was Captain De Faria. "Sir, what reaction should we expect from the Paraguayans when they receive your answer?"

"If Lieutenant Balduino and the Anhambai do as I say, they will know that we rejected the subpoena before the messenger delivers them the note." Portocarrero had a good-natured half-smile, contrasting with the severity of the situation. "My answer is just for Barrios to know who he's dealing with."

"Vicente Barrios, the Paraguayan Colonel? Does he know you?"

"We are old acquaintances, Captain."

***

The Paraguayan colonel strolled in the upper deck of the steamship Paraguarí while reading a piece of paper. A man near his forties, with a dense black beard. His bicorn hat, like those worn by admirals, covered his semi-bald head. A silver-handled saber slung from his waistband, almost touching the ground. The clatter of his tall black leather boots resonated in the wooden floor.

A dozen officers watched Vicente Barrios read the note silently with the Brazilians' answer for their subpoena.

After a minute, he folded the paper and shook his head. The name of Colonel Hermenegildo de Albuquerque Portocarrero, Brazilian commander of the military district of the lower Paraguay, was familiar to him.

They had met twelve years earlier. At that time, the enemy was the Argentinian dictator Rosas. Paraguayans and Brazilians were allies. The empire sent the colonel and a group of officers to Asuncion, together with weapons and ammunition, to teach locals how to build an army. One student was Carlos López, the father of dictator Solano López. Another apprentice was Vicente Barrios himself. Both referred to Portocarrero as *mi maestro*.

On that December morning, the Paraguayan command already knew that the Brazilians refused to surrender. Before Portocarrero's reply arrived, the cannons from the Anhambaí gave the answer by firing at the Paraguayan flotilla.

Surrounded by his officers, Vicente Barrios clenched his fists at the realization that his former *maestro* commanded the fort. Even with twenty soldiers for each Brazilian, the discovery posed a problem for the Paraguayans. Inside Coimbra, the once brilliant professor became a formidable foe.

During the previous two years, Paraguayans sent spies disguised as farmers and merchants to map the fortress and its officers. He heard no mention of Portocarrero. One of these spies was Lieutenant André Herreras, now part of the invading force.

"Lieutenant Herreras, your reports mention a captain commanding the fort, correct?" Barrios asked.

"Affirmative, sir. Captain Benedito de Faria. "

Still furious, Barrios thought twice before blaming the lieutenant. "Something has changed then, Herreras. The officer that answered my subpoena has a rank higher than captain and the skills of a general."

The lieutenant, confused by the announcement, tried to defend himself, but the colonel signaled with his hand that it was unnecessary. "How many fort defenders you reckoned on your last mission?"

Herreras recovered from his memory the last time he was spying on Coimbra. He had met Captain De Faria before when disguised as a farmer selling food for the fort. "Sir, by their livestock orders, they have no more than 200 men."

"With an officer like Portocarrero in the place, it is possible that they have more men than that."

"Do we proceed with the attack, Colonel?" asked one lieutenant on the deck, until then merely a listener to the entire conversation.

"Yes. If I hesitate, the *Mariscal* puts me in front of a firing squad. Start the siege with artillery and prepare to land Luiz Gonzales' infantry."

Chapter IV

Unlike the previous day, that 27th had clear skies. From the hilltop, one could see several leagues downstream.

Nopitena and Luis arrived on time to witness Lieutenant Balduíno firing his ship's cannons against the Paraguayan squadron. The first ball hit the water. The Brazilian gunboat corrected its angle, and the second projectile hit the bow of a Guarani schooner.

Between shots, Lieutenant Balduíno noticed that the enemy vessels were almost empty, and they were disembarking at the river's edge, preparing to attack the fort. When the Anhambaí began to return, Paraguayan artillery nearly hit the ship's hull.

During the river confrontation of the Brazilian gunboat and the Guarani cannons, Luis was sketching in the notebook he carried in his bag. He drew enemy artillery pieces and made calculations about the invading battalions, keeping track ofhow many men he could see and the type of artillery used

After a few minutes of observation, they returned to the fort faster than any patrol had done over the last two years. On the way back, Nopitena asked the single question disturbing everyone's mind.

"Chief, how long do you think the fort can resist?"

Luis Caetano concentrated on rushing his horse, thought for a second. "As long as we have ammunition, food, or water, whichever ends first."

They kept silent. The only noises were the snorts and hooves of the horses galloping through the road back to the fort. But before they arrived at the northern gate, Nopitena spotted two boys from his tribe. Two little ones, barely twelve years old. They often came in the morning to bring fodder for the army's horses, and in return, they got fresh meat or coins to use in Corumbá.

"Chief, I need to warn these two to leave before the Guaranis arrive."

Luis nodded. "Do it fast, Anspeçada."

Nopitena turned his horse and trotted the road toward the boys. He approached them in Kadiwéu language, telling them to leave because the Guaranis were near. The boys were familiar with the stories about these people, enemies who invaded the Guaicuru villages to enslave the innocent.

Before the kids ran away, Nopitena remembered the lieutenant's words about lacking water during a siege. The first to suffer are animals because humans have their canteens and water jugs. Nopitena got off his mount and handed the horse over to the boys, telling them to take it to their village.

The soldier ran the rest of the way on foot. Almost at the gate, the noises of cannon fire roared between the two armies.

The siege began, and there was no one to open the northern gate to Nopitena.

The Indian pondered what terrorized him more. To be captured by the Guaranis, or his lieutenant to think he was a deserter, a coward?

***

Luis entered the fort and left his horse at the stable. He hurried to the captain's office, gasping for air after running through the courtyard.

But the office was empty. A janitor told him the captain went to the southern wall.

The Lieutenant rushed to the place, guarded by Lieutenant Melo and his men. The air turned gray with smoke from battery cannons blasting against the Paraguayans. The captain and the colonel were close to the artillerymen, adjusting the aim of a 24-pounder cannon. Meters from there, on the very top of the wall, Lieutenant Melo distributed fierce orders to the soldiers.

"Sir, permission to report observations from the hilltop!"

The captain nodded, and Luis handed over his sketches with the Paraguayan positions.

"Good job, Lieutenant Gomes." Portocarrero grabbed the drawings. "But time is short. Make a verbal report."

"Sir, the enemy has around three thousand men, camping between one and two leagues, with sets of mobile artillery."

Portocarrero turned to De Faria. "How many men do we have, Captain?"

"One hundred fifty-five, sir, of which 115 are soldiers, and the rest are Indians, prisoners, or civilians."

Then the Colonel turned back to Luis. "How many vessels did you see Lieutenant?"

"Eight steamships, some flat canoes and two schooners, including one hit by the Anhambaí," said Luis.

Lieutenant Melo left the wall to listen to Luis' report and heard that the Anhambaí hit a Paraguayan schooner.

"No chance my men will dispatch less Guayos than Balduino!" Melo turned to his men at the wall, and living up to the nickname of Bravo, shouted:

"Your *mulambos*, the Guayos sent only thirty men to each one of you! Lucky us, unlucky them! I will lash any soldier that is not stinking of gunpowder!"

Luis, with his rifle in hand, watched the scene. Melo Bravo's insults inflamed the soldiers. *Damn, even I want to go to the wall to fight at his side.* Luis thought. He asked for the captain's permission to assist in the defense with his Kadiweu soldiers.

The captain nodded. Luis gathered all his men, except one: Nopitena.

He didn't want to imagine that his most loyal soldier, after years of service, fled at the first sign of battle. The lieutenant led the Indians to the wall and ordered them to carry cannonballs to the battery gunners.

In the thick forest covering the fortress' southwest, seven hundred fifty Guarani soldiers moved. The sixth battalion, commanded by Luis Gonzalez, had the best men among over three thousand invaders. They slipped through the trees to make a contour outside the lawn facing the southern wall.

A wise strategy. To advance through the forest was slower than going over the grass, but the tree cover protected the soldiers from cannon fire. If the Paraguayans pushed through the open field, the fort's batteries would slaughter them. But not in the trees.

Melo Bravo and his soldiers knew the enemies were advancing under the trees, halting their march just a few meters before the wall.

"Each pawn with a rifle on his shoulder, now! And if ammo is missing, spit on the bastards! Your dirty breath will kill more Guaranis than any rifled cannon," shouted Melo Bravo to the soldiers.

Seconds later, the first wave of Paraguayans appeared in a crimson red uniform, running and firing against the fort defenses. The front-line men, led by a young lieutenant, came forward, grunting indecipherable words. The Brazilians answered with a cannon volley of grapeshots, an ammunition consisting of small-caliber solid balls packed into a canvas bag.

The bags disintegrated with the explosion, so the numerous lethal metal balls left the cannon flying everywhere. It tore apart the first batch of invaders.

The second Paraguayan wave followed almost immediately, jumping and sometimes trampling their wounded comrades. The fort's gunners needed time to reload, so it would be up to the rifles to fight them.

"Sit fingers on the triggers!" The shout of Melo Bravo was the last thing anyone heard before the twenty-something Brazilian rifles howl against the invading red mass. A cloud of burned gunpowder covered the place.

Luis Caetano and a pair of riflemen positioned themselves as sharpshooters on the wall's parapet, providing cover for his Kadiweu fighters that carried cannon ammunition. The batteries fired a few more grapeshots, each of them mowing multiple Paraguayan soldiers. The fort, however, had a limited supply of it. Coimbra's batteries existed to fight invading ships, not infantry, so most of the balls were solid shots.

Soon, Paraguayan infantry reached the wall, and the fort's defenders were shooting almost vertically at any red shirt who tried to climb the bulwark.

"Prepare bayonets! Chop the Guayos until they fit in a ration bag!" shouted Melo Bravo, as he fired, hitting a Guarani on the arm and tearing his limb apart.

The metallic clatter of bayonets being attached to rifles announced the bloodiest of all combats: hand-to-hand fight.

The invading battalion of Luiz González came too close to the walls for cannon fire to hit it. The red-coated soldiers formed a living mass climbing the slope to the fort. Luis Caetano ordered his Indians to drop some of the solid iron balls from the top of the wall, grinding whoever was on the way. The idea worked, and apart from saving gunpowder, each solid ball took at least two Paraguayans out of battle - dead or injured. His improvisation surprised even De Faria. The captain and his detachment were ready for the next enemy wave against the southern bastion.
However, no one noticed that meters away, at the lowest point

of the barrier, eight Paraguayans jumped into the fort across a spot guarded only by two sentinels.

A terror shriek came from one sentry, while the other didn't even notice what hit his head. The watchman's cry alerted the other soldiers, who advanced with bayonets on the invading Paraguayans, opening their bellies and chests. The two injured sentinels, however, lay dead.

On the south wall, invaders used the bodies of fallen fighters to climb faster, but with no success. Meanwhile, bullets coming from the Paraguayan rear, invisible in the cloud of burned gunpowder, buzzed over the heads of the Brazilian riflemen.

Lieutenant Melo continued to shoot any piece of skin that tried to climb the facade. His bravery- as well as his threats - ignited the fighting fury in the Brazilians of the southern wall. Each private aimed, fired, reloaded, and fired again with Napoleonic agility. The rifle barrels were already steaming hot, but Melo's soldiers ignored the pain of burning their own hands as they reloaded their weapons.

On the opposite side, Paraguayan officers signaled to retreat. A moment of brief silence came as the invaders regrouped their platoons while the defenders ran for more ammunition.

Luis Caetano, positioned at a tower top and acting as a sniper in the entire battle, counted at least three kills. He had the chance to make four, aiming his rifle at the back of a

Paraguayan captain. The lieutenant heard a soldier call him: Luiz González. *A captain that displayed such a courage leading his men doesn't deserve a shot on the back,* he thought. *Besides, they are already retreating.*

The Paraguayan Luiz turned, and his eyes met his Brazilian namesake pointing a gun to him, but without shooting.

From a distance, the two Luises saluted each other in mutual respect after a day where both sides fought bravely but with no conclusion.

Minutes after nineteen o'clock, the last shot was fired. The invaders returned to their camp, leaving behind the dead. Brazilians counted casualties and remaining ammunition. Luis Caetano, meanwhile, wondered in which *quinto-dos-infernos* was anspeçada Nopitena.

Chapter V

The smuggler Gaspar Picágua moored his boat on a riverbank miles away from the fort.

He and his older brother, Friar Pedro, were going downstream toward the border that morning. Later, however, they spotted the invading flotilla and the beginning of hostilities between Brazilians and Paraguayans. The first reaction of the brothers was to turn around and sail upstream about two leagues, from where they could see all the strife.

"Christians killing each other...For what?" Friar Pedro Picágua wondered, shaking his head in desolation.

He was the auxiliary deacon from the Itatí parish, an Argentinian village near Corrientes. The same Itatí where the brothers grew up. Pedro had nothing to do with Gaspar's clandestine activities but accompanied him under the pretext of ministering to isolated communities along the river. The truth is that he still hoped to influence his brother to live a better life in the eyes of God.

"No, Pedro. These are Paraguayans and Brazilians killing themselves and interrupting my trip." Gaspar said. After selling almost all his stock of alcohol and tobacco, he wanted to return to Corrientes, taking the skins bought in Corumbá. In Corrientes, he was going to deliver the leather pieces at Amaru's Warehouse. He expected two good payments for the service. One in coins and another for his eyes, by seeing Amaru's daughter, the young Aramí.

Gaspar continued his monologue. "If we go down the river, the Guaranis will think we are their soldiers fleeing the fight and hang us. If the Brazilians see us before the Paraguayans, they will take us for Guaranis and make a sieve out of our boat.

"But we are Guarani, brother." Pedro's eyes watered in sorrow while watching the slaughter from a distance.

"We are Correntino Guaranis, not Paraguayans, Friar." Every time Gaspar called Pedro a *friar*, the cleric put a smile on his face, remembering all the less praiseworthy nicknames his brother gave him during childhood. "This war is not ours. Between a Paraguayan rope around my neck and a Brazilian bullet, better sail up the river, back to Dourados." Gaspar grabbed a banana from his sack. "Who knows, maybe there is still good business out there."

They untied their chata at dusk. The shooting in the battle for Coimbra stopped. Nearby, a detachment of Paraguayan Guarani men invaded a village of Guaicurus-Kadiwéu, looking for slaves. Some Indians fled in canoes, seeking refuge in the fort.

"We should help them," Pedro said, looking for the desperate Indians escaping from their ravaged village.

"Did you already forget what I just said? To expose ourselves could mean our own death." Gaspar laid in the barge, preparing to sleep at a safe distance from all the conflict.

The friar shook his head, as if giving up on expecting any braver behavior from his smuggler brother.

The next morning, Friar Pedro and Gaspar Picágua headed north, fleeing problems and a war that was not theirs—at least for now.

***

"Coelho, gather a group of civilians to care for the wounded and bury the dead." Captain Benedito de Faria ordered when approaching the officers in the courtyard. Some soldiers were sitting and cleaning their rifles. Others struggled to wipe their irritated eyes and skin—many had blackened faces after gunpowder residue. The men had a savage but also tragic appearance. "Lieutenant Gomes, Lieutenant Melo, to my office."

As they accompanied the captain, Luis noticed Coelho resented not being called to the officers' meeting. *I hope he takes that as a lesson of humility…prick*, he thought.

Colonel Portocarrero was also in the captain's office, visibly tired. Despite his age, he engaged in the battle, using his artillery knowledge to aim the cannons, resulting in accurate shots already on the second attempt.

"Lieutenant Melo, I want a report on our gunpowder and ammunition supplies," the colonel said, "Lieutenant Gomes, gather all adults who can walk and are not sentinels. Captain Benedito, please check the condition of the combatants and report any deserter."

Upon hearing that the captain would investigate the defections, Luis Caetano already knew he would need to explain how Nopitena disappeared under his command.

"Gentlemen, I believe no one is deluded into thinking this is the last Paraguayan offensive," said Portocarrero. The officers nodded. "It was just one division. According to Lieutenant Gomes observations, there are at least two others camped. Tomorrow they will come up again, with even greater strength. Bring your reports in one hour."

Leaving the room, the two lieutenants walked in the same direction. Melo Bravo broke the silence. "It won't even take an hour to find out the obvious." Luis understood what Melo meant. There was still some gunpowder, but no more cartridges prepared for the rifles.

"Melo, we can order the men to fill cartridges," Luis said.

"For that, we would have to reassign even the sentinels, and the Paraguayans left a platoon of eavesdroppers in the woods." Melo pointed in the forest's direction. "If we let our guard down, they jump over the wall during the night and set fire on our gunpowder warehouse."

The ability of Melo Bravo to foresee enemy tricks made Luis confident, with a side-lip smile.

An hour later, the officers gathered again in the captain's office. Melo was the first to report. "Sir, of the twelve thousand cartridges in our arsenal, there are less than three thousand left."

"Three thousand?" Portocarrero raised his eyebrows. "Did we spend nine thousand bullets in one afternoon? Did your men fire almost two thousand shots per hour?"

"Either we did that, or the Paraguayans would jump over the wall to kill us all and...do all kinds of diabolical things to our families."

Like Portocarrero, Melo Bravo's wife and daughter, baby Josephina, were also in the fort. Portocarrero understood the lieutenants' motivation and warmongering fury, but it was difficult to explain how Coimbra had such a precarious supply.

"How a fort that is the empire's first line of defense had only twelve thousand cartridges! We've never had enough for more than a day of battle! Captain, did you request the ammunition restock?"

"Sir, it's been two months since I asked Corumbá to send more," replied De Faria.

"Corumbá?" The colonel rolled his eyes. "It smells like Oliveira's ineptitude." Portocarrero meant Carlos Augusto de Oliveira, a bureaucrat colonel based in Corumbá, responsible for the local logistics. The suspicions about Colonel Oliveira's negligence were the reason Portocarrero visited the border garrisons.

Thinking for a few minutes about how to solve the problem, the Colonel had a Eureka moment. "If we have gunpowder and empty cartridges, that means we can improvise ammunition ourselves."

"We could, but the ensign reported that the wounded men are in terrible condition, and the healthy are busy watching over the fort," Melo replied. "The Guayos are close in the jungle and can jump over anytime."

"*Mas que merda*. Captain Benedito, your report. Give me some good news."

Luis' pulse accelerated, alarmed that the captain would list Nopitena as a deserter. How to justify that one of his soldiers ran away under his watch? A lieutenant's first duty was to serve as an example. For a recently promoted officer, to have a deserter among his men demanded explanations and raised an equal amount of doubts.

"Sir, the information I bring is a double-edged sword," Captain de Faria said, "it is about the Indian Nopitena from Lieutenant Gomes' patrol."

Luis couldn't look at the captain. His eyes lowered to the ground in shame. The treason and deception from his trusted Kadiweu filled him with anger.

"The soldier with white drawings all over his torso?"

"Yes, himself. The Indian returned to the fort, accompanied by more than a dozen Natives. Almost none are good for combat. Mostly women or kids, but I agreed to give them shelter," said the captain. All that Luis heard was that the Indian returned. It was enough for the lieutenant to relax his muscles.

"Why did you allow them in?" Portocarrero's tone was not of disapproval but curiosity.

"I know this brings more mouths to feed. But Lieutenant Melo said we don't have enough hands to fill cartridges. Indians can do that. There's no use for food if we don't have bullets for the Paraguayans tomorrow."

"Indeed, captain. Lieutenant Gomes, you get along well with the natives, so put them to work." Portocarrero punched the table, surprising those present in the room. "All of you, Nessum Dorma!"

"Nessum, what?" Luis asked.

"Nessum Dorma. It means Nobody sleeps in Italian."

With no knowledge of foreign languages, Melo Bravo made his personal interpretation "Neither in *talian* nor in Coimbra captain. Nobody sleeps until we have bullets enough till the last Guayo!" Melo and Luis saluted, clicked their boots, and left the room.

Alone in the office, the captain and the colonel walked to a window and stared at the courtyard. They saw the officers excited to solve a problem considered impossible hours before.

"Sir, you know Barrios. Do you think that a good bash tomorrow will force him to give up?"

Portocarrero sighed and thought for a few seconds. "Give up? I taught this man to chase the enemy until the grave pit. Do you know Osório?"

"Our Osório? The general of forty-two battles?" Captain De Faria widened his eyes.

"Yes. Barrios doesn't have Osório's brilliance, but he is just as obstinate. He doesn't give up, hunting his prey until the nest. And for that, the bastard will use everything I taught him."

***

"Nopitena, you son of a harlot! What happened?" Luis asked, relieved that the Kadiweu did not betray him.

"Chief, I warned the kids on the road to stay away from the fort so they wouldn't be a target for the Guaranis. Then I remembered you said that this entire mess would last until the water finishes." Nopitena answered, reminding the lieutenant of his own words. "I didn't want my horse to die thirsty, so I left the animal with the boys to take it to the village and came back on foot." Nopitena faced Luis with a straight face and no signal of guilty. Instead, his eyes looked firm, as if he was even proud of what he had done.

Luis knew of the sentimental connection the Kadiweus had with their horses. There was a reason white people called them the Indian knights. "I understand that, but why didn't you come back? Did the shots scare you?"

"I tried to, but the gate was closed, with no one to open it. I hid in the ravine because if the Paraguayans saw me, they would kill me for being a Guaicuru, and if a Brazilian saw me, he would think I'm a Guarani."

Luis laughed at the clumsy but innocent situation that the Kadiweu described. "All these people, where did they come from, soldier?" The lieutenant asked, pointing to the refugees.

"When I was hiding in the ravine, they arrived in canoes. They spoke my language and asked for help."

"Did they explain why they came?"

"Kaiowas arrived in their village, and when they show up, everyone knows it is an expedition to catch slaves."

Luis recalled that the Kaiowas, a local type of Guarani, were mortal enemies of the Kadiweus. *Are the Kaiowas helping the Paraguayans?* Luis thought. If so, it meant the refugees had plenty of reasons to fight and defend the fort, as it was the only thing separating them from being captured by the hands of the rival tribe.

"All right, anspeçada. Can you teach these Indians how to fill ammunition cartridges?"

Nopitena nodded. The lieutenant ordered every civilian to assemble in the main square next to the arsenal and start working. The night was going to be long. With only 3,000 cartridges, the defenders of Coimbra did not have enough ammunition even for two hours of battle.

***

The allied Indians, the officers' wives, and inhabitants from the fort's vicinity gathered in the main square. Besides the one hundred fifty soldiers, Coimbra now provided shelter for nearly one hundred civilians. A crowd that occupied nearly every meter of the dirt courtyard floor. Their curled lips and tired-eyed pleaded for protection. Protection from an enemy hungry after a long march. An enemy not acting under the civility conventions.

The sweaty smell didn't bother anyone, on the contrary. It masked the even worse stench from the human remains beyond the wall, where bodies with intestines exposed by bayonet cuts rotted in the damp night.

Luis, standing in front of the crowd at the open-air courtyard, called everyone's attention. "Gentlemen, and ladies, the Coimbra fort, under the service of the Brazilian Empire, welcomes you. Unfortunately, today we cannot provide you with the comfort worthy of the best resorts." A laugh erupted with the ironic commentary. "Our Guarani neighbors visited us with no invitation, but today we gave them a beautiful jab."

A man shouted, "Long live the Empire!" and the others—except the Indians—repeated the catchphrase.

"They believe that tomorrow we will surrender!" The spectators laughed in scorn, and Luis continued. "Today, we lost two men, but for each one of us, they lost twelve!"

"Long live the defenders of Mato Grosso!" yelled another civilian, followed by even more effusive applause.

Luis pointed to his colleague Melo Bravo and continued the speech. "Lieutenant Melo here knows how to hail lead on these dogs! But now we need more cartridges for the rifles because tomorrow the bastards will come again!"

This time, the audience remained silent. A woman with a baby in her arms hugged the little one close to her chest, waiting for the worst.

Luis realized that the slightest hint of hesitation would make the refugees' hands tremble, and therefore useless for handling gunpowder. "You, ladies and gentlemen, have the arms we need tonight." He took a breath and gazed with firm, confident eyes in the face of each present. "Each cartridge filled by your hands will kill a Paraguayan. A Paraguayan that would dishonor your wives or kidnap your children! Each piece of fodder prepared by your fingers will guarantee the freedom of your villages! Every ammunition you make will water our gardens with Guarani blood!"

When Luis mentioned the rival tribe, the Kadiweus shouted with enthusiasm and anger against the Paraguayans, Guaranis, Avás, or any term used for the invaders.

After Luis' improvised speech on the main square, civilians and soldiers, whites and natives, became united in a frantic task force.

From a distance, Portocarrero and Benedito de Faria witnessed the euphoria caused by the Lieutenant's speech.

"Has the boy always been that skilled with words, captain?" asked the colonel.

"First time I see him doing that, but he was always good at dealing with foreigners and training Indians."

Within hours, female hands manipulated the gunpowder with a lightness that surprised even Captain De Faria. Dona Ludovina, Portocarrero's wife, guided the volunteers, dividing the larger caliber bullets into smaller ones suitable for the *Minié* rifles.

Later that night, the tireless Portocarrero summoned the officers to his quarters. The Colonel started the meeting by asking Ensign Coelho about the wounded.

"Sir, apart from the casualties we already know, the rest of the injured will survive. I fear, however, that we may lack water because of the useless...additions to our population." Coelho's gaze denounced his contempt for the indigenous and civilian refugees.

"One problem at a time, ensign. If there is no water tomorrow, find two men, a pair of buckets and go get water from the river without being shot." The Colonel's words drew smiles from Luis and Melo. "Call the musician Verdeixas to help you, Coelho. With his drummer's arms, he can carry two buckets, and you carry one."

Being compared with the soldier-musician Verdeixas, whom Coelho also considered deadweight, hurt the snob ensign's ego. Portocarrero returned to the subject, "The useless people you are referring are out there, working all night, ensign. Lieutenant Luis, what about the ammunition?"

"Sir, we filled over two thousand cartridges, and we still have gunpowder available, but..."

"But?"

"The paper is over."

The cartridges for the Minie rifles were made of paper. None of the officers expected anything so trivial to be an obstacle that night. Perhaps hands, gunpowder, even lead could be missing. But paper?

Melo Bravo broke the haunting silence of the room. "Let's use fabric instead! May women tear up their skirts and dresses!"

Captain Benedito de Faria, aware that one of these women was the colonel's wife, got ready to reprimand Melo, but Portocarrero interrupted him. "The lieutenant is right. Mrs. Ludovina has plenty of dresses. Donating some for our resistance is a minor effort."

Luis Caetano, standing at Melo's side, thought about his half-sister, Joana Augusta—or, as he called her, Joau. She knew how to convince her father and her late fiance to give her more dresses than she would wear in a lifetime. Ripping her garments to use the fabric for cartridges could make ammunition enough for an entire battalion. Fortunately for Joau, her luxurious costumes were safe in Rio de Janeiro.

In the following hours, the sounds of fabrics torn apart filled the patio. The women's garments, including Ludovina Portocarrero and Maria Melo—Lieutenant Melo's wife—

turned into raw material for cartridges and fodder so that soldiers could keep fighting the next day.

Or on that same day, since dawn was breaking.

Chapter VI

After hearing their mother's voice, a boy and a girl ran toward the entrance arches from the center of the mansion's white-walled living room. In the center of the room, motionless but with a smile on her face, was the children's tutor, Joana Augusta Gomes de Carvalho.

Joana had a dress divided into two parts. The upper section, a floral bodice with a modest neckline—if it could be called a neckline. The skirt had a beige color, light enough to reflect the powerful tropical sun. Over her head, a sennit straw boater hat gave the young lady a Venetian look.

The children's mother was Ana Francisca Alves de Lima e Silva, the Viscountess of Ururai. The aristocrat strolled across the mansion entrance hall, wearing one of her heavy satin gowns, with a dark blue color. Over her shoulders, an emerald shawl with golden fringes. A style more suited to the temperate climates of Europe than to tropical Brazil.

"The children behaved very well today, lady Ana. I think the heat made them a little worn."

"I'm glad they behaved, Joana. That's why you look as rested as early spring," the Viscountess said. "Do you have classes with Mr. Almeida Rosa today?"

"The children don't make me tired. They have their mother's cleverness with their grandfather's discipline." Joana's' compliments made Ana chuckle. "And yes, today I have a law class with Mr. Almeida Rosa."

Watching her children quietly in their beds, the viscountess whispered, "Don't you think it is curious to spend the morning tutoring the grandchildren of a conservative senator and take classes in the afternoon with a liberal?"

Joana, not knowing if the viscountess' comment had a substance of repression, grinned and shook her head, "The professor leaves politics aside when he teaches us law. Do you know that one of his good friends is also a conservative, just like your father?"

"I don't doubt it. Otaviano has open doors everywhere. He is a purebred diplomat. Who would that friend be?"

"His name is Alfredo, he is the son of a Frenchman, but born in Brazil. The teacher said that he will introduce me to him one day because politics aside, he is a beneficial influence."

"Oh, Taunay!" The viscountess tilted her head, staring at Joana with a wide smile. "I know him. He reminds me of you. You two have the same aristocratic air, a taste for the arts, and a round cheek. And he is single as far as I remember." Ana Francisca winked.

Joana Augusta blushed. For her, the Viscountess was almost a maternal figure, given that her mother died at childbirth. The two women left the children's chamber and went to the living room. A maid placed a teapot and cookies on a table with four chairs. "Are you going to receive visitors, my lady?" Joana asked.

"Yes, the two Marias: Paranhos and Saraiva. If you can skip your class, you are welcome for our tea. Both of them bring rumors about the end of the war in Uruguay."

Maria Paranhos was the daughter of the Viscount of Rio Branco, a former minister from the conservative party. Maria Saraiva was the niece of José Saraiva, a former minister from the liberal party. Both relatives from politicians who worked together to solve the Uruguayan civil war. A conflict that ended with the victory of the *Colorado* party—supported by Brazil and Argentina—against the *Blanco* party, supported by Paraguay.

It puzzled Joana how people like Almeida Rosa or the Viscountess could so easily mingle among members of both parties. Parties whose most ardent supporters exchanged punches in the streets.

"Thank you for the invitation, but today the teacher is waiting for me," Joana said.

On the way to her class, she reflected on the Viscountess' words about Taunay. Not that she was interested in him. She hadn't even met him yet. But maybe it was time to stop mourning her late fiancé. The guilt she carried, however, pointed otherwise.

The girl arrived at the old manor with Doric columns and a well-groomed front garden. Classical sculptures decorated the lawn. A house that could be seen as ugly and displaced by the new-rich in Rio, used to import ephemeral fashions from other cultures. But for men of exceptional intellect, this garden was the harbinger of good taste.

She knocked on the door, and a gentleman in his forties opened it. A thin face, trimmed beard, short hair. But none of his features drew more attention than the gigantic eyes, which looked even bigger behind the oval spectacles.

"Joana! How are the tutoring activities at the Viscountess?" Francisco Otaviano de Almeida Rosa asked.

"Going well. My affection for children helps, but I'm still not sure if I deserve to be called a tutor."

"Perfect, modesty is a significant step in good diplomacy, and in these times of war, diplomacy is imperative."

To not be disturbed by any noise during his studies and lectures, Otaviano covered the floors of all hallways and rooms with plush carpets. It caused a sepulchral silence. A person could not even hear his own footsteps, so Joana's mind wandered back to the conversation she had with Ana Francisca shortly before.

"Mrs. Ana told me about rumors that the war in Uruguay ended in our favor." She said.

The phrase caught the teacher's attention. "The Viscountess is the daughter of Caxias, so she must know more than I do. Have you ever heard of the short blanket analogy?"

Joana, an admirer of arts but not fluent in colloquial language, shook her head while holding a sneeze. In the same way that the carpets absorbed the noise, they also accumulated dust.

"It's when you can't cover your feet and head at the same time," the teacher answered. "This is the case of the Uruguayan war. A favorable outcome for us and Buenos Aires means a disaster for Paraguay."

"Do you think they can do something unexpected?" Joana sat in one armchair.

"Unexpected? Maybe. Paraguay has been reinforcing its military for years. They threatened the Marques de Olinda, a civilian ship! Losing the Uruguayan ally is the spark that Solano Lopez needs to fire cannons against our borders."

When Joana heard about cannons at the borders, one thing came to her mind: her brother, who would soon be transferred from Coimbra back to their home in the 3-Estados farm.

At least, that was what Joana Augusta Gomes de Carvalho believed.

Chapter VII

The first morning lights painted the white fort in a golden hue. After two poorly slept hours, Captain Benedito de Faria met Luis and Melo Bravo at the fort's battery. Both lieutenants had sleepless faces and large dark circles around their eyes but waited for the captain with a triumphant grin.

"Good morning Lieutenants, how are we with men and ammunition?"

"Over 4,000 cartridges manufactured, sir," said Luis in a firm tone, "thanks to the work of women and Indians throughout the night, led by Dona Ludovina Portocarrero."

"Who could think that the colonel would contribute tonight by taking care of the children while his wife worked?" commented the captain with a grin "Melo, do you believe that what we have enough to repel one more attack today?"

Melo, with an erect posture and firm eyes, took a step forward. "I don't believe, sir, because to believe would mean I am not sure. We will beat the Guarani again."

The Captain widened his eyes, admiring the officer's boldness. He asked how Melo Bravo planned to react to yet another enemy offensive.

"Each shooter must wait until the red shirts come near the wall. I will organize my men in a double line." Melo

60

pointed in the bastion's direction. "When the invaders arrive, the first line fire, retreat and reload, making room for the second line."

Luis, listening to his colleague's explanation, recalled the classes at the military school. There was a similar Napoleonic tactic used by the French to conquer Europe. The difference was that Melo Bravo wanted to wait for the enemy to get close. Very close. Fewer shots would miss the target, and hits from a short distance were lethal.

"But what if they climb the walls, Melo?" the Captain asked.

"Bayonets attached, sir. Then, instead of making holes in them, we tear them up."

Luis, listening to Melo and De Faria closely, made a step forward. "Gentlemen, what if we show the Anhambai the place of the Paraguayan offensive and thus have their artillery support?"

The idea attracted their eyes. Luis continued, "Someone must remain on the edge of the wall receiving the enemy attack, with a red flag. When Balduino sees the flag from the Anhambai, he fires in that direction."

"Who's mad enough to serve as a bull's eye for cannonballs?" asked the captain.

"Me and my Guaicurus, sir," replied Luis.

De Faria raised his eyebrows at Luis' suicidal fearlessness. "For someone who wanted to leave until two days ago, now you want to serve as cannon target? What has changed, Lieutenant Gomes?"

"Sir, I still want to leave, but first, we need to chase the Paraguayans out of the way."

"I agree, lieutenant. You can go ahead with your plan. Good luck and stay away from the cannon shots."

Luis saluted the captain and left the room, walking toward Nopitena at the main square.

"Anspeçada, I have a task for you," He tapped the shoulder of the Indian. "Go to the Anhambai and inform Lieutenant Balduino that every time he sees a mast with a red flag raised in the Fort, he must fire the cannons in that direction, calibrating it to hit twenty yards ahead of the flag."

"Flags? Who will hold these flags?"

"Aha! We will!" Luis laughed. "Go, Nopitena, we have no time."

The Kadiweu rushed to the north gate and then to the pier. There he found a dinghy and rowed toward the Brazilian ship, protected from the Paraguayan flotilla by a river bend.

When Balduino heard the plan from Nopitena's mouth, his first reaction was a grimace. "Anspeçada, your lieutenant must know that, at this distance, a fart would be enough to change the cannonball course and decapitate the flag holder, right?"

"Yes, sir. It is a risk we will take. We count on your good assessment of the winds."

Fascinated by the risky mission of the Guaicurus and Lieutenant Gomes, Balduino accepted the responsibility of providing artillery support with the Anhambaí - if the wind helped.

***

Still early in the morning, the first red uniforms appeared at the forest's edge. As on the previous day, the Paraguayans used the dense vegetation as cover against the fort's cannons.

Colonel Portocarrero and Captain Benedito de Faria joined the men at the fort's battery. The cannons were of little effect against soldiers hiding in the jungle but still useful to prevent Paraguayan vessels from approaching with reinforcements.

Melo Bravo guided the riflemen on the wall, while Luis Caetano placed a Kadiweu soldier every twenty meters. Each carried a stick with a red cloth tied at the end. It would be too generous to call the rags as flags, but the sticks were tall enough to be seen from the river by the Anhambaí crew. The lieutenant instructed them to raise the poles if enemy soldiers came less than twenty steps from the wall.

"Chief, where are you going to stay?" asked Nopitena.

Luis pointed to the lowest part of the wall, a stretch less than two meters high. "I will be at the side of Lieutenant Melo's shooters."

The anspeçada raised his eyebrows, horrified. "That is the most dangerous place to be today!"

Luis nodded. "I know it. It is where the Guaranis will attack, so this is where I need to be. In addition, after signaling, I can get a rifle and help Melo Bravo's soldiers."

"Better send an Indian instead of you. If the worst happens, we still have a chief."

"And which of the Kadiweus can shoot? If I put a rifle in your hand, you may hit your own balls." The lieutenant's joke had a pinch of truth. With his poor aim, Nopitena couldn't hit a Capybara at close range.

They walked to opposite sides, exchanging wishes of good luck.

Luis stood in his place at the wall. On the opposite side, red patches moved, protected by the trees in the jungle. A light wind ruffled the lieutenant's sweat-damp black hair. He looked around. The Kadiweus were already at their posts, each with their own flag and their uniforms unbuttoned to relieve the heat, exposing the geometrically patterned white tattoos.

Feeling the breeze touching his face, Luis also opened the top buttons of his uniform. *If death comes today, let it be under the gentle touch of the westerly winds,* he thought.

The women and children who all night long worked noisily in the courtyard retired to the halls of the fort. The only sound heard was the croaking toads at the riverbank.

Minutes passed in silence.

Less than sixty meters of open land separated the jungle from the fort's wall. Sixty meters of unpaved, steep terrain. The same sixty meters that on the previous day were the last stop on earth for so many dying Paraguayans today promised to be the scene of an even more brutal battle.

If the Brazilians wanted to, they could risk random shots toward the trees. There were so many Paraguayans that they might hit one. The order, however, was to save ammunition and fire only when the enemy came close.

Both parties did the same for the first morning hours of December 28.

They waited.

Until trees screamed something incomprehensible.
Mba'apo poi!

The Guarani war cry. This time, Captain Luiz
Gonzalez's ferocious 5th battalion had reinforcements. The
soldiers of the sixth and seventh battalion sprinted toward
Coimbra. The number of attackers surpassed 1,500 men
against the less than fifty defenders of the southern wall.

Luis knew that when the red-shirted mass advanced
against him, he needed to raise his flag at the right time. Only
then the Anhambaí could calibrate its cannons and fire against
the Paraguayans. Enemy bullets and bayonets could end Luis'
life in the same way as an inaccurate shot from Lieutenant
Balduino's vessel.

Mba'apo poi!

Again, the Guarani war cry echoed on the battlefield.
The red crowd left the jungle, and in seconds they covered the
open space separating the forest and the fort.

"Wait for the Guayos to come! Shoot only when you
can already feel their dirty breath!" Melo Bravo shouted to his
men.

The enemy came closer, rushing on the open field. The
defending riflemen remained motionless, with fixed gazes and
attentive ears, waiting for the command to shoot.

"Now, shooters! Now!!" Melo waved to his soldiers.

Soon the Brazilians fired the first shots, and in a matter of seconds, a second and third volley. The system adopted by Melo Bravo worked like clockwork, with sequential lines of a dozen snipers, alternating between reloading and firing.

The efficiency of Melo Bravo's soldiers almost hypnotized Luis until he raised the flag. Time for the Anhambaí cannons to pound the enemies.

But no cannon sounds echoed. Luis looked up at the top of his wooden staff to make sure that the cloth was visible. The red fabric swung violently. *Maybe Balduino is delaying the fire because the wind is too strong, and the cannonball may hit the wrong target,* he thought.

In a few seconds, he heard the first explosion. The shell crossed the sky and blew up a hole in the floor a few meters from Luis, in the open ground, injuring no one. *Balduino is measuring the distance for the next shot! The Anhambaí joined the fight!*

The second cannon shell crossed the air with a tight curve, hitting a group of Paraguayans a few meters from the fort. It cut one in half and took three others out of service. The hit of the Anhambaí cannonade motivated the defenders.

Wanting to end the fight as soon as possible, the Paraguayans shouted, "Surrender!"

But Melo Bravo's men responded with cries of "Viva o Brasil," "Viva o Imperador!" and aimed down in the face of any invader who tried to climb the bastion.

The Anhambai fired a dozen times more with great accuracy, but the mass of enemy soldiers came too close to the wall, and the balls were no longer hitting anyone as they fell into the rear field. Lieutenant Luis Caetano lowered his signal flag, took his rifle, attached the bayonet, and moved to reinforce the side of Melo Bravo.

A Guarani, who appeared to be the same age as the lieutenant, climbed the short wall. Luis ran from his spot, stabbing him with the bayonet in the femoral artery and impaling the man.

The pressure of the open artery produced a gush of blood that hit the lieutenant's eyes. For an instant, his vision turned red, and the smell of raw meat entered his nose. Luis took out his bayonet from inside the red-shirted soldier, whose face was pale, deadly pale.

The viscous, warm red liquid that splashed on Luis soaked his hair and made his hand slippery enough to drop his rifle on the floor.

The lieutenant took a step back, wiping his hands on the uniform. Unsheathing his saber in a single movement, he advanced against another Paraguayan who jumped inside the parapet. The blade slashed through the foe's abdomen. While Luis pulled his sword from the mess of skin and intestines, a push threw him to the ground. During the fall, a bayonet blade missed his arm by a few centimeters.

"Watch out! They will stab you, chief!" Nopitena came from his signaling post to support the defense.

The Paraguayan with the bayonet still tried to enter the parapet. Nopitena took Luis' rifle from the floor, holding it in the hot barrel, and hit the buttstock on the invaders' head.

Luis heard a snap, a sound similar to a twig breaking. *So, this is the sound of cracking a skull?*

Meters from there, perceiving the chaos of gore and dying bodies raining from the southern wall, the Paraguayans retreated to the jungle to organize a new offensive.

The floor under the Brazilian soldiers was as wet as if it had rained, soaked with the blood and sweat of combatants who fought for hours under the scorching heat. A rifleman shouted for water; a request gradually repeated by others. Luis, who at that point looked like a careless butcher, told Nopitena to go to the warehouse to fetch some gourds of water while the soldiers recovered their breath.

The next attack would come, and thirst was just one problem.

***

"*Dona* Ludovina, the chief sent us to take water for the men." Nopitena entered the storehouse, accompanied by two other Kadiweus carrying empty jugs.

Ludovina—Portocarrero's wife—had no idea who was the *chief* the Indian referred to, but she took him to the water tank. Near it, Ensign Coelho, albeit reluctantly, fulfilled his duty to care for the wounded. The musician Verdeixas helped him, ignoring Coelho's insults about how useless an artist was during battle.

Nopitena and the woman inclined at the tank to fill the jugs, but it was nearly empty.

"Where's the water, Coelho?" Ludovina asked.

Coelho turned to the woman and shrugged his shoulders. "This is all we have, madam." Pointing to the wounded soldiers, he added, "I don't know how we can help them if we run out of water."

Nopitena still tried to fill the gourds, but Ludovina's hand prevented him.

"This is not enough for even three soldiers." Ludovina released the arm of Nopitena. "If you take this to the wall, half of the men will kill each other to drink, and the other half will desert to not die thirsty."

Verdeixas listened to their conversation, keeping a fixed, attentive gaze. He came closer, took a long breath, and volunteered to go fetch water at the river.

"If you leave this fort, you will not make three steps alive," Ludovina predicted, "only divine protection can save you." After uttering these words, her eyes deviated to the chapel next to the warehouse. "Maybe that's just what we need."

The woman remained in silence for a moment, then explained to Verdeixas her plan and asked Coelho to find two women with powerful arms.

***

After removing two wounded men from the bulwark, Luis, Melo Bravo, and the soldiers cleaned their weapons, placed cartridges within reach, and kneeled on the narrow parapet from which they defended the fort.

"Ready for one more, Melo?" Luis asked while cleaning the enemy's blood that smeared his rifle

"If there is no gunpowder, I will use steel," Melo grabbed his saber hilt. "Until I dye my blade in red." Both knew that the ammunition boxes prepared during the night were again nearly empty.

On the grass field between the wall and the jungle, several mutilated men howled in pain. Dozens of wounded

Paraguayans cried for rescue. Most of them did not have bullet holes but maimed limbs, evidence that the Brazilians were already out of ammunition, resorting to bayonets and swords in the desperate defense against an army twenty times the size of their own.

A gunner pointed to the Paraguayans hiding at the edge of the forest. The red-shirted combatants were all staring at the fort and making the sign of the cross.

"What is that supposed to mean?" Luis asked. The Brazilian riflemen whispered that maybe the enemy saw supernatural signs.

Luis turned around and understood the reason for the invader's commotion.

On the opposite side of the fort, at the riverside wall, Verdeixas carried the image of Our Lady of Mount Carmel. The statue from their chapel. The musician held it over his head so that the Paraguayans could see the saint.

A red-shirt soldier shouted "¡*Viva Nuestra Señora!*" followed by a similar exaltation on the Brazilian side, "Viva Nossa Senhora do Carmo!"

The fight, instead of re-starting, was delayed. A truce. A truce declared not by officers and their words, but by common soldiers and their prayers.

Verdeixas left the fort, accompanied by two women - Aninha Cangalha and Maria Fuzil, both soldiers' wives blessed with washerwoman's arms. They went down to the river and filled several gourds with water. Once the gourds were full, they returned in the same way they left: under the saint's image.

Verdeixas, under the applause of the thirsty soldiers, whispered when he passed by Ensign Coelho, "I think this useless man here brought water to you."

Nopitena distributed filled mugs to the riflemen and battery cannoneers. They still heard some bangs that afternoon, but after the truce, spirits cooled, and the warlike atmosphere relaxed. Paraguayans fired more out of obligation rather than out of a desire to kill.

Tired, the invaders returned to the camp, leaving the decisive attack for the following day.

"These last few hours didn't look like a war between Guaranis and Brazilians," Nopitena said, standing on the parapet next to Luis Caetano. Both stared at the blood-stained dirt floor outside. Days before, fluffy grass covered the soil, but it became a mud of bodily fluids. "It seemed like brothers fighting."

"Because it is a brother's fight." Luis replied, "That is what it has always been, Nopitena. The problem is when the brothers are Cain and Abel."

"Cainha what?" the Indian asked.

"Forget it. Let's help the wounded."

***

The Brazilians brought to the fort eighteen wounded Paraguayans, left behind after the enemy retreat. Some had wounds that would make normal men howl in pain, yet they mostly remained silent, like stones, except for occasional groans. Although their short stature made them look younger, the Guaranis revealed the bravery of seasoned soldiers on the battlefield.

The wounded men occupied the fort's largest storeroom, also known as the arsenal. It had almost no supplies after two days of intense combat. The odor of open wounds and urine was far worse than the intoxicating gunpowder smoke of the battle. Colonel Portocarrero, Captain De Faria, and Luis Caetano entered to interrogate the prisoners and gather intelligence.

One of the Paraguayans lay on the floor, silent, in a distinctive red-gold uniform. Likely an officer, probably a lieutenant. His bloody right arm had a deep bayonet cut. If left untreated, it meant unavoidable amputation.

De Faria, knowing the bargaining power he had, asked him in fluent Spanish, "*Señor, si dejamos este corte sin tratar, perderá su brazo en el mejor de los casos. En el peor, la infección le quitará la vida.*" Pointing to Ensign Coelho, who carried a piece of bandage, the Captain continued, *"pero te podemos ayudar."*

The captain bent down and, closer to the man, whispered, *"Entonces, por favor dígame: ¿Quién es usted y cuántos hombres tiene Barrios?"*

The red-shirted officer, gasping for breath after losing blood, replied that there was still a reserve apart from the 5th, 6th, and 7th battalion. The Brazilians knew the Paraguayans had three battalions. The officer's words matched the observations of Luis and Nopitena from the hilltop.

"If these are the 5th, 6th, and 7th battalions ..." Portocarrero said, taking a step forward to not trample the leg of another injured man, "where are the 1st, 2nd, 3rd, and 4th?"

The red-shirt officer turned his eyes in the voice's direction, confused by the presence of a Colonel. *"La última vez que los vimos fue aun en Concepción,"* he said, groaning with pain from the slit arm. *"Fué cuando el Mariscal López advirtió a todos que Brasil nos había declarado la guerra."*

From behind, Luis twitched his facial muscles in surprise. "War? Did we declare war?"

"Sí, eso es lo que dije." The enemy officer replied, *"¿Eres sordo o simplemente estúpido? Ahora hagan su parte y obtengan alguién para cuidar de mi brazo."*

Portocarrero stood up and signaled to a caretaking woman and Coelho to treat the Paraguayan's arm.

"Sir, permission to ask." Luis Caetano knew that in critical moments, respect for the hierarchy demanded from a lieutenant to save questions for his superiors. "Did we declare war on the Paraguayans? I thought they attacked first."

"There is no war declaration from us," Portocarrero replied as they left the room to get fresh air in the courtyard. "On the contrary, my orders were to prepare for a war proclamation from them against us because of the Uruguayan situation."

Luis was not aware of the situation in Uruguay, but the captain told him something about the Brazilian and Argentine intervention in the neighboring country. The results displeased the Paraguayans, so they assaulted the Brazilian ship *Marquês de Olinda*.

In the courtyard, the three officers continued to talk while dusk arrived in Mato Grosso. "I bet Solano López invented this war declaration to motivate the Guaranis," the captain said, looking toward the river. "He wants his soldiers to think they are resisting against the empire, when in fact they are the invaders. Somewhat astute this Mariscal."

"Solano Lopez's cunningness will be judged at the end of this war," replied Portocarrero. "What concerns me is the existence of four other battalions somewhere around."

Luis gave himself the luxury of finishing the colonel's words. "Sir, if they unite and attack us, any resistance will be futile."

"Lieutenant Gomes, with no ammunition, there is no resistance. Find Lieutenant Melo, make an inventory of what we still have. We meet again in sixty minutes."

Luis saluted Portocarrero and left. The colonel then turned to Benedito de Faria. "Captain, inform Lieutenant Balduino at the Anhambaí that I also want him in the meeting. See you all in one hour."

***

The officers met at the captain's room at 20:00. Portocarrero stood at the side of the mahogany desk, consulting a large map of the military district. The colonel began by asking Ensign Coelho about the injured soldiers.

"Ours are recovering well, but two of the Paraguayans need extra care," Coelho answered without hesitation between words.

"Good." The colonel nodded. "Lieutenant Gomes, what about the ammunition supplies?"

Luis Caetano took a deep breath before giving the news. "Between rifles and pistols, we have less than a thousand cartridges, a little gunpowder, and no other material to improvise."

Captain Benedito de Faria and Portocarrero looked at each other. The captain wrinkled his forehead while the colonel ran his hand through his hair. The other officers knew the colonel caressed his beard when satisfied but touched his hair when facing a complicated decision. The silence in the room created an atmosphere as dramatic as an Italian opera.

"If on the first day we fired two thousand rounds per hour," the captain said, padding in circles around the room and looking at the ground, "then our ammunition is enough for another half hour of combat."

"Sir, our bayonets are sharp!" The simple suggestion that resistance was unfeasible exalted Lieutenant Melo Bravo. "Today, our gunpowder scared the Guayos, tomorrow they will bleed on our steel!"

Portocarrero raised his hand as if signaling to everyone in the room to be silent. "As head of the military command, it hurts me to admit we have no conditions for resistance." He took a step forward and put his right hand on the shoulders of the exalted Melo Bravo. "But we fought a good fight and delayed the Paraguayan advance by two days. Lieutenant Simas, by now, must be in Dourados, alerting the garrison about the invasion."

Portocarrero's words calmed Melo, as Coimbra's efforts were not in vain.

"Resisting without ammo will not only risk the lives of our families, but it will bring certain death to our men."

Portocarrero walked closer to the bookshelf, one of the few pieces of furniture in the captain's spartan office. "These men will be important in the coming war."

By mentioning the coming war, the colonel ensured they did not plan to surrender and become prisoners.

If both surrender and resistance are ruled out, what we are going to do then? thought Luis, standing still at the exit of the dimly lit room. The only sources of light were two candles placed on the shelves and an oil lamp near the entrance. Most of the fort's lamps were at the arsenal, used by the woman who tended for the wounded.

"Did any of the Paraguayan vessels try to force the passage upstream, Balduino?" asked Portocarrero to the commander of the Anhambaí, who stood in the back of the room together with the other officers.

Balduino replied that none of the Paraguayan vapors attempted to sail upstream since the first day when they got too close and received fire from both the fort's batteries and his ship.

The colonel made a couple of slow-paced steps toward the officers near the door. His eyes examined each one of them as if seeking how much fear rested in their souls. Expectation for drastic decisions filled the room.

"Luis, Coelho, and Melo: divide all the fort population into three groups." The colonel sat in a chair near the door, displaying both mental and physical exhaustion. "Each one of you will lead one group to the Anhambaí. We need to sneak in absolute silence. Starting in one hour."

The two lieutenants and the ensign saluted and left. In the backyard, Melo turned to his colleague, "Luis, do you think it is a good idea to hand over the fort to the Guayos? Go down in history as cowards, runaways?"

Luis Caetano tapped his colleague's shoulder. "My friend, think about your family and soldiers. This country, these people, will need Melo Bravo, more than once or twice. There will never be a single paragraph in history containing your name and coward in the same sentence."

"So be it."

Lieutenant Melo Bravo would, in fact, never be called a coward.

Meanwhile, Lieutenant Balduino left the captain's office and ran to the fort's pier. Protected by the darkness, he ran to prepare the Anhambaí for the retreat.

In the office, only Benedito de Faria and Colonel Portocarrero remained.

"Do you think Barrios will notice that we are retreating during the night?" The captain asked.

"He was an excellent student and knew by heart the best of military history." Portocarrero, sitting in the brown leather armchair behind the table, gave a nostalgic sigh, recalling the lessons he gave to his pupil, now their enemy. "I will use this to our advantage." The colonel rolled some tubes with maps of the region and threw them in a bag. "Captain, have you read about the Battle of Aix Island?"

"When Lord Cochrane, during the night, sent ships full of gunpowder toward the French fleet to set them on fire...Bomb ships, what a genius! But we don't have enough gunpowder for that, sir."

Portocarrero put his elbows on the table, and resting his head on his hands, replied with the shrewd look of a wolf, "True. But Barrios doesn't know that."

Chapter VIII

From the northern gate, anyone could see the river waters shining like crystal pebbles, only interrupted by a small island and the shape of the Anhambaí. The hot air, in contact with the water, created a dense fog. Sometimes, this fog endured just a few hours at dusk, sometimes the entire night. It looked frightening at first sight, but if one closed his eyes, the silky touch of the mist was the closest you could be to the comfort of a mother's hug.

Inside the crowded main square, however, a less tranquil scene. The sweat in spouts and the annoying mosquitoes were enough to make any kind soul nervous, but the necessity to withdraw in complete silence, with only one's own clothes, turned the place into a powder keg.

Before leaving to the ship, Lieutenant Balduino warned Luis and Melo that all the fort's residents should wait in the northern courtyard of Coimbra. Each group should form a single line and walk sideways, with their backs against the wall, contouring the building until they reach the river's edge. There, two longboats had to transfer them to the Anhambaí.

They needed several boat trips to carry everyone to the ship. To decide which group would go first, the officers took their luck using two dice Luis carried in his uniform pocket.

With a double six, Melo and his group had first place, followed by Coelho and Luis. Ironically, luck decided that Melo Bravo, the officer wishing to remain in Coimbra to tear up Paraguayans with his bayonet, would be the first to withdraw.

Melo's group was already near the gate, followed by Coelho's. Luis and the last batch were still at the courtyard when suddenly two maids—soldiers' wives or companions—slapped each other over a pair of pans. The lieutenant rushed to them.

"Either you both have some composure, or I lock you in a cell and leave for the Paraguayans to free you!" said Luis, with a whispered scream to the two brawlers. "No one is going to take any pan! The order is simple, no extra articles on the ship! No extra weight!"

Luis Caetano took a breath and turned to the group. "Nobody takes any personal articles. With so many people in the Anhambai, we will be lucky to move it upstream without being captured!" He said with harshness but less anger.

He just finished his sentence when Captain De Faria came from behind. "Lieutenant, order your Indians to load in the last barge six empty barrels from our arsenal and tie them to the Anhambaí's bow."

"What? Captain, I think I got it wrong," Luis said, confused by the bizarre order he received. Perhaps the fatigue of fighting three days, the melting tropical climate, and the cannon explosions affected his reasoning.

"What did you not understand, Lieutenant Gomes? Tell your men to carry empty barrels to the ship and tie them to the bow. Colonel's orders."

Luis nodded. He knew there was no time for explanations and that it was best to focus his efforts on keeping the women and children silent. Portocarrero was a high-ranking officer for a reason. During his days at the fort, the colonel fascinated everyone with his knowledge of military organization.

While the first group boarded, Luis and Portocarrero's wife, Dona Ludovina, as well as her children, waited for their turn in the pitch dark northern gate yard. A cloud of flies and blood-sucking insects flew over them. Ludovina had a little baby on her lap. The infant grimaced, annoyed as the escape disturbed his peaceful sleep. Sometimes, the small child tried, in vain, to nap in his mother's arms.

A metallic noise reverberated. *Again, they are fighting over the pans!* thought Luis. The baby began a high-pitched, continuous cry.

Luis ran toward the feuding women. "You pair of rowdy cows! I told to leave the pots behind! You will make the Paraguayans know we are leaving and kill everyone here!"

Luis turned to Nopitena and ordered, "Anspeçada, call the other Indians, tie and gag them both!" The Kadiweus advanced on the women. The two ladies, under protest, admitted it was a bad idea to fight over the pot. On the other side, Colonel Portocarrero, in his official uniform, ran to see from where the noise came.

The little baby still screamed. He was the son of Ludovina and Portocarrero, and the Colonel worried that the blood of his blood would risk the lives of all Brazilians in the fort. He turned to Ludovina, with eyes as cold as a glacier.

"Madam, either you shut up this child, or I will!"

The musician Verdexas, standing next to the woman, began to whistle at low volume, in the child's ear, a melody that sounded like a solemn march. Luis Caetano identified the song. One of his sister's favorites.

The baby swallowed the cry, smiled, and fell asleep.

"For the second time, you saved us, Verdexas. Which music is that?" Ludovina asked the versatile musician-soldier.

"It is a piece from Maestro Francisco Manuel da Silva. A trivial song, but it makes the children happy, Dona Ludovina."

Everyone embarked. The last group comprised the Indians with the empty barrels, the two quarrelsome women, Dona Ludovina, and the children. Only Portocarrero was missing. Fearful of leaving the Colonel behind, Luis left the group and went to the officer's quarters. He found the commander writing a note on a piece of paper and hiding it under his pillow. *Better not to ask what is this paper.* Luis clicked his boots to announce his presence.

"Sir, the last longboat is leaving."

"Excellent lieutenant, I will accompany you there."

They left the room and went to the pier. Luis, recalling the earlier events, whistled quietly the baby-soothing song.

***

Portocarrero boarded last on the Anhambaí, greeted by the crew and saluted by Lieutenant Balduino, the officer responsible for guiding everyone safely to Corumbá.

The Anhambaí was anchored in a river bend, behind an islet that sheltered it from the Paraguayan sight. But once the boilers turned on and the ship left the bend, Paraguayan observers would see it and give chase.

The English-made, 130 feet long ship usually had less than fifty sailors on board. However, that night, with the addition of the refugees and civilians, it had five times that number. The fort's inhabitants settled on the stern and lower deck, leaving the bow almost empty. To move up and down the river, the Anhambaí relied on two sails and a steam engine that powered two side wheels. The vessel's armament comprised two 32-pounder cannons. Cannons which, in the previous days, had been used to exhaustion, making the Paraguayans believe it was a warship with more guns than just two.

"Sir, welcome on board! I am sorry to be the bearer of disturbing news!" said Balduino.

"Already?" Portocarrero widened his eyes.

"Yes, sir, we are at the weight limit, and the bad news is that the Paraguayans left their steamboats ready to sail upstream." Balduino walked to the bow, alongside Portocarrero and Luis Caetano, careful to not trip over anything on the dark bitumen night. He pointed to the end of the islet that hid the Anhambaí. "As soon as we get out of here and make the curve upstream, they'll spot us."

"Just by a miracle, they will not reach us..." Luis said.

But neither Luis nor Balduino knew that the colonel already had a plan. Captain De Faria and Melo Bravo joined them, so all the officers, except Coelho, walked in silence to the front of the ship.

"Luis, did your men hang the empty barrels on the bow?" The colonel asked while inspecting the ship's upper deck.

"Yes, sir, they are all hanging from the hull."

Portocarrero ordered one of the Indians to bring the small box placed near his baggage.

"Balduino, we must sail now toward the Paraguayan flotilla instead of escaping. In absolute silence, with the boilers quiet, carried only by the river current."

The idea bothered Balduino. Luis clenched his jaw.

Captain Benedito remained calm, aware of Portocarrero's ingenious plan.

"Place this box next to the big barrels at the bow. When we get closer, less than five hundred yards from the Paraguayan ships, light that wick and get away."

"Sir, permission to ask," Luis said. "Why the empty barrels? Is this box some kind of new weaponry?"

The Colonel stroked his thick beard, amused by the question. "New? On the contrary. This is one of the oldest weapons of mankind: the bluff."

Portocarrero turned to De Faria and asked him to share the entire plan with the rest of the soldiers while he checked on Ludovina and the children.

***

The Anhambaí, with all the lamps off and in complete silence, left the river bend with a light kick of the steam engine. She moved with the currents toward the Paraguayan flotilla, anchored two miles downstream.

Not even a cigarette light. The officers inspected each side deck, stern, and bow so that everyone remained muted. Contrary to what happened at the fort, this time, no one cried or quarreled as they all hid.

The ship needed to create an image of being unmanned. When Captain De Faria explained to Luis about Portocarrero's plan to pass as an explosive ship, the lieutenant remembered the military tales told by his father, Dom Caetano.

It was a bold plan, based on the belief that the Paraguayan commander, Vicente Barrios, would remember the lessons he had from Portocarrero. After seeing the Anhambaí with barrels tied to the hull, Barrios would think that the Brazilians turned the Anhambaí into a bomb vessel. Just like Lord Cochrane had done at Aix half a century earlier.

Portocarrero knew that Cochrane was one of Barrios' favorite heroes.

He expected Barrios to order the Paraguayan flotilla to retreat to escape from the bomb ship, leaving their advanced position. The Anhambaí would then turn around and gain time to escape to Corumbá.

"Sailor, throw a little wood on the boiler, enough only for us to start moving. Not a single pound more!" Balduino ordered from the command room using one of the communication tubes that carried his voice to the boilers on the lower deck.

The Anhambai moved with a gentle kick of the engine and a slow turn of the wheels. Then the sailors halted the boilers. The ship glided through the waters, carried by the current, like a boa constrictor through the jungle bushes— silent, slow, frightening.

The vessel left his cover behind the islet. The moon's glow marked the ghostly silhouette of the apparently dead Anhambai.

It took several minutes until one of the enemy observers noticed a floating shape on the horizon, two miles distant.

From the Anhambaí, hidden on the deck, Luis heard the enemies shouting, "*Barco a la deriva! Ojo! Barco a la deriva!*"

"They took the bait!" Luis said to Nopitena, both crouched at the bow. Only the duet, responsible for lighting the explosive box, and Balduino, handling the rudder, were on the top deck. They crouched, otherwise the Paraguayans could see them.

"Bait? You mean fish food?" Nopitena spoke Portuguese but knew little of popular expressions.

Luis frowned. "No, I meant...well, forget it. If we can hear them, it is because we are close enough." The lieutenant crawled to the gunpowder box.

In the darkness, the wick cord was nowhere to be seen, so Luis touched the ground with his hands until he found it. He lit up and ran back to his shelter.

The explosion of the little box echoed for miles. The impact destroyed one of the empty barrels. On the Paraguayan flotilla, alarmed sailors screamed. The screech of frightened birds from the adjacent jungles made it impossible to hear what the Guaranis shouted.

The red-shirted captains aimed their sailing telescopes in all directions until they encountered the fearful shadow of the ghost ship. The Paraguayan steamboats turned on the boilers, and the schooners hoisted sails. The enemy flotilla started to retreat to avoid the fake bomb vessel.

"The Paraguayans are retreating! Fire in the boilers, sailors! Give steam to this ship!" shouted Balduino on the communication tube. The Anhambaí needed, at all costs, to turn around to not get too close to the Paraguayan flotilla. If that happened, a collision would be the least of the problems.

Sailors, soldiers, and even civilians rushed to the ovens, throwing coal to raise the boiler fire fast enough for the wheels to move and turn the ship. However, the river current gave no respite and continued to take the ship dangerously close to the Paraguayan flotilla.

The Paraguayans moved their vessels, taking parallel positions on both sides of the riverbed, forming a lethal *corredor polonês—a corridor that reminded how carriages opened the passage for ambulances or kings to pass undisturbed.* An enemy corridor that could sink the Anhambai. Balduino needed to counter-steer the ship in time. Otherwise, that river stretch, just in front of the Coimbra fort, would become their graveyard.

The current kept dragging the Anhambai. The Brazilian ship slid closer and closer to the angle of the Paraguayan cannons. Either they halted it, or they would be sitting ducks for the enemy guns.

The boiler ran almost at full strength. Sailors threw the best quality of firewood available. The steam chimneys spit a dense fog. Balduino, openmouthed, raised his hands to head. Luis unsheathed his saber, preparing to fight any red-shirt that dared to board the ship, with Nopitena at his side. The Anhambai came so close to the Paraguayan flotilla that enemy faces were visible from the main deck.

The violent water currents looked determined to deliver the brave defenders of Coimbra to their deaths at the invader's hands.

Suddenly the ship stopped. The engine at its maximum power made the whole vessel shake. Sounds of the metal hull formed a terrifying symphony, a dramatic dance. Every bolt, nut, and metal sheet clicked, scratched, and writhed. The chimney expelled dark clouds in the sky as if the river itself was on fire.

The Anhambai started to move in the opposite direction, slowly taking distance from the Paraguayans and moving upstream in the mighty river, defeating the fierce currents.

From there, they shouldn't stop, and no boiler rest, until they reached Corumbá.

Chapter IX

Vicente Barrios, with pupils dilated and pulse accelerated, observed the Anhambaí vanish on the horizon, realizing it was no bomb ship. "Sentries, signal to the flotilla to head to the fort." He told the men in the upper deck. "Cannons ready! Their ship is running away! Time to take Coimbra, time to take prisoners!"

By the time he finished the sentence, the sailors at the bow and stern of the Paraguayan flagship repeated the message to the rest of the flotilla.

"Sergeant, bring me a canoe! I will march with the infantry to the fortress' walls!" Barrios differed greatly from his brother-in-law Solano López. While Solano preferred to command from the rear, to give orders from far and expect everyone to comply, Barrios rode with his cavalry, sailed with his sailors, and marched with his soldiers. While Solano used his intuition, Barrios used the knowledge of military science gained over years spent with great masters.

One of these masters was now at the Fort, waiting to surrender. At least that was what Barrios thought. If the Paraguayan colonel conquered the fort and Portocarrero surrendered his sword to him, it would be an emblematic case of a pupil surpassing a tutor.

Barrios, however, had enormous respect for Portocarrero. He wished to accompany the land troops and salute the former master for sharing such fierce combat, worthy of the most celebrated records in military history.

"Sir, what about their ship? Do we allow them to escape?" asked a lieutenant escorting the Paraguayan colonel.

"That ship doesn't matter. It must have only a handful of sailors seeking help. Our prize is the fort and the prisoners." Barrios said as he walked to the canoe. "For now, bomb them! The fire of our cannons will soften the Brazilians. When our infantry arrives, the surrender will be immediate!"

The dark night beckoned it was not even three in the morning when the roar of the Paraguayan cannons plagued the entire jungle. The fire opened by the Guaranis against the fort was so concentrated that it took time for the artillerymen to notice that the Coimbra's cannons did not respond to the attack.

One of the Guarani infantry sergeants camped at the riverside cheered, "they gave up! They are not returning fire!"

Gonzalez, who in the previous days had led three different battalions to take the fort with no success, left his tent. "Soldiers, to arms! We will march to the fort in a matter of minutes!"

The Paraguayan column left camp before five in the morning, reaching the walls with the first sunlight. The place's stillness made the officers believe it was a trap. Barrios, however, did not hesitate and, along with a pair of young soldiers, jumped over the low wall first. The same wall that in the previous days so many Paraguayans died in the futile attempt to conquer. Now at their reach.

Barrios went up, and standing on the parapet, in his red and golden gilded uniform, looked around and shouted, "Brazilians, you fought bravely, now surrender with dignity!"

But only nature responded to the Colonel. Croaking frogs, buzzing cicadas, and screaming parrots. The soldiers could hear the metallic clanks of their own sabers and bayonets.

Aware of the silence, Barrios ordered the scouts to enter the fort with him, and so the Paraguayans entered Coimbra for the first time.

An eerie emptiness. Empty of people, gunpowder, and bullets. In the whole main courtyard, the only thing breaking the monotonous red of the dirt floor was a couple of pans left behind.

Vicente Barrios blinked repeatedly. His triumphant expression from hours before was gone. The fort looked like a ghostly place. A lieutenant approached him with a piece of paper in his hands.

"Sir, you have your name written on that envelope." Barrios, moving his head on dismay, took the envelope in his hands, opened it, and noticed a hurriedly written note:

"On the Isle of Aix, the barrels of the great Lord Cochrane were full of gunpowder. Ours are nothing but deception. I am glad to see you became a colonel. *Su Maestro.*"

At the top of the Coimbra fort, Barrios realized Portocarrero's trick. Using his admiration for Lord Cochrane, the Brazilian Colonel managed to escape with all the fort's inhabitants, except for a few wounded Paraguayan soldiers the Brazilians rescued from the battlefield. Among them, a lieutenant with a carefully bandaged wounded arm.

Looking at the river, he ordered, "Prepare the boilers! We chase them to Corumbá!"

The Brazilians deceived him, but Barrios consoled himself, reminding that at least it was a master like Portocarrero who tricked him, not some ordinary captain. However, he still wondered what Solano López's reaction would be if he received the news about the escape.

Vicente Barrios needed to capture prisoners and achieve greater victories if he wanted to appease the *Mariscal*'s warmongering fury.

***

The sun high on the horizon indicated almost ten in the morning. The brightness of the day revealed how overpopulated was the Brazilian ship. The trip to Corumba would take a few days, making it necessary to deal with less heroic matters such as excrement disposal or food storage. Otherwise, disease and pestilence would spread like wildfire in that compact human mass.

On his way to the Anhambaí cockpit, Luis Caetano passed by Ensign Coelho, still caring for the wounded in one corner. Since the first day of the siege, the Ensign had changed from a pink-cheeked spoiled youngster to a dedicated soldier helping the injured men. Perhaps, thought Luis, the boy was not that futile.

"Coelho, officers' meeting now. Come." Luis said.

"Another meeting where I will be a dead weight, with no right to a hoot," grumbled the young officer. He turned to one infirmary helper, "Dona Madalena, get the gauzes and please change the bandage of this corporal." Coelho pointed to a blood-stained soldier lying on the floor and accompanied Luis.

The wheelhouse, illuminated by three windows, was relatively tidy compared to the rest of the ship. The wooden wheel used to steer the vessel elegantly occupied the frontal part, while maps and navigation plans covered the side walls.

When Luis and Coelho entered, the other officers were already reunited. Among them, Lieutenants Melo and Balduíno, Colonel Portocarrero and Captain De Faria, who was the first to voice his concerns.

"It is likely that the Paraguayans are chasing us by now." The captain interrupted his speech, gulping water from the mug he held. The baking weather made thirst a constant sensation. "We must prepare men for the defense of Corumbá. God willing, Lieutenant Simas arrived in time to gather reinforcements and alert the people."

After De Faria finished, Portocarrero's boots' sound against the wooden floor echoed in the small room. The colonel, hitherto quiet in a corner near the wheel, walked with his hands behind the back and with an open chest. He passed by the captain and came close to the three lieutenants and the ensign.

"Barrios will chase us to the north, but it is still necessary to warn the southern garrisons to stay on maximum alert." Portocarrero faced the four subordinates, ready to announce the reason for the meeting. "I need one of you to disembark and go to Miranda and Dourados. The volunteer can take as many soldiers as he considers necessary."

Miranda and Dourados were the two other border garrisons under the authority of Portocarrero. Both were military villages composed of soldiers, their families, and surrounding civilians. Miranda was more than one hundred kilometers far away from Coimbra. Dourados, twice this distance. That meant hundreds of kilometers of swamps and wild steppes under the threat of enemy soldiers and hostile indigenous tribes.

Of the four candidates to disembark, the first discarded was Balduíno because of his position as ship commander.

Melo preferred a thousand times more to die by the enemy sword than lost in the jungle. Coelho was still a boy with aristocratic tendencies, no match for the Pantanal marshes.

"I will," Luis said. "I need to take only one of the Indians with me. The others may stay on board and help the ensign in the infirmary."

"Lieutenant Gomes, do you think you can do a twenty-league walk through the jungle, and a few days more in the *Cerrado* steppes, accompanied only by an Indian?" asked an incredulous Captain De Faria. "Do you think you are some sort of Ulysses?"

Luis grinned. The comparison with the Greek epic hero was flattering, but the sobriety of the meeting asked for an explanation.

"No, sir. It is not any Indian that will come with me, but the Kadiweu Nopitena. He knows the marshes. Plus, he can talk to any Guiacuru villager we find on the way, so we can get a pair of horses to go faster."

Luis's idea made sense. To disembark with only one companion meant fewer mouths to feed on the long journey. Besides, if they got a pair of horses, they would be in Miranda in a dozen days.

Portocarrero nodded, "Fine. The sooner we can pull over for you both to disembark, the better since we're going in the opposite direction."

"Sir, we don't have dinghies on board," Lieutenant Balduino recalled an important detail. The dinghies used to transport and disembark passengers remained in Coimbra. Without them, either the ship needed a pier to stop, or volunteers had to jump straight to the water. There were no piers anywhere near, and jumping in the river could be deadly. The December current could drag a Peroba trunk as if it was a piece of bamboo.

"Balduíno, I will ask the Indians, there must be a village nearby or some fishing canoe," said Luis.

"Alright, but warn the Kadiweu that it will be a quick maneuver."

Luis left the wheelhouse while the rest remained to discuss bureaucracies such as food rationing and hygiene on board.

The Indian soldiers commanded by Luis were at the bottom deck, helping to separate fuel for the boilers. When he approached, he noticed the terrible quality of the wood available. "My Lord! They will arrive in Corumbá with this rotten wood only if they go down to push the ship!"

"But how can someone push the ship, chief?" Nopitena asked. Luis didn't explain that it was just figuratively. The time was too short for a semantic lesson.

"It does not matter. We, you and I, need to disembark and proceed to Miranda." Noticing the other Kadiweus around, Luis opened the conversation to the rest of the men. "Any of you know exactly where is the closest village between Albuquerque and Coimbra?"

"My village is halfway to Albuquerque, chief," replied a chubby Indian soldier called Nadedi.

Luis sighed in relief. If his village was halfway between the two settlements, it meant only a few leagues ahead. "Nadedi, Nopitena, come with me to the upper deck."

Luis walked with the Indians to the cockpit. When the two Kadiweus arrived at the door and saw only officers inside, they hesitated to enter, intimidated by the uniforms and insignias.

"Come in, you both," Captain De Faria said.

The two Indians looked at Luis, waiting for his command as if he had more authority than the Captain. A result of the closeness and confidence his men had in him. "Come in, soldiers," repeated Luis.

Inside the room, Nadedi spoke about his village. The Guaicuru did not know exact distances—not for his demerit, since even some officers were confused between the Portuguese measures and the new metrics taught in the school benches. Nadedi described that his settlement was on the opposite side of an elongated islet.

Balduino identified the location. "If it's there, we need to shut down the boilers in less than twenty minutes!" he said, signaling to one of his sailors in the room to inform the boiler crew. "You both prepare your baggage because we will soon divert to the margin."

The call depended on Luis Caetano. At his signal, Balduíno would reduce the boat's steam, allowing the approach of a canoe. Above everything else, the entire movement needed to be extremely quick. Every minute wasted on that brought the enemy closer.
Luis and the two Indians left the room to start preparations, and on the way, Nadedi explained that the village was about thirty minutes walk toward the sunrise. Once there, they should ask for two horses but in return give a small box to a woman named Niwaalo. Nadedi took the tiny box from his haversack and handed it over to Nopitena.

"What's in this box?" Nopitena asked.

"Just a few teeth. The person to whom you should deliver it will understand." said the plump but helpful Nadedi.

Minutes later, Luis and Nopitena returned to the upper deck. The lieutenant carried his rifle, officer's saber, and a brown side bag with ammunition and personal items.

Nopitena carried a canvas sack with food and the box from Nadedi.

On the same deck, indifferent to Luis and Nopitena, men fished, and women cooked. People tried to live with the bare minimum dignity in the overpopulated ship. Another day with no clouds.

Meters ahead sailed a Pirogue with a Guaicuru and a child. The Anhambaí approached the boat, and the waves from its iron hull cruising against the current almost knocked the child out of the canoe. The distressed father yelled an insult while waving for the ship to get away.

Nadedi shouted a few words to the fisherman, in a Guaicuru dialect familiar to both, and the canoeist calmed down.

"What did Nadedi tell to that fisherman?" Luis asked Nopitena.

"He told him that we need help to bring two men to the shore, and we would pay for the service."

"Pay?" Luis snorted. "There go my coins."

The canoe glided closer to the Anhambai, still at least twenty meters distant, when a sentry shouted from the observatory tower.

"Smoke downstream! Three to four leagues distant!"

On a clear day, smoke seen from afar meant only one thing. The Paraguayan flotilla was coming, although still at a safe distance. From that moment on, every second with the boilers turned off increased the risk for everyone on board.

"Nadedi, tell him to come faster!" Luis shouted at the Indian, who then yelled in a Guaicuru dialect to the fisherman.

The Brazilian ship practically stopped, with its engine generating only enough power to not drift away with the current. Near the margin, tree trunks were half-submerged due to the recent rains that filled the river.

"Nopitena, do you see these half-sunken trees?"

"Yes, chief."

"If I lasso one of these logs, we can tie ourselves with the rope and use it as an anchor, so the current doesn't take us away. Then we wait outside for the fisherman, and the Anhambai doesn't waste more time."

"We are going to become Surubim food, chief," Nopitena said, alarmed to hear the lieutenant's idea, "but if you go, I will follow."

"Will you?" Luis grinned. Nopitena nodded.

The Kadiweu asked the sailors for a cord, a material that any navy ship had in abundance.

Luiz hurriedly prepared the knot, remembering the old days at the 3-Estados farm, tying cattle together with his friend Primo. He twirled the noose over his head twice, and during the third time, he threw it.

The noose flew the ten meters that separated the ship from the tree trunks with a hiss, wrapping one of them elegantly. "As for a rifleman, you are a good cowboy!" Melo Bravo celebrated while tying the rope around the waist of Luis and Nopitena.

"My friend, I'm leaving, but you give the Guaranis a smack for me." Luis shook Melo's shoulders, bidding farewell.

"No doubt about it, Lieutenant Gomes. Good luck walking through the jungle. I don't know if I could do it."

"You underestimate yourself, Melo. If I had to choose someone to save these people from the Guarani paws, it would be you."

Nopitena finished his preparations. Luis took his place to jump. "May everyone have a pleasant trip to Corumbá. I am leaving for a stroll through the jungle!" He turned to Nopitena. "Anspeçada, at my call, we both go."

The muddy waters of the Paraguay River bubbled while tapping the ship's structure. The lieutenant looked toward the woods, where a flock of Maritacas took flight from the top of one tree.

"Now! Jump!"

As if trying to imitate the birds, the Lieutenant and the Kadiweu leaped out from the Anhambaí, splashing into the nut-colored river.

Almost immediately, the currents dragged Luis and Nopitena to the rope's limit. The fisherman supposed to pick them was still ten meters away.

The rope tied to their trunk stretched, tightly gripping Luis's torso.

Breathless, he looked back and saw that Nopitena was in a much better position. Since the Kadiweu was at the other end of the rope, all the cable tension applied right at the middle, at the lieutenant and his ribs.

He panted, gasping for air. Passing out now, even for a few minutes, would mean to sink his head into the water and drown.

Luis glanced at the ship, trying to see his companions from Coimbra for the last time. Lieutenant Balduíno, Captain Benedito de Faria, Portocarrero, and the Guaicurus he commanded for over two years. But the air did not reach his lungs. His vision blurred, and even the sounds of the rapids were fading. Tied to the rope, Luis Caetano collapsed.

Chapter X

The smuggler Gaspar Picagua and his brother, friar
Pedro, turned upstream. The direction change was to avoid the
skirmish between Brazilians and Paraguayans. Instead of the
way back to Corrientes, they arrived in an effervescent
Corumbá. Platoons marched, moving cannons at the port.

The war blocked their way to the south. In Corumbá,
hundreds of soldiers eager to drink and purchase small
luxuries gave Gaspar a chance to profit. He sold the few
bottles he still had in a matter of hours for customers who
paid several times the usual price.

He left the square after a series of successful deals and
waited for Pedro's return. The friar went to the town church,
still under construction, to greet the local priest and offer his
help to attend confessions. In the face of danger, people
rushed to ask for God's forgiveness.

While resting under a palm tree, Gaspar thought about
the contrast between him and his brother. One, a willful soft-
voiced friar, eager to help anyone seeking salvation. The
other, a sneaky smuggler profiting from the vices of the
riverside villagers. If not for the blood ties, and the fact they
were the only family left for each other, they could be rivals.
Each soul saved by the friar was one less drunkard.

Gaspar's ramblings prevented him from noticing an
officer in a blue uniform approaching.

"Peddler, do you have a bottle of bagaceira to sell?" the man asked.

"No, sir, only cachaça, and it's almost gone." The smuggler raised the hat covering his face and looked to the officer. "Wait, I know you!"

It was Lieutenant Simas from Coimbra, a frequent buyer of Gaspar's products. The lieutenant's presence in Corumbá explained why the smuggler saw a boat passing upstream near the fort at breakneck speed.

"You are the Guarani who sold pinga in Coimbra!" Simas said. "Don't you know we are at war with your people? Are you a spy?"

"I am a Correntine Guarani, sir, not a Paraguayan Guarani. This war of yours is not mine." Gaspar said before his origin raised any suspicion. The only metal the smuggler wanted were coins, not bullets, for he had no military inclination. "Why so many people around here?"

"When I warned the local command about the Paraguayan attack, they decided to evacuate." Simas took a few coins out of his pocket to buy one of the last liquor bottles, "So, as soon as they get more boats, everyone will leave."

"All these soldiers and no one will fight the Paraguayans? Is everyone really running away?" Gaspar squinted his eyes. He didn't care about war motivations but knew that an evacuated city was bad for business.

"I asked myself the same question when I heard Colonel Oliveira saying that he wanted to leave before seeing the first Paraguayan." Simas shrugged his shoulders in disdain. "What Portocarrero had of bravery, this one has of wimpiness," he whispered.

"What about the people that live here?" Gaspar asked as he delivered the bottle to Simas.

"If it depends on Oliveira, it is each man for himself. But I guess you will still make money from it." The lieutenant put the liquor flask in his side bag, bidding farewell.

Gaspar looked around. Nearly Everybody was leaving the city only with the clothes on their backs. Many would be glad to sell their valuables at a bargain price. Things he could resell down the river.

The Correntino smuggler just found a way to make money from the conflict. From a war that was not his.

***

Slapped in the face, Luis Caetano woke up, ignoring the aggression but turning his eyes upwards. A Jaburu in the canopy of an Ipe at the river's edge attracted his attention. The vision made him ignore the burning sensation on his face and the pain in his chest. Still dizzy after blacking out in the river, his thoughts wandered. *What a strange animal: half body as a stork, and the other half, black as a nightmare. The two parts separated by a scarlet necklace as if the breeder was putting together pieces of multiple species in the same animal. And yet, the result is majestic. A bird as large as a well-nourished child.*

"Chief! Chief!" a voice said. Two more slaps hit the lieutenant's face. "All in order?" Nopitena asked, accompanied by the fisherman who brought them to the shore.

"Yes, anspeçada. Later I'll pay you back for these slaps," Luis replied, sitting on the sand of the riverbank. Looking at the horizon, he could still see the Anhambaí turning in a curve.

"The imperial army has a debt with you," Luis said to the fisherman, who understood nothing. Nopitena repeated the lieutenant's words in the Guaicuru idiom. The man uttered something.

"What did he say?" asked Luis, as he dried his wet boots by hitting them on a rock. "How much money Nadedi promised him?"

"You can keep your coins, chief. He said that the Guarani are already bringing terror to the villages downstream," Nopitena had tense, twitching eyes, "And the debt is paid if we chase them away from here."

Luis shared Nopitena's concern. The Kadiweu's settlement was in the same region as the Guarani raids. The lieutenant nodded to the fisherman and said goodbye with a touch on the cap. "Time to go to Nadedi's village to deliver the box and pick horses," said the lieutenant as he stood up.

Nopitena touched his uniform repeatedly as if missing something.

They advanced into the woods and, minutes later, met a group of children climbing onto a log.

"Ligotis, chief."

Luis understood it meant the same as kids. The Indian asked the children something, and one escorted them to his village while speaking continuously with Nopitena.

Less than ten minutes later, they arrived at the settlement. It had five square-shaped *ocas,* indigenous huts made of wood and straws, arranged in a semi-circle, forming a large dirt yard in the middle. Around the settlement, unclothed men prepared the land for crops, while in front of the huts, young women cooked or weaved straw. Children ran, played, and fought each other without anyone bothering them. Two huts had small stables attached, where the Indians kept their horses, and a shallow stream with crystal clear water ran on the right side of the terrain.

Nopitena asked for Niwaalo, the woman to whom they should give the box. The workers pointed to the central *oca*, where women prepared food pots over a fire.

"Niwaalo?" Luis also asked.

The Indian girls stared at him, then called an elderly and chubby Indian woman carrying wood to feed the blaze.

"She is Niwaalo, chief," Nopitena said.

"Finally. Anspeçada, give her the box and ask if she has a pair of spare horses to us."

Nopitena walked a few steps toward the woman and started talking. *Wait, where is the box? Why his hands are empty?* Luis asked himself while watching the scene.

The Kadiweus' conversation took longer than expected. The lieutenant, understanding nothing, contemplated the young Indians preparing the food. It had been a long time since he saw a female's breast. In fact, it was a long time since he saw a woman as a woman. In the fort, female presence meant soldiers' wives and daughters, and, as a matter of respect, he looked at them as men. For this reason, the view of those rounded, puffy reliefs carved in cinnamon skin was a visual feast.

Nopitena returned. The lieutenant, openmouthed, watched the bare-chested women at work.

"Chief?" The Kadiweu cleaned his throat, "They will give us one horse, so we still need one more."

Absorbed in his admiration for the girly grace, Luis stuttered. "Um, well, one...One is better than nothing." He shook his head, regaining his composure. "Did you give her the box?"

"No, chief, it must have fallen into the river."

"What?" Luis raised his hands in the air, not understanding how the soldier could be calm about it.

"It is not a problem. Before, Nadedi told me that the box had only teeth inside. Niwaalo is his mother, and that signaled he is alive and well. The teeth were his when he was a child." Nopitena exhibited the satisfied grin of a person who solves a problem he just created.

"No surprise she and Nadedi are so similar, at least in waist size," Luis said, resisting the urge to look back at the naked Indian girls.

"They also offered us food and shelter until tomorrow. Do we accept, chief?"

"It is impossible to ride at night. We can stay a bit more and enjoy their...hospitality."

Nopitena gave him a side look but said nothing.

"We leave tomorrow at dawn. Two people on a single horse will not be comfortable, but better than walking," Luis said.

At sunset, they ate together with the Kadiweus. After supper, Nopitena took the animal to graze. The beast needed strength for the long journey. Luis sat near a hut, listening to the bubbling of the stream waters. After a chaotic day, the moisture scent from the creek and the breeze from the jungle comforted him. He closed his eyes for a moment.

Some noises came from inside the trail. Perhaps a bush pig or some of the various nocturnal animals. *But what if it was a Guarani platoon?* Luis reached for his rifle and the ammunition box he stored in his shoulder bag.

Suddenly a fist hit his temples. The lieutenant, still dizzy, responded with a jab in the chin of the dark figure. He took the stranger's arm, twisted the aggressor's hand, nearly breaking it, and threw him on the floor.

A childhood of fighting alongside (and sometimes against) his friend Primo taught him how to dodge and connect punches.

"Who are you? What do you want?" Luis asked.

The stranger shouted something incomprehensible while trying to get free, but Luis mounted on the man's back.

"Are you a Paraguayan? Where's the rest of your band, filthy scallywag?"

Nopitena and two other Indians approached the brawl. "Chief, let him go! He is one of us, speaks our language!"

Luis hesitated to release the person who smacked his head minutes earlier. When the man stood up, a circle of spectators formed around the two.

"Nopitena?" said the stranger. His condition was pitiful. Wounded, half-naked, and with a runaway's decrepit gaze.

Nopitena frowned at the wretch. The full moonlight revealed the newcomer's face. "Natena!" They hugged. The decrepit man, after recognizing the old friend, had a broken voice and trembling hands.

"Is everything fine?" Luis asked while checking with the hand if his head was bleeding after the fight. Only a few curious bystanders, mostly girls, remained, trying to understand what had just happened.

Nopitena explained that Natena was his childhood friend and lived in his village. Days before, he saw the Paraguayan attack against the fort from afar and thought that Nopitena got caught in the fight.

"Well, he was almost correct," said Luis. "But why is he here if he is from your village?"

The soldier did not know why, so he asked his friend. Natena recounted the reason for his arrival, and with each word, Nopitena's face changed. First, eyes opened in fear, passing through teeth clenching in unease and ending with the purest, indescribable form of terror.

Nopitena sat on the floor, and the other Kadiweus around him showed compassion. Women mourned while some men shouted *Nidelakadi! Nidelakadi!*

Luis had heard this word before. His platoon of Kadiweus shouted the same while defending the fort. It meant *war*. War that had reached these Indians. In their case, however, it was a tribal conflict much older than the skirmish between Paraguay and the Empire.

"Chief, they invaded my village. They took some people away, killed others. Natena escaped, but he doesn't know anyone else who made it." The Indian explained with a pale expression, eyes full of desperation as Luis never saw before, "Chief, they took Nialigi..."

Luis turned to the young women, looking for an herbal infusion to calm his soldier. The girls, knowing what had happened, gave him a filled pot. The concern for his friend was enough for the lieutenant to ignore the naked breasts that earlier won his admiration.

Minutes after drinking the herbal liquid, Nopitena fell asleep.

***

"Anspeçada, wake up!"

Nopitena grunted after hearing the order. He fidgeted, opening his eyes on the straw bed the Indians placed him the night before. The first sunlight brought back Natena's escaping story, and all the memories were fresh as the morning breeze. The Guaranis invading his village, attacking the elders, and kidnapping Nialigi, the girl he had always had deeper feelings for.

"Get up. The horse is ready. Let's see what happened to your village," Luis said, walking toward the Indian bed. The Indian soldier looked outside the Oca and saw a saddled horse. Outside, peasants were already at work in the fields, and the sun was rising high on the horizon. Whatever they gave him to drink the day before made him sleep too much. "Chief, my village is downstream. We should go east to Miranda." Nopitena sat down, rubbing his eyes and drinking from the water bowl at his bedside.

Luis took a twig and began to draw on the floor. "Miranda is to the southeast. Your village is to the south. Only a minor detour." He made a big circle and a straight line passing under it. "If after your village we go straight to the Bodoquena ridge, we avoid the marshes of the Miranda River and ride on dry ground. It will be faster than going straight from here."

The lieutenant ingenuity eased Nopitena, who sighed in relief. Then the Kadiweu's face straightened, and staring to the draw in the sand, he asked, "What if we find Guaranis along the way?"

"One problem at a time." Luis chuckled, almost as if the idea of another fight amused him.

They left that same morning, arriving at Nopitena's village late afternoon when the sun was already descending on the firmament.

Silence filled the place. No child screams, no cries, no despair. Anyone who could escape has fled, abandoning everything behind. Two bodies laid near the stable, with the blue countenance of the dead and blow marks on the head. Nopitena recognized one of them.

"Warriors. I guess they stayed behind so the others could gain time to escape."

The Kadiweu walked around his deserted village. No cooking fire or sounds from any livestock. If it wasn`t for Natena, telling him what happened the day before, one could imagine that the village was abandoned for weeks, maybe months. His bare feet stepped in something warm.

Fresh manure, still warm. By the size and greenish color, it was either from a wild capybara wandering the village or from a larger, herbivorous animal.

Luis entered each of the huts and collected any food the former residents left. From there, they had a long journey to Miranda. Behind one of the ocas, he found a shed with tools, grain bags, and a brown, four-legged silhouette.

A moving, large shade.

Quietly, the lieutenant went to the central yard, "Nopitena, come here!" he whispered.

They returned to the grain shed, and Luis pointed to the animal, nearly twenty steps away. A beautiful stallion that, despite their presence, kept eating from the grain vases with the composure of a princely mount.

"Chief, I think now we have horses for both of us," Nopitena said, reaching into the corn bag that Luis carried.

The Kadiweu stood up, attracting the horse's eyes. He extended his arm, hand splayed in the air at chest height, displaying an ear of corn.

Nopitena resembled a fencer in a fighting position - one foot forward, followed by the other that dragged behind him. In a silent ballet, the Indian approached the animal, who continued to stare at him.

His hand neared the stallion's nose so close that the animal's breath dampened his fingertips. The horse tilted its head and looked at the corn.

A Bite.

The animal was still chewing the grains when Nopitena turned his own body to the side, placing his other hand on the stallion's chest, feeling its heart. Hugging it. It was as if through that embrace, all the sadness from seeing his village devastated and all his torments were healed. Healed by the horse's heat, by his calm indifference, and by his powerful muscles.

The Kadiweu had great mounting skills. But that was beyond a skill. It was a gift. A gift that formed an alliance between man and beast. An alliance that even the Guarani would fear.

Chapter XI

Corumbá was not large, but among inhabitants, soldiers and Indians, it had over two thousand people. Nearly all of them wanted to escape. Any object that floated and could navigate became a tool to evacuate the place.

In those early days of January, shortly after his arrival, the smuggler Gaspar Picágua still profited even after selling all his cargo. He bought precious goods for peanuts from the fleeing residents, who were afraid of the imminent Paraguayan arrival. He also earned from transporting people.

Families from riverside settlements asked the peddler for help. He used his boat to take the locals to the port, where they attempted to buy a seat on the Jacobina or Anhambaí ships. The latter had arrived days before, with the inhabitants of the Coimbra fort.

Gaspar knew one officer who arrived on the Anhambaí. Lieutenant Melo never bought a bottle from him because the others insisted on paying his bill. A well-regarded man. Nearly everyone owed a favor to the diligent Melo Bravo.

The place where Gaspar negotiated his services was next to the city's arsenal—close to the church under construction, where his brother Frei Pedro assisted the parish priest. That afternoon, when almost all the inhabitants had already left the city, Melo Bravo came with a platoon.

"Get away, *muambeiro*! Let's blow this place up, so no Guayo uses Brazilian gunpowder!"

Gaspar stared at the man. Melo's clenched teeth and frantic gestures gave him an appearance between bravery and hatred-fueled hallucination.

"You're out of your mind, Lieutenant! It will blow up the entire city!" Gaspar said.

Indeed, Gaspar's assessment was correct since the ammo deposit had enough explosives to level the quarter and damage nearly every house in the port's vicinity.
A few meters from there, a Portuguese man who lived in Corumbá repeated Gaspar's words. Like other foreigners, he saw no need to leave the city since he was neither Brazilian nor Paraguayan.

"Colonel Oliveira ordered everyone to evacuate. I leave against my will, 'cause I am boiling to fight for every inch of this land," replied Melo Bravo to the Portuguese. "But...he is the colonel. If we are going to withdraw, at least the Guayos will not benefit from it."

"Just throw all the gunpowder into the river," Gaspar said with a smirk.

The lieutenant and the other two soldiers glanced at Gaspar. It was a safe plan and needed little effort, as the river was right there.

"Good idea. You would be useful in the imperial army, *muambeiro*."

"Thank you, Mr. Melo, but this war is not mine," replied Gaspar.

The next day, Gaspar kept on carrying people from nearby villages to the port using his barge. All passengers wanted to buy an escape ticket to Cuiabá on board the schooner *Jacobina*.

It became clear, however, that the Jacobina became too heavy to sail upstream. The officers had the idea of towing the schooner using the Anhambaí. But no one questioned whether the Anhambaí, also packed to its maximum capacity, could handle this Herculean task.

Friar Pedro finished his work after most of the faithful left for the ships. He spent time at the port watching the improvised river taxi from his brother. "Gaspar, where they will put so many people? How is this Brazilian boat going to sail upstream with such a weight? My Lord!"

The words from Friar Pedro were prophetic. Even at full steam, the Anhambaí did not have strength enough to move the Jacobina from its place. Colonel Oliveira ordered the men to cut ropes and let the Anhambaí go alone, leaving the Jacobina to its own fate. Local fishermen, arriving at Corumbá from downstream, warned that the Paraguayans had already taken Albuquerque and headed for the town.

Gaspar delivered his last two passengers to the Jacobina. He then noticed a skiff approaching with the same lieutenant who a day before wanted to blow up all the city's gunpowder. Like other officers, Melo Bravo had a reserved place on the Anhambaí, but he couldn't stand to see the schooner's passengers abandoned.

Melo returned for the Jacobina, climbed at the bow, and ordered everyone to be silent so he could speak.

"Inhabitants of Corumbá, the Anhambaí heads to Cuiabá. They promised to return to help you, but I fear that there will be not enough time, as the enemy is coming."

Sorrowful cries resounded on the Jacobina's deck. The lieutenant made a gesture asking for silence and continued. "Anyone who wants to leave the city by land, especially women and children, follows me. The remaining soldiers and I will march together and give protection to whoever is with us."

The escape plan to march across flooded swamps under the scorching sun sounded suicidal, but it was the only alternative. It was either that or certain death for the man and slavery for women and children under Paraguayan hands. Gaspar, with his boat meters away from the schooner, listened to Melo's words. *Walk through the marshes with so many people? They nicknamed him wrongly. It's not Melo Bravo. It's Melo Loco!* The smuggler returned to the port and recounted the story to his brother.

"Like Moses leading the people through the desert to flee from the Pharaoh," the friar said.

Some of the passengers from the Jacobina followed Melo, but many stayed, waiting for the promised return of the Anhambaí. Gaspar remained in the city, making money out of others' despair. Besides the improvised river taxi, he still made trips back and forth across the river, carrying food that he bought for a few dozen réis in warehouses outside the risk area. Stuff he sold with enormous profits in Corumbá, where markets were empty.

Three days later, in the morning, the smuggler stopped at a pier a few leagues to the north. He negotiated with farmers to buy corn sacks and dried meat to resell for the fugitives in Corumbá. Peeking at the river from afar, he saw the Anhambaí returning to the city. *They really came back*, thought Gaspar. "I better hurry before they take away what's left of the city."

Gaspar closed his deals, and by the end of the afternoon, he loaded everything into his flatboat and left. As he returned to Corumbá, a cannon reverberated. On the horizon, three columns of smoke closed the distance. *They are here.*

After a river curve, he witnessed two Paraguayan steamboats harassing the Anhambai. The Brazilian ship tried frantically to leave the enemy's reach, but without success.

The brave Anhambaí fired its stern cannon at the enemy steamers. The invaders responded with artillery fire and musket balls from deck shooters. The three ships sailed slowly as they went against the current, while Gaspar's flat-bottomed boat dashed in their direction. The smuggler tried to control his vessel to avoid approaching the floating duel, but the speed of the agile *chata* hindered his efforts.

The Anhambaí, perhaps with all the remaining gunpowder, fired a cannonball that killed a Paraguayan lieutenant by cutting him in half, cracked down the ship's hull, and fell into the river less than two feet from Gaspar. Albeit successful, it was the Brazilian ship's last shot.

Uncertain if the ball hit his boat or if the waves from the battle turned him, the last thing the Correntine felt was a plunge into the fresh water and the impulse to move his arms and feet to return to the surface. Startled, Gaspar didn't realize that something pinned into his submerged thigh.

***

Gaspar woke up near the port, still inside his boat. A fisherman towed the smuggler's chata from the battle zone shortly after the fight. Two men were bandaging his left thigh. At their side, a blood-stained cloth.

"See, brother? The fight you want to escape always finds you back," friar Pedro said, with the reassuring voice of a priest and an older brother. After bandaging Gaspar's leg, one man—probably a foreigner, because of the sunburned red

127

skin contrasting with his blue eyes—warned that the Correntino had lost some blood.

"It must have been the side of your boat that hit your leg, or maybe some twig," the friar said.

Gaspar's memories, however, returned. He recalled feeling a bite. It was not metal or wood but teeth.

"An Ariranha bit me." The smuggler had deep resentments against such animals, nicknamed by foreigners as *river panthers*.
The Ariranha, a local type of giant otter, with its slender black body, aquatic habits, and size of a large dog, was one of the river's most feared predators. Not because of its agility, much less than that of a jaguar or its bite, timid if compared to an alligator. But because of the insane aggressiveness with which entire groups attacked anything that they considered a threat. An attack from those creatures almost took his life during his childhood, forcing his father to jump into death to save his son. A tragedy he witnessed alone.

"The Ariranha legend again? I already told you this is something in your head," replied Pedro in a harsher tone. "Rest. I'll tell someone to fix the boat and bring you water and food." The friar stood up and helped his brother to sit down.

"How can we leave with this skirmish on the waters?" Gaspar asked, not realizing that peace returned to the place. No more shots or explosions. The battle ceased.

"We are leaving tomorrow at the early sunrise. Now you need to rest." The friar perceived that the after-battle silence still confused his brother. "The fight here is finished. Whoever was on the Brazilian ship, if didn't dive into the river, was arrested or killed. Happy the ones who fled through the jungle with Lieutenant Melo."

"And I thought his plan was mad..." Gaspar observed the port movement. His eyes reached the pier nearby. The Paraguayan steamers Yporá and Rio Apa and then the Brazilian Anhambaí slowly approached, looking like ghost ships.

No Brazilian flags were visible anywhere, but only soldiers in scarlet red uniforms. On the sail strings of the Iporá, small pendants shaking.

Severed ears.

Chapter XII

Nopitena's bowl-shaped black hair covered his eyes as his brown stallion galloped across the low grassland. The Indian, riding the steed he found days before in his abandoned village, gained distance from Luis Caetano and his silver-haired horse, gifted by Niwaalo. Both bolted from a hilltop toward a tiny course of water in a valley.

The Kadiweu reached the stream first, winning the informal race. He did not hide his satisfied gaze after defeating the lieutenant. They dismounted near the creek, and Luis greeted the Kadiweu.

"Incredible, incredible. It was as if you both floated over the bush."

This compliment, coming from Luis, was no small feat, for the lieutenant was also a competent horseman. The easy victory of the Kadiweu and his animal tested the best qualities of both men and beast.

Nopitena, despite his connection with the agile light brown horse, did not bother to give him a name. Every time he wanted the animal to move, the Kadiweu shouted *Eka, Eka,* so Luis decided that this would be its name—even though *Eka* was just a command to move in the Kadiweu language.

The lieutenant's own horse had a similar size and was named *Nickel*. A metal that Luis never saw, but according to how his father described it, it had a similar silvery color.

The pair stood a few kilometers from Miranda. After leaving the village, the two had some tough days. They rode across wetlands and dodged flooded regions on several occasions to avoid alligators or ariranhas who could attack the horses. That didn't avoid, however, the mosquitoes that came from everywhere.

The obstacles encountered in the swamp doubled the pleasure of leaving the marshes and entering the *cerrado*, a dry-soiled savanna. The cerrado had its dangers, but the animals' pace increased. A welcome speed since they were short on food supplies.

"Chief, there are some Jenipapo trees a few meters from here. Their fruits are good as fish bait. I will try to catch something," Nopitena said.

"Great. We camp here today. Tomorrow we arrive in Miranda." Luis, exhausted by the late afternoon sun and long horseback riding, reclined under a tree and took a nap, wishing to wake up only with the scent of roasted fish.

The lieutenant fell asleep with a hat covering his eyes. The fatigue of riding ten days with almost no rest, plus the nights tormented by mosquitoes, put him in a deep sleep. He had a vivid dream. A dream of his adolescence at the Três Estados ranch. The afternoons listening to the stories from his father. He also remembered his trips with his friend Primo to the nearby cities, sometimes causing problems with the locals. But he didn't remember his mother.

A metal clatter woke Luis up, prompting him to unsheathe his saber. Still reclined on the tree, he sought for anyone who dared to disturb his sleep. But it was only a child, paralyzed by the glow of the lieutenant's sword. A kid of only ten or eleven years old, with a disheveled appearance, making it difficult to tell if it was male or female.

"No! He's just a boy! He is my son!" A desperate woman voice from the edge of the stream made Luis turn his head. She ran in his direction. "Please, don't hurt him. We're leaving."

"Calm down, lady. Why are you leaving?" Luis asked as he stood up.

"By the grace of the Virgin Mary! You are Brazilian!" the woman said, ignoring the lieutenant's question.

"As far as I know." Luis took his hat and adjusted it over his head. "But why are you leaving?"

"Because there is nothing left in Miranda. The Paraguayans took it." The woman had swollen eyes and a starving face. "They came for us after Dourados."

"Dourados?" For a moment, Luis thought he had heard the wrong word.

"Yes. They killed almost every soldier there, including my husband."

The woman's words echoed in the lieutenant's head like a blow. The catastrophic news so baffled him that he used the tree trunk for support.

"But, but...how? We came from Coimbra using the fastest way, and yet they overtook us?" Luis stammered, staring at the horizon as if either his mind or his geography knowledge betrayed him. *Is there a faster passage that allowed the Guarani to arrive earlier?* he thought.

Nopitena returned with two fish on a line, both medium-sized *pacus*. The little starving boy saw the Indian bringing food and ran to him.

"Coimbra? No sir, they came by Ponta Porã. The Guaranis spared only a foreigner, who later told us everything. My husband was part of the cavalry regiment. They tried to defend the settlement, but there were too many of them. About 100 for each Brazilian," said the woman, revealing her sad face. "It was a carnage. They massacred even the Indians who resisted."

"Ponta Porã? How come...Oh...Good grief! Two columns!" The lieutenant punched the tree where he rested minutes before. "They invaded us with two columns!"

"Chief? Can I light the fire to roast the fish?" asked Nopitena, not knowing what was going on but realizing they had a problem.

"No. If the Paraguayans are in Miranda, a campfire here will attract their attention."

"I'm going to do it on the tree leaves, then. Who are these?" Nopitena asked.

"They will eat with us. Give my fish to them." The bad news took the hunger out of Luis. If Miranda had fallen, Dourados probably had the same bad luck, or worse. Dourados' garrison commander was Antônio João Ribeiro, a good friend of Luis. *What fate did he have? How much did he suffer?* the lieutenant thought.

Nopitena grabbed some leaves from a nearby banana tree, wrapped the *pacus* in it, dug a hole in the ground, and lit a low fire. He put the fish inside and covered it with large green leaves so that the ember gleam was invisible. The continuous breeze quickly dispersed the thin smoke.

A bright full moon softened the darkness, reflecting like a pearl in the stream waters and casting shadows under the tree. The Indian gave the fish to the youngster, as Luis wished. He ate as fast as a grasshopper.

"Kid, leave some for your mother!" the lieutenant's low but harsh voice scared the little one, who gave the woman the rest of his food.

"You are lucky enough to have a mother, and you want to starve her?" Luis scolded the child.

"It is ok, sir, it is ok," the mother tried to calm the lieutenant. Nopitena knew that Luis' irritation was not only with the brat's selfishness but with the child's privilege of having a mother by his side.

"Madam, where do you intend to go next?" The lieutenant calmed down and asked the woman.

"To the Maracaju ridge. The Kinikinau went there first when the Guaranis attacked. They found a good place. It is safe and with fertile land." The woman took another bite of the roasted fish.

"Kinikinau, strange-speaking people," Nopitena said while playing with the boy, using moonlight to make shadow figures with his hands.

"If the evacuees from Miranda escaped to the mountains, I believe we can go there too." Luis ate some of the flour he had. The hunger finally hit the lieutenant, but now the fish was gone.

"Chief, what about Dourados?" asked the Indian, recalling the original mission they received from Portocarrero.

"Our mission was to alert Miranda and Dourados about the Paraguayan invasion. If their second column invaded Ponta Porã and arrived in Miranda, it can only mean that..."

Luis did not want to say out loud the bad news. "We are going to the hills. There we ask if someone knows about Dourados." Luis turned and saw the woman and the child, who, after playing with Nopitena, rested on his mother's lap. Indifferent to all the disasters that surrounded him. Indifferent to the fact that his father died defending the Empire.

"You can come with us. Two people can fit on each horse. In two days, we arrive in the mountains." The lieutenant told the woman.

Her eyes filled with tears of relief. Hours before, she had been unsure that she and her son would survive another day. Now they had full bellies and a ride to safety.

"Yes. Yes, of course," the woman said, holding in joyful sobs.

***

For two days, they rode under the blazing sky of Mato Grosso. Streams and creeks along the route provided enough water for the horses. Two more fish caught on the second day interrupted the monotony of eating corn from the sacks they carried. Additional flavors came from local fruits, such as gabirobas and bocaiuvas. They also found a *graviola* tree with ripe fruit, a rarity in January. Its refreshing flavor enlivened the exhausting journey.

During the trip, the group met other exiles who explained the path to the refugee camp, located on a mountain plateau. They arrived there around eleven in the morning. Luis and the woman on the silver-colored Nickel, while Nopitena and the child rode on Eka. During the way, the Kadiweu taught some words of doubtful meaning to the little one.

Meters ahead, three Indians guarded a thin road and interrupted the passage.

"Who are?" one guard asked.

"We are looking for the Kinikinau camp. We just want to rest and bring to safety this woman and her child." The Indians approached and inspected their bags. They tried to speak to Nopitena, but he did not understand.

"Kadiweu?" a guard asked. Nopitena nodded. It was easy for the sentry to guess his tribe: rarely natives rode horses as smoothly as the Kadiweu-Guaicurus.

Another guard accompanied the group to the camp, telling in broken Portuguese that they should speak to Pacalalá, the settlement's chief and leader of the Kinikinau tribe. Near the entrance, inhabitants opened clearings to make space for crops. The camp arrangement was similar to what they saw in Niwaalo's village but larger.

The Kinikinaus inhabited the Miranda River region, and their language had nothing in common with either the Guarani or the Guaicurus. As they lived between ridges, they had limited contact with other tribes and understood little of the Portuguese language.

The biggest difference, however, was in the residents. As much for the diversity in their appearance as for their meager bodies, with slender faces and sunken eyes. The crops were their hope, but the field demanded time and sweat.

They tied the horses to a stump and looked around. Nearby, a white man helped a woman to build a frugal shelter out of wood and thatch. Luis asked him about Pacalalá. The man pointed to another clearing some 400 meters ahead.

Luis and the woman went to the place and found an oca, where dozens of Kinikinau men slept side by side. *Should I wake them up?* Luis thought. The lieutenant cleared his throat, trying to awake them with the hoarse sound. Nothing. He repeated the noise more forcefully, and one man woke up.

"I am looking for Pacalalá," Luis said.
The Kinikinau shook another native, a taller Indian with red paintings over his body, and uttered something in their language. The painted man woke up, turning to the two newcomers.

His body painting was irregular, different from the white, geometrical tattoos of Nopitena. His height was like Luis Caetano and taller than most natives. But instead of a muscular body like the lieutenant, he had a slim figure.

"Yes?" Pacalalá said, rubbing his eyes and stretching.

"The guards told me to get your permission to sleep in the camp. My name is Luis Caetano, lieutenant in the fort of—"

"Lieutenant? Are you a deserter?" Pacalalá wrinkled his nose in contempt. "We want peace, but we don't share our roof with cowards."

"You are right to do so. I am not a deserter. I am on a mission toward the southern garrisons. This woman and her child are fleeing from Miranda." Luis pointed to the woman. "I only need to rest for a night and see if anyone knows what happened with Dourados."

"There must be someone here who knows about Dourados. Did you bring anything to help the camp?" Pacalalá became more receptive to the Lieutenant's stay, knowing it was going to be short.

"No, but my soldier and I can help you with whatever you need," Luis replied.

"Do you know how to capture cattle and horses?"

"I was born and raised with a rope lace in my hand. My soldier is also good with horses."

"So rest. At night we go out to grab Paraguayan cattle at their camp."

Luis nodded.

Pacalalá prepared to return to his sleep, "You can sleep around here in our hut if you wish. The oca for women and children is on the opposite side."

Luis thanked him but went back to Nopitena. He explained to the Kadiweu that at night they would join a group to capture cattle. The lieutenant went to sleep in a clearing next to a hut.

The idea of stealing cattle from Paraguayans encouraged Luis. It was a chance to help these poor people to have meat or milk. It was also a chance for revenge, albeit symbolically, against the invaders who spoiled his transfer from Coimbra to an undemanding job in the National Guard. That was hard to forgive.

***

Luis and Nopitena got up before the other volunteers to capture cattle. The men formed two bands. One group was tasked with stealing a cow, while the other should bring one or two mares from the invaders' military garrison. Animals intended to plow the land.

They discussed the activities while sitting and drinking coffee around a campfire. A damp night brought hazy weather, and the firmament still had a pitch-black color.

"Anspeçada, you join the group that will bring the mare. I will go with the others." Luis said.

"All right, chief. But what if something happens?" Nopitena held a coffee tin mug with both hands. A mist covered the place. It was impossible to see anything beyond the distance of three arms.

"Nothing that shouldn't happen is going to happen tonight." Luis grabbed his rifled, verified his saber, finished his coffee, and stood up.

Before two in the morning, they joined their respective bands, taking distinct directions. Luis went toward the barn, where the Paraguayans guarded the livestock. Animals that the invaders stole from the local farms. *If they stole that cattle from Brazilians*, Luis thought, *we are not stealing anything but taking it back. It is a Brazilian herd, after all.*

The group descended the plateau and found the stable. A lamp illuminated the building facade. The mist made it impossible to see any sentinel on guard, but it was not the first time these men captured cattle. Sentries were always there. Their rule was to create a diversion, any distraction for the guards. The Paraguayans had so many animals that they couldn't notice the herd decreasing one by one as the days passed.

The group hid behind thick bushes on the upper side of a hill. The fog began to fade.

"What do we use today to distract them? The piggy?" said a middle-aged man, referring to the idea of releasing a baby pig from the bush toward the sentinels so that the swine's cry would cover any noise the men made while stealing the cow.

"No, I brought no piglet today. The Captain will be the distraction." The man leading the group tapped Luis' shoulders. "He will go there, to the other side of the slope," he pointed to the right, in the direction of some bushes two hundred meters farther. "He shoots from there, and the soldiers will chase the noise."

"Chase me?" Luis lifted his eyebrows. Nobody warned him about turning into bait.

"Calm down, captain, just shoot and run," said another white man. The Kinikinaus spoke little. Many of them barely knew Portuguese.

The lieutenant was so taken aback by the plan that he ignored them calling him captain. At least that didn't bother him.

Luis checked how many cartridges he had in his shoulder bag. *Enough.* The lieutenant walked to the east side of the cowshed and stopped at a tiny mount. The group leader said it was easy to run back to the camp from there. He only needed to go downhill and follow a water stream.

Crouched on the spot, Luis filled his rifle with gunpowder but no bullet. Even if he wanted to knock a sentry, the fog made it impossible. The intention was just to make noise. He cocked the hammer, and aiming upward, squeezed the trigger.

The rifle fire scared the sentries. Their confusion lasted for a few seconds, but the babbling of the birds, flying in a screaming cloud, took much longer to fade. Instants later, Luis Caetano looked to the shed. Two men from his group used a rope to pull a cow.

The moonlight also illuminated the two sentries, running toward him while leaving the cattle unguarded. The plan to use him as bait worked, but now Luis needed to rush for his life.

He hurried down the opposite side of the hill, arriving at a stream. The lieutenant followed the watercourse in the path to the camp, but he noticed a soldier already on the hilltop. The Paraguayan saw him too and shouted something in Guarani while aiming his rifle.

Luis jumped into the stream, wondering if the soldier could see him or not.

The lieutenant kept going, water at the height of his hips. The darkness and the ravine covered his escape. If he walked through land, the soldiers could trace his steps, and the Paraguayans would discover the refugee camp. A Paraguayan bullet could also find his back, so he continued inside the stream, with his body completely soaked but out of enemy sight.

***

When Luis opened his eyes, the dawn showed its first colors. He glared at the horizon. The sky shifted to a cobalt blue tone. No clouds. At his feet, the sounds of the water hitting the boulders. The moist scent invited him to take a deep breath.

Better go before it becomes too bright, he thought. He still had to walk near twenty minutes through the open field following the stream course, where he was at significant risk of capture by the Paraguayan soldiers. After that, another half-hour trek in the forest, where trees and vines provided some cover.

The lieutenant walked in the shallow waters of the stream to make his way in the shortest time possible. After reaching the forest, he sighed, relieved. From there, he continued at a leisurely pace to the refugee camp.

Luis arrived at the settlement when the women prepared breakfast. It was remarkable how whites and Indians, all victims of the Paraguayan invasion, formed a community, sharing tasks and building a new life in that forgotten place

Impressive how these people, in this situation, and after surviving so many terrors, still make an organized settlement. This place shall prosper, he thought. He was sure that if Mato Grosso reflected the cooperation established at the Maracaju Ridge, it could be a model province for Brazil.

"Look! It's the captain! Did you ride a sloth to take so long?" a settler said while preparing to sleep. Luis understood why many of the men slept during the day. Tired, he fell asleep right there, near a woman cleaning fish.

Hours later, a kid woke up the lieutenant: the refugee child they brought to the camp days before. The boy said something unintelligible. Luis deduced it was some course Nopitena taught him.

"I don't speak Guaicuru, boy." Luis stretched his arms. The child pointed to a fire with pots cooking meat.

Near there, on a low grass field, Nopitena played with the youngsters. Some of them curiously touched the Kadiweu's geometrical white tattoos in his back, shoulders, and chest.

The refugee mother from Miranda helped the rest of the women—white, *caboclas,* and Indians—to prepare manioc and salted meat. When Luis approached, the child pointed to Nopitena, who turned and noticed the lieutenant's presence.

"Good morning, Chief! I see everything went well yesterday. You arrived on time to feast! "

The cattle captured the day before had already succumbed to the settlers' appetite.

"Did you do your part and catch a mare for them?" Luis got curious about how his soldier worked with a group of Kinikinaus who could barely understand him.

"One? He caught two horses," said a third voice, coming from Luis's side. Pacalalá. "It is the first time I admire the skills of a Guaicuru. The men recounted how he approached the mares, and almost magically, the animals obeyed him," said the camp chief.

"Excellent, I guess we paid for our stay then." Luis had a sardonic smile, remembering that the day before, Pacalalá doubted they could help the camp.

"It's more than paid. To make justice, I told the women to dry a few pieces of meat and pack in a cotton bag, so you have food for your journey." The Kinikanau leader spoke Portuguese with a strong accent, but understandable.

"Very grateful. I still need to find out what happened to Dourados," Luis recalled that their mission was not finished yet.

"I know someone who can help you. José, come here! Zé!" Pacalalá shouted toward the oca.

A man came running with a half-limped leg. He looked as battered as a war refugee could be. "José arrived last night, coming from Dourados, together with people who escaped from there," Pacalalá introduced the man to Luis Caetano.

The man's jacket, in a woeful state, had the insignia of a private. "You are not a civilian, I imagine." The lieutenant suspected the soldier could be a deserter.

"No, sir, they ordered me to guide the civilians to safety." José had the appearance and accent of a caboclo, the half-native, half-white inhabitants from the region.

"What happened to Dourados?"

"It is a long story. Do you have time, sir?" José asked.

Luis took two mugs and filled them with coffee. He gave one to the man and sat on a bench of stumps near the central clearing. The heat was mild because of the clouds announcing a late afternoon rain.

"Spill everything out, private. We both have plenty of time today," said Luis to the man. Sitting, José said he served in Dourados under Lieutenant Antonio Ribeiro.

"Antônio João Ribeiro?" Luis asked, and the man nodded.

The lieutenant still hoped some good news could come out of the soldier's ragged mouth. He silently prayed that his dear friend from the times of military school survived.

"Lieutenant Ribeiro received a letter from a Paraguayan captain named Urbieta, asking for our surrender." José paused and sipped the coffee, whose smoke rose vertically from the cup on that windless day. "They said that another Paraguayan, Colonel Resquin, already took Nioaque and Miranda, and their battalion would take Dourados by force if needed."

"And what did Ribeiro do?" Luis asked before drinking from his mug.

"He instructed me to gather all the civilians wishing to escape at the main square and lead them to Miranda's garrison to get protection. But when we arrived at Miranda, it was destro—"

"I know what happened to Miranda." Luis interrupted the story. "Keep talking about Dourados, private."

"Before I left to guide the civilians, lieutenant Ribeiro gave me this note. I should deliver it to Colonel Dias da Silva, who would be either in Miranda or Nioaque, but, well..." José got quiet, confused by a mission that could not be completed since both Nioaque and Miranda had fallen. Either Colonel Dias da Silva was dead or retreated in the face of Paraguay's devastating numerical advantage. "Lieutenant Ribeiro told me that if I didn't find the Colonel, I should handle the message to the garrison's highest-ranking officer," completed private José.

"As the garrison no longer exists, and unless there is a captain around here, I believe I am this officer," Luis said. The man nodded, relieved, for at least he accomplished his mission. He gave the letter to Luis and thanked him.

"I am the one to thank you, soldier. Not only me, but the imperial army is grateful. You did an excellent job bringing these people here safe and sound. You may rest."

Luis took the letter in his hand and opened it.

To your Lordship Lieutenant-Colonel Dias da Silva

Today we received a summon of surrender from the Paraguayan Captain Martín Urbieta, part of Colonel Resquin's invading column.

I told the peasants and civilians, around fifty souls, to evacuate under the care of one of the soldiers.

The subpoena I vehemently refused. We expect at least two hundred members of the Paraguayan cavalry to attack us. We are fifteen Brazilians defending this post.

I know I will die, but my blood and that of my companions will serve as a solemn protest against the invasion of our country's soil.

Lieutenant Antonio João Ribeiro, commander of the Military Colony of Dourados

Luis Caetano folded the paper and put it inside a pocket. The name of his friend was now in the hall of the fallen heroes. Until that moment, Luis thought only of fulfilling his last mission and returning to the comfort of his house. His chest tightened in shame, and his throat went dry with doubt. He feared if one day he would understand what led men like Melo Bravo or Antonio Ribeiro to exhibit the bravery of mythological beings.

The Paraguayans planned their invasion so that vast forces surprised small or isolated garrisons of Brazilian soldiers, like in Coimbra, Dourados our Miranda. They wanted to crush the defenders' morale, forcing them to surrender, and used all sorties of cruelties to whoever was brave to resist. The thoughts of what the enemies did to his friend Antonio Ribeiro tormented Luis. The images of human ears hanging from the Anhambai ship after the battle of Corumbá returned to his mind, and he gulped.

"Chief, the food is ready," Nopitena said from nearby.

The settlers gathered in the central square of the camp and shared roasted meat and cooked cassava.

Pacalalá sat down next to Luis. He saw a certain fury in the eyes of the lieutenant.
"What are you going to do next?" The Kinikinau chief asked.

"What remains for us is to rush to Rio and spread the news about the aggression suffered by Mato Grosso." Luis took a bowl of manioc and a piece of meat in his hands. "If the Paraguayans sent two columns to invade a province in the middle of nowhere, God knows what they are planning for the rest of the border. The empire is still asleep, and we are going to wake it," Luis said, much to Nopitena's surprise, who, sitting at his side, almost dropped a food bowl.

"Chief, are we going to Rio? I need to look for my people."

"Kadiweu, if the Guaranis are attacking even the Terenas and Kinikinaus, I wonder what they did to your tribe, with whom they always had bad blood," said Pacalalá, referring to the eternal tribal conflicts. "You will find death if you go out looking for your people in a place full of enemies."

Pacalalá had reason. The Kinikinau chief explained to Nopitena that the best way for him to help his people was to join Luis, and together with the Imperial forces, fight the Guaranis until maybe one day liberate the captives from his village—if they were still alive.

But the Kadiweu needed time to think, so Luis resumed his conversation with Pacalalá "What is the fastest way to go to São Paulo?"

"São Paulo?" Pacalalá had no idea what that meant. Luis realized that using white-people geography would not work, so he rephrased the question. "I mean the Paraná river. What is the shortest way to there?"

"Paraná...far away, but with a simple path. Go straight toward the rising sun for about thirty days." The duration he meant was by foot. On horseback, the time would be at most a third of that. The Kinikinau continued, "Avoid crossing the south side of the ridge. There is the land of the Kaiowas." completed Pacalalá.

The Kaiowas were natives close to the Paraguayan Guaranis. There were rumors that many of them took the side of the invaders. Luis didn't know if he should believe the rumors, but just in case, it was worth the caution.

Pacalalá gave one last piece of advice while finishing his meal "This uniform of yours is no good. Change your clothes if you don't want to attract attention. If you want to sleep around here, there is a place for you. "

Luis thanked him, informing him that they would depart the next morning.

Before dawn, the lieutenant and the Kadiweu saddled horses. Luis exchanged his military boots with a refugee, getting a pair of sandals and pawn clothes. They prepared in silence to not awaken whoever slept, but a boy came running toward Nopitena. It was the same child they brought to the settlement days before.

Nopitena realized he did not know the little boy's name.

"What it is your name, fellow?"

"Pedro," the child replied, "are you leaving?"

Nopitena nodded.

"Stay. We can climb the trees and go fish." The boy had a whispered, bitter voice and watering eyes. His little hand reached Nopitena's right arm.

"You are becoming good at catching fish. I'll give you my line and hook." Nopitena took from his pocket a skein of fishing line and a hook made of wire. "But remember to always leave some for your mom. Deal?"

"Right. Thank you." Pedro nodded and grabbed the gift. The kid had a half-smile, mixed with sorrow for the friend's departure.

Luis mounted Nickel and ordered the horse to move. Nopitena petted Pedro's head before turning to follow the lieutenant. They rode, as Pacalalá instructed, toward the rising sun, toward the Paraná River. Toward São Paulo.

***

The piano's notes sounded slower than expected in the visiting room of the Viscountess house in Rio de Janeiro.

"Very well, Aninha. Try again, but a little faster." With a light tone of voice, Joana Augusta taught piano to the ten-year-old girl.

Early afternoon sunlight flooded the dining room, penetrating the large windows and reflecting on the white walls. In the center, a ten-year-old girl, with a lace dress and hair tied, strummed the piano keys while Luis Caetano's sister watched her progress.

Joana knew Aninha liked melodies from Robert Schumann, cheerful and easy to learn. At the entry arch, a silhouette stood still and watched them both, not entering to avoid disturbing the class.

When the girl hit the last note, both tutor and pupil heard clapping sounds from the room entrance.

"Excellent, excellent! My compliments for helping her to develop so much, miss Joana. Maybe at the next dinner, she can play a recital for the guests." The female voice was from Ana Francisca Alves de Lima e Silva, the viscountess of Ururaí. "Aninha, how do you call this song?"

"Fro...Frau...hmm, teacher?" Aninha looked at Joana.

"*Fröhlicher Landmann.*" Joana helped her student to remember the song's name. "It is a Germanic composition, but we can call it the Happy Farmer."

"Better the translated name. Perfect choice. Who would think that Prussians can create such light, joyful music!" The Viscountess approached her daughter. "Aninha, your brothers and cousins are playing in the garden. Join them."

The mother helped the girl to descend from the Piano bench, excessively high for a small child.

Only Joana remained in the room when the joyful expression of the Viscountess disappeared. "Joana, have you heard anything from your brother?"

"No, lady Ana. The last letter came almost three months ago." Weeks before, Joana realized it was taking too long to receive any correspondence from her brother. Letters usually took around a month to arrive from Mato Grosso, not three. "I thought about it a few days ago. His last letter was about a promotion and transfer back home. Maybe he forgot to write with so many things happening?

"This is what I wanted to talk about." The Viscountess sat on the piano stool. "I dined with my father yesterday and asked him about the border. Since Paraguay blocked the river for Brazilian ships, communication is only possible by land. It may take months."

"I see. At least now I am sure he didn't do something stupid that put him in a military prison." Joana let out a sigh of relief and remembered her brother's impulsiveness. "It's just a barrier from the Paraguayans. I think I should wait longer for a letter then."

The Viscountess lowered her eyes, almost closing them, as if in doubt or holding something. "There's one more thing. My father received reports, still from December, that Paraguayan troops gathered at various points along the border of Mato Grosso."

Joana Augusta was not familiar with military arts. She preferred law, rhetoric, and music, but she knew that no country mobilizes soldiers without reason. Her heartbeats accelerated. "My lady, isn't there any more recent information?"

"No, my dear. As I said, with the river blocked, every message from there takes more than a month to arrive." The viscountess stood up and put her hands on Joana's shoulder. The tutor had her eyes frozen on the wall, lost in thoughts about Luis Caetano's fate.

"Do you know what would be a good idea? Come with me for a tea, the two Marias will join us," said Ana Francisca, referring to Maria Paranhos, daughter of the Viscount of Rio Branco, and Maria Saraiva, niece of counselor Saraiva.

Joana recovered her posture as best as she could and accompanied lady Ana Francisca to the entrance arch. Before leaving, the viscountess came closer to her.

"One last thing: please, do not tell this information to Almeida Rosa. Maybe he already knows, but if not, let's keep it only between us."

She nodded, promising to not share a word with her law professor about the prelude of war.

A war that already devastated a province 1,600 kilometers away but still unknown to most politicians in Rio.

Frontiers of Fire

Chapter XIII

After departing from the Maracaju ridge, Luis and Nopitena had a smoother journey, except for the scorching heat. It took twelve days on horseback to reach the Paraná River. To cross it, they paid a ferry using the coins Luis carried in his pocket since Coimbra.

Later, they continued along the Tietê and Jacaré-Guaçu rivers. To ride near water meant guaranteed food through fishing, as well as refreshment for the horses.

"Chief, when we get to this Rio de Janeiro city and tell them about the war, what happens next?" Nopitena asked while they traveled on the riverside path. At the waters, a barge navigated to the south, transporting coffee and goods.

"First a banquet. Then, maybe a promotion to first lieutenant." Luis Caetano smiled, anticipating the credit he would receive after informing the empire about the Paraguayan attack.

"But what about the Guard?" Nopitena reminded Luis of his plans to transfer to the National Guard. An event that, during months, the lieutenant expected with excitement.

"My transfer to the National Guard can wait until we've spent a few weeks enjoying what Rio de Janeiro offers us." Luis grinned. "Still curious to see the ocean, Anspeçada?"

Nopitena never took much interest in the womanizing stories the lieutenant recounted about his holidays in big cities. But when the Kadiweu heard something about the ocean, he raised all kinds of questions. Luis described it to him as "a body of water so large that would take months to arrive at the other side." Its vastness grabbed his curiosity. The waves too. When Nopitena heard about waves, he asked if their size depended on the ocean's mood. Luis never laughed so much.

After seeing the ocean, however, Nopitena planned to rejoin the army and maybe, one day, free his people from the Guaranis who had attacked his village.

As Luis fantasized about the urban bohemian life and Nopitena tried to imagine the ocean, they heard a scream coming from ahead. Both continued on their path, advancing toward the noise. After a curve at the corner of the dirt road, two men were beating another some two hundred meters ahead while a third thug drew a machete.

Luis held his rifle, loaded it with a bulletless cartridge, cocked, and fired a warning shot.

The three men glanced at the lieutenant while the victim remained on the ground, covering his head with his hands. The aggressors were bulky, brawny men, slightly bigger than Luis, with hairy faces and disheveled hair. A kind often hired for dirty jobs, like what they were witnessing before them. The third man, carrying the machete, was smaller and bald. All the three wore white shirts and brown pants, reminding clothes that farmers provide to employees. Meters behind them stood a cart pulled by two mules.

"Keep moving, you two, nothing to see here." the bald man holding the machete said. The other two henchmen stared, with eyes thirsty for violence.

"What has this wretch done to deserve this?" Luis asked.

"He didn't pay his debts, and the Vergueiro family doesn't forgive debtors." The bald brawler grinned. He had at least half of his teeth missing.

"This bastard is too young for debts. Gambling?"

"I told you, it doesn't matter. Ditch from here, trooper. This fellow isn't worth a fight." Only the bald responded. The other two troglodytes peered at the victim, so he didn't escape.

"Leave him. How much he owes you? I can pay it." The lieutenant reached into his pocket, pulling out some coins. There was still a decent amount of money he brought from Coimbra in his jacket.

"This isn't about cash anymore. It's a lesson." The bald thug kicked the boy on the ground, who groaned agonizing sounds. The man pointed his blade to Luis. "Get out!"

"Oh, mate, you don't want to swing that machete at me," Luis said to the lackey of the Vergueiro family.

The Lieutenant threw his rifle to Nopitena, who grabbed it in the air.

"Chief, why bother? Let's continue. There's a long way." The Kadiweu didn't understand why the lieutenant would pick a fight between people he'd never seen, and that only slowed them down.

"I don't know, Anspeçada. But I don't refuse that kind of challenge." Luis unsheathed his saber and tapped Nickel's side with his spur. The horse darted toward the machete man.

The gallop raised dust in the almost fifty meters' distance that separated them. Luis Caetano held his saber rigid, pointing straight at the height of his eyes. He could not see left or right, for his vision turned into a tunnel finishing at the henchman who dared to challenge him.

The man with the machete held his blade high, preparing to slash either Luis or his horse. "Soldier, you're going to die for nothing!"

Nickel's gallop covered the entire distance in a few seconds. The lackey and the lieutenant got close. Luis made the first swing with his blade, drawing an eight in the air. Then another swing.

For a split second, they stood side by side, then the horse galloped away. The henchman's machete flew away, hitting the floor meters farther. Next to the machete, an amputated hand.

The mutilated ruffian kneeled near the mule cart and grabbed a piece of cloth, trying to stop the blood from coming out of the severed limb.

Luis turned his horse around, holding his bloody saber. One of the standing henchmen realized the lieutenant got the better result from the duel. The thug grabbed a rock and threw it, hitting the lieutenant's head. Luis fell off Nickel's back.

The troglodytes ran toward the lieutenant to finish him, but the Kadiweu, holding the gun of Luis, loaded the rifle and fired against the bandits. Nopitena terribly missed the target, but the noise scared the two thugs. They ran to the mule cart, where the mangled bald man sat waiting, and left.

The beaten boy uncovered his head and stood up. He was a slender figure with fair skin, blond, almost silvery hair, and grayish eyes. Nopitena rarely saw such people—later on, he would describe him as a talking ghost. The Indian dismounted from Eka, asking the boy for help to carry the lieutenant. Luis, lying unconscious, had a wound on his forehead spouting blood.

***

The coolness of a mild morning, the smell of wet earth, and the noise of bubbling water mixed with distant talking voices. It felt very familiar. For a moment, Luis thought he was back home, at the Mantiqueira ridge.

Unable to open his eyes, the lieutenant didn't know if he was awake or dreaming. Good heavens, he barely knew if he was alive! Maybe it was how the path of this world to the next one starts.

The coffee scent stirred his senses. It was the impulse a once dying person needed to open his eyes. He touched his head and felt the smooth texture of a bandage. It still ached, worse than the worst hangover he'd ever had.

"Look who woke up." A soft voice in a foreign accent attracted Luis Caetano's eyes to a room corner. His vision, still blurred, focused on a light-skinned girl, around nineteen years old, with golden hair and simple clothes. In one hand, she carried a tin mug, exhaling the caffeinated scent that gave Luis the energy to return to the world of the living.

"Franz, he woke up. Bring him some coffee, too," the girl said in a gentle voice. Luis still tried to understand where he was. White-painted walls, slightly stained by the red dust of the region. On the room's opposite side, a portrait of a man with a thick mustache and a strange helmet—it had a spearhead on the top.

A stripling of thirteen or fourteen years old entered the room, carrying a coffee mug for Luis. "I made it with my selected beans, the strongest. You'll get better fast." He placed the mug on the edge of the bed. Like the girl, he also had a peculiar accent.

Together, they helped Luis to sit up to drink. The lieutenant, holding the mug in both hands, took a couple of sips.

"What happened? Where am I?" the lieutenant moaned his first words.

"First, you should ask what day is today." The boy giggled.

The girl also laughed at Franz's answer. However, seeing how disoriented the lieutenant was, she promptly explained. "Two days ago, you and an Indian saved my brother from the Vergueiros' henchmen. One of them hit your forehead with a stone before he fled." The girl approached and pulled up the blanket to cover Luis as he was bare-chested.

The lieutenant noticed, ashamed.

"Your Indian and my brother brought you here, and the least we can do is to accommodate you in his room, so you can recover," she said.

"And what is this place? Who are you?" The lieutenant, still disoriented, began to recover the memories of his feud with the henchmen.

"Felicissima farm, house of the Schmidts. This little coffee scholar here, Franz, is the son of the house owner." The young blond woman stroked the child's equally blond hair. "I live here as aggregate, as well as my brother Martin. I take care of the boy and help Mrs. Gertrud while Martin works with Mr. Jakob on the farm."

The lieutenant reclined on the bed and glanced at the girl. Since Luis left his house, he had never felt such a coziness. Maybe it was the symphony of the falling rain and the smell of wet grass. Maybe it was the coffee aroma and the velvety voice of that figure. Maybe it was her oceanic-blue eyes, very different from the gray, ghostly iris of her brother Martin.

An alarm rang in the lieutenant's head. Thousands of kilometers away, the Paraguayans spread terror in Mato Grosso without the empire noticing.

"I need to leave. I need to go to Rio." Luis made a sudden movement, placing the mug at the bedside drawer.

"Herr Jakob, bitte!" the girl called at the room's entrance. Seconds later, a gentleman around fifty years old came. He had an impressive white beard and sunburned skin. The gentleman observed with condescension Louis's foolish attempt to rise. The Lieutenant's waning strength barely allowed him to get out of bed, let alone ride over four hundred miles on horseback.

"Good Morzing, Herr...?" asked Jakob Schmidt.

"...Gomes. Good Morning, Mr. Schmidt," Luis said, giving up the pathetic attempt to get up, reclining back on the bed.

"Herr Gomes, you are no good to traffel or walk yet." the man spoke with an accent even thicker than the girl. "Vesterday, zee doktor vas here, und said you had luck. Zee two hits in head could make you zilly foreffer."

Luis laughed when the foreigner underlined he could be silly forever, but this meant serious sequels. His head was hit twice: first by the stone, and then when he felt from Nickel.

"I understand, Mr. Schmidt. Thank you for your generosity. Could someone please call Nopitena?" asked the lieutenant.

"Call what?" Franz and the girl asked at the same time.

"The Indian."

The Kadiwéu arrived at Luis' room with clean clothes and a restful face. Luis was left alone with his soldier.

"Welcome back to our world, chief!"

"Anspeçada, has anyone been here to examine me?"

"Yes, yesterday, late in the afternoon, a man came on a carriage. He told us it will take another three days for you to be fine." Nopitena's response confirmed that, in fact, a doctor had said Luis shouldn't leave.

"Did the doctor bandage my head?"

"No. When he came, you already had it. It was Miss Sophie. She came several times to bring food, water and change the gauze."

Sophie! So that is her name! Luis thought.

"We'll need to speed up on the road later. Meanwhile, help the owners of the house with whatever they need." After giving the orders, Luis Caetano turned around to rest. His head seemed to explode in pain.

***

Outside Luis' room, Nopitena met Martin on the way to the tool-house, where both slept since the Lieutenant's arrival. Ceding his room to Luis was the least Martin could do after being saved from an assault that could end in a tragedy.

Since the Kadiweu arrived, he helped at the farm, doing chores familiar to him, like feeding the horses and milking the cows. He also transported things around with the help of Eka, his horse. Nickel, the lieutenant's mount, rested in the stable.

In the toolroom, apart from the two makeshift beds, there were also the Indian's belongings and Luis Caetano's rifle. The last shot fired with that gun scared the Vergueiro's henchmen, saving both Luis and Martin's lives. An excellent result, considering how the Kadiweu missed the target by a large margin.

Nopitena searched among the tools for a brush to comb the horses when he found Jakob Schmidt examining Luis's gun.

"Interesting herr lieutenant's rifle. He takes good care of it." The farmer ran his hand over the side of the gun, brushing away the dust and examining the details. "Belgian manufacture. Liège always makes good veapons. But I belieffe it should take ein while to load, nein?"

"No, sir. In our fort, soldiers loaded it before one could count to twenty." Nopitena said, remembering the mind-blowing reload speed of Lieutenant Melo Bravo and his riflemen in the Coimbra combat.

"Drei times, ein minute...Zis is time consuming." The foreigner's words made Nopitena raise his eyebrows in curiosity. Mr. Schmidt continued, "Und what if I say it's possible to make zee rifle fire up to seven times ein minute?" the German said, not looking at the Kadiwéu but devoting all his attention to the gun.

"I don't know how this is possible, sir. But I am not good with guns, so maybe there is a way." Nopitena, by accident, revealed his flaw as a weak rifleman.

Jakob Schmidt, the immigrant from Thuringia, scratched his bearded chin. "You don't know how to shoot, but you are a gut horse rider. Opposite of Martin." The German smiled. "He not know how to zit on a horse zaddle, but he hits a flying pigeon hundred yards far."

During their conversation, Martin also entered the tool house. Taking advantage of the fact that both were in front of him, Jakob Schmidt revealed his idea. Certain that their guests would remain for a few more days, he told Nopitena to teach Martin how to ride, a useful skill at the farm. In exchange, Martin could teach Nopitena how to shoot.

"But how am I going to teach him to shoot, sir?" Martin asked.

"Take zee Dreyse from your father," Mr. Schmidt replied.

Martin's eyes lit. Mr. Jakob allowed him to use the spectacular weapon he inherited from his father.

Minutes later, outside the tool house, preparing his cart to go to town, Jakob called the Indian. "One last question. If not ein problem, I can improve zee lieutenant's rifle, making it faster."

Nopitena thought for a few seconds. "Um...if it's for the better, I think there's no problem, sir."

"Sehr gut." Jakob Schmidt took his hat, greeted the two young men, and left.

It was just noon. Outside, pleasant weather, a few clouds, and a mild breeze. Ideal for Nopitena to give his first riding class. While saddling Eka, the Kadiweu glanced at the young German. A creature so skinny and tall that the Indian feared the horse would be frightened by thinking Martin was a scarecrow or a phantom.

***

After a four-hour nap, Luis woke up. On that late afternoon, sunlight streamed through the lace curtain, drawing geometric shapes on the floor.

Time for a walk, he told himself. The lieutenant couldn't, however, wander around shirtless. With no idea about where was his clothes, he shouted for Nopitena, with no success.

But someone else heard his voice.

Sophie entered the room, bringing a small vase with violet flowers.

"They will help you rest and recover." She placed the blossomed pot on the window parapet.

Her golden, swirling hair and the colorful plants hypnotized the openmouthed lieutenant. His frozen eyes gazed at the girl, the window, and the flower. His thoughts wandered to the rhythm of her mellow voice.

"Am I bothering you?" She shifted her eyes to the silent lieutenant.

"Uh…No, no!" Luis shook his head, returning to reality.

Sophia's face reddened, and she took two steps back. The lieutenant did not understand why. The girl pointed to his torso. Luis, charmed by her presence, didn't realize he was half-naked.

Different from the girl, Luis' olive skin was not the type that gets blushed, so his embarrassment came as an "Oh!" and the convulsive move to pull the bedsheet and cover his body.

"No, I just...I just need my shirt."

The girl nodded and walked to a wardrobe in the room's corner. It had the same walnut wood color as the rest of the furniture. She opened it and took a hanger with his white shirt, clean as if someone washed it carefully and with patches over the former holes and torn fibers. It was still a pawn shirt, the one he swapped with a refugee at the Maracaju ridge to not look like a Brazilian officer. The shirt, however, looked now at least decent and smelled like fresh cotton.

Luis stood up, grasped the shirt, and dressed up as quickly as he could. When pinning the buttons, he suddenly got dizzy and wobbled. Sophie, in a reflex, took him by his waist, avoiding the tumble for an instant. The lieutenant, however, was heavy for such a delicate girl, and both almost fell until his hands gripped the wardrobe's door.

Back to normality, the girl's arm was still around the lieutenant. Her cheeks reddened as she released him.

"...I don't think you are ready to walk alone," she said, taking two steps back.

"After two days lying down, it's normal to stumble a little. But some exercise helps to recover." The lieutenant tried to plant his feet on the room's wooden floor. One step after another, frowning with the effort. "Where is the Indian?"

"He and my brother went to the town to make a delivery, and later, he will teach Martin how to ride." Sophie looked at the lieutenant sitting, now fully dressed. "If you wish to go for a walk, I can lend my arm to give some support, Lieutenant Gomes."

The way Sophie pronounced Luis' surname echoed in his ears. The G whispered like K. *Lieutenant Komes.* He wished to hear that again. The formality of using surnames, however, increased the distance between them—a distance that he wanted to reduce.

"Excellent, miss. I would appreciate it if you just called me Luis."

They linked their arms and advanced with slow steps, first through the room and down the small corridor leading to the yard.

A few meters ahead from the terrace was a lush coffee plantation. On the right, a perch with some chickens and a corral with two cows. On the left, a warehouse that could be a barn or toolshed. They walked around the yard, almost silently, interrupted only by the occasional sound of the farm animals. A few meters further, they saw Franz.

The youngster sat on a stump, and at a makeshift plank table, he selected different roasted coffee beans.

"Hello, buddy. Is it some kind of game?" asked Luis, recalling the days in the fort of Coimbra, where Indians and soldiers, to avoid boredom, invented games with pebbles, seeds, and whatever they could find.

"No. I'm sorting the coffee to find out which tree gives the most bitter or sweet types." The boy talked with a tone that did not sound like a child but an expert passionate about the subject.

"And is there a difference? I always thought coffee was all the same." Curious, the lieutenant squinted his eyes to observe the grains.

"Smell this one." The boy took a handful of grains from each of the two separated canvas pouches and approached Luis, "and then this one."

While the first had a lighter scent, the second smelled like wood.

"Taste varies a lot too," said Franz. "I'll make one for you, from the best! If an ordinary type woke you up, imagine what this one is going to do." The boy grabbed the two coffee pouches and ran to the kitchen grinder to mill the grains.

"He likes you. Nobody pays much attention to his ideas. But he's a good, smart boy," Sophie said as they leisurely strolled through the yard. Luis remembered what the girl said about her and her brother as aggregated to the Schmidts' house.

"You told me about Martin. But what about the rest of your family?" the lieutenant asked when they stopped in front of the chicken patch, observing two chicks fighting over a grain of corn.

"It's a long story." Sophie pushed with her foot an entire corn ear toward the chicks to stop the fight.

"I have time. It looks like I'm going to stay here for a few more days," replied Luis.

Anticipating the lengthy family memoir, the young woman took a few steps to get out of the afternoon sun and protect her pale skin. Pale, like the pages of an unwritten book.

The family of the Werther twins came from a Thuringian town called Weimar. Their father, Wolfgang Werther, a former member of the German army, moved to Brazil as part of a mercenary corps called Brummer. The Emperor hired them to fight in the Platine War. Wolfgang brought his wife and the two five-year-old kids to Brazil.

He died during the war. Sophie shared this information with little emotion, much to Luis's surprise. Her mother and kids moved to Senator Vergueiro's family farm. The Vergueiros preferred to bring European immigrants to work on the plantations instead of slaves, so they were praised by the imperial family and celebrated as abolitionists.

But the foreign workers employed by the Senator were not free either. Immigrants needed to work in a strenuous rhythm to pay a debt—created under the pretext of covering for the housing and work equipment—that never ended.

Influenza killed their mother when the kids had only twelve years, so the twins fled to the Felicissima farm, welcomed by the Schmidts.

"I assume the debt was never forgiven, and that's why the Vergueiro's henchmen assaulted Martin," Luis said after hearing the whole story.

"Correct. Even though we have paid this debt several times, *mit arbeit*." Sophie sighed.

Thoughts tangled with memories in Luis's head. Who could guess that the family of Senator Vergueiro, the abolitionist, hailed for preferring paid workers instead of slaves, in reality, abused immigrants?

They kept their calm stroll, distancing themselves from the chirping chicks.

On the horizon, a man with white tattoos on his upper body was giving instructions to another who, awkwardly, tried to mount a horse. At each attempt, the animal moved a few steps away, avoiding the phantasmagoric individual from placing his oversized foot in the stirrup.

"Isn't that Nopitena, and..." Luis narrowed his eyes to understand what happened, "what is that weird, scraggy thing trying to jump on his horse?"

Sophie laughed. "My brother."

Chapter XIV

The next day, Luis woke up with the smell of melted butter and fresh bread, indicating that breakfast would be ready soon. He lumbered to the kitchen. His steps were already firm on the floor, but his head still ached when he sat or stood up. A minor nuisance that could become a torment with the horseback rattle.

Mrs. Gertrud Schmidt prepared the kitchen table. The woman had a rustic appearance, completed by a headscarf and apron in floral motifs. She brewed coffee, boiled milk, and placed a large piece of cheese on the table. The boy, Franz, sat at one chair and cut a slice for himself. Dona Gertrud left to tell her husband in the tool room that the coffee was ready. On the way out, she met Luis standing still at the kitchen entrance and invited him for breakfast.

Luis, only at the company of Franz, asked the boy, "What about Miss Sophie? She will not have breakfast with us?"

The blonde kid peered at the lieutenant, trying to understand why he asked about the girl. Seconds later, Franz grinned. He understood the reason behind the question.

"Sometimes, she doesn't eat breakfast." The kid took a bite of his slice of cheese. Luis did the same.

Franz sipped his coffee and looked again at Luis. The boy enjoyed the lieutenant's company, who liked the dark, bitter liquid as much as him. Something in common between the battle-tested soldier and the ingenuous teenager.

"I have an idea," said Franz. "In exchange for your opinion about the two types of beans that I separated, I can tell her you wanted to take a walk around the farm but have no one to guide you."

The lieutenant laughed at the boy's offer. Not because it was foolish, but because it was too smart for a country child. *How cunning this kid*, he thought. If the plan worked, he would gain another chance to stroll around with Sophie, with no need to ask her directly. Of course, to justify the requirement for her help, the lieutenant needed to exaggerate his medical condition. Otherwise, Martin's sister would think that the lieutenant had no reasons to request her help except the most dubious one.

Luis asked Franz to pass him a slice of bread, and they closed the deal.

The lieutenant returned to his room and took a map out from his bag.

The worn-out item looked like it came from the battlefield. Which was the case since it was the same map he brought from Coimbra. It had water stains from his dive in the Parana River, but it was still useful to check the way to Rio. A way that naturally passed through the 3-Estados farm, owned by his family. A stop that would give them a chance to resupply and rest the horses.

How many days to get there? Luis pondered about the journey, aware that his recovery was nearly complete, needing two days more at most. He felt his chest tighten, not knowing why.

To leave the Felicissima farm was the way to fulfill a greater duty of alerting the empire about the invasion and then return to the comfort of his home, perhaps with a medal on his uniform.

But the lieutenant remembered he had never felt so cozy as when he woke up in Martin's bed, with the smell of wet grass and Sophie's velvet voice. A sugary sound that it made him forget about the bombs and screams of the Coimbra siege. His mind sunk into the memory of her celestial eyes.

Franz entered the bedroom, interrupting the lieutenant's reverie. The boy carried an aluminum mug, from where a trickle of smoke danced in the air. The young man passed it to Luis's hands. A nutty aroma filled the room.

"It's the best blend I've ever done. If I give it to Mom or Sophie, they won't be honest with me, but you will." Franz stood at the side of the bed, anxious about Luis's assessment.

Leaning against the headboard, Luis took the first sip. The voluptuous, dark liquid passed over his tongue with the vigor of river rapids, warming his neck and leaving a noble bitterness.

It was bitter but not brutal. One could even doubt his own senses and think it was sweet.

"Perfect," said Luis.

"Thank you, Mr. Gomes, but I disagree with that. I'm still far from perfect." The little German relaxed his shoulders after the approval of his creation. "Now, I'll do my part of the deal." Franz left the room while Luis remained reclined on his bed, wondering if the boy could convince Sophie Werther to take another walk with him.

***

Martin woke up in silence, taking care to not disturb his roommate. In vain, because the timid flame light from the oil lamp he lit interrupted Nopitena's sleep.

The Kadiweu and the German prepared their tools and saddled Nickel and Eka. The day before, Nopitena asked Luis if they could ride Nickel. The lieutenant agreed, as long as they avoid dangerous terrain and give the silver-haired animal a proper rest.

Martin took out the Dreyse and a dozen cartridges from a storage box. Nopitena glanced at the box and raised his eyebrows after seeing what looked like a second rifle. Anyone would suspect a peasant owning such a powerful gun, let alone two.

The Kadiweu contemplated the weapon in Martin's hand. The rifle was about the same size as Luis Caetano's but had a strange silver horn in the middle. The trigger and the barrel bands had a distinctive golden color that glowed over the gun's walnut wood and shone like little stars every time the dawning sunrays entered through the window. On a small metal plate, just above the trigger, an enigmatic inscription: Zündnadelgewehr.

They packed up and went to the Schmidts' house for breakfast with bread and cheese and left shortly, surrounded by the early morning fog, typical in the Mantiqueira ridge at that time of the year.

The path crossed was on flat terrain, on the edge of a river called Monjolinho. The way had minor obstacles that served as good training for Martin. He almost fell off the horse more than once and, insecure, asked Nopitena if it wasn't better to just walk. The Kadiweu said no every time.

"If you fall from the horse, you go back and try not to fall again. It is simple," Nopitena said.

After arriving at an open field, they dismounted, and Martin turned from student to master.

"There are some birds around, but first, we shoot fixed targets. The trees near the stream." Martin pointed with the right index finger. The two stopped in a meadow under the shade of a banana tree. The German took the rifle in his hand, aiming for woods some 200 meters away.

He took a cartridge out of the bag. To Nopitena's astonishment, Martin twisted the metal horn instead of loading the ammunition down the rifle's muzzle. A breech opened in the gun's chamber, and he inserted the cartridge on it.

Tuck Tuck.

The solid sound came from the gun's iron bolt moving. First forward and then to the side. The two moves closed the Dreyse chamber breech.

He fired.

The echo of the mighty German rifle roared over the meadow. The once clear sky darkened with frightened birds fleeing the trees. Martin noticed the Kadiwéu's surprise.

"Where did you put the bullet?" Nopitena examined the Dreyse with widened eyes.

"Here in the breech." Martin pulled the iron lever again and opened the ammo compartment.

Nopitena had served the army for years but had never seen a weapon like that. The shooter did not need to insert gunpowder or bullet in the muzzle, neither push everything using a ramrod like in the rifles he saw his entire life. The rifleman also could remain in a kneeling or prone position, without the need to stand up to reload.

All thanks to the mysterious mechanism that opened a breech to insert the cartridge straight into the rifle chamber.

How deadly would be an entire army carrying this gun? The Indian thought.

Something broke the silence and crashed on the floor a few hundred yards from there. It was a bunch of bananas that fell from the tree, shredded by Martin Werther's surgical shot.

"Now, it is your time. Aim at one of those bananas around the one I hit." The German handled the gun to Nopitena.

"It is heavier than the Chief's rifle." The Kadiweu said, holding the weapon.

He repeated Martin's movement sequence, pulling the iron horn, opening the breech, and putting a cartridge from the pouch into the gun's chamber.

Tuck Tuck.

Nopitena pushed the bolt, closed the slit, squinted his eyes at the iron sight, and pulled the trigger.

A thunderous sound echoed once more across the field. The Dreyse's stock hit Nopitena's unaccustomed shoulder, jerking his body backward as if he'd been pushed by a wild horse. Gunpowder smoke from beneath the rifle's silver horn filled his nose with a sulfurous smell. Smoke entered his mouth—open in astonishment at the mighty weapon—and left a metallic aftertaste.

Nopitena opened his eyes, not knowing where his shot had gone. He was certain he hit nothing.

"You held the rifle's kick well, not bad. But...is it normal for your people to shoot with closed eyes?" Martin said.

Even though the German asked with no malice, Nopitena took the question as a sarcastic mockery of his people. *What an idiotic comment,* he mumbled. The Kadiweu knew, however, that the question made a certain sense. Why did he close his eyes when firing? Perhaps that explained his appalling performance as a marksman.

Before the Indian reloaded the weapon to shoot again, the German called for his attention.

"Nopitena, do you remember when my horse started to swerve, and you said it was my loose grip on the reins? You told me that the animal always will follow the rider's hands."

"Yes?"

"Like the hands of the rider guiding the horse, your eyes guide the bullet. If you close them, you'll end up shooting nowhere."

After hearing the commentary, Nopitena felt ready to shoot again. This time, with open eyes.

The next shot still missed the target, but for a much smaller margin.

"Now, it is a matter of practice. You need to improve the firmness of your grip, the feet position, breathing pace, and in the end, you must learn how to shoot between heart beats." Martin said, enumerating each topic with fingers raised.

"What? Heart beats?" Nopitena arched his eyebrows.

"Yes, but this comes last because it needs body and mind to work together. Today we focus on aiming."

After practicing, they stopped to rest under the banana grove. The morning fog and fresh breeze were long gone. The blue sky and the strong sunshine took their toll of sweat. Nopitena asked Martin where he learned to shoot like that. The boy, both in appearance and age, had certainly never been in combat but shot as good as the best of Coimbra's marines.

"My father was in the military, so since I can remember, we've been around soldiers. After he passed, we moved to the Vergueiro's farm with my mother. A few men from my father's battalion lived there, and they took me on hunting trips. At some point, I learned how to shoot," Martin said, peeling and eating a banana he took from a nearby tree.

"What happened to your father?" Nopitena also grabbed fruit from the bunch.

"He died in the war he came to fight, not able to fire a single shot." The tone in Martin's voice denounced that this was a difficult topic for the young man.

Nopitena wanted to change the subject. "I hope I don't have the same fate," he said.

Martin asked what would be the next steps of the lieutenant and the Kadiweu. Nopitena recounted the plan to go to Rio and alert the empire about the invasion. He also described the fierce battle in Coimbra and the escape on board the Anhambai.

"I wish one day I could be part of such feats." Martin's eyes sparkled with tales of bravery from men like Lieutenants Melo Bravo, Balduino, and Luis Caetano.

"The army could make a good use of a shooter with your skills," said Nopitena, eating another banana.

These words remained in the pale - but sun-reddened - head of the gaunt Martin Werther. What was the point of wasting such a talented marksman on farm labor, running away from henchmen and debts?

***

Luis Caetano rested in his bedroom at the Schmidts' house during the early afternoon. If in recent days the rain had brought mild temperatures, on that day, the January summer revealed its strength on the Felicissima farm.

"Lieutenant?" a mellow voice came from the entrance. A voice that Luis had gotten used to in the last few days. "Franz said he planned to walk with you through the coffee fields, but he asked me to apologize. He can't go because of...an unpleasant condition with his belly." It embarrassed Sophie to explain that the boy had diarrhea.

"Oh, heavens...In the morning, he looked fine. Hopefully, the kid gets better. I was curious to visit the coffee plantations. What a pity," the lieutenant said with a crocodile sadness.

"I guess I don't know as much about coffee as Franz does, but I can go with you if that's fine."

"It is a good idea." Luis agreed with Sophie's proposal, which he indeed expected beforehand.

"The sun is strong outside. I'll get you a long-brimmed hat."

She left the room for an instant, and the lieutenant smiled, noticing that the girl no longer called him by rank or other formalities. The plan he and Franz created worked.

The pair walked across the porch and then through the coffee plantation with arms intertwined. They talked about the battles in the fort and the cattle laced in the Maracajú mountains. Luis Caetano told the complete story that led him there, but the golden-haired girl kept her mysteries.

"And you, my lady? What do you think about life here?" Luis asked as they walked down a corridor among the green coffee groves.

"You can call me Sophie since I call you by name too" the girl's invitation to abandon the typical formalities between strangers cheered Luis up more than expected. "But life here...it is not the one I would choose to live."

Unlike Martin, she showed a certain bitterness toward Brazil. The country where she lost her mother. The country where they were mistreated by the Vergueiros, living a life of semi-slavery. It was as part of the army of that country that her father died. The girl never voiced it, but every syllable she intoned expressed regret at living in tropical lands.

"So, do you think about leaving?"

"Not now. My brother and I live in a comfortable house, and we lack nothing, thanks to the Schmidts." Sophie looked to the farmhouse. "I owe them my gratitude."

They stopped and turned around.

"Please tell me more about your sister and the place where you came from," Sophie said, resting her hand over Luis's arm. As she touched the lieutenant's battered hand, the girl's satiny skin made him lose himself in thought. Weeks before, his arm was soaked in Paraguayan blood at the Battle of Coimbra. Her touch seemed to absolve his hand of any crime committed.

Luis looked for words to describe the 3-Estados farm—which was not really a farm but just a ranch. It surprised him that the girl who spoke with such contempt about Brazil asked about his typical Brazilian countryside childhood.

As he recounted his father's tales, they saw two horsemen approaching from the west, riding in the open fields. It was Martin, riding Nickel and Nopitena with Eka.

"My brother finally mounted a horse." The girl chuckled.

When Nopitena saw the lieutenant in the distance, he rushed Eka. First, from a walk to a trot, then to a fast gallop. To make a show of his talent, he darted over the grasslands and tipped his body over the side, out of the saddle.

"The galloping bite," Luis said, watching the Indian stunt.

"What?" Sophie asked.

"It's a riding maneuver his tribe does. He will suspend himself, hanging with only his legs in the saddle and one hand holding the horse's neck." The lieutenant placed his open hand over his eyebrows, blocking the sun to better watch the dexterity demonstration from the Anspeçada. He still left his other hand over Sophie's.

"And why do they do it?"

"Because this way they have one hand free and the body is much closer to the ground. They can use their free hand either to hunt an animal like a wild boar or to stab an enemy with a spear." While Luis explained, Eka and Nopitena dashed at full speed. "The faster the gallop, the more powerful the blow."

Nopitena, however, had a terrible aim, and even with his superior horse riding skills, it would be unlikely to hit a smaller target with a dart.

The scorching afternoon still held a surprise. Sweat made Nopitena's palms wet. The hand holding Eka's neck during the daring technique began to slip. Realizing it, the Indian tried to decelerate the animal. When Eka reduced to the rhythm of a trot, the Kadiweu dropped to the ground, tumbling uncontrolled over the grass. All one could see were legs and arms and chunks of soil in the air.

"Damn!" Luis released the girl's hands and ran to his friend.

When she saw the lieutenant running at complete ease, Sophie Werther smiled, realizing that the officer pretended to look weaker than he really was.

"It was nothing, chief, just a graze here and there," Nopitena said.

"You almost did the fastest galloping bite I've ever seen." Luis laughed at the scene of the Kadiweu spitting the grass that entered his mouth. "Hope you will live enough to try it again someday."

Luis looked back and saw that he was several meters far from Sophie. *She saw me running! What a moron I was,* he thought. *But maybe that is for the best. We plan to leave tomorrow, anyway.*

A long way to Rio still awaited the lieutenant and the Kadiwéu, and apparently, memories of tender walks and painful tumbles.

***

With Franz's help, Madam Gertrud Schmidt took the table to the backyard, extending its size by using a wood board supported by two tripods. They enlarged the table so everyone could dine together. It was the last night of Luis and Nopitena at the farm.

A pleasant breeze eased the heat. At dinner, they shared stories and washed down the feast with beer that Mr. Jakub brought from another German immigrant from the neighborhood. After the meal, the lieutenant, the Kadiweu, and Martin remained seated on the veranda, drinking from the keg offered by the Schmidts and talking about the riding and shooting practice.

"Sir, I believe there are still things to teach and learn," Martin told Luis before gulping one-third of his beer.

"I have no doubt about it, but we leave tomorrow at dawn." Luis took another sip of beer.

"I meant…Sir, I want to join. Anspeçada Nopitena saw how I can help the army and this country that has welcomed me." Martin's eyes shone, his chin pointed upwards, and his chest squared open. There was not a single sign of hesitation in the young man's face.

"You have skills, but you are still a boy. Besides, we are not going to war. We are just messengers." Luis filled his mug with beer. "We'll go to Rio, pass the message, maybe win a medal, and then I'll go back to my house."

"Nopitena said he's going to fight the Guaranis," Martin said.

"Really?" Luis recalled Nopitena's promise to wage war and hunt those that devastated his village. The lieutenant thought it was just an impulse caused by the hatred of the moment. Now he realized the Kadiweu was determined about fighting. So was the German. "Martin, talk to your sister. The Schmidts need you. War is no place for teenagers."

The lieutenant believed that with this answer, he had put an end to Martin's stubbornness. They shared a few more stories, finished the keg, and went to bed. The next day, the trip started early and with more surprises.

***

By six in the morning, Luis and Nopitena moved around the farm, packing their belongings in sacks and bags, which they hung on the horses for the journey.

"Anspeçada, where's my rifle?" Luis Caetano asked, inspecting his stuff on the grass yard in front of the house. Since he was a cadet, the lieutenant had never been so long apart from his gun. His walks and conversations with Sophie Werther made him forget for a few days what is a soldier's best friend: his weapon.

"Mr. Schmidt has it. I'll go get it." Nopitena went inside the house, giving no time for Luis to ask why the farmer had his gun.

The Kadiweu returned minutes later. With company.

Gathered on the porch, next to the Indian, a few faces. Martin with a leather bag, Mrs. Gertrud, with two mugs of hot coffee, one in each hand, and Mr. Jacob Schmidt, with Luis Caetano's rifle hanging from a leather bandolier.

Behind all of them stood Sophie Werther. The girl's blue eyes and rosy—but sleepy—face in that bucolic farm setting filled the lieutenant's soul with serenity.

"Lieutenant, here's zee rifle. Clean, repaired, und with ein modest improvement. Perhaps ein shot before leaving to bring good omens?" said Jakob Schmidt.

Luis removed a cartridge from his bag. When he tried to load it through the muzzle front, as he always did, the German settler interrupted him.

"Nein, Lieutenant. Now you don't need to put ammo in zee muzzle." Mr. Jacob took the rifle back and pointed with his finger to a sort of small metal box with a silver bolt on the top of the hilt.

That wasn't there before. Luis frowned.

Tuck Tuck.

The farmer pulled the silver bolt, cocking the rifle, and opened the metal box with his fingers. In the opened box, he inserted a bullet directly into the rifle's chamber. The process was almost like Martin's Dreyse, except that the Dreyse opened the breech in a continuous movement, while the improved rifle from Luis needed two independent movements, taking a few seconds more.

"Maybe not fast as zee Dreyse, but it can fire much faster than before." The bearded German gave the gun back to Luis, cocked, with a bullet in the chamber and ready to shoot.

Luis pointed the rifle to the front, to an open field ending in a pond. To all the present, he aimed to nowhere. But in his eyes, he saw himself again on the bulwark of Coimbra, confronting the tireless troops of the 5th Paraguayan battalion under the command of the resolute captain Luiz Gonzalez. Luis Caetano, on another occasion, spared the life of the retreating captain. But next time, things would be different, and whoever pulled the trigger first, whoever aimed more precisely, would come out alive.

He shot. The noise of his rifle's new version had more powerful basses than before, as the box in the breech allowed the sound to evade the gun barrel. Not only did the sound come out of the rifle's metallic device, but also a wisp of smoke from the burnt powder.

"Impressive. Thank you, Mr. Jakob. I don't know how to repay for this and all the hospitality," the lieutenant said, still examining the new device on his rifle.

"Eazy, take care zu Martin does nothing foolish on zee way," replied the settler, to Luis' confusion. It was the first of many surprises during that February morning.

"Are you coming with us? Do you have a horse?" Luis asked Martin.

"Even better. I have a carriage." Martin pointed to a comfortable carriage he owned. Luis wondered why a young man with a sophisticated weapon and a vehicle like that one still needed to run from debtors.

"Good. Some comfort is welcome for the rest of the trip."

When they finished the coffee, Jakob, Gertrud, and Franz Schmidt said goodbye to the trio.

"Are you recovered, dear? I see you still do not walk well." Mrs. Gertrud asked Luis in a motherly tone.

Nopitena chuckled. The old woman was referring to the typical open-legged monkey-gait the lieutenant had. Luis tried to explain that this is how he always walked, but this time, he avoided mentioning his balls.

Next, it was Sophie's turn to bid farewell. She hugged her brother Martin, urging him to send letters. Then she handed him a red handkerchief and whispered something into the boy's ear. The girl also said goodbye to Nopitena and asked him to take care of her brother.

Last, she went toward Luis Caetano.

"We hope you enjoyed your stay, Lieutenant Gomes." Sophie smiled after breaking the agreement to not call Luis by his rank anymore.

"I would like to stay a few more days. It was amazing for my recovery. But I take the bright memories with me and the hope to come back." The lieutenant replied, looking into the girl's eyes.

"I won't count on that. Soldiers often don't come back." Sophies' reference to her father's death tarnished the tone that Luis intended to give to the occasion.

"I'll do my best, miss." The lieutenant kissed Sophie Werther's hand and said goodbye, leaving behind some of the best memories he would have for years to come.

Chapter XV

March 1st. Rain poured over the imperial capital. Inside the Guanabara bay, ships sought refuge from the ocean swell.

In a bright dining room with white walls and massive arched windows, a few women shared a table, enjoying tea and biscuits. Among them, only one had plebeian origins. Joana Augusta Gomes de Carvalho, invited because of her friendship with the Viscountess of Ururaí, lady Ana Francisca Alves de Lima e Silva.

The friendship with the aristocrat brought Joana to the group. The following invitations arose from her refreshing presence that charmed the ladies from the refined circle. She was a talkative girl with a delectable cultural background that worked as a magnet in the high-society circles of the capital.

Joana shone like a baroness. Still, she had a plebeian surname, being the youngest daughter of an engineer who, by his own sweat, raised funds to educate five children, including her brother Luis Caetano.

The rainstorm over Rio prolonged the afternoon tea, which shortly turned into a soiree, animated by melodies from Portuguese guitars. Joana sat near a small table, next to the Viscountess and Maria Carolina Saraiva, Councilor Saraiva's niece. The latter made up, together with Maria da Silva Paranhos, the closest friends of the Viscountess, whom she fondly called the Marias.

Once the Viscountess invited Joana into the group, the two Marias esteemed her for the variety of subjects the girl discussed with ease.

That day, perhaps influenced by a talk with Almeida Rosa days before, Joana realized that not all could be said in that circle. Something she learned after mentioning that the war in Uruguay was over, thanks to Minister Paranhos' diplomatic prowess.

Maria Paranhos liked the idea that her father solved the Uruguayan conflict. For Maria Saraiva, however, this was an insult.

"To claim that the merit of peace is only from Minister Paranhos is to neglect my uncle's contribution," said Maria Carolina Saraiva. "This is as correct as saying that a carriage runs because of the wheels and not thanks to the horses pulling it."

Joana couldn't find words to argue with such a comparison. Except for the implied malice, it was an analogy as brilliant as those made by rhetoric masters like her teacher, Otaviano de Almeida Rosa.

"It is not worth discussing who had more merit in the crafty peace treaty the Empire signed in Uruguay. Both Saraiva and Paranhos acted in the maximum fulfillment of their duty," said the Viscountess, calming everyone. "Besides, there are other issues more urgent for the government, such as the Paraguayan threat."

"Threat, Lady Ana? It's already a reality. Yesterday my father told me he received a letter about a fort invaded on the Mato Grosso border." Maria Paranhos said, leaving behind any animosity with Maria Saraiva.

"Excuse me, I think I misheard. Did you say that Paraguayans invaded a fort in Mato Grosso?" Joana asked, inclining herself toward Maria Paranhos.

"Yes, Dad told me that he even received a letter listing the survivors who took refuge in Corumbá and then escaped to Cuiabá."

"Do you remember the name of that fort?" Joan pushed her cup away. The last things she would think at that moment were tea and biscuits.

"I believe it was something like Corimba. I am not sure. But why? Do you know anyone on that end of the world?" asked Maria Paranhos.

Joana had mentioned once to the Marias about her brother in the army but never got deeper into his location. The Viscountess, however, understood the fear in the girl's face, expressed by her trembling fingers.

"Coimbra? Was it Coimbra?" Joana's pulse accelerated.

"Yes! That's right! Fort of Coimbra." Maria Paranhos had her Eureka moment, aloof to the apprehension in the eyes of her friend.

Joana squeezed a handkerchief. Her cheekbones turned pale, not resembling the cheerful tutor who taught aristocratic kids to play joyful melodies.

She asked to leave for a moment. The two Marias didn't understand what had just happened or what caused the girl's sudden mood change, but the Viscountess explained that Joana's brother was an officer at the invaded fort.

"Do you have the list of survivors in your house?" lady Ana asked Maria Paranhos.

"No, my dad just told us he saw the list, nothing more. But Ana, I believe that your father, being who he is, should already have all the information."

They were close to the Viscountess's family house. The rain stopped, so lady Ana left the place, asking the two Marias to wait until she came back.

Joana returned, and Maria Saraiva tried to comfort her, bringing hot tea and a slice of cornmeal cake to the girl.

"Did lady Ana tell you?" asked Joana.

Both Marias nodded and changed the subject, but the conversation didn't flow together with smiles and jokes anymore, except for one and other malicious remarks about guests' clothes. Most of the time, the three women only listened to the melodies from the Portuguese guitar.

The Viscountess came back and asked her friends to accompany her to the terrace.

On the open-air mezzanine, they had a splendid view of a rainbow over the bay and sat on rattan chairs under the shade of an ornamental lemon tree.

Indifferent to the post-storm spectacle, the Viscountess held Joana's hands, and told that she went to check with her father knew about the list. Lady Ana saw it with her own eyes but found no Gomes de Carvalho among the survivors.

The Viscountess's gesture made explanations unnecessary. Joana knew how to read the nuances of human expression. She knew that her brother never arrived in Corumbá.

***

Joana woke up in her comfortable bedroom at the Viscountess mansion. Instead of an ordinary servant's accommodation, she had one of the spacious rooms reserved for guests. But despite all the luxury that day, she had a sleepless night.

She turned and tossed on the white linen until daybreak, wondering about the fate of her brother. She didn't know what was worse about his absence among the survivors. For her, either Luis perished fighting for the Empire, or the Paraguayans captured him to be a slave with a short lifespan.

Before starting the Portuguese lesson for two of the children—José de Lima and Aninha Francisca—Joana visited the dining room. The Viscountess was having breakfast and invited her to the table to spare some minutes chatting.

While stirring the sugar in her coffee with milk, Joana took a breath. "Lady Ana, there's something I'd like to ask you. Of course, if you don't accept it, I'll understand, but—"

"But you need to return to your father's ranch and tell him the grievous news in person?" Ana Francisca guessed the plead. After all, it was the only thing someone with common sense could do when carrying tragic news.

Surprised by lady Ana's insight, the tutor confirmed that this was indeed what she wanted to ask.

"Joana, I would never put obstacles to such an important task. In fact, I got you a seat in a senate carriage that leaves tomorrow for São Paulo. It will stop at the village of Queluz."

Joana widened her eyes, amazed at how the Viscountess made her life easier by using her influence as a senator's daughter. With the conflict in Uruguay and now the Paraguayan threat, the steamship service between Rio and São Paulo had an irregular schedule, and to travel by land would cost Joana almost all her savings. But not anymore.

"I don't know how to thank you enough, lady Ana, except for ensuring my devotion in caring for and instructing

your children to the zenith of my ability." Joana smiled
gratefully as she cut a piece of carrot cake served for breakfast
at the plentiful table.

"I have one request, though," Viscountess Ana said.
"Today, when you give the children their last lesson, tell them
it will only be a vacation, that you will return, so they will not
be sad with your absence."

Joana grinned, flattered that the little ones would miss
her presence. "Of course, my lady. It will only be a vacation."
She winked and asked for permission to leave the table. The
children waited for her near the piano.

Before she left the dining room, Ana Francisca called
her again, "My dear, I almost forgot. I guess you won't have
time to visit Otaviano before your departure, correct?"

"Oh, I don't think so." Joana realized she needed to
cancel her next class with her law and diplomacy teacher.

"I believe he will be at an event my husband and I will
attend tomorrow. If you permit, I can explain to him what
happened." Ana Francisca once again made Joana's life easier
without her even asking.

"Yes, please. Very kind of you, lady Ana."

"Do you know who else will be there? Remember
Taunay?" The Viscountess grinned.

"Teacher Otaviano's elegant friend?" Joana let out a compliment. Lady Ana giggled at the girl's choice of words.

"Yes, himself. I can also send him your greetings," said the Viscountess as she raised her tiny cup.

"Sure, why not? I will be grateful." She left the bright, white dining room and went to give the last class to the children before a few weeks' break to visit her father.

***

Seven in the morning, Joana already waited in front of the Conde dos Arcos Palace—the seat of the Federal Senate. It was the departure point for the senatorial carriage to São Paulo. The tutor was elegantly dressed in a light yellow lace and floral dress, a beige scarf around her neck, and a hat adorned with a lily.

A young man holding a briefcase also waited at the same place, apparently one of the parliament secretaries. Next to him, a gentleman in a gray suit, with a shiny bald head framed by sparse white hair, revealing his nearly fifty years. *This one looks like a senator*, she thought. Together with him was a woman, and the rings showed they were married.

They all greeted each other and waited, in silence, while the streets of Rio became livelier as the morning passed.

The senate carriage arrived, pulled by two horses. After everyone settled inside the car, another occupant turned up with a senatorial posture and was just as bald as the gray-suited gentleman but wearing a black coat and hat.

The journey's first day had no hindrances. The fatigue of quickly packing suitcases and waking up early left Joana in a state of semi-drowsiness, ignoring the other travelers. After an overnight stay in a roadside inn, the carriage resumed its course. Rested, Joana saw the two older men chatting. They knew each other.

They talked about the end of the Uruguay war. The black-suited passenger praised the gray-suited one for the peace treaty he signed in Buenos Aires.

"Treaty signed in Buenos Aires? Minister Paranhos signed the treaty in Buenos Aires, not this man. Unless..." Joana told herself. She glanced at the man and recognized in him and his wife, the same facial features of her friend Maria Paranhos.

"Sir, madam, apologies for the inconvenience, but are you by any chance Mr. Minister José Paranhos?" Joana asked.

"In-person, humble servant of the Brazilian empire and imperial majesty." The minister made eye contact with Joana and smiled. "To whom do I owe the honor?"

His companion, sitting by the side, cleared her throat and stared. To appease any jealous impulse from the woman, the minister also introduced her. "And here is lady Teresa, my most dignified wife."

"Lady Teresa, Maria's mother, she told me how you taught her to play piano," Joana said.

The couple cocked their eyebrows. "Do you know our daughter?" asked the minister's wife.

"Yes, I meet her often at the house of the Viscountess of Ururaí, during our tea parties and soirees."

To know that she was a friend of her daughter was enough to open multiple conversation topics between Joana and Lady Teresa for the rest of the day. They talked about music, literature, and of course, suitors - although Joana never revealed the tragic story of her engagement.

Lady Teresa also introduced her to the other man in the car, João Vanderlei, the Baron of Cotegipe. A member of the conservative party, like Paranhos, but with distinct ideas from her husband.

Meanwhile, the two senators discussed matters of state between themselves, with punctual participation from the young parliament secretary also on board.

A few days into the trip, expected to last a week in fit weather, the two politicians read newspapers bought at the Pouso Seco station.

"The Emperor's call for volunteers is working," said Cotegipe.

"Indeed, the imperial majesty's request and his own enlistment as the first volunteer caused an impact. The barracks in Bahia are so crowded with volunteers that there is no space for more recruits," Paranhos replied in a joyful tone.

"What about the National Guard? I don't understand the need to mobilize so many inexperienced volunteers when we have the Guard!" replied Cotegipe.

Joana listened to the conversation and knew the answer to Cotegipe's question. The Guards did not want to fight. Although considered a military force, the National Guards were from wealthy families and preferred easier jobs closer to their homes. Colonels from the guard often used the title to get personal advantages. Joana knew this very well because this was the path her own brother planned when he asked to transfer from the Army.

"The Guards, my dear co-religionary, are too fat to get on a horse." The comical insult made by the otherwise refined Paranhos made even the shy secretary chuckle.

"You are right. Still, recruiters are filling our army with caboclos. And it will get worse! There are rumors that soon they will put slaves in soldier's uniforms under the promise of freedom!" Cotegipe's nostrils flared with annoyance. "Freedom! Can you believe it? It's not enough to assemble an army of worthless people. They want to steal hands from the farms!"

"Vanderlei, we already agreed to disagree with the slavery subject. Our lands are fertile. Whatever we plant on it grows, regardless of the hand that plows, whether captive or free. We don't need slaves."

The Minister's words did not surprise Joana. Maria Paranhos, at one of their meetings, talked about her father's abolitionist positions. Paranhos was not alone inside the Conservative party.

Joana pondered about how remarkable was the political diversity one could observe in Rio. Figures such as Taunay, Minister Paranhos, or the Viscountess herself were strongly connected to the Conservatives. Others, like professor Otaviano or the niece of councilor Saraiva, had links with the Liberal party. But they treated each other with due respect, often forming supra-partisan ties of friendship.

The only thing common to all of Joana's social circles was the absence of slavery advocates. Some acquaintances were openly against it, like Maria Paranhos. Others were indifferent, as the Viscountess. But none defended the captivity system. The Baron was the first pro-slavery character the girl had ever met.

"And you, miss." The Baron interrupted Joana's thoughts. "What do you think about this madness of giving freedom to black people if they fight Paraguay?"

Both senators tried to involve Joana in the discussion about the enlistment of slaves, and both thought she would pend to their side.

"Your Excellencies told that the National Guard is reluctant to go to war despite their obligation with national defense, right?" She asked.

The two politicians, Paranhos and Cotegipe, nodded.

"Your Excellencies also said that mulattos filled the barracks in Bahia, ready to fight after the Emperor's call. Is that true?"

The two lawmakers agreed one more time.

"Very well. So free those who respond to the fatherland call. In their places, captivate those who refuse to fulfill their duty, like the fleeing members of the Guard." Joana delivered her conclusion with a bubbly, triumphant voice.

As soon as the sentence finished, however, she pondered if her words went too far, even more after the Baron of Cotegipe frowned at her bold remark.

To talk about liberating slaves in front of a politician like Cotegipe was, at least, insolent. At worst, dangerous. Even worse was the suggestion that instead of blacks in the sugarcane plantations, fugitives of the National Guard should be used. That was an inconceivable audacity.

"Brillant!" said José Paranhos, breaking the moment of silence. "The imperial house is in a hurry to end slavery, and your solution would fall well into the ears of his majesty!" concluded the minister.

For a moment, Joana worried about her nonsensical opinion circulating in the imperial palace. Luckily for her, the laughter of Paranhos and Lady Teresa denounced it was just a joke. Or not?

***

Days later, in the early afternoon, Joana arrived at Queluz. The fresh air from the Mantiqueira ridge had nothing in common with the atmosphere from Rio. Hills were everywhere, and the neighs from the horses zigzagging on the road curves bloomed her childhood memories. The same could not be said about the Baron of Cotegipe. The politician vomited twice at the curviest points of the road.

During other times when she traveled between Queluz and Rio, the trip seemed longer. Perhaps the conversations with Lady Teresa Paranhos or the gazettes bought at the road stops provided enough distraction to make the time go by faster. Perhaps, however, it was the fact she bore tragic news for her father.

The carriage stopped smoothly in front of the chapel of Saint John the Baptist. She wished goodbye to Minister Paranhos and his wife and greeted the secretary, the carriage driver, and João Vanderlei, the Baron of Cotegipe. Despite the harsh look, the latter seemed to no longer remember the debate with Joana days before. The senate car disappeared on the horizon toward its last destination, the provincial capital.

She walked to a point in the chapel's square where it was possible to hire drivers and carriages for a day. The shoemaker close to the square, the same who repaired her sandals several times during childhood, had his workshop open. Inside it she saw a beggar in rags, maybe imploring the man for a piece of bread.

Joana greeted the cobbler from a distance. But he didn't recognize her. Perhaps the tragedies of losing a fiancé and then a brother had weighed on the girl's face, making her unrecognizable, far from the effusive teenager of the past.

Close to the rental carriages, two strangers talked to each other.

For Joana, it was as if they were characters from a painting by Hieronymus Bosch, such their aesthetic oddness. The first, wearing a ragged shirt, had short stature, brownish skin, and a broad nose. His straight black hair was cut in the shape of a bowl, looking like a black potty on his head. The other man was pale, with a ghostly appearance. But it was a ghost that evoked concern, not fear, for he looked undernourished, almost squalid.

For a moment, she hesitated to go to the carts, repulsed by the idea of approaching the strangers. She saw drunks and sailors in Rio, but she never got within a dozen yards from them. *And yet*, thought the girl, *a sailor at least still resembles a person, unlike those misfits.*

She noticed that the larger of the two, the one with ghostly features, had his pants ripped, almost showing his underwear. *Maybe they are perverts? What kind of barbarians, or idiots, arrived at Queluz?* Joana thought about going to the militia sergeant to report the two vagabonds. But that would only delay her arrival home.

The tutor approached a driver to ask for the price of a ride to the 3-Estados ranch.

"Chief, we're hungry here!" The man with the bowl-shaped hair shouted from a dozen meters away.

Why is this savage talking so loud if his unearthly companion is right beside him? She thought.

"Bite your own arm!" said a third voice from across the street.

Even though she was busy negotiating prices with the cart driver, the answer caught Joana's attention. *Bite your own arm.* That's what she used to tell Luis when her brother complained he was hungry.

The tutor turned her head, looking for the voice. It came from the beggar she saw in the shoemaker store. She squinted her eyes, focusing on it. Behind the dirty clothes and untrimmed beard was someone familiar.

The man, however, recognized her first and called her by the childhood nickname.

"Joau!"

Chapter XVI

Joana and Luis traveled in a hired carriage from Queluz to the 3-Estados farm. Martin's vehicle carrying the German and Nopitena, followed behind.

Joau, as Luis called her, insisted on traveling in a carriage separated from the foreigner and the Indian, using the excuse that it would be faster. The lieutenant accepted, knowing that, in reality, she wanted to keep a distance from his strange friends. Men that, just like the lieutenant, smelled like a dirty corral.

Luis explained why his name was never on the list of survivors who reached Corumba. His sister relaxed her countenance, relieved to find her brother before passing the news to Dom Caetano. Dom Caetano was not exactly healthy, and perhaps such tragic information would be too much to bear. He had six decades of life, and until his late fifties, had an incredible vigor. Diphtheria, contracted shortly after Luis Caetano's departure for Coimbra, took a high toll on his vitality.

The lieutenant, therefore, had never seen his father—a former army engineer turned businessmen and passionate about history and woman—as frail as he was. After the death of his wife, the mother of his first three daughters, he became involved with the woman who gave birth to Luis, the first and only boy.

Dom Caetano also forbade anyone to inform his son about his fragile health.

The rancher knew Luis's imprudence, and if he heard about his father's illness, he would leave the fort and end up accused of post abandonment. Joana, also aware of how reckless her brother could be, supported her father's decision to hide the disease. The only one who never liked this story of keeping secrets was Francisco Aparecido, an orphaned mulatto who grew up in the 3-Estados ranch to become Luis's closest friend. The lieutenant even called him Primo, meaning cousin in Portuguese.

"Joau, what do people in Rio know of the Paraguayan invasion?" Luis Caetano asked, trembling in his seat. The carriage jiggled on the road like a leaf on a windy day. The horses made an extraneous effort to drag the weight of Joana's luggage, plus the passengers. Meanwhile, behind them, Nickel and Eka moved Martin's car with relative ease. Neither the German nor Nopitena carried many belongings.

"Everyone knows Solano invaded our borders since an eyewitness rode all the way to alert the capital. But details are still unknown." Joana talked while tolerating the trepidation from the irregular road stretch to the 3-Estados farm. "The emperor created the Fatherland volunteers, a special military body composed of civilians from all over the country to fight the invaders. His majesty enlisted himself as the first volunteer."

"That changes everything." Luis lowered his head, angered with himself. First, he arrived late to alert the Miranda and Dourados garrisons. Then another messenger reached Rio before him. Any hope of a medal vanished for now. "It is the second time I show up too late to complete my mission. Who alerted the capital about the Invasion?"

"A farmer named Gomes da Silva. He rode on horseback for almost fifty days from Corumbá to Rio. Arrived there on February 22." Joana recalled what she had read in the newspapers. "The Paraguayans killed one of his children."

"Poor man." He sighed. The lieutenant reflected on the reason for the farmer to travel so fast: avenge his children, murdered by the invader. Meanwhile, Luis was doing it for a medal. *Maybe his motives were just stronger than mine*, he thought.

Suddenly, a hiss split the air.

Fiiiiiiiiuuuuuuuuuiiiii!

The Lieutenant's eyes narrowed. He turned his face and lifted his cheeks—slender after the long trip—with a wide grin. Placing his thumb and forefinger between lips, the Lieutenant answered with another whistle:

Fuuuuuuu!

The sounds were a code Luis Caetano and Primo used during horseback rides. A method to not lose each other under

217

the mountain fog or under the alcoholic torpor after drinking nights.

A brown horse reached the siblings' wagon. On the animal's back was a mulatto with simple cotton clothes and a straw hat—like any peasant in the region—dark, curly hair, narrow face, and unshaved beard. He had the same height as Luis but with a slightly younger appearance.

"What a day! The presence of two heirs!" The horseman tipped his hat, greeting the siblings. "Why are you using these rags, Louy? Did you fight with a jaguar? And..." The mulatto sniffed. The stench of the unbathed lieutenant forced him to cover his nose with a hand. "What is this smell?"

Primo spoke with the same strong retroflex R of the lieutenant. In fact, nearly everybody in the countryside of Sao Paulo talked with that R, except Joana, who changed her accent—it would be eccentric to speak like a country girl in the social circles of the capital. Primo Francisco also had the discomforting habit of finding his friends pet names. Luis found a coin in the road? Primo called him Lucky Louy. Luis complained he works too much? Labor Louy. Luis was dumped by a girl? Loner Louy—he got a punch after saying this one.

"Good afternoon to you too, Primo, you dirty vagabond. This smell results from hard work, something that you don't know what it is."

Mutual offenses were the mark of their friendship, a reciprocal confidence that emerged from the dawn of childhood.

"Hard work? Since Dom Caetano had this idea of a banquet, he gave me a lot of work. I kept going here and there, from the ranch to Cruzeiro and back," replied Primo, releasing his halter and pointing in one direction and the other, as if no one knew where Cruzeiro was. "All the time buying things for that dinner party. Now I see it's going to be a fine thing, even you both came."

"Dinner party?" Luis and Joana said at the same time.

"That is what I said, miss. I have to hurry to deliver this thing here." The mulatto pointed to a bag he carried. "see you at the house. Hop!" With a slap on the horse's rump, he rode to the ranch.

Half an hour later, they arrived at the main farm house. A freed black servant, the house cook, greeted them. A gray-haired, good-humored man, maybe fifty years old, but with a solid physique. He cleaned fish and prepared the fire to roast a pig.

"Old Manuel! Remember to separate the loin for me!" Luis said to the man.

But it wasn't necessary. Seu Manuel knew by heart which cuts Luis liked. The cook worked for the family even before Dom Caetano's children were born.

"Oh, Luisinho! Even you came! And you too, Miss Joana!" said the cook as he removed the fish entrails. He turned toward the house, addressing his kitchen helper, "Almir, call Dom Caetano. The children are here."

While the group removed their luggage from the vehicles—mostly Joana's suitcases—a man opened the porch door.

He had hair as white as rice and supported himself with the help of a cedar cane. Apart from the visible physical difficulties, he had a natural elegance, enhanced by good clothes, including a black top hat and a brown satin vest. More than sophistication, he had an air of wisdom, like distinguished men of science in Rome or Byzantium.

"Manuel, I think I am seeing things." said the gentleman at the porch, rubbing his fingers over his eyes as if to wake up from an illusion.

"No, Dom Caetano, it's Luisinho and Joana!" Manuel left the knife and fish in the backyard basin, washed his hands in a gourd, and went to help the troupe carry the luggage.

"*Meus filhos*! What a pleasure. You both combined to come together?" said Dom Caetano before inhaling the unpleasant body odor that accompanied the cart. "What the heck is that smell?"

Both Luis and Manuel guffawed. The rancher did not mince his words, a characteristic that Luis inherited from him.

Even Joana, with all her politeness, had a bit of her father's spontaneous side. A side she showed with her ironic reply to the Baron of Cotegipe days before.

"It was a long trip, Dad." Luis tried to justify the reek.

"I imagine it was long," Dom Caetano said. "But your sister carries the light scent of a baroness." The rancher hugged his daughter, who smiled with the compliment.

"I am glad you both are here." Dom Caetano looked back to the lieutenant and adopted a serious expression. "But, my son, did you run away from duty? That wasn't the case, right?"

"No, dad." Luis shook his head, denying vigorously, "but it's a long story. Months ago, there in Mato Grosso..."

"Wait, wait. We have guests for dinner today. I'm sure your story at the fort will be the highlight of the night!" Dom Caetano interrupted, placing his wrinkled hands on Luis's sweaty arms. "Now, son, you need to go take a bath, as well as your...who are they?" The rancher pointed to the two strange types waiting at the door, Nopitena and Martin.

"They're my friends," Luis said.

Dom Caetano stared at the peculiar folks.

"Uh.. right. Go get clean because soon even the pigs will faint with this smell," the rancher said, with the joyful humor of a parent visited by his offspring. "Guests arrive at seven in the evening."

Dom Caetano then turned to the kitchen. "Almir! Put two more seats at the dinner table and prepare food for four more!"

    ***

The trio bathed in a pond in the farmhouse's vicinity. The mountainous region was not as hot as Mato Grosso but warm enough to make the water tepid. When the lieutenant, followed by Nopitena and Martin, arrived in the dining room, Manuel—who, that evening, besides cooking, would also serve the guests—discreetly called Luis to come closer.

"Luisinho, your two friends can eat with Almir and me. There's a table at the kitchen veranda." The sexagenary, deep-voiced cook leaned toward the lieutenant. "But here in the dining room, Dom Caetano told us to put places just for you, Miss Joana, and the guests."

Luis stared at the servant for a few seconds.

"Seu Manuel, they are my guests."

"Boy, your friends are an Indian and a foreigner." The black servant adopted a posture of paternal authority. "I always told you that each person has their place in this world. Don't make it difficult."

"It's fine." Luis resigned, remembering that, as a child, he enjoyed eating with the servants at the same kitchen veranda, a pleasant place during warm nights. "But open a bottle of the good kind for them."

"Oho! From the best ones," said Manuel, returning to the final dinner preparations.

The trio went to the veranda. A large wooden table with two long, white-painted benches, one at each side, occupied half of the space. A meter further, two rocking chairs. Primo occupied one chair, with his feet on the rail, holding a glass of cachaça and smoking a straw cigarette.

"Will you eat with us, like in the old days?" the mulatto asked.

"No, but they will." Luis pointed to the Indian and the German, taking their places in the benches around the table. "I'll stay here until the guests arrive."

"These two guys, do they speak our language?" Primo asked.

"If your language is Portuguese, I think we speak better than you," said Nopitena.

"My virgin! A talking Indian! Would you like a cachacinha? And what about the wasp poke stick over there?"

"Ahem. My name is Martin." The German responded with his thick accent.

"What a beauty, Luis! Nothing like the lieutenant to bring the strangest blokes of the empire and break the tedium of the ridges!" Primo filled four short glasses with cachaça and raised his own. "A toast to Dom Caetano's best son and to the weird guys walking behind him!"

Luis Caetano grinned at his friend's sarcastic toast. Of course, he was his father's best son, as he was the only one. Drinking the liquor, he looked at the road and saw the first guests.

A spectacular carriage, made of walnut wood, painted red and gold, pulled by two stallions adorned with colorful wreaths approached. The coachman wore a black suit and an English top hat.

"What's that on the horses?" Nopitena asked Martin and Luis.

The German said he had not seen such luxury on the farm where he lived.

"Flower ornaments. A nobility thing, so they must be big people," Luis replied.

"Dom Caetano said something about the daughter of a commenter coming," Primo said as he grabbed some peanuts from a tin at his side.

"I believe you mean commander, or maybe commendator?" Luis grinned at his friend's mistakes.

"Yes, commentre." The mulatto snorted. "Posh people."

A gentleman, apparently less than forty years old but already bald, descended from the gilded carriage. Behind him was his wife, in a light blue dress and long hair, modeled in a sophisticated bun. Holding her hands, two carefully dressed children

Seu Manuel, neatly changed from a chef to a butler, received the family while another carriage approached from behind. This time a more ordinary coach.

"And who are these?" Luis asked Primo.

`Hum...He is the militia captain of Cruzeiro. You know who else comes along, right Louy?" Primo blinked at the distracted lieutenant.

"I know. Why do you think I am bathed, perfumed, and with new clothes?" Luis smirked while breaking a peanut shell.

"Good luck, Lewd Louy."

Along with the captain, two other individuals left the carriage. The first, a plump, pink-skinned man in his mid-twenties, wearing a neat uniform. The second, a brunette young lady with straight, long hair, wearing a lacy beige corset and a thin red shawl over her shoulders. The warm weather forced her to use a handkerchief to wipe the humidity from the forehead and from the curves of her cleavage.

"Têtê is getting more and more...healthy" Primo was never shy in his comments about the opposite sex, but he took special care with Teresa, the daughter of the militia captain. He knew how the lieutenant had been interested in the girl since their teenage years when they met at family dinners and local events.

Luis Caetano got up from the rocking chair, waved to Teresa's father, and then, walking toward the brunette, greeted her by tipping his hat.

***

All the guests took their seats around the oak dining table, decorated with azalea floral arrangements. Manuel—the cook, turned waiter—served wine and refreshments. As an appetizer, a wooden board with fruits from the Mantiqueira sliced Minas cheese and ham.

At the right side of Dom Caetano sat the militia captain and his wife, while on the left, the mysterious guest of the luxurious carriage and his austere-looking wife.

Joana Augusta arrived at the table at last. She had an ordinary beauty, not sufficient to draw attention, but her presence, bubbly voice, and peaceful rhythm of speech made people forget about time when talking to her. Besides, she knew how to dress well, wearing a turquoise dress with a discreet neckline - at least much more discreet than Teresa's - and an amber tiara. Her gracefulness caught the table's attention, and her arrival halted the conversations.

"My distinguished guests," Dom Caetano cleared his throat, "let me make the proper introductions." Both Joana and Luis already knew the militia captain and his two children, the sumptuous Teresa and the well-nourished Aureliano. The host introduced to them also the mysterious guests from the luxurious carriage.

"Here is Mrs. Francisca de Paula Santos, daughter of the most dignified imperial commendator Francisco de Paula Santos, along with her illustrious husband, Henrique Dumont."

Heirs of an imperial commendator! That explains the pompous carriage, thought Luis.

Dom Caetano explained that Henrique Dumont was one of the most promising engineers in the empire and a potential director of the São Paulo railways.

Railroads were one of Dom Caetano's greatest passions. Through the common interest, the rancher and Henrique Dumont developed a friendship. Engineer Dumont's children played in the adjacent room with toys that once belonged to Joana and Luis.

The lieutenant and Teresa sat on opposite sides, but their legs accidentally—or not—met under the table. The girl, perhaps remembering Luis as a childhood friend, decided to have fun by kicking the lieutenant's shin. Luis, startled, spilled his wineglass. The accident made the guests surprised, except for Teresa, tittering proudly.

There will be a payback for that, Tetê. Luis stared at the giggling girl.

Seconds later, a child approached Henrique Dumont, showing a little toy train he found. The kid, about eight, had a white shirt with short pants and wasn't intimidated by the adults around.

Luis, to disguise his embarrassment after spilling wine, struck up a chat with the boy, by asking his name.

"My name is Henrique, just like Dad."

The lieutenant greeted the child as if he was an adult.

"Oh, it is a pleasure to meet you, Mr. Henrique Santos Dumont. My name is Luis Caetano Gomes de Carvalho."

"Nice to meet you, Mr. Luis. Is this your train?" the little boy asked.

"Yes. Do you also like trains?"

"Uhum, does it fly?"

Luis grinned at the unusual question.

"Trains do not fly, buddy. Maybe you are confusing them with balloons."

"Hum.. maybe. I will go back to the toy room. Excuse me." The boy returned to the adjacent room, where his sister played with Joana's dolls.

"For an eight-year-old boy, he has the elegance of an ambassador," Joana said to the child's father.

"Thank you, Miss. While diplomacy is a noble profession, I dream he will become an engineer, like your father and myself. But if not him, maybe the next ones," Henrique Dumont replied.

Dom Caetano tasted some of the ham served. "Do you have plans for more kids, Henrique?"

"Yes. If we have another girl, Virginia. If it's a boy, Luis or Alberto."

"Let it be, Luis, because Luis Santos Dumont sounds more adequate for a commendator's grandson than Alberto Santos Dumont," said Henrique's wife, Francisca.

It flattered Luis Caetano to know that his first name was suitable for a commendator's grandson.

The waiter Manuel brought to the table the first dish of the evening—boiled veal. Meanwhile, the captain of the militia turned to Luis:

"Have you already transferred out from the army, Lieutenant? To take up your post in the Queluz National Guard?"

'It's a long story, sir.' Luis sipped his wine.

"So tell us, please! I insist, and we're all curious to hear it!" Teresa said with a provocative smile.

Dom Caetano also encouraged his son to describe the adventure from Mato Grosso to Sao Paulo.

Luis started with the battle in Coimbra, the escape aboard the Anhambaí, and the nights at the refugee camp of the Maracajú ridge. He also told how the fight with the Vergueiro's henchmen to save Martin resulted in a concussion and a few days of recovery at the Felicíssima farm.

While the lieutenant recounted his adventures over the past two months, the second course was served, and the wine flowed freely on the table. Manuel filled the glasses with no one realizing his presence.

"And that's how we three ended up back here," concluded Luis, referring to him, Nopitena, and Martin.

"Fate wanted you to come home, Luis. Whether planned or unforeseen," the militia captain said, with an expression already softened by the rounds of wine, "Service in the National Guard is easier. At most, you will have to select volunteers for the war. And there are so many people volunteering that there's no room for everyone."

"How different is the situation now," said Dom Caetano, reminding that in previous conflicts, like the Platine war, the lack of soldiers forced the empire to recruit mercenaries from abroad. The rancher asked what caused such an increase in the numbers of men willing to risk their own lives.

"The Emperor's call. He enlisted himself as the first volunteer," Joana replied.

The militia captain gave a skeptical, sideways smile.

"Yes, some volunteers are indeed coming because of the emperor's call. But not all. Blacks enlist because it is a chance for slaves to gain freedom. Peasants volunteer because it is a chance to earn five hundred reis a day, three hundred thousand more when they return after the war, and additional fifty thousand square meters of land." The militia captain interrupted his explanation to eat a spoonful of the doce de leite served as dessert in individual porcelain bowls. "Nobody expects to die in a brief war against Paraguay. The payment is a fortune for such an insignificant risk."

The captain's optimism, certain that the war would be short, was equal to what Joana saw in Rio. But her employer, the Viscountess de Ururaí, the daughter of a distinguished general and senator, did not share this optimism. For Joana, the wary approach of a well-informed woman as Viscountess Ana was a bad sign.

"For the officers, it's also an excellent deal. The time needed for promotion is cut by half when you are on the battlefield," said Aureliano, the son of the militia captain. He was also an army officer stationed in Cruzeiro as a recruiter. "Not to mention the chances of making a good impression on a colonel and advance even faster." These words sounded like a siren song for Luis. Still a second lieutenant, the war could help him add one more star to his uniform. Better payments, prizes, and an even more comfortable life. *What are the risks of a war against Paraguay?* He thought, considering the possibility of delaying his transfer to the Guard. A better salary and a fancier rank tempted him.

"Money, promotions, manumission. Are those the reasons our soldiers fight for?" Dom Caetano said with a guttural voice, raising his hand in a gesture of supplication. The words from the rancher interrupted the optimistic tone of the table. "Machiavelli once wrote that a state relying on mercenaries is neither firm nor safe, as they are disunited, infidels and cowards ante the enemies."

The rancher lowered his hand and looked at his plate, resigned. Then he concluded, bitterly, "our men will fight for money and land. The Paraguayans, meanwhile, will fight for everything they love. Each of them will be worth five of ours."

The pessimistic monologue caused a mournful silence, interrupted only by the noise of the children's spoons, sitting on the mat and devouring portions of doce de leite from little bowls.

"At least the government has plans to strengthen the Navy," said Henrique Dumont. The engineer had good contacts and insider information. "But I believe this will take some time. I don't think the war will be that short."

Luis received Henrique's words as something positive. If battle time counted twice for the period necessary for promotion, a long war could help him jump ranks instead of slowly climbing the hierarchy.

The lieutenant imagined that even a promotion to captain would be possible. *Captain Luis Caetano Gomes de Carvalho*, he thought with a grin.

***

The first guests to leave were the Dumonts, with their children already falling asleep. Both Dom Caetano and the Militia Captain went to the porch to say goodbye to the family. When the luxurious carriage left, they preferred to stay a bit longer to have a smoke, enjoying the freshness of the night.

Luis left the dining room and walked to the kitchen veranda. From a distance, he heard the festive noises of the veranda feast. Certainly, those not allowed to sit in the main room had enjoyed it as much as the guests. No doubt Manuel opened a bottle of the good liquor for the boys.

On the way to the veranda, he noticed, in a corner, Joana talking to Aureliano, the son of the militia captain. He was a little older than the lieutenant, almost the same age as Joana. Luis wondered for a moment what they were talking about, then walked straight to the porch.

"Blondie, you're making this up!" Primo said to Martin as he filled the glasses with one more shot to each.

"No, Francisco, that's the rule of the game," the German replied.

Noticing the Lieutenant's approach, Nopitena and Martin welcomed him with a Good Evening, Chief. That amused Luis. So far, only Nopitena used to call him Chief but somehow, Martin followed his colleague's custom.

Primo didn't bother to greet Luis but pointed to the cards on the table.

"Louy, the blonde bamboo stick is teaching us some game from his land. Jucapil something. But I think it is all made up."

"Juckerspiel." Martin couldn't understand why it was so difficult for them to learn the game he played at the Schmidt's.

"After emptying a bottle of cachaça, it's hard to understand the rules of anything, Primo." The lieutenant sat at the table and asked for a glass for himself.

Nopitena drank little to nothing, as he was weak to alcohol. Martin and Primo, however, already looked like soakers, with swollen eyes and slurred speech.

Luis raised his glass and asked for a toast to celebrate the end of the evening at the veranda, or as Primo called it, the commoners' corner. Manuel joined in the toast, as his services as a butler were no longer needed.

Primo leaned toward Luis.

"How was the dinner with the fine ones?" The mulatto tried to whisper the question, but the ethyl in his blood caused the words to come out crooked and almost screaming.

"I spent a lot of time recounting the story about how we got here," Luis said.

"Ahh, your pet Indian told us everything! So you took a stone in the head?" asked Primo, referring to what happened at the Felicissima farm. Nopitena stared at Primo, and his eyes warned it was not a good idea to call him a pet Indian.

"I hope the hole they made in your head hadn't leaked out the rest of your reasoning," Primo smirked.

"Look who's talking about reasoning! The worst drunkard of the Paraíba valley!" Luis responded to his friend, holding the almost empty bottle of liquor.

"I was the worst until you brought this spooky chap over here!" Primo pointed with his thumb to Martin, who sat behind him, "Have you seen how he dries glass after glass?"

Luis looked with curiosity at Martin, and the German just shrugged his shoulders.

"What did they tell you of the war?" Primo asked.

Luis repeated what Aureliano said about the volunteer benefits: regular payments, the promise of a piece of land, as well as faster promotions. The list of advantages attracted attention not only from Primo but also from Martin and Nopitena.

"Sounds good, but not for me. My life here is peaceful. I earn something helping Dom Caetano from time to time, and I have a girl waiting for me on the weekends." Primo lighted his cigar. "Two girls, indeed. One in Queluz, and another in Cruzeiro."

Nopitena and Martin, meanwhile, pondered about the lieutenant's words.

"Chief, what's your plan then?" The Kadiweu had a low tone of voice and heavy eyelids. He wasn't used to staying up this late.

"I am still thinking about it." With no answer to give, he drank his shot of cachaça.

"If you go, I will," Martin said.

"What if I don't go?" Luis turned his head, peering at the young European.

Martin looked at Luis, then at Nopitena.

"I will still volunteer, but I will need to find another officer to lead me." Martin got up and went to sleep. The resolute posture of the young immigrant perplexed Primo, but not Nopitena, who ended up snoozing in the chair.

Primo lit another straw cigarette. He and the lieutenant remained up late under the moonlight, exchanging insults and reminiscing about passages from adolescence.

Martin's words echoed in Luis's head. *I will still volunteer, but I will need to find another officer to lead me.* That fellow, who until weeks before was a complete stranger, trusted Luis enough to guide him to the front line. Just like Nopitena trusted. But while Nopitena accepted Luis' leadership because of rank, Martin respected the lieutenant because of a single act that saved his life.

Luis had no pleasure from leading. After witnessing how heroes of the lineage of João de Oliveira Melo or Hermenegildo Portocarrero led their men at the Coimbra fort, he concluded that this was not for him. But that night, Martin's eagerness to serve under his command made him think that maybe one day he could be like Melo Bravo.

"Where are you going next?" asked Primo as he chopped tobacco.

"I don't know yet. I'll give the boys a few days to think about what they want."

Chapter XVII

Luis drank a cup of black coffee, ate a piece of cornbread from the kitchen, and filled a canteen with fresh water.

From the window, early morning brightened the sky, coloring it in rosy tones. A spectacle that sometimes the Mantiqueira ridge boasted to its visitors as if the mountains were a living creature with its own dignity.

"Hey jug head, what are you doing at this hour?" a female voice coming from the kitchen entrance caught Luis' attention. "Are you going to visit Teresa in Cruzeiro?"

It was Joana Augusta, who the day before went to bed much earlier than the lieutenant.

"Uh...Joau? Well, it wouldn't be a bad idea to visit Tetê after seeing how she, huh...changed." The lieutenant had dark circles around his eyes, a signal of how little he slept.

When Luis and Joana were still teenagers, Teresa tried to befriend them. As she was a few years younger, they rejected her company. But the girl grew up, and from an inconvenient juvenile, she turned into a magnet for the Lieutenant's eyes.

"I'm going with you. It's good to breathe some fresh air." Joana took a piece of cornbread for herself and put several more in a bag.

"Just get a horse." The lieutenant left the kitchen toward the stable.

On the way to Cruzeiro, Joana told Luis what she had heard in Rio about the war. How volunteers from all over Brazil crowded the barracks, enlisting to fight the invader. She also mentioned that the tales of the Coimbra Fort, resisting against thousands of Paraguayans, lit a patriotic spark in every heart.

"Joau, if only they saw what I saw…They'd think twice before enlisting." Luis sighed and inhaled the pure breeze of the ridge as he searched for words to describe the battle terrors. "The bodies piling up on the edge of the wall, the smell of piss. Joau, do you know that when a bullet or a blade kills a man, he ends up pissing himself, right?"

Joana Augusta didn't know. She has no idea, thought Luis, confirmed by the look of disgust on the girl's face. "The only thing worse is the smell of…" Before Luis could complete what he would say, Joana raised her hand, signaling she had enough descriptions.

"Would you rather transfer to the Guard, who won't go to war because they are too paunchy to ride?" Joana used the same mockery against the National Guard she heard on the way to Queluz.

Luis kept silent. The National Guard's lag to engage, while civilians—from slaves to freedmen—complied with the emperor's request, could give them a poor reputation.

"Even if you conquer Teresa," Joana had a crooked smile, signaling that a new provocation was coming, "when the war ends, and the first veteran with a medal on his chest appears, he takes her from you right away, cuíca."

One of the several nicknames Joau gave to her two-years younger brother referred to the little Brazilian wild animal—the cuíca—whose wide black eyes reminded her of the lieutenant as a child.

"You have a point, Joau. A medal turns fine what is gross. And there's still the money, promotions..." Luis added to his sister's words. "What will be the role of the father of your lady? Is he the one who will command the Imperial forces?"

Luis couldn't hold his curiosity about the legendary figure. The Viscountess' father had a reputation that preceded his name. The crowds called him The Peacemaker for the many wars he had ended.

" I don't know. But if they put the army on his hands, this war will not last long." Joana replied while they rode under the eight-in-the-morning sun, already halfway to Cruzeiro. "Yesterday, Aureliano asked me the same thing. We chatted about the fight against the Paraguayans." She removed the canteen attached to the horse's saddle to take a sip of water.

"And...? I see how the lad is interested in you." Luis smiled.

"If he loses some weight, maybe I would consider. Still, that was not the reason for our conversation. Aureliano told me that even he would like to join the platoons going south."

"But...?"

"But since he's a recruiter, he can't, right? They need him to stamp paperwork in Cruzeiro. He thought, however, that you were going to join the fight."

Aureliano, apart from being Teresa's brother, was also an army lieutenant. But differently from Luis, he never served in any outpost or witnessed any battle. His father's position as a militia captain ensured him a snug post as a bureaucrat officer in Cruzeiro. Despite that, Aureliano was cordial and diligent, unlike the spoiled young officers relying on family influence like Ensign Coelho. The only thing similar between Coelho and the recruiter is that both were out of shape.

"Why did he think I would join the fight?" Luis asked while their horses crossed a trickle of water that descended from the mountains to the Paraíba do Sul River.

"He said you're lucky to have men who follow you so far. That there is no greater joy than fighting side by side with those who trust you." Joana said.

Luis remembered Martin's words about going to war under his command. Or Nopitena, volunteering to ride with the Lieutenant from Mato Grosso to the capital, even after seeing his village razed.

Aureliano is right. Lost in his thoughts, Luis didn't notice that a girl with a flowery dress, black hair, and curvy shape waved to him from a ranch near the river.

Joana and Luis rode toward Teresa. The girl invited both for refreshments in their summer garden. It was almost ten in that warm morning, so they gladly accepted it.

Teresa, once an insipid teenager, had blossomed into adulthood. Her questions sometimes provoked Luis, sometimes made him suspicious of what she meant. Joana, a young woman herself and excellent at reading the subtleties of human intention, knew exactly that the girl was trying to arouse her brother's interest.

"Time to get back home. Thank you, Tetê." Luis stood up from the table in the ranch's garden. Clouds formed in the sky, bringing the possibility of late afternoon rain.

Joana nodded and joined her brother on the way out.

"When will we see each other again, Luis?" Teresa asked. The two Gomes de Carvalho siblings turned their heads and glimpsed the girl after the unexpected question. Teresa tried to amend. "And Joana, of course. When will I meet you two again?"

"When the war finishes, I think," Luis replied.

Joana looked at her brother with eyes wide in amazement. As much as she knew how to predict reactions, she didn't expect that her brother, until then doubtful about joining the war, would change his mind out of nowhere.

But maybe it was not out of nowhere. Maybe it was not even because of Teresa.

"I hope the victory comes quick. I am not used to waiting so much." replied the flowery-dressed girl, wishing goodbye to the siblings.

Wait for what? What did she mean this time? Luis again caught himself in one of Teresa's riddles.

"She wants you to return from the battlefront directly to her." Joana read the confused expression on the lieutenant's face and replied loudly to his thoughts. There was an almost telepathic bond between the two. "What about your decision to go south? It is not only about a medal to impress the girl, is it?"

"No, Joau. There is the money, the promotions. It is also because of the lads. Aureliano was right." Luis' said, with a firm voice and tense muscles, pulsing with energy from his sudden decision to go into battle.

"Fair reasons. It should be a brief war, anyway. Even a sluggish jughead like you should be back from there in a few months." The random insult exchange expressed the friendship between the siblings. Something non-existent with Dom Caetano's other three eldest daughters.

"Sluggish? Catch me before Queluz then!" Luis spurred Nickel's haunches, setting off the horse. His sister smiled and followed close behind. The two Gomes de Carvalho kids, in an improvised race, raised dust on the sandy road.

***

Closer to the ranch, the siblings spotted Nopitena returning with Martin from a nearby meadow called Campo Alegre. They halted and waited for the Indian and the German to approach. It was still mid-afternoon, and the clouds provided some shadow while the horses drank water in a creek.

Luis noticed that Martin, riding awkwardly on a nag, carried his rifle. The cartridge belt had some empty spaces, meaning he used part of the ammunition.

"Armed, but returning with no game, Martin? Bad day for a hunt?" Luis asked as they arrived.

"No, sir, it was Nopitena who shot," Martin said.

"That explains everything. He aims like a drunk pissing in the dark."

Joana and Martin laughed, but not Nopitena.

"He is learning. Maybe until we get into battle, he can hit a target" Martin's defense of Nopitena was more embarrassing than helpful. "It is a pity that you may not see it, sir. I will send you a letter when that happens." While Martin often missed understanding a good joke, he knew how to use some sarcasm.

"Won't need it. I'll go to the south." Luis passed on the decision he took hours earlier.

Martin looked at the Lieutenant with wide eyes in amazement, and a large grin opened from side to side in the face of the otherwise serious Prussian. The surprise was greater for him, as Nopitena sensed the lieutenant would not refuse a good fight.

"Martin is your name, right?" Joana asked the German.

"Yes, madam."

"Where are you from? I assume you're German for the accent."

"I was born in Weimar, Thuringia, but I came to Brazil still very young."

"Oh, a German. On the way from Rio to here, I read about a battalion of your people assembling in the south, in Blumenau, to join the volunteers."

"Blumenau?" Martin repeated the name in a ringing tone of voice.

"Yes, it is a village built by Germans near Itajaí. It is like a piece of Prussia in Brazil. Immigrants who fought for us in the Platine war settled there." Joana told Martin a little of what she had read in the newspapers during her travel.

Luis also paid careful attention to Joana's explanation. He remembered when Sophie told him the story of their father. He was one of the Germans hired by the empire to fight at the Platine conflict.

"Miss Joana, sorry for the inconvenience, but I have a question."

Joana chuckled with the excessive respect coming from the skinny, pale German. She admired European manners and politeness, but seeing such a shabby-looking young man with proper etiquette felt like a satire.

"Do you know who is organizing these battalions?" Martin asked.

"I'm afraid not," replied Joana, as they passed through the gate to the ranch, "but I remember they were called the Von Gilsa Volunteer Corps, so that must be the commanders' last name."

"Von Gilsa...My father had a commander with that last name. How can I go to Blumenau?"

Martin's question coincided with their arrival at the farmhouse of the 3-Estados ranch.

"It is a long way. First, you need to reach Santos, either by land or by a boat departing from Paraty." Joana replied while getting off her horse. "After, board a ship to Itajaí, heading south,"

Luis, hearing her answer, had an idea. Even though he decided to go to war, it still bothered him to take an inexperienced young man like Martin to the gates of death. Therefore, the lieutenant thought about traveling south with the same ship that made a stopover in Itajaí. Once there, Martin could disembark and join the other Germans, who would train him until he was ripe to battle. Meanwhile, Luis would continue his trip only with Nopitena.

At the farmhouse, Luis Caetano sought Manuel and asked about Primo Francisco. The cook pointed to the porch, where the mulatto smoked a straw cigarette and watched the sun go down.

"Primo, do you know where I can find the timetables for the vessels leaving from Paraty?"

"People write this stuff is in newspapers. I can't confirm because reading is not my favorite thing," replied the mulatto "sit there, let's smoke a cigarette."

Luis hadn't smoked for a while, but he gladly accepted it, given the chance to talk to his friend.

"When you go to Queluz," Luis said, "can you find out for me when is the next transport to Santos or Itajaí?"

"What do I get?" Primo asked, scratching the scant hair that grew on his chin.

"A bottle."

It was a good prize. Good enough for Primo Francisco to leave for Queluz the next morning and bring the information that in eight days, a steamboat would depart from Paraty to Santos and then to Itajai. If the trip from 3-Estados to Paraty took three days, then they still had five to rest.

Luis told Nopitena and Martin about the departure in five days to board a ship heading south with a few stops along the way.

That night, Primo called the three of them to share the bottle of cachaça—or what he left of it—that Luis gave him after the favor and asked Martin to teach him again how to play the Juckerspiel.

***

On the eve of their departure, the trio enjoyed another feast sponsored by Dom Caetano. It was a farewell to one more period of absence of his only son. This time he hoped it would last much less, maybe only a few months.

From all the motives that pushed the three men to a faraway conflict, Luis' goals were the easiest to achieve, and that is why his father hoped that his boy's return would not take long. All he had to do was take part in a couple of battles against the Paraguayans, earn a medal, wait for a promotion, and return as a hero after the Empire removed Solano from power.

Martin and Nopitena, however, had less concrete reasons. The first went for the honor of his father, to erase the image of a Prussian soldier that died before the first shot.

Nopitena had the most dangerous motive: revenge and freedom. Revenge against the Guaranis who destroyed his village and freedom for the Kadiweus enslaved during the enemy raid.

"Primo, have you ever thought about joining the volunteers?" Luis asked as they drank after dinner.

"For what? I am a farmhand with no mother or father, but still with a roof and food. I don't need to throw myself in front of a cannon." Primo took a sip of liquor. "Here, my worst risk is a bad hangover after drinking shitty pinga in the town bar."

"You have a point. Take care of my father while I'm gone. He got a lot worse since I departed. I hope to spend more time with him after my return."

"Don't worry, Louy." Primo Francisco tapped his friend's right shoulder.

Luis dried his glass and went to his room. Nopitena and Martin left earlier to sleep. The next morning they would need to wake up early to pack supplies, bid farewells, and begin a new journey in their lives.

Primo, who had nothing to do on the next day, remained on the veranda. The summer night breeze carried the freshness of the nearby forests, making the scene delightful. In the sky, the moon hopped between rapidly drifting clouds that moved much faster than time passed down there.

Life in Mantiqueira ran slowly, and to contemplate the hills under the moonlight enjoying a cigarette and a good Pinga was the program that Primo planned to repeat every night as long he could live. He didn't need anything more, although the presence of his friend Luis turned great what was already good.

While the mulatto smoked his last cigarette, gazing at the ridge that separated the State of Sao Paulo from Minas Gerais, a female figure approached.

"Joau, you around here? I will not offer you a cigar because you're too refined for that."

"This thing stinks, but make good use of it. Luis already went to sleep, right?"

Primo Francisco nodded.

"I have a favor to ask, or rather a proposition," Joana said in a whispered voice while standing near the parapet.

"Oh, another favor." Primo sighed. "It will be the second favor someone requests me in a matter of minutes. I hope it's easy, or at least well paid," replied the mulatto, with a roguish glance.

"Well paid? Sure, and not just in cash. But I will not call it easy."

"So tell me what your proposal is, Dom Caetano's little girl."

Chapter XVIII

The three men packed their stuff inside the stagecoach. Luis and Nopitena planned to leave their horses—Nickel and Eka—in the ranch, under the care of Primo.

The carriage would take them to Paraty, and from there, they should board a steamboat to Santos and then another vessel to Porto Alegre, passing through several stopovers. Luis didn't bother to inform his two companions about the itinerary details. If everything worked out, they would arrive in Porto Alegre in a month, in the second half of April.

Dom Caetano, Luis' father, weakened by age and sickness, approved the decision of his son to re-join the army rather than becoming a good-for-nothing officer in the National Guard. The rancher was a model patriot who appreciated the Imperial family, though he had seen the Emperor less than a handful of times.

Luis' father loved the Emperor for his abilities and because it was his majesty that allowed Dom Caetano to become who he was. If it weren't for the emperor Dom Pedro II's efforts to modernize the country's infrastructure by opening roads and developing machinery, the rancher would never have accumulated his wealth. The wealth that he invested in the 3-Estados farm and to support his five children.

Deep down, however, fatherly love squeezed his heart. Disturbed him the insecurity that maybe the war wouldn't last only a few months, as everyone thought. He feared he might never see his son again—not only because of the enemy bullets but also because he felt that his age advanced faster than it should.

"Prepared for the trip, son?" Dom Caetano, supported by his cane, approached the porch, where the trio organized their baggage. "Won't you saddle the horses?"

"We're going by carriage, father." the lieutenant replied. The cost to transport a pair of horses by ship would just be too high. Their plan, instead, was to use the stagecoach pulled by a pair of mules and sell them at the port of Paraty.

"No, Luis. Saddle the horses and take them with you. I will cover the costs. They brought you here. During battle, there is nothing better than a horse already used to a rider." Dom Caetano reached out and gave Luis a purse with coins. It was more than enough to pay for the transport of Nickel and Eka.

"Thanks, father, but that's a lot of money. Does it make sense to spend all that?"

"If something happens to you...," Dom Caetano placed his hand on Luis' shoulders, "there's no point in saving money while risking a child."

The lieutenant put the coin purse in his bag. They prepared Martin's carriage. Instead of the two mules, they harnessed Nickel and Eka. With such sturdy animals, they would arrive at the port even faster.

Arrangements finished before eight in the morning, and the group prepared to leave. Joana, Dom Caetano, and Manuel stood at the porch, but Primo was missing. Luis Caetano noticed the absence of his childhood friend and wondered if he had a hangover from the night before.

But breaking the solemnity of the moment, the missing mulatto jumped over the handrail from the kitchen veranda and walked toward the carriage, bringing a bag.

"Is there space for one more in this cart, or do I have to go on the roof?"

"Did you change your mind, you low-life loafer?" Luis exhibited a satisfied smile, welcoming his friend.

"I wanted to stay to take care of your horses, but if they're going, then I'm going too." Primo threw his cloth bag on the vehicle's roof. "It is too tedious here. Maybe the south and your band of weirdos can provide me some fun."

Luis raised his hands, shaking his head at Primo's nonsensical answer. The lieutenant had, however, a satisfied smile.

"Who's going to take care of my father?" asked the lieutenant.

"Manuel, the jughead here is asking who will take care of Dom Caetano!" Primo told the cook.

"Never mind, Luisinho. Me, Almir, and my grandson can take care of everything." replied the black caretaker.

"I even don't need this much help." Dom Caetano waved his supporting cane.

Luis then hugged his sister. He did the same with Dom Caetano, holding his father longer than usual. At last, he thanked Manuel with a friendly pat on the back. Meanwhile, Nopitena and Martin thanked their hosts for the unexpected hospitality the two peculiar types received.

Joana approached Primo to bid farewell. "Don't forget about our agreement," she whispered. Primo shook his head up and down, confirming that he got the message.

The quartet then left for a long odyssey toward a distant front line.

Each one of them carried his own reason. The Lieutenant seeking to become a captain. Nopitena with a thirst for revenge. Martin with the desire to use his father's Dreyse for the sake of honor. And Primo, whose interests were known only to himself and Joana.

***

"The farmhouse is so peaceful, so silent now," Joana said during lunch with Dom Caetano, hours after the boys left.

"They were not that noisy," the rancher replied as he cut a slice of ham. Joana knew her father hated rowdy places, but his son was a good reason to tolerate even the loudest conversations and card games on the veranda.

"Do you know what surprised me, *filha*? Until yesterday Francisco was firm in his decision to stay at the farm, even though Luis invited him to join them as a volunteer. Then in the next morning, he changed his mind, out of nowhere." Dom Caetano laid the cutlery on his plate, rested his palms on his chin, and stared at his daughter. "Strange, isn't it? Almost as if someone had made him a very tempting offer."

By Dom Caetano's tone of voice, it was clear the rancher suspected something caused Primo's sudden change.

"Daddy, I asked him to take care of Luis." Joana gave up her secret. She moved her plate to the side for a moment. "Luis is my only brother."

"And what did you offer?"

"Money, if Luis returns safely. And the truth about his origin." Joana confirmed Dom Caetano's suspicions.

"Filha, can you imagine how Luis will react if he finds out you paid a bodyguard for a grown man like him?" The rancher knew that his son's temper would consider Joana's action an insult.

"As long as he's alive, that's what matters."

"Honestly...if I were him, I would be furious, but if I were you, I would do the same." He turned his head to the kitchen and called loudly, "Manuel! Bring us a bottle of Jerez, so I can drink with my little girl."

Jerez Brandy was Joana's favorite liquor. She had a sophisticated taste for imported goods. Dom Caetano, although far from his youngest son, had a chance to enjoy the company of his daughter for a few days more.

***

From the ranch to the Paraty port, the trip took three days up and down the mountains. In the region, it is normal to rain at least a third of the days in March. Torrential showers, not drizzle or sprinkles, but the type of storm that covers the sun and turns the afternoon into night. This downpour came on the third and last day. The horses and wheels moved slower on the wet mud. They arrived in Paraty several hours later than expected. They sold the cart at a port's workshop and boarded the steamship heading to Santos, their first stopover. Luis used part of the money from Dom Caetano to pay the passages for the group and the two horses.

The ship arrived in Santos after a day. The next morning, they would board a much larger steamship departing to the main southern ports, among them Itajai and Porto Alegre.

While searching for a place to sleep near the harbor, among coffee sacks carried by dockers, the group found a small inn between the dirty bars. A most ordinary place, but enough for a night.

After disembarking, Luis left the group. He needed to report to the artillery captain of the nearest garrison—Fort Augusto, a few kilometers from there—to know which battalion to join in the Rio Grande do Sul and fill the paperwork to volunteer himself as an officer and the other three men as enlisted soldiers.

Nopitena, Martin, and Primo remained at the port, playing cards, eating sardines and fried mackerel at the old Caiçara's inn. The ship they would board the next day anchored just fifty yards away from them, with grains and goods loaded on the deck.

The Kadiweu met the ocean for the first time. The limitless cerulean water and the impossibility to see beyond it dazzled him.

Meanwhile, Martin noticed a sign written in German hung a few yards away on a decrepit building. A bodega designed to sell goods to European sailors who docked at the port.

"I will buy beer," the gray-eyed German said, getting up from the table after finishing another gambling round. Primo tossed Martin a coin, asking the German to buy one for him too.

"Indian, how it was to work with Luis?" The mulatto pulled a chat with Nopitena as Martin walked away. "All our youth we spent with booze and games, but never at work."

"He risks too much, listens too little, and disliked the life in the fort. But he was a good chief," replied the Indian, leaning in his chair.

The Kadiwéu's response surprised the mulatto.

"How is he a good commander if you just said bad things?"

"I didn't say he's a good commander." Nopitena shrugged. "I said he is a good chief, and that means he is a good man, of courage. But to be a commander, it's a long way off."

"That's right. To take a rock on your head while fighting for a stranger takes courage," Francisco said, nibbling on pieces of fried sardines. Nopitena separated the cards for another game.

Shouts came from the bodega where Martin went to buy beer, followed by the noise of falling objects.

Both rushed to the spot.

The bar's wooden counter and the suspended shelves with aligned bottles on the wall were the only organized part of the joint. A dozen clients, drunkards mostly, sat on backless benches distributed chaotically in the space. The floor had stains of liquor, dirt, and who knew what else. The whole place stank of pickled sausage.

On the center-left, three men were threatening the German lad after he spilled beer on one of them. The ruffians wore striped shirts, like sailors, but their faces had a dirty, roguish appearance.

The skinniest of them lifted a bench to hit Martin's head. Primo grabbed one of the bench's legs and tumbled the delinquent to the floor. The second man, with long hair and a scar on his face, went after Primo. Nopitena jumped behind him, pushed him by the arm, and pulled out a pocketknife he carried. From behind, the Kadiweu touched the cold steel of his dagger in the delinquent's neck.

The third striped-shirt man was bald and bulky, with slower movements because of his large size but with arms powerful enough to crack a skull. He also went for Primo, with his wrists raised, but froze when the Kadiweu waved his knife.

All the bar stared at Nopitena with his blade pressing against the throat of the long-haired, face-scarred brute.

"Calm down, everyone. We don't want any problem," Nopitena said with a smooth voice that contrasted with the whole situation. "We'll pay for whatever damage our friend caused," Nopitena turned to Martin and told him to give a coin to the striped shirt trio.

The Indian lowered the blade, and the three men reluctantly calmed down. The long-haired fellow, the one with a scarred face, took the coin and stared at the Kadiweu.

"This pay for the spilled beer. But one day, you will pay for touching my neck, Indian."

The gang left, leaving the turned tables and chairs behind.

Primo took the beer mug that Martin held and downed half of it. "The one you spilled was yours. This one is for me."

They returned to the table in front of the inn, only to witness the three striped-shirt brawlers boarding the same ship they would take the next day.

Luis returned late afternoon and found the trio at the table, resting after rounds of beer, shots of brandy, and more fried sardines. The prices were affordable, considering the generous amount of coins that Dom Caetano gave them.

"What a surprise. Everything here looks so calm." Luis said when approaching the group.

"But hours ago, I went to that bodega..." Martin started to speak, but Primo kicked him under the table, and the German shut up.

"No problem at all, except for the weak liquor they sell...sir." Primo called his childhood friend Sir in a tone full of irony.

Luis smirked.

"The captain of Fort Augusto assigned us to a regiment assembled in Rio Pardo, near Porto Alegre. That's where we're going." Luis delivered the news to the men and pointed to Nopitena, calling him for a private conversation near the pier.

"Nopitena, I also asked about news from Mato Grosso."

The Indian did not understand how this related to him.

"What about it, chief?"

Luis took a long breath, closing his eyes for a second.

"The Guaranis took Corumbá. Locals reported they had around a hundred Indians as captives. Kadiwéus. Women and children included."

"If they took Nialigi or the ligotis, chief..." Nopitena stared at the vastitude of the ocean. His lips twisted in anger. "I will make them pay with blood."

Chapter XIX

"Aunt Joana is back, Zezinho! In the piano room!" The oldest of the Viscountess' kids took her younger brother by the hand and ran together to the mansion's main hall.

Joana Augusta waited for them. It was remarkable for her that lady Ana Francisca's children called her their aunt. She knew the family for years and taught the children Portuguese language, music, and etiquette. But still sounded unusual that she, the daughter of a small landowner from São Paulo, was considered part of the family of the greatest military hero in the country.

After their class, lady Ana returned and invited Joana for tea to catch up on the news.

"I see you recovered well from your grief," Ana Francisca said, reclined at one of the rattan chairs on the balcony.

Joana, at first, forgot why she should feel any grief but then remembered why she left Rio weeks before: to tell her father about Luis Caetano's disappearance and likely death.

The tutor recounted to lady Ana the story of her trip, about how her brother was alive but never reached Corumba because of his mission to warn the other military garrisons.

"I'm glad that he's alive and can spend some time with your father." The Viscountess's well-rounded face, a feature typical of the wealthy, turned relaxed with the positive outcome of Joana's story. She knew the girl had a tempestuous relationship with her three older sisters and that losing her cherished younger brother would be devastating.

"He stayed just for a few days, but now he's heading south," Joana said, with her usual glowing, optimistic tone, while pouring a lump of sugar into her coffee. "He thought it was an excellent opportunity to take part in a war that shouldn't last long. After all, what dangers do the Paraguayans offer, right?"

Joana's last sentences erased the smile from Lady Ana's face.

"Oh no..." the Viscountess whispered, holding her hand over the mouth and bending her head down.

"Lady Ana? Did I say something wrong?"

"Yes, Joana. This war..."

"What about it, my Lady?"

"I don't know if I can tell you much. It hangs on the mutual trust we've built."

Joana nodded, confirming that the Viscountess could trust her.

"My father told us that everything we know about Paraguay is wrong. The fault of our ambassador there, Viana de Lima. The Paraguayan police watched him closely since he arrived in Asuncion last year, so he never gave accurate information."

"I read about him saying that ten thousand Brazilian soldiers could defeat Solano Lopez," Joana remembered the newspapers she read on the road to Rio, always belittling the enemy forces.

"That is what I mean. The same drivel from the same ambassador who said in October that Paraguay would not dare provoke Brazil, and here we are now." The wide gestures made by the Viscountess translated her revolt. She barely tasted her tea, leaving the cup untouched on the table. "The Emperor is considering your teacher, Otaviano, to negotiate an alliance with the Argentinians."

It was not a surprise that Joana's teacher, Francisco Otaviano de Almeida Rosa, was a strong candidate to represent the Empire. Aside from his good grasp of Spanish, he had rare rhetoric skills, capable of convincing even the most stubborn general.

"Is it possible that their military strength can rival us?" Joana asked, her neck stiff and knuckles clenched with tension.

"Possible? Father said that, in reality, Solano Lopez has an army of almost 60,000 men! Apart from a dozen of ships and formidable fortifications. Strongholds built by us, Brazilians, when we were allies."

Joana understood the part about forts and ships, but the number 60,000 meant little to her. Not without knowing the size of the imperial forces.

"My lady, how many soldiers the Empire has?"

"Real soldiers? Around 15,000. They are working on a plan where we may raise the number to 50,000, with an intense volunteer enlistment campaign."

The Viscountess's response caused a momentary silence on the veranda of the Ururaí's house. Teas and biscuits remained untouched.

Seconds later, Joana, staring at the floor, murmured something.

"My goodness."

***

At eight in the morning, under cloudy skies, a ship left Santos, heading south. Onboard, an unusual quartet—a young officer, an orphaned immigrant, a mulatto, and an Indian.

Dignitaries occupied the more expensive rooms on the steamship's upper deck. Luis could take a room for himself, but, accustomed to the spartan life of the Coimbra fort, he judged this to be a waste of money. He and Nopitena went for the cheapest place of the ship, the general area, on the lower deck. There, crowds of passengers slept in hammocks on one side while animals and livestock occupied the other. During the day, the noise reminded an open-air fish market. At night, snores and farts drummed and mingled with the sound of the water hitting the ship's hull. The least irritating smell was horse manure.

Luis and Nopitena chose hammocks close to Níquel and Eka to calm the animals during the long journey.

Nopitena took a spot next to the door, something he always did at the Fort dormitories. Once, he explained this was a Kadiweu warrior custom, the place of the bravest, the first to fight if someone invaded the hut. Luis never took it seriously. If he wants to sleep at the door, let it be, the lieutenant thought.

Primo and Martin took their places on the deck's opposite side, along with several other passengers. People that, unlike Luis and Nopitena, preferred to sleep smelling human reek instead of animal dung.

"Hey, dried face!" Primo Francisco shook Martin at his hammock, calling him one of several nicknames he had already invented for the slender foreigner. "Check out there, in the corner. Aren't those the three thugs from the bar fight?" The mulatto pointed to three individuals sitting over wooden boxes on his left side, twenty feet away. Half a dozen other passengers laid between them and the strangers. Although the lower deck was dark even during the day, Primo's eyes were correct.

"Yes, it's them." The German nodded.

"Damn...well, they won't cause trouble in front of so many witnesses, but don't get distracted," Primo said, turning back for a nap.

Nothing happened on the first day nor on the first night. To break the trip's stagnation, on the second day, Luis exchanged one of his coins for a bottle of pinga. Card games rolled free on the upper deck.

"Martin, are you coming with us?" asked Luis Caetano. "The cachaça is on me."

The foreigner looked around. Two of the three striped-shirt rowdies from Santos were still there, sitting on the wooden crates and peeling oranges.

"I'll stay here, sir, to watch our things."

"Watch our things?" Luis frowned.

Martin nodded to the left side of the room. Although the lieutenant didn't know about the fight in Santos, Luis noticed that the gentlemen in the corner looked suspicious—strangers handling knives and avoiding eye contact. Weird fellows.

"Take care. If you need anything, go upstairs."

****

Martin laid in his hammock, letting his thoughts drift away to the story Joana told him: a German town built in the South. His sister, Sophie, always talked about returning to Europe, but he wasn't fond of the idea. He came to Brazil as a toddler and felt attached to the land. A German settlement in Brazil was perhaps a happy middle way—good enough for both.

"Hey, you are the chap who spilled beer on us at the bar, right?" A man approached him unnoticed and stood next to him.

"Yes, it was me. Why?" In vain, the German lowered his right hand to the sack under his hammock, trying to find a knife or something to defend himself.

"I wanted to apologize for what happened there," the man said. It was the skinny, short-haired member of the gang. Unlike the other two, he didn't have any visible scars and his clearest feature, besides the squalid figure, was an unbearable garlic breath.

At least he apologized, and thugs don't do that, Martin thought. The German accepted the apology and offered a handshake.

"It is ok. My name is Martin, what about yo—"

270

A sudden blow to the back of his head, coming from who knows where, knocked out Martin Werther.

Chapter XX

April first had an unusual atmosphere in Rio.

Contradictory news about the war, troops, and leadership movements were everywhere. To add confusion, it was prima aprilis, a European-imported custom of inventing rumors on that exact day. Nobody, except for a few, knew what was true, what was false, and what was a joke.

Among the few truth knowers were both the Viscountess Ana and Francisco Otaviano de Almeida Rosa.

Joana knew that in the capital, these were the two of the voices to be trusted. She departed earlier to her class with Otaviano that day, to use the extra time to ask her teacher about the veracity of the things she heard and read.

The tutor took a taxi. The sound of the horse's hooves pulling the carriage served as a backdrop to her thoughts. Vendors buzzed on the streets, but their shouts did not penetrate Joana's head, occupied by guesses and doubts. She arrived at the place where Otaviano met with his students—a selected group. A group that she had the privilege to be part of, thanks to the potential that the lawyer saw in her.

Joana knocked on the door. A familiar voice invited her to go inside.

The spacious room had an elegant decoration. A large panoramic drawing of colonial Rio adorned the left wall. Cherry wood furniture created a graceful ambiance, necessary to teach the subtleties of diplomacy and the intricacies of the law.

The teacher sat on a bergère chair with white upholstery. On the dark-brown leather sofa, another person was having a tea, this one much younger: Alfredo Taunay, the son of French aristocrats, with a passion for arts common in Otaviano's social circle. Taunay had a short, dark mustache, equally dark hair, and the same rounded cheeks and smooth skin of the Viscountess, quite distinct from the skinny shape and elongated face of Otaviano.

"You arrived earlier than expected, Miss Joana. You can join us if you don't mind." Almeida Rosa adjusted his rounded glasses to look at the room entrance.

"If I am not bothering, it will be a pleasure." She approached them and sat on a chair opposite to Taunay's sofa—who she greeted politely. "Teacher Otaviano, I came earlier to ask about the rumors people are spreading in the streets."

Joana, without quoting sources, asked if it was true that he would soon head south to serve as a diplomat with the Allied governments.

In silence, Otaviano looked to Joana for a few seconds. Slowly, a smile came to his face.

"You didn't hear that in the streets, Miss Joana. Almost no one knows about my appointment yet."

Joana said nothing, but looked to the floor, searching for an excuse to hide who told her about the nomination.

Too late. The girl knew how to guess what others meant by their gestures, but Otaviano was a master on that—after all, he was the one that taught Joana how to read people like a book.

"I believe you heard it from the Viscountess, as her father is one of the few well-informed." He adjusted his glasses. "It's true, I accepted the nomination to replace Saraiva as imperial envoy to Argentina."

Joana raised her eyebrows. They nominated her mentor for a tremendous task, even more so replacing the notorious counselor Saraiva.

"Congratulations, I am speechless! You have all the merits for such a worthy assignment."

"I am not sure yet if this job is a reason for congratulations or condolences." The commentary caused laughs both from Taunay and Joana.

The girl then asked about the murmurs of how unprepared the empire was and how rushed things were.

"As for the rumors about the gravity of the war, they are real," Otaviano said, "We just don't know how serious it is yet, but urgent enough for the farewells to begin today."

"Farewells? Are you departing already?" Joana asked, looking around. There was no luggage in the room.

"Not yet, but I'm not talking about me." Otaviano stood up and went toward Alfredo Taunay, sitting on the leather sofa and just listening to their conversation. "Alfredo leaves tomorrow. He will join Colonel Manuel Drago's expeditionary column to free Mato Grosso from the invaders."

"It's a long march," Joana said to Taunay.

The young man nodded with a smile.

She admired the youthful aristocrat's bravery but could not see a soldier in him. At least not one to endure a months-long march into such a wild place, against such a mysterious enemy.

Alfredo Taunay was the son of a talented painter. At twenty-two, he already completed three degrees—literature, mathematics, and natural science. Almeida Rosa praised his writing style. An intellectual, for sure. But Joana doubted how effective intellectuals were in the war carnage. *At least he can write a decent war diary*, she thought.

Taunay, having a few errands to do before departure, said goodbye and promised to send letters from the front.

Otaviano de Almeida Rosa and Joana remained in the room, and the diplomat confirmed to Joana that everything the Viscountess told her about Paraguay was true. He then took an envelope from his desk.

"The Emperor asked me to set up a small staff team to assist me in negotiations. Only one or two people, of my greatest confidence because of the secrecy and seriousness of the matters to be dealt with." Otaviano had a serious face. Still, sitting in his armchair, he looked at the door where Taunay had left minutes before. "One of them would have been Alfredo, but his departure caught me by surprise."

Joana smiled discreetly at the idea that a member of the liberal party, like Almeida Rosa, could trust so deeply a conservative like Taunay. Intellect and good taste created a bond between them that overrode the worldliness of politics.

"Do you have another candidate, Professor? Anyone else you trust?"

"Yes." Francisco Otaviano handed over the envelope to Joana. She didn't understand what she was supposed to do with it.

He nodded for her to open the envelope.

She pulled out a letterhead with an invitation to serve as secretary to the plenipotentiary minister to the Platine nations.

The name Platine referred to the Prata river, and the Platine nations were the Empire's southern neighbors: Argentina, Uruguay, and Paraguay—all of them had a hectic history with Brazil. Friends in a moment, foes on the next.

"If you accept, we leave tomorrow. Apologies for the late notice, but it was also abrupt news for me," Otaviano said.

Joana faced the possibility of being an insider in the negotiations of the largest alliance on the continent. She was invited to witness history being written.

There were still two problems. The proposition assumed a relocation to Buenos Aires. This would force her to resign again from tutoring Lady Ana's children. Even worse: she also needed to move to the site of a personal tragedy from her past.

***

"Kackwurst! My family no longer owes you anything! Get out of here! Hurensohn!"

Luis Caetano and Nopitena looked at Martin, lying in the hammock and raving about things no one understood. The steamship's nurse applied a bandage on his head. A swollen bump above the neck showed how strong was the blow.

"We'll have to wait until he recovers to understand what happened," Luis Caetano observed the condition of the slender German, who, over six feet tall, barely fit in the small hammock of the crowded dormitory.

"I don't think we'll have to wait long," interjected Primo, descending from the stairs that connected the upper deck with the compartment where they slept. "The box that used to be under his hammock is no longer there. Someone stole it thinking it had valuables inside." The mulatto looked at Luis as if the lieutenant knew what the German was carrying.

"Box? What was that box like?" Luis asked.

"Long, narrow. I think it's a little bigger than an arm and made of wood," Primo answered while carrying a cup with a transparent liquid. It didn't have the burning smell of cachaça, so Luis assumed it was just water.

"Hmm...the Dreyse!" Luis recalled that Martin carried his magnificent weapon inside the box and always kept it in his sight. That's why they hit him from behind.

"Primo, you are the only one here who remembers this box. Find it, and the boy will have a debt with you."

"Debt? I heard he has a problem with paying debts." Primo's joke, referring to the Werthers' debt with the Vergueiros, made Luis stare in disbelief. With Martin injured at their side, the moment was just inappropriate. "Bleh, I will try. Ask him who was here when he was attacked."

"Do you think he can tell us anything? He's talking gibberish!" Luis shook his head, annoyed by Primo's lack of awareness and compassion. Nopitena, meanwhile, put his hand on the forehead of the German to check if he had any fever. Nothing.

"Oh, is he a little dizzy?" Primo said. "Whenever I'm groggy of cachaça, old Manuel has a way to put me back on track at the ranch."

"What is it? Any herb or tea?" Nopitena turned to the mulatto with a serious tone.

"No, water." Primo suddenly threw the liquid from his cup in Martin's face.

The German tilted his head back, turning the face to the opposite side. With a groan, he opened his eyes, scared and drenched.

Luis and Nopitena were still processing Primo's behavior. Throwing cold water on a knocked-out lad seemed cruel. But somehow, it was efficient cruelty because Martin regained his consciousness.

"Who was here when you got hit?" Luis asked.

"Argh...Nobody. No, No. There was someone...one man from the pub gang." Martin sat in the hammock, closing and opening his eyes, trying to recall what happened. He looked to the spot where he saw troublemakers. But there was no one else there, not even their stuff.

"So it was them!" Primo chuckled, realizing that it got a lot easier to find the gun, and started hunting for the stolen Dreyse rifle.

"Nein! It wasn't them! The man came to apologize to me."

"Apologize to you or to distract you?" Luis rubbed his chin. "If every European was foolish like that, Brazil would still belong to the Indians."

"What?" Nopitena asked.

The Kadiweu's serious face made Luis notice the faux pas.

"Nevermind, Nopitena," Luis replied.

***

The lieutenant and the Indian took the blonde foreigner to the upper deck to visit the doctor's cabin.

"He can't take any other hit on the head, especially in this place." The doctor pointed to the lower left side of Martin's head. "It is the joint of the Occipital and Temporal bones, a sensible part. Another blow here can be fatal."

Luis nodded, and Nopitena remained quiet. Martin, still sitting on the doctor's chair.

"How long it will take for him to recover?" The Lieutenant asked. Meanwhile, Primo entered the doctor's room.

"A few days of rest will do the job. He blacked out because fainting is a way our body protects us from the worst," replied the doctor, who wore civilian clothes and rounded glasses. "Why is he wet?"

Luis shrugged his shoulders and looked at Primo.

"See, Blondie, you need to stop getting into trouble!" Primo smirked.

"But I did nothing," Martin replied, downcast but getting up from the doctor's chair. His golden hair fell over his face as he slowly tried to stand on his feet. "They robbed me..."

"Who robbed you?" the doctor asked.

Luis asked Nopitena to help Martin go outside and breathe some fresh air. In the room only with the physician and Primo, the Lieutenant explained the whole situation from the morning and described the stolen object.

"The only sure thing is the thieves are still here. It is a ship, after all. Nobody leaves in the middle of the ocean." The doctor sighed, sitting on the chair behind his desk. "Still, it surprised me that a group of strangers occupied the cabin next to mine, minutes ago, in the middle of the trip. Curious, isn't it?"

"A group? Were they three scoundrels wearing rags?" Luis frowned.

"No. In fact, they were three well-dressed men." The doctor replied, not suspecting that he had given them a lead.

Luis spent a few hours with Nopitena and Martin on the upper deck. The sea breeze and balmy sun helped to cool off after the troublesome day. Dusk fell while the steam was already at the height of Cananéia, bordering the coast on its way south.

The lieutenant went downstairs and found Primo peeling an orange with his penknife as he sat on a crate. It was forbidden to eat in the dorms, but he didn't care. He ate there so that no one would ask for a piece of his fruit.

"Primo, what do you think about these strangers the doctor mentioned?"

"Oh, three men change compartments in the middle of the trip. How convenient. Orange?" Primo offered a slice of his fruit.

"No, thanks."

"Anyway, I'll get the blondie's rifle back." Primo stretched his neck before eating the piece rejected by Luis.

"How?"

"Just like when we were kids, and you lost your slingshot at the Sergeant's farm." Primo grinned. "I got it back."

Luis recalled when he lost a slingshot, but he didn't remember how Primo recovered it. His only memory was of his friend returning him the toy and young Luis owing a favor.

Primo did not join the group for breakfast the next morning. Perhaps the bread, coffee, and butter didn't attract the mulatto, so he went to search for something better.

Martin spent the time until early afternoon searching for the Dreyse. Luis never shared the lead about the assailants' whereabouts, as the foreigner would go there to recover the gun and get beaten again.

By midafternoon, the weather turned damp, and the thick clouds no longer allowed the three men on deck to see the shore. Surrounding the ship, only the white veil of sea mist.

"Where do you think we are, chief?" Nopitena asked, standing on the upper deck.

"Perhaps near the coast of Santa Catarina. We should get to Itajaí in two or three hours if we don't get a downpour weighing the sails and delaying us."

Just when the Lieutenant finished his phrase, they felt the first water drops on their heads.

"Better go down. We should pack our things for disembarking and prepare the horses."

They gave the remaining fodder to Nickel and Eka, so the horses arrive well-fed, with no extra weight to carry. Luis and Nopitena picked up their sacks and went to the other side of the compartment.

Primo was snoring in his hammock.

"Looks like he did not recover the Dreyse after all," mumbled Luis Caetano, wondering if he should wake up his friend to confirm the obvious.

He didn't have to. The mulatto opened one eye and smiled. "It is under the yolk-haired boy."

They turned and peered at the place under Martin's hammock.

The Dreyse was there. Without the box and chained to the hammock pole so no one would try to take her again.

"Slicker. You got her back, but how?" Luis leaned against a pillar.

"As I told you, the same way I brought back your slingshot. I opened their door as they left for breakfast. They didn't even bother to lock it." Primo recounted his achievement with a brooding touch of pride and satisfaction. "I searched under the bed. The box was there. I took the gun and left the box so they wouldn't suspect. The nitwits won't even notice it's empty."

Luis shook his head, amazed with the mad imprudence of Primo. His friend invaded the room of three criminals as if he was stepping into a roost of tamed chickens. *Maybe we are ready for whatever the future brings*, the lieutenant thought.

Chapter XXI

The steamer arrived in Itajaí under the evening orange sky, a prelude to a chilly April night on Santa Catarina's coast. The ship moored in the city's harbor to refuel and change crew. She would set sail on the next day to the Rio Grande do Sul, the last destination.

"Where are we now?" Martin walked down the ramp toward the port.

Luis, walking right at his side, replied, "Itajaí."

"I've heard that name before..."

"My sister told you about it. It's close to Blumenau, where your people are forming a battalion."

"Viktor Von Gilsa's Battalion!" Martin remembered the story Joana told him at the 3-Estados farm. The so-called promised land German settlers were building on Brazilian soil. It was right there.

Luis looked around for Nopitena and Primo. They were right behind him.

"You two find a place for us to stay. Tomorrow at sunrise, we return to the ship." Luis gave his luggage to Nopitena. "I'm going to the port's quartermaster with Martin." The lieutenant was wearing his uniform, for this would help to convince the port bureaucrats to give the information he needed.

"What about his baggage, chief?" Nopitena pointed to Martin.

"He will take his stuff with him," Luis answered.

Nopitena, knowing what that meant, raised his eyebrows. Primo ignored Luis' explanations. Meanwhile, Martin had a constant half-smile on his face, satisfaction exhilarated by the imminent encounter with Von Gilsa.

If there was a place where they could discover Von Gilsa's whereabouts, it was at the port's administration. In a city like Itajaí, there was nothing the dispatch bureaucrats didn't know.

They approached the gray, modest building, lit by two torches. At the door, a pair of well-dressed men chatted. The twilight, broken only by the dim flame lights, made it impossible to recognize the details of their uniforms, except that one of them had golden embroideries on the shoulders. *Probably ship captains waiting for the revenue procedures to continue their journey*, Luis thought.

Luis and Martin greeted the two gentlemen at the door and entered the office.
Inside, the port administrator yawned behind a simple desk with piles of paper. He was a middle-aged man with dark circles under his eyes. He starred at the two visitors for a

second, making them feel like intruders. With slurred words, the administrator asked what they wanted.

"We are looking for a man called Von Gilsa," Luis said.

"Does it look like I know him?"

"No, but it looks like you forgot how to respect an officer of the imperial army." Luis avoided using his rank to get favors, but the short time to find Von Gilsa and leave Martin before departure asked for energetic gestures.

"All right, sir officer. What is the person's full name?"

"Mr. Viktor Von Gilsa, the commander from a volunteer battalion forming in this region."

"Mr. Von Gilsa..." repeated the bureaucrat, blinking slowly with his heavy eyelids.

"Yes, Von Gilsa," Luis said.

"Mr. Von Gilsa!" the administrator repeated in a louder voice, almost jumping from his chair.

"Are you brain-dead? How many times will I have to repeat his name?" Luis took a step closer to the bureaucrat's desk while Martin remained silent.

"I'm not talking to you, Lieutenant. I'm calling him."

A man with a thick beard opened the door and entered the room. The golden-embroidered uniform made Luis recall he was one of the gentlemen chatting on the front porch.

"What now, Geraldo?" the thick-voiced man asked the administrator.

The yawny public servant pointed to Luis and Martin and returned to his bureaucratic duties.

"Mister Viktor Von Gilsa?" Luis extended his hand to the man, who responded to the greeting.

"Captain Viktor Von Gilsa. To what do I owe the honor, Lieutenant?" he replied, recognizing Luis' rank based on his uniform's insignia.

As they introduced themselves, Von Gilsa led them outside. The office dampness was suffocating, different from the light, refreshing sea breeze from outside.

"I assume you want to join our battalion." Von Gilsa said, before introducing the other man he chatted with minutes earlier. "Here is Lieutenant Emil Odebrecht, one of our officers."

"Ca...Ca...Captain Von Gilsa, I...I am...I am Martin Werther." The young foreigner stuttered during the unexpected encounter. Martin had an exaggerated respect for military ranks, a heritage from his father, which added

embarrassment to the whole situation. "I am Ludwig
Werther's son. I want to join your men."

"Ludwig Werther? I had a soldier with that same name
at the Platine war." Captain Von Gilsa twirled the mustache
with his finger while recalling the memory of Martin's father.
"An ill-fated fellow, a victim of the front line diseases, like so
many other good men."
"Yes sir, der brummer you sir commanded was my father. I
still carry his gun, eagerly awaiting its combat debut."
"Sickness kills more than bullets during wars on this side of
the world," Von Gilsa looked at the young blond stripling,
"and yet you want to join us?"
Martin nodded. Emil Odebrecht, standing next to Von Gilsa,
had a mustache as thick as the captain but no beard. He
looked at the boy's face, glowing with pride under the
lamplight. "Der junge would be a fine addition to my platoon,
Captain Viktor."

"Great. Captain, Lieutenant, my task is finished here."
Luis Caetano touched his cap, greeting the two officers, "I
leave the best possible references about the lad, Martin. He
still needs to improve his horse-riding though, but the rest of
his qualities make a decent soldier."

Luis turned to Martin and shook his friend's shoulder.
"Take care of yourself, Tedesco, because I won't be around to
save you."

The German smiled.
On the way back to the inn, Luis walked in silence across the

dark alleys, recalling Lieutenant Odebrecht's satisfaction when he saw Martin's willingness to fight. Even though they knew each other for a short time, there was a bond between them, as if the skinny, weird foreigner was the innocent but loyal younger brother Luis never had. A bond built after a life-saving gesture.

Luis wasn't fond of the idea of leading men, but if necessary, he wanted all of them to have that impetus. The impetus of Martin, who, from now on, would no longer be under his command.

Maybe it is better this way, Luis tried to convince himself.

***

The first hostel Nopitena and Primo visited at the Itajai Port was not expensive and had rooms available. They almost chose it until they saw at the reception the three robbers from the steamship. The thugs also recognized them back. The long-haired, scarred-face leader of the bandits made a gesture, passing his forefinger around his own neck as they exchanged glances with the mulatto and the Indian.

A threat.

If it was up to Primo, they would have stayed there, never minding if he would get into a fight, not caring if they may beat him, given their brutal size. Nopitena, fond of parsimony and undisposed to deal with cowards that attack from behind, had enough of brawls during the trip. Because the Kadiwéu was carrying the money, his word was final, and they moved to the next lodge.

Primo and Nopitena left their sacks in the room and sat on the sidewalk. They talked about the situation. Would the three miscreants follow them to Rio Grande do Sul? And what were they doing traveling so far? At least Luis left Martin there with the other Germans, so there was no longer any Dreyse around to provoke the greed and desire of the thieves.

The lodge was just a few dozen meters from the sea. Nopitena observed the ocean's vastitude. At his side, Primo opened a half-empty bottle.

"Where did you find that?" the Kadiweu looked sideways to the mulatto.

Primo shrugged, as if creating liquor from thin-air was a magic trick he could always perform.

Time flew in the rancid but relaxed harbor. Both forgot, however, that when Luis came back, he would look for them in the first inn.

Hours later, the lieutenant asked the first lodge's owner if an Indian and a mulatto booked a room there.

The innkeeper thought it was a riddle. "You mean an Indian, a mulatto, and a Jew, right? That's how the joke starts."

Luis returned to the street, where he found his companions drinking on a nearby sidewalk.

Nopitena explained why they chose the second inn. Luis ignored the bandits' threat. Perhaps the troublemakers were just sailors and remained in Itajaí. At least that's what it looked like. Besides, Martin was not with them anymore. Luis, Primo, and Nopitena knew how to defend themselves.

On the next day, light rain was falling over the port. While returning to the steamship, they saw the striped-shirt gang boarding just ahead of them, straight to the private cabins of the upper deck.

"At least this time we will not share space with these rats," Primo said while climbing the ramp that led to the ship.

"Should we take their threat seriously, chief?"

"Threat? If they want to try it, let them do it. What do you think, Primo?" Luis laughed.

"I take the larger one. You and your pet Indian have fun with the others."

Instead of anger, Nopitena just sighed after the mulatto again called him a *pet*. The Kadiweu already realized that there was no escape from Francisco's mischievous nature.

The trio heard a cry coming out from nowhere.

"Wait! Wait!"

They turned necks round to see where the shouts came from.

A young man ran toward them with the excitation of a small wolf cub meeting his pack, but that figure had nothing of small. The blond hair, gangly manner, and typical paleness revealed his identity.

"What is he doing back?" asked Luis

"They gave him back to us, like a lame horse." Primo chuckled, pleased by the return of the prime target of his mockery.

Martin reached them in the middle of the ship's ramp. Luis raised his hands with palms up as if asking the foreigner to explain why he returned.

"They are still going to train and drill for a long time before marching south, not moving to the front until end-of-year. I don't want to wait."

Nopitena smiled. He knew why Martin wanted to go to the war as soon as possible—the lad told him during one of their shooting practices. His father died before battle, and the German refused to give a chance to bad luck. The sooner he got to the front, the better.

Luis Caetano took a deep breath. "Darn...well, we had paid for your ticket to the Rio Grande, so I guess you can continue with us. But watch your own back."

The lieutenant turned and continued his way to the ship, hiding a smile. Deep down, it flattered him that Martin chose them instead of joining Odebrecht's German platoon.

Chapter XXII

The barge of Gaspar Picágua and his brother, Friar
Pedro, descended briskly on the Paraná River. That torrential
river stretch was the fastest-paced from the entire trip from
Corumbá to Corrientes.

This journey lasted over three months. It was in the
distant January when Gaspar witnessed the Coimbra siege. He
had the same ethnicity as the invaders—although he was not a
Paraguayan Guarani, but a Correntine Guarani, so he
supported no clashing side. The invasion, however, damaged
his leather business.

Gaspar returned to Corrientes, knowing that it would
not be possible to continue his trade unless the conflict ended.
That irritated him more than any war.

At least, within a maximum of two days, they would be
back home, thanks to the powerful river current at the height
of the Humaitá fort.

The immense Paraguayan fortification was less than
eighty kilometers from the Argentine city of Corrientes. The
formidable construction, revamped by European engineers
and Brazilian military consultants—when both countries were
still allies—stood on a sharp river bend in a U-shape. Its
batteries had enough guns to destroy any hostile fleet that
tried to invade Paraguay from Argentina. Men and nature

presented terrible hardships to anyone who tried to reach the hearth of the Paraguayan lands uninvited.

After praying his morning rosary, Frei Pedro looked at his brother, who was piloting the boat.

"It was here." The priest made on himself the sign of the cross.

The smuggler repeated his brother's gesture, more out of obligation than belief. It was in that place that Gaspar lost his faith. It happened years before, during the fort's reconstruction under the command of President Carlos Lopez—Solano Lopez's father.

The Picagua brothers, still children, accompanied their father, a construction worker building the massive fortress walls. While adults worked, kids played at the nearby beach.

On a silly dare, Gaspar swam to a part of the river far from the other children. The boy never noticed that nearby was a nest of Ariranhas, the aggressive carnivorous otters from the Pantanal.

The animals attacked the kid. His father ran to help, moved by the shouts and cries of desperation. The child had only a few scratches because his parent protected him with his own flesh. The Correntine construction worker had his skin and muscles ripped by the sharp claws of dozens of swimming predators. Infections over the multiple wounds and days of excruciating fever followed and killed him in less than a week.

The death of his father weighed over the shoulders of Gaspar. He never understood how God could create such a hideous animal. Hideous enough to attack a child and kill his parent. After that, he and Pedro were alone in the world—or not, since they had each other.

The orphaned brothers did well. One was one of the most beloved friars in his hometown of Itatí. The other made more than enough money as a merchant—or smuggler—on the Paraguay River.

"Cursed animal," Gaspar muttered as they passed the now empty otter's burrow just below the imposing fort.

"They are God's creatures, acting by instinct, not malice," Friar Pedro said.

"As Paraguayans and Brazilians kill each other by instinct?"

The Friar decided to not enter the discussion. They were close to home, and it frustrated his brother that they carried much less leather than he expected to resell in Corrientes. Pedro changed the subject.

"If the Brazilians try to go upriver here, they will have an outstanding obstacle. Ironically, because of the fort they built for the Paraguayans." Pedro looked toward the Humaita fort while standing in the bow.

"And the currents. It is so strong that sometimes feels like the river is alive." Gaspar glanced at the foam created by the speeding barge.

The accelerated water movement was the reason behind the name of the place: Corrientes. The problem of having almost no leather to sell meant money losses. Gaspar bought whatever he could in Corumbá, as the Brazilian merchants evacuated before they arrived. It was just a fraction of the amount he normally transported. Unless the smuggler increased his prices, the sales would barely cover the journey costs.

"What I should do? If I raise the prices, *Dom* Amaru will think I'm a cheater." Gaspar asked while operating the boat's rudder at the stern.

Friar Pedro sat in the barge's bow, about eight meters away, balancing his weight on the vessel so that it would not rear up while they darted across the river, "I suspect that more than Amaru's opinion, you care about what his daughter will think."

Gaspar sighed, and that was enough to confirm that Pedro was right.

What afflicted the smuggler, more than the financial strain, was the risk to his reputation. Not complying with his agreement to the warehouse owner would blur his image in the eyes of Arami, Amaru's daughter. Among all the Correntinas, none had attracted Gaspar more than her.

Arami used to help her father at the store. When Gaspar returned from his smuggling trip, to see her was as pleasant as the profitable leather sales. But this time, he faced the dreadful idea of earning less or being called a swindler by Amaru and his daughter.

"Tell the truth. That will be enough." Friar Pedro replied. "Tell them we couldn't bring more because of the war between Brazilians and Paraguayans."

"And do you think he will believe, Pedro? In the villages that we passed from Asunción to here, no one knows about any war." Gaspar replied with a tone of contempt for the Friar's simplistic solution. "In the past, I told more credible lies to Amaru, and still he suspected me. Imagine that!"

"The difference, brother, is that now you will tell the truth." The Friar waved to a group of children playing at the riverbank. "God protects the innocent and the honest in heart."

***

Two days later, on April 12, the Picágua brothers arrived at their homeland, in Itati, a tiny riverside village less than seventy kilometers from Corrientes. Despite the small size, it was one of the oldest settlements in the entire Corrientes province.

The village started as a Jesuit settlement during colonial times. The Iberian priests catechized the Picágua's ancestors. In 1615, an apparition of the Virgin Mary turned the place into a pilgrimage destination. By the time they arrived in the village, it was the busiest period of the year: Holy Week. Passion Friday would be on just two days.

"Today is the sermon of the seven sorrows of Our Lady. Are you coming?" the Friar asked the smuggler.

"I need to go home, change my clothes."

Pedro smirked, resigned to his brother's excuse, and walked to the church.

Gaspar strolled to their home. Years ago, their mother also lived there, before smallpox took her life. A yellow-painted house in such a good condition that stood out among the forty or fifty shacks in the village of Itati.

The profits from the skins and liquor trade up and downstream ensured that the smuggler had a solid roof, although the foundation was still of the simple hut built decades earlier by their parents.

From the front door, it was possible to see the river, the border between Corrientes and Paraguay. Gaspar noticed an abnormal movement of boats on the Paraguayan bank, in a region called Ñeembucú.

The smuggler arrived at the chapel during mid-mass.

"Stabat autem iuxta crucem Iesu mater eius," Friar Pedro proclaimed in front of the simple wooden altar. The faithful solemnly bowed their heads. Many of them grew up with the Picágua brothers. Others were pilgrims from towns in Corrientes or Misiones. All devotees of the Saint who appeared centuries before, in the time of the Jesuits.

Gaspar forgot to bow. He came to the church more out of respect and gratitude to his brother than out of faith. Gratitude that the Friar, months before, had accepted the smuggler's request to accompany him on the river trip. The loneliness of making such a long journey with no one to talk to—or grumble to—afflicted the peddler. The brother accepted the invitation with kindness, as long as Gaspar stopped at the riverside villages by the way so that the priest could attend confessions and celebrate a Mass here and there.

Stops along the way were convenient for Gaspar. Friar Pedro received multiple meal invitations at the riverside villages, and he always took his brother with him. The smuggler never spent so little on food.

"Is it nothing to you, all you who pass by? Look around and see. Is any suffering like my suffering, that was inflicted on me?" Pedro's energetic voice during the first reading contrasted with the attentive, fixed eyes of the faithful. The once sympathetic friar changed to a fierce herald during the narration of the mother of Christ's suffering.

The crowded church had a silent, dramatic atmosphere during Pedro's sermon. Gaspar's thoughts floated between his brother's words and the memory of agonizing screams and mutilations from Coimbra and Corumbá. Memories that the smuggler soothed by convincing himself that he had nothing to do with it, as he was a Correntino, not a Brazilian or Paraguayan.

"And thus, brothers, the prophecy of Simeon was fulfilled: A sword will pierce your own soul," Friar Pedro said, standing at the front of the faithful, who knelt. Gaspar, with a noticeable delay, followed the crowd.

Still tired from the lengthy journey, the smuggler felt his limbs wobble. His legs ached even more because of kneeling so often during the sermon. After the Mass, several devotees approached the Friar, greeting him back from the long absence. Near the exit door, Gaspar remained standing in silence.

Pedro attended to a young lady asking for the blessing of her toddler and then turned to his brother. "You stayed until the end this time. I'm glad."

Gaspar shrugged. "Do you need that much kneeling?" The peddler pointed to his trousers, with knees dirty from the repeated contact to the dusty floor.

"Not really," Pedro grinned. "But the most dignified suffering is the one we accept and are thankful for receiving." the Friar said, returning to the gentle tone that diverged from the heated old-testament preacher he impersonated minutes before.

"I will never understand this taste for self-sacrifice." The smuggler shook his head, glancing to the people leaving the Mass, back to their homes across the sandy streets of Itati.

Pedro tapped Gaspar's shoulder. "I think you will, brother. Before you even realize it."

***

At the dawn of the next day, the brothers left Itatí for Corrientes, the capital of the province with the same name. The barge carried the leather pieces. Along the way, Gaspar again noticed an unusual movement on the Paraguayan riverbank, more intense than on the previous day. Hundreds of men carried crates and boxes into chatas, barges similar to the one they sailed.

"What do you think is happening there, Pedro?"

"Soldiers going upstream?" The Friar focused his eyes on the boats at the opposite bank.

"No. They are not using uniforms. They are merchants or supply transports." Gaspar answered while holding the rudder.

The trip's quietness was only interrupted by chirping birds or the wind shaking the sail. Gaspar used the silence to consider the excuse for charging Amaru a higher price than agreed. He recalled Pedro's words days before: stick to the truth. Maybe then he could get divine help not to irritate his buyer, who was also Aramí's father.

They saw the store from the pier. A large warehouse selling non-perishable goods: lamp oil, salt, leather, textiles, and even furniture. On its walls, multiple wooden placards announced prices and products.

"Dom Amaru?" Gaspar entered through the half-open wooden door, followed by Pedro. Salt sacks, fabric rolls, and oil jars cluttered the corners. The center and the area in front of the counter, however, were neatly organized.

"Welcome, merchant from Itatí." From behind the counter, Dom Amaru greeted the siblings and bowed his head to the clergyman. "And please bless me, father."

"God bless you," Pedro, with his right hand, made in the air the sign of the cross.

"High time for your arrival." Amaru had a smile on his face while guiding the brothers to the counter. Over the desk were a used notebook and a gourd of yerba mate releasing a minty scent. "Some people from Ñeembucú visited and bought all the leather I had. Everything!"

Pedro and Gaspar exchanged glances. Ñeembucú was the region on the opposite side of the river, where they saw all the movement in the morning. Things just got stranger.

"Why are the Paraguayans coming here to buy leather?" Gaspar asked.

"For boots and uniforms, they say. Who knows?"

The warehouse owner looked to be around fifty. He had a whitish mustache but black hair like a young Indian. His mood and attitude depended on if he was selling or buying. The salesman Amaru had an affable approach to customers. The buyer Amaru, not so much. It was the second that Gaspar would face when informing about his price increase.

"Maybe because of the war..." Gaspar threw a bait to start the entire story about the war and the lack of leather supplies in Mato Grosso.

"War?" Amaru looked to the smuggler, putting aside a notebook where he scribbled numbers and names.

"Yes, the one between Brazilians and the Paraguayans."

The store owner looked in silence to Gaspar, as if demanding with his eyes a further explanation about the unknown conflict.

Gaspar made a long description of all he witnessed: the siege at the Coimbra fort, the capture of leather-supplying farms by Paraguayan soldiers, and the exodus of Corumbá emptying the warehouses. He recounted an overly graphic depiction of the combat between the ships Yporá and Rio Apa against the Anhambaí, where the Brazilian crew was massacred, their ears cut off and attached to the sails of the captured vessel.

Amaru remained in silence, awestruck. Behind him, a few meters from the counter, Gaspar noticed two honey-colored eyes watching the conversation. Eyes dumbfounded by the macabre story. Eyes from Aramí.

"Is this true, Father?" Amaru asked Friar Pedro, still assimilating the terror of the narrated battle scenes.

The friar nodded and wrapped his fingers around the crucifix he was carrying around his neck. "May God protect us."

"Amen," Amaru and Aramí responded at the same time.

To not look strange, Gaspar also uttered the same.

"That's why, Dom Amaru, we weren't able to bring everything that was arranged." Gaspar delivered the bad news in a hurried tone. Each word almost jumped out of his mouth, as if wanting to make that moment as brief as possible. "But the travel costs were the same, so I have to raise the prices per leather piece."

Amaru raised his head, nostrils flared with each gulp of air. If before he expressed dismay at the tragedies described by Gaspar, now severity filled his face.

Gaspar took a step back while the Friar remained in the same place, with the same taciturn but calm posture.

"Smuggler, you're kidding, right?"

The flat, harsh tone of voice and the emphasis on the word *smuggler* scared, but at the same time revolted Gaspar. Had Amaru not realized that the problems they had on the trip were beyond their reach? Or maybe the warehouse owner wanted the brothers to sell the leather at a loss? No, that was something Gaspar would never do. So he adopted a new line of reasoning.

"Dom Amaru, you told us that leather is sold out everywhere. What prevents you from selling it at a higher price as well?" He took a breath, giving the man time to assimilate the idea. "That way neither I, nor you will lose anything."

"Daddy, this might be usury," Aramí approached, joining her father behind the store counter. Gaspar turned his head to see the girl. Waist-length black hair, silky, peanut-colored skin, and teeth as pale as the feathers of the white *monjita*. She carried on her neck a silver crucifix similar to Pedro's but with a shiny green stone in the center.

"My apologies for the intrusion." Pedro attracted their attention after breaking his contemplative silence. "But in this case, it is not usury. It is a necessity."

Perhaps it was the soft tone of the Friar's voice, but at that moment, Amaru calmed dawn, unclenching his fists and sipping his *yerba mate*.

"It is an acceptable solution," Amaru said.

For him, one of the city's oldest and most respected merchants, raising prices was agonizing. His activity at the warehouse went beyond pure commerce. It was a social landmark. The locals respected him almost as an authority. People like him made Corrientes what it was—a city where whites and Guaranis had been living almost always in peace since the times of the Jesuits.

"We brought little but of the best quality. Who will complain about paying more for such fine goods?" Gaspar offered a handshake to close the deal.

Amaru hesitated. "Bring the pieces here, so I see them first."

Gaspar agreed, satisfied. It was a positive signal that he could unload the leather items from the barge and take them for inspection. He knew that once inside, the merchant would accept the product—not only out of respect but because their quality was indeed outstanding.

Pedro remained in the store, talking to Amaru and Aramí about the holy week's festivities, while Gaspar left to fetch the leather. The pier was less than sixty yards away. It was a small volume of products, but he still needed two rounds to carry everything.

He made the first round, bringing half of the leather rolls wrapped in a canvas sack, dragging it on the dusty road. Outside the warehouse, a familiar face was glancing at him.

"Hey, is this that heavy, or are you becoming weak?" Aramí said with a smile that paralyzed Gaspar.

"Oh no, no. I am just careful. And how are things going here?"

"Boring. Moara left to live in Ñeembucú." Aramí referred to their childhood friend, a neighborhood girl that had a crush on Gaspar's brother. Pedro's vocation for a religious life destroyed any hope the girl once had. "It's been a while since I talked to you."

"We are talking now," Gaspar said as he approached Aramí and ran his fingers over the girl's long, dark hair. They approached each other until their breaths mixed in the air.

"My father is waiting for the leather." Arami pushed the smuggler away. "Take it to him, and then we'll talk."

"I'll make two rounds. After I bring what I have to him, I'll stop by here." Gaspar smiled.

A smart plan. With Amaru entertained by his conversation with Friar Pedro and the meticulous analysis of the leather quality, he would not notice that his daughter was talking outside with the smuggler.

"Okay, now go." Arami nodded.

Gaspar entered the warehouse, left the canvas sack in the middle of the room, and tapped the large bag twice, saying, "If the Paraguayans are buying leather for making boots, warn them that these products are too good for foot soldiers. It is General's material."

Amarú grinned, entertained by the typical smuggler's sales pitch.

Gaspar returned to the boat, passing by Aramí on the yard and telling her to wait for him.

He grabbed the second canvas sack from the barge and then looked back to the warehouse, fifty meters away.

From a distance, he saw a group of red-dressed soldiers entering Amaru's warehouse.

Paraguayans.

Chapter XXIII

Gaspar dropped the canvas sack on the pier and hastened back to the store.

Before he arrived, a male shout came from the inside. Sounded like a soldier barking orders in a Guarani accent that was not his own. *Certainly Paraguayans, but what was their business in Corrientes?*

Aramí was not waiting outside anymore. The smuggler jumped over the backyard fence and then climbed onto a pile of bricks at the side of the warehouse until he could look through a small window and see inside the store. Only the area behind the counter was visible, but not where the soldiers stood.

Still, Gaspar could hear their voices with clarity, disturbed only by his pounding heart.

"Old bastard, don't you realize we're doing this for you? You are a Guarani like us," said the voice with an unusual accent.

"Sir Sergeant, I have no problem selling my goods to your platoon, but we only accept *Correntine* pesos. No Paraguayan money."

The only person Gaspar saw from the window was Aramí, standing with her back turned to him. She didn't notice he was observing the wrangle.

Click

A metallic sound, as a lever being pulled. Aramí covered her face with her hands.

"Either you sell the leather to us, or you will be treated as a traitor to the *Guaranies*! Soldier Kerana, what do we do with traitors?"

"Uh...uh...We shoot them, sir," said a third voice, muffled and thick.

In a second, Gaspar's thoughts clarified. A cocked gun was pointed at the merchant.

"I have no problem selling to you if you pay me with *Correntine* money." Amaru's voice sounded anxious, despite his effort to stay calm.

Idiot, give them the leather. They are armed! Gaspar thought, pressing his face to the narrow window while trying to identify the shadows inside the warehouse. But only Aramí's back was visible.

"Are you Guarani or not?" shouted the Paraguayan sergeant.

"I am..." Amaru's voice stopped halfway. "I am a *Correntino*."

"No, *Papá!*" Aramí screamed. "Do what they want!"

"If I do it now, they will never stop."

A bang echoed through the warehouse. A dull noise of a falling body reached Gaspar's ears.

Aramí bent under the table. Looking for a way to escape the soldiers, the girl glimpsed the window facing the backyard, ten feet away. The same window through which Gaspar tried to observe what he could from the situation.

Their eyes met for a moment. The smuggler saw, for the first time in her delicate face, an expression of the purest agony and terror.

"Help me," Aramí's lips moved while she hid under the counter.

Gaspar nodded and looked around to check the fastest way through the warehouse's entrance to reach her. On a last glance through the window, he noticed another man trying to help the girl. His brother, Friar Pedro.

The smuggler grabbed a brick from the pile. He ran, leaping from the wall, hurting his feet, but despair numbed all the pain. He rushed toward the door, but before getting there, another gunshot noise cut the air.

Gaspar stopped. *Am I running to suicide?*

The soldiers left the store to light torches in the yard. The smuggler passed unnoticed through the door.

Inside he found only one Paraguayan, with a sergeant uniform, and Pedro, fallen to the ground with a stain on his chest that resembled a large red flower.

Gaspar, still holding the brick, dashed inside and hit the Sergeant's head.

He raised his arms to strike the soldier one more time.

"Don't!" Pedro, in an agonizing shriek, stopped his brother from murdering the unconscious soldier.

Smoke invaded the place. The Paraguayans he saw before used their torches to arson the warehouse roof and left.

Gaspar pulled Pedro outside the building, out of reach of the spreading flames, and laid him below a lime tree on the street. Neighbors abandoned their houses for fear of the spreading flames.

He pressed his hand over his brother's wound.

"Get out of here. It's my time to go, Gaspar."

"Don't talk nonsense. Don't you believe in God? Now it is time for him to change our luck."

"I couldn't have better luck, brother. But Aramí...." Pedro took a breath to say something to Gaspar, but the bleeding was exhausting his strength.

"What about her?"

"They took her."

"I will find the girl later." Gaspar tore a piece of cloth from his trousers and attempted to stop the Friar's bleeding. The crimson liquid soaked the dusty soil. The bullet pierced Pedro's body, exiting through his back, where blood still leaked. "No, No...We need to stop it. I need to save you."

Pedro pulled his brother's hand.

"Gaspar, first you have to save yourself. I will pray for you from there."
"There where?" The desperate smuggler asked.

The Friar exhaled. His eyes took on an opaque glass appearance. Gaspar looked into his older brother's face and wept, not caring about the blistering heat of the fire that surrounded them.

Meters from there, Paraguayan soldiers entered the burning warehouse and rescued the sergeant with his head bloody from the brick hit.

Gaspar took one last glance at his brother, committing the Friar's face to memory. He took the silver crucifix from Pedro's neck and ran toward the river, to his boat.

Ran like he had never run before.

***

Gaspar forgot to eat or drink until early evening, when his boat reached halfway to Itati. The wind blew loud in the opposite direction, forcing the smuggler to put all his strength in the rowing paddles. The paddling came with a painful cost, resulting in erupted blisters on his hands.

When night had fallen, the Correntine took the barge to a sandbank and slept right there, on a small beach hidden in the meanders.

Gaspar awakened when the darkness of the night turned into the fluorescent pink of the Pantanal morning. Next to him, several trees with a ripe fruit called *laranjinha de pacu*. It had a sour, acid taste, so people rarely consumed it and instead used it as fish bait.

Before the tragic events at Amaru's warehouse, he and Pedro planned to eat something before departing from the Corrientes port. They didn't, and now Gaspar was starving. He ate the fruit, ignoring the acerbic, pungent flavor. Later, he picked up some extra laranjinhas, put it in his barge, and went back to rowing. *I must arrive in Itati before noon before the soldiers reach there,* he thought.

The food and a night of sleep recovered his strength. After a river bend, when the sun was already at its highest point, Itati appeared on the horizon. Locals and pilgrims were heading to the church.

Good Friday. The faithful expected to see Friar Pedro celebrating Christ's passion. Vain expectation.

The smuggler squinted his eyes, noticing among the pilgrims dozens of red-uniformed men, just like the cursed ones who had murdered Pedro and Amarú the day before.

They are here.

Gaspar still had at his side, in the barge, the second canvas sack with the never-delivered leather pieces. He remained in the boat instead of visiting Itati for fear that the invading soldiers could confiscate the remaining items. It was all he had now. They could also recognize that he was the one who hit a brick at a sergeant in Corrientes, and that would get him executed.

On a river bend near Itá Corá, his barge crossed ways with five Paraguayan military steamships.

In the late afternoon, he moored his boat in a riverside village. The locals, Correntinos like him, cried in sorrow. Some men were seriously injured. When the smuggler asked what happened, they told him the Paraguayan sailors from the steamships looted everything.

"Food, candles, even wood. They took all we had!" A young woman sobbed, with tears running down her face. "They beat anyone who opposed the looting, saying that the food and animals were for Meza's flotilla, that would liberate the Correntinos."

Liberation from what? thought Gaspar. The Correntinos lived in peace until yesterday, until the red-shirted soldiers crossed the river.

The smuggler wrinkled his brow, thinking if the Meza's flotilla were the ships he saw that day.

"How many ships they had?"

"Five large steamers. A soldier asked if anyone wanted to join them to go downriver and finish the *Porteños*."

The smuggler, versed in the regional nicknames, knew that *Porteños* meant Argentinians from Buenos Aires.

If they are targeting Buenos Aires, that means this war is no longer only between Brazil and Paraguay, he thought. Gaspar recalled that in Corrientes, there were two Argentine warships, the Gualegay and the 25 de Mayo. *Poor bastards. Against the flotilla of five Paraguayan ships, these two Argentinian steamers do not stand a chance. They will share the same fate as the Anhambaí.* Gaspar remembered the savagery witnessed months earlier in Mato Grosso.

In this war between three nations, Corrientes and its people would be under crossed-fire.

Soon, soldiers would be everywhere—the sergeant that murdered his brother among them.

Gaspar wanted revenge, but for now, he had to get out of there.

He returned to the boat and continued to row. Sleeping on the beaches, eating fruits he found at the banks and food he got by exchanging, one by one, the leather pieces that remained in the barge.

He rowed and rowed, as far as his arms allowed, always to the east. Rowed until he no longer saw a single Paraguayan, or Porteño, or anyone else.

Chapter XXIV

Joana took no pleasure in saying goodbye to the children.

The support from Lady Ana softened the sorrow of another farewell at the Viscount of Ururaí's house. For the Viscountess, Joana's opportunity to join Almeida Rosa in his diplomatic mission to Buenos Aires could make the girl witness history at the very place where it would be written.

"Just do not join the liberal party under Otaviano's influence!" the Viscountess said with a laugh during Joana's farewell.

The warning was unnecessary. Joana had no interest in any specific party. Even if she had, her convictions were far more influenced by lady Ana Francisca de Lima e Silva, daughter of the greatest exponent of the conservative party, and by her father, also a conservative. She was little to nothing attracted to the liberals, and the only member of this party she knew was Otaviano, who never tried to lure her into politics.

After arriving in Argentina, they checked in at the renowned Hotel de la Paix, in the heart of Buenos Aires' cultural life. Less than five minutes away from the Plaza de Mayo and the Teatro Colón, inaugurated years earlier with a sumptuous exhibition of the opera *La Traviata* by Giuseppe Verdi.

Joana always appreciated the arts and social life that Rio de Janeiro provided her, so the first impression of Buenos Aires couldn't be better. The first day had no official agenda. It meant free time to explore the surroundings.

Still thrilled by the European architecture and lavish gardens, she entered her room and left the suitcases on the floor, observing the refined furniture. A spacious cedar bed covered with layers of white-linen perfumed with lavender aromas. On the opposite side, an oak dresser with a gilded-frame mirror.

Joana looked in the mirror. Lips curled upwards, drawing a soft grin.

She reprimanded herself. How dare she show any happiness in THAT city? A city that stole so much from her.

A place that erased from her life possibilities far greater than any opera, opulent theaters, or Greek-roman columns. A place that took her fiance, Fernando Tavares.

The young man who loved Joana more than his own land, more than his own family. They met when she was just sixteen, and two years later, he asked for her hand.

At eighteen, however, Joana was already familiar with Rio and experienced the luxury of the nobility. Her father, Dom Caetano, was not poor either and spoiled his youngest daughter, fulfilling her desire for extravagant dresses, perfumes, and holidays at the capital.

Fernando was born in a middle-class family. To accept his marriage proposal, Joana demanded that he find means to support the girl's lifestyle. "I am not a frugal lady," she highlighted to him many times.

The young Tavares learned Spanish from an Argentine he met in Cruzeiro and got a job at the Baron of Mauá bank. During an international expansion, the bank sent a few of his employees, including Fernando, to work in Buenos Aires and Rosario in 1858.

In the same year, a yellow fever epidemic devastated the Argentine capital. A disease that was flying in the air—an example of the gloomy sarcasm of death, since the city's name meant good air—and killed the rich and poor, young and old, guilty and innocent.

The fever also took the life of Fernando, who moved to these far-away lands only to get the resources to keep a spoiled, capricious girl. What he found was only death.

Since then, Joana began a relentless quest to develop any talent that allowed her to pay her own bills. Years later, she became the tutor of the grandchildren of a senator and a student of Rio de Janeiro's most renowned diplomat.

This led her, in one of those life's ironies, to Buenos Aires. To the same place where her fiance perished. Joana Augusta could not hide the ocher taste of remorse that the memory brought her. Her lips curled downwards, and she peered the gleaming wooden floor with watery eyes.

She changed her clothes and left the hotel, heading to
Calle Cangallo, building 103, located less than three hundred
meters away, toward the docks. The local supposed to be the
headquarters of Banco Mauá. A place where she would face
her demons.

Someone there could know more about Fernando's
death, Joana thought. His family never told her much about
what happened—they cut off relations with the girl, whom
they blamed. An accusation that she plead guilty to.

The financial institutions that occupied both sides of the
street—the bank of Buenos Aires, the Banco Nacional, and a
few others—were cramped with elegantly dressed customers.
Not even in Rio de Janeiro had she seen such a flow of people
depositing money and opening accounts.

*Is this a normal day? Looks like everyone is rushing to
the banks*, she thought.

Joana stopped in front of a beige building. The Banco
Mauá, MacGregor & Cia sign showed that it was the right
place.

At the entrance, a man greeted her at the elegant clerk's
counter.

"I'm with the Brazilian diplomatic mission. How can I
open a deposit account?" Joana assumed the clerk understood
Portuguese. The question about opening an account was just a
pretext. She wanted to see a director and knew that a clerk

would call his superior when facing a member of a diplomatic mission, and that is exactly what happened.

Down the stairs, a gentleman came in a dark suit and a butterfly tie. The banker was slender, tall, and had a big, thin nose. He greeted Joana, inviting her to a meeting room with brown leather chairs and mahogany furniture. From the armchair, she noticed that, under the dimmed lights, the whole place looked like a Diego Velázquez painting.

"I'd like to open an account."

The banker smiled. "It will be my pleasure to assist you, lady. We are here for years serving the Brazilian interests in Argentina," he said with an accent. He was not Brazilian but spoke Portuguese as good as someone that learned it many years before.

"Your Portuguese is excellent. Did you work with the first Brazilian employees of the Banco Mauá six years ago?" For an instant, she hoped the banker knew her late fiance.

The gleam in the banker's eyes disappeared, and he looked down, placing a hand over his forehead as if supporting his skull on it.

"Six years ago...I don't know anyone from that time. They either died during the fever or moved to Rosario."

"Oh..." Joana let out a frustrated interjection.

"Bad for them!" The banker recovered the uplifting, business-making mood. "There has never been a better time for business than now in Buenos Aires! The Empire is spending everything and a little more to supply the soldiers, so whoever can sell something to them has a direct path to wealth!"

The suited manager stood up and, strolling to a window, looked at the street.

"Come here, look."

Joana walked to the same window. A line of people was waiting to enter the bank and reach the counters, showing no discomfort with the humid heat of Buenos Aires.

"These are merchants. People who sell horses for Osório's corps, rations for Paunero's soldiers, equipment for Mitre's recruits. Everyone is profiting. And they trust their profits to us." said the banker, with a gleam in his eyes worthy of a dazzled child. "What a fabulous moment!"

Joana winced with the distasteful observation. That merchants and bankers were going to profit barbarities from the war was no surprise. But talking about the military slaughter as something positive disgusted her.

She got disgusted because she was acquainted with greed.

It was greed, arrogance, and a desire for luxury that, six years before, took the life of the man who loved her. Seeking vain desires, she charmed Fernando Tavares into a journey with no return. Remorse was the price she would have to pay. The banker's greed was a demon with whom she was familiar.

With diminished hopes to know more about Fernando's demise, Joana thanked the man for the attention, telling him she would return another day to open the account, and left.

***

Luis woke up, washed his face, and left the inn where the group slept for a few days after arriving in the Guaiba River port—the steamship's last destination. There were still a few days of travel by land until reaching the military camp. He carried his luggage, signaling to the innkeeper that this would be their last day at the place.

The time spent at the Guaíba's inn was beneficial to exercise the horses in the nearby fields, since they got soft after the long steamship trip to the south. The thugs who assaulted Martin and stole his gun no longer caused any problems. Luis and his men saw the robbers for the last time after disembarking, when the delinquents took a carriage heading west.

In front of the inn, Primo Francisco was saddling a smoky black colt.

"Where did you get that horse, Primo?" Luis asked.

"I won on a bet!"

"Really? And what did you bet in exchange?" Luis frowned, wondering what Primo could risk since he had nothing as valuable as a colt. Only an idiot would bet a horse against nothing—and in the ports, there weren't many idiots.

"I bet your horse against this sweety here."

"Did you bet...Nickel?" Luis widened his eyes. "Did you bet something that isn't even yours?"

"I knew I was going to win. There was no way the other idiot could have a hand better than mine."

Luis Caetano clenched his fist and shook his head, furious with his friend's insolence in betting Nickel on a card game. Even so, the lieutenant deep inside knew that if Primo lost the game, he was cunning enough to get around the situation and solve it with no one noticing.

Besides, the extra horse was useful to them. They still needed to ride to Rio Pardo to join their assigned battalions. With three horses for four men, only one would carry an extra person each day, so the group could move faster.

They arrived in Rio Pardo in five days instead of the six planned and joined the spacious encampment under the command of General João Frederico Caldwell. The site stretched across a vast plain, looking more like a permanent citadel than a makeshift camp to gather soldiers for the impending frontier battles.

The campground had tents, shops, and a lively, even exuberant commerce. Besides the military personnel, the population comprised also cleaning servants, food peddlers, apothecaries, and many other people that found a way to subsist in the place.

The civil inhabitants, the hangers drying clothes, and the festive bonfires made Luis raise his eyebrows at first sight. The lieutenant thought they would be late arrivals to the camp, so they rode at a forced trot since Porto Alegre to not miss the departure to the battlefield.

"With all this buzz and laughs around, I doubt they plan to march anytime soon," Luis said while riding down the hill that led to the camp entrance.

"And all the haste for nothing," Primo replied.

Luis Caetano sought the local intendancy office. He had several questions, such as which battalion he would join and which soldiers would be under his command. But the biggest question was why there was no sign of movement, and everyone seemed so accommodated.

However, in the intendancy, there was only one private attending to the newly arrived officers. He barely looked eighteen. There was no chance the lad knew why no one marched to defend Brazil while thousands of Paraguayans threatened the country. The only reason the secretary-soldier was there was to give basic directions about tents and write complaints.

The junior officers' tents were near the soldiers' grounds, where Nopitena, Martin, and Primo would sleep. Luis also was informed that he would have a tent-mate, another lieutenant.

A young officer, around the same age as Luis, was polishing his boots at the entrance. His appearance, however, was quite distinctive. While Luis had a muscular figure, his tent-mate was slender like Martin, though not as tall. Instead of Luis's scruffy beard, the man had a carefully shaved face adorned by a fine, well-groomed mustache.

Certainly an officer zealous of his appearance. Even too zealous.

Luis himself enjoyed regular baths or clean clothes but scorned cosmopolitan, silk-skinned schoolboys like that. A disdain translated by a sideways stare. Interrupted by the visitor's shadow over his boots, his tent mate finally stood up with a bright smile.

"Good Morning! How can I help you?" he asked, offering a handshake.

"My name is Luis Caetano. The intendancy told me I will share tent 43 with you."

The young officer grinned, shaking Luis' hand with force and effusiveness.

"Welcome, Lieutenant. Your bed is on the left. If you need anything, just ask. We have plenty of time here, my friend."

My friend? Luis thought. They barely met, and the individual already treated him as if they were gambling & liquor mates for years. The overly warm reception was so strange that he forgot to ask the tent mate's name.

For his luck, he didn't even have to, because almost in sequence, the young officer amended:

"Ah, my name is Gabriel. Lieutenant Gabriel Martinez, but you can call me Martinez, or the *Ginete*, which is how they know me around here."

Luis smirked after hearing the nickname. Before, Martinez's informality and ease were strange to Luis, but now it amused him. Maybe it was not that bad. The lieutenant left his luggage on the tent's floor and walked back to the entrance.

"Why Ginete?" Luis wished to know the reason his tent-mate was nicknamed with a word used by Iberian horse-masters.

"Because I've tamed almost every wild stallion in this camp. There is no horse I can't ride." Gabriel replied while sitting on a wooden bench and polishing his already shining saber.

"One of my men is also an excellent rider," Luis said as he sat down on the grass next to Martinez.

"Really? Where is he from? From the Pampas? A trooper from São Paulo? Or is he a Prussian mercenary?"

"None. He is an Indian. A Kadiwéu."

"An Indian horse rider?" Martinez had a laugh burst, almost dropping his saber from the knees. "I would like to see that."

Luis nodded with a smile but then remembered the question that had been nagging at him.

"Martinez, why everything is so still here? The military command from Santos sent me to join Caldwell's men, supposed to march to the border at the end of April."

"You heard the same thing we've been hearing for almost a month. Every week the camp commander tells us that soon we will march." Gabriel Martinez chuckled. "Who knows what they mean by *soon*."

"Hum. So we rushed like idiots for nothing," Luis said.

Gabriel returned his now shiny saber to the sheath. "That is what the army is about, my friend. Rushing, and then waiting."

"And why wait here for so long?"

"Each time they make an excuse. This time they say we march as soon as General Caldwell arrives from Porto Alegre, in about ten to fifteen days."

Luis shook his head. *Ten to fifteen days is too much.* Still irritated with the unnecessary suffering imposed on the horses by their hasty trip, Luis reminded the one positive thing about the stagnated Rio Pardo camp: the time there was already double-counting for his next promotion.

Gabriel stood up and pulled on his now gleaming boots, then asked Luis if he wanted to take a walk around the camp. Luis nodded.

While passing by the soldiers' tents, they saw Primo playing cards with some recruits. No signal of Nopitena and Martin, who perhaps were resting inside. Everywhere they saw soldierly excitement. Volunteers from all over the south. Men played and laughed everywhere.

"Gabriel, why is everyone so animated?"

"Because we are volunteers at the request of His Majesty, the Emperor, why else!" He turned to Luis as they walked through the corridors formed by tent rows and said,

"And the promise of money and lands means a lot for these men."

"Not for you?" asked Luis.

"Let's say my family has the means to provide for me. For money I wouldn't need to be here, but I want to serve." Gabriel looked at Luis with the optimistic glow of an inexperienced officer. "I believe you think the same, right?"

Luis, who already witnessed the battle's carnage and the death smell, preferred to not discourage his fellow. "Yeah, kind of."

***

Back at the Hotel de la Paix after the brief visit to Banco Mauá, Joana took out her shoes. Walking barefoot across the beige floral-patterned carpet, she opened the curtains and glimpsed at the street. Then she threw herself on the spacious bed, covered in silky cotton bedsheets, and breathed the room's mahogany-scented air.

In a few hours, she and her professor-turned-employer had dinner scheduled with the admiral who commanded all the Brazilian naval forces in the region.

High-rank commanders were everywhere in Rio, but Joana never saw admiral Tamandaré in person. Because of his age and responsibilities in the southern regions, he rarely took part in the social events of the Capital.

But Tamandaré's fame preceded his persona. Still a teenager, he fought in the independence war. During his early career, he was a pupil of the legendary Thomas Cochrane and since then contributed to the empire in all the major naval conflicts.

Joana shut her eyes to rest before the important occasion. Instead of sleeping, she recalled an unusual event of minutes before. While passing through the hotel lobby, she saw a man in a navy uniform asking the receptionist:

"Do you have any letter or telegram for Mr. Otaviano de Almeida Rosa?"

"I'm sorry, sir, we have nothing in that name." The receptionist said after searching through a bundle of papers.

Who was that man? Why was he asking for Otaviano's letters? Joana asked herself questions impossible to answer there, in her bed. She decided to inform Otaviano when they meet in the lobby before the dinner.

After a brief nap, Joana got dressed and went down to the lobby. The dinner was at nine o'clock, but she arrived almost thirty minutes earlier and found Otaviano, sitting in one of the leather armchairs, cross-legged and reading some documents. With the eyes focused on the papers, he hardly noticed his secretary.

"Mr. Otaviano, good evening." Joana approached, announcing her arrival to the diplomat.

Almeida Rosa put down the papers and greeted her. Before they walked to the dining hall, she halted.

"The hall is in that direction." He nodded. "We are a few minutes ahead of schedule."

"There is something I need to tell you before we meet the Admiral."

Almeida Rosa looked to the girl. "Yes?"

"I left the hotel in the morning to visit the Mauá bank. When I returned, at the reception, I saw a navy officer asking if there was any message for you."

"For me?" Almeida Rosa pushed his glasses up. "Did he find anything?"

"Nothing. I think this is good, right? Better than someone stealing your letters."

"On the contrary, Miss Joana. This is a bad sign."

"Why, professor?"

"The reason for tonight's dinner is for the Admiral's staff to hand me guidelines for negotiating with the Argentinians and Uruguayans." Almeida Rosa resumed the walk to the restaurant. "They were looking for letters addressed to me because they don't have any additional information to give me."

"Will you wait for orders from Rio to start the negotiations?"

"Time does not allow such luxury." Almeida Rosa took a deep breath. "I will have to act on my own."

They entered the restaurant several minutes before nine and sat at the table reserved for the Brazilian diplomatic mission and Tamandaré's staff. The cream-colored walls of the large dining hall reflected the dancing lights from the crystal chandeliers. As requested to the hotel, their table was in the corner, separated from the other guests that had already filled the place. Spies or journalists should not hear their conversation.

"Very well, miss Joana. Thank you for the information." Otaviano settled into an emerald green chair cushioned with floral motifs. "How was your visit to the Mauá Bank?"

"I believe you already know why I went there." Joanna grinned, but not with a joyful grin.

And indeed, Otaviano de Almeida Rosa knew. Before Joana became his student, he was the teacher of her late fiance, Fernando. A young man so promising that he stood out even among the pupils handpicked by Otaviano. The professor saw in him a potential ambassador or minister. But that never happened.

Brazil could no longer rely on the talents of Fernando Tavares, and Joana felt indebted to have deprived the country of such a skillful young man. That guilt pushed her to ask, almost beg, for Fernando's former teacher to accept her in his place as a diplomacy and law student.

"You are right, miss Joana. I know why you went there. Have you ever read Aeschylus' work?"

"No, little I know about Greek tragedies."

"In his Oresteia, he wrote..." Almeida Rosa tilted his face to the ceiling as if the chandelier's light helped him recall the ancient Greek verses. The words came to his mouth, and he chanted slowly:

"*Wisdom comes through suffering. Trouble, with its memories of pain, drips in our hearts as we try to sleep. So men against their will, learn to practice moderation.*"

When Otaviano recited the last verse, a tall, uniformed officer appeared at the hall's arched entrance. He had an elderly image, a white beard but no mustache, and walked in slow but firm steps. At his side, a much younger man, also in a navy uniform but with a thick black mustache. The same person Joana saw at the hotel reception, asking for Almeida Rosa's letters.

"Mister Admiral! How nice to see you!" Almeida Rosa greeted the most senior officer of the two.

"There are only two people that say this without sounding fake, Otaviano. One of them is you. The other is my secretary, Lieutenant Artur." Tamandaré nodded to the man at his side, introducing him to the present. In the sequence, Almeida Rosa also presented Joana to both Navy officers.

Waiters brought the first glasses of Malbec, a wine variety that had just arrived in Argentina at the hands of French agronomists.

"It is impressive how European sophistication is so present here in Buenos Aires." Joana risked starting a conversation. "From the wine to the architecture and arts... one could not differentiate here from a city of the Old Continent."

"Except for the mosquitoes..." Artur said with a smile.

"I agree with Mrs. Joana, and I dare to say that things will become even better to our southern brothers." Almeida Rosa captured the attention of the presents at the table. "The Argentinian president, besides being a gifted military leader, is also a talented statesman. How lucky they are by having a president like Mitre!"

Admiral Tamandaré frowned on his chair. "Do you say all this just because of the wine?"

"No, mister Admiral. I say that because of everything around us. His military talent was clear when he defeated

Urquiza at Pavón, and his genius is behind the prosperity of this land."

Otaviano's words carried some historical truths. In Pavón, during the Argentine civil war, Mitre's Buenos Aires army won a resounding victory over Urquiza's Argentine Confederation.

"Still, we helped Mitre win his domestic war, and we turned the tide in Montevideo," said Tamandaré. "If we left Mitre to solve the situation in Uruguay by himself, Aguirre would still be the president, not our friend, Venancio Flores."

"No doubt, mister Admiral. The peace in Uruguay did not come at the hands of Mitre. It came thanks to Osório, Mena Barreto and," Almeida Rosa paused mid-sentence, raising the expectation for his next words, "more than anyone else, thanks to you, Admiral. The great Tamandaré, distinguished student of Thomas Cochrane."

Joan held back a laugh until her cheeks turned red. She recalled an afternoon when Almeida Rosa explained to her how diplomacy often involved stroking egos. Even more so for high-ranking military and politicians. Otaviano's unexpected praise liquefied the Admiral's grim expression.

"Well, I did what I could," Tamandaré grinned, inclining in Otaviano's direction.

"You set the record straight." Almeida Rosa raised his glass, offering a toast to Tamandaré.

"I appreciate the recognition," Tamandaré tasted his wine as he sat down again. "You are better than any other diplomat the empire sent before."

Tamandaré referred to the now ex-minister Paranhos, with whom he had a conflictual history.

During the war against Aguirre in Uruguay, upon seeing enemy supporters burning an imperial flag in Montevideo, Tamandaré positioned the powerful Brazilian fleet to bombard the city. The reprimands of Paranhos, who opposed bombing a capital full of civilians, held him back. Tamandaré obeyed the orders of the then minister but told in his face that only a soldier could know what an insult to the flag means.

For Otaviano, however, Tamandaré's criticism against his predecessor was unfounded. It was Paranhos who coordinated the peace agreement in Uruguay and prevented further bloodshed. And like Otaviano, Paranhos was a supporter of fraternal relations with Argentina.

"Is there any news or guideline from the Empire about the negotiations with Mitre and Venancio Flores?" Otaviano opened the subject of the alliance with the Argentinian and Uruguayan presidents.

"Sadly not. I believe you will have to use your best judgment, minister."

Otaviano sighed.

"This negotiation with Mitre is a mere formality," Tamandaré said. "Viana de Lima informed me that the Paraguayan forces are so rickety that with ten thousand soldiers, we will finish Solano Lopez!"

"Viana de Lima said so?" Otaviano adjusted his glasses with his right-hand indicator.

"Yes!" The Admiral banged his wrists on the table and guffawed. "We don't need allies to defeat the Guaranis, Otaviano! We will wipe them out!"

Otaviano, however, wasn't on the same optimistic wave. Viana de Lima, the former Brazilian ambassador to Paraguay, was unreliable and failed to alert Brazil about the invasion. Solano López placed him under surveillance years before, filtering his letters and crippling his intelligence.

"The Paraguayan army is way stronger than Viana de Lima or Tamandaré think," Otaviano told Joana when both Navy officers went for cigars. "We need an ally like Mitre, even under the risk of offering terms without Imperial consent."

Chapter XXV

Morning, May 1st. Chilly winds roamed across the wide boulevards of Buenos Aires, with gardens colored by the yellow shades of autumn. As every Monday, the city woke up to work. Carriages and horses trotted along Calle Cangallo. The bells of the *Iglesia de La Merced* tolled.

Inside the Hotel de La Paix, Joana descended the wooden stairs to the lobby. Below her right arm, she carried a brown leather folder.

After the dinner with Tamandaré, Otaviano knew that there were no Imperial guidelines or terms to negotiate with the Argentines and Uruguayans. When the Emperor nominated him as a *plenipotentiary minister*, possibly His Majesty took the word *plenipotentiary quite* literally.

Since then, the diplomat and Joana had worked for days, weaving an alliance treaty with terms acceptable to all parties. Every day, he sent emissaries to the representatives of Mitre and Venancio Flores—the Argentine and Uruguayan presidents—asking whether one clause or another would be acceptable.

The leather folder Joana carried contained the treaty's final version.

The clatter of her shoe hitting the wooden stairs muffled as she reached the lobby, covered in a reddish carpet.

As in on other occasions, Otaviano was already there, sitting in one of the wide armchairs, with his legs crossed and reviewing a never-ending list of papers. But there was some impatience in the serene posture of the former professor, now a diplomat. He adjusted his glasses incessantly and ran his fingers along the paper lines as if looking for some lost word, some hidden paragraph.

"Professor, is there anything that still worries you?"

"Tamandaré. The treaty needs his signature too. He can put everything to waste."

As much respect as Otaviano had for the Admiral, it was visible that age was taking its toll. Besides, among the various glories of the old sea lion were two wars against the Argentinians.

"It's been a tough task to convince the Admiral to ally with a country he's fought twice." Otaviano raised his eyes to his secretary, "Too tough. We need help."

"Professor, what about Artur?" Joana sat on the opposite armchair, still holding the leather folder under her arm.

"The admiral's protégé? I know he is a well-educated officer. But how could he help?"

"The Admiral trusts him. And Artur admires you." Joana recalled that during the dinner, the young lieutenant showed great interest in Otaviano's translations of literary classics. "Maybe he can help us convince Tamandaré."

"It's a wonderful idea." The professor snapped his fingers. "I have a plan."

The treaty signing ceremony would start in less than two hours in the congress building, a seven-minute walk from the Hotel de la Paix.

"Tamandaré will go by foot to the congress. Despite his age, he likes to exercise and will use the chance to socialize with other military and prominent political figures." Otaviano said. "As a typical Gaúcho, he enjoys this windy weather."

The professor stood up and made a gesture for his secretary to follow him to the Hotel's entrance. There, he asked for a cabriolet taxi to stop.

"Please, drive her down Calle Bolívar to Parroquia San Ignacio de Loyola, and then up through Calle Defensa." Otaviano told the driver and gave him two coins. "This way, you arrive at the backside of the congress."

"Why all that, professor?" Joana frowned.

"Miss Joana, when you arrive at the congress, Tamandaré's staff will be there, but not the Admiral himself, because he will be walking across the park. I will meet the Admiral on the way and try to delay him." Otaviano stopped his explanation and offered a hand to help Joana climb into the cab. "Deliver the papers to Artur and explain to him that without the Admiral's signature, there is no treaty."

Joana nodded, and the cab departed.

Otaviano saw the carriage gain distance, adjusted the blazer on his thin body, and set off on a walk toward the congress.

    ***

As planned by Otaviano, Joana arrived at the backside of the congress building. There, she found two members of the Admiral's entourage. Artur was one of them. He wore the same navy dress uniform he had at their dinner days before. A blue jacket with a high collar and golden shoulder pads bearing his first lieutenant's insignia. Nevertheless, the most contrasting feature of the junior navy officer's uniform was the white linen pants. Such a white that it gleamed under the Argentine morning sun.

"Mister Secretary to the Admiral?"

"Yes, Miss Secretary of the Minister?" He turned to the familiar voice coming from behind his back. "You can call me Lieutenant Artur. How can I help you?"

Artur offered his hand to the girl to get out of the car.

"Minister Otaviano asked me to deliver you this so you can read it as soon as possible." Joana took a sheaf of papers from the folder and handed them over to the Lieutenant.

"You mean the Admiral should read it, right?"

"No, Lieutenant Artur. You."

He rose his eyebrows. "Why me? I am not the one making decisions here."

"The minister believes you have excellent skills to translate to the Admiral any point that is not clear to him."

He grinned. He understood what that was all about. Tamandaré had a history full of military glories, but he despised intellectual efforts. In fact, there were even rumors he was a slow reader. The Admiral made up for these flaws by hiring staff with distinguished academic abilities—like his secretary.

He opened the unsealed envelope. Under the shadow of the tall, lush trees lining the sidewalk, he skimmed the document. After turning a few pages, the Lieutenant shook his head as if disagreeing with something.

"Miss Joana, these numbers conflict with what we received. Is the Minister sure about them?"

Joana did not know what was on the paper, but she knew Otaviano.

"The Minister would not write any number based on unreliable sources, Mr. Secretary."

He sighed. "Please, you don't need to call me mister, miss. Lieutenant Artur is enough."

"Lieutenant Artur, this document is of paramount importance. The reason Otaviano asked me to deliver it to you is because, trusting your intellect, he believes you will convey this information to the Mr. Admiral in the most..."

"Convincing way? I get why he wants my help. Let's be honest. No problem on this point, since I agree with the minister's position. I will report to the Admiral the facts set out here."

Joana thanked him and turned to walk back to the congressional waiting room.

"Miss Secretary! I still have a question."

"Yes, Lieutenant Artur?" She turned around.

"Did the minister Otaviano really say he trusts my intellect?"

"Ah...yes, he said."

Artur put a wide smile.

Joana couldn't recall if Otaviano praised Artur's intelligence or not. She remembered, however, how praises and mutual admiration can cement alliances.

Meters from there, Tamandaré chatted with Otaviano as they crossed the Plaza 25 de Mayo and arrived at the congress. Both went straight to the session room, while Joana remained in the galleries, appreciating the European architecture, the arches, and columns that adorned the Italian-style palace.

Half an hour later, after an announcement in the corridors, the guests entered the session room. There, Argentine, Uruguayan, Brazilian, and even European journalists crowded the hall's upper arcades. Joana, Artur, and the other members of the Brazilian delegation took their places in the side chairs.

In the frontal stage, near a pulpit, only three men. Rufino Elizalde, Argentina's foreign minister, his Uruguayan counterpart—Carlos de Castro, and the familiar face of Otaviano.

Elizalde made a brief speech, followed by an even shorter commentary from Castro. Otaviano was the next to address the public and the three nations, so he took his place at the pulpit. Contrary to the energetic words of the Argentine and Uruguayan diplomats, the Brazilian started with a smooth voice and tranquil tone.

"Of all the articles in this treaty, the one I most celebrate today is the seventh. 'For this is not a fratricidal war, but a war against a man, Solano Lopez. A war to put an end to the aggressions he committed against us and against his own people'. Let us remember it every moment we face our Paraguayan brothers."

Claps echoed in the room. In seconds, it turned into a standing ovation, resounding like a storm coming from the palms of spectators enraptured by a brilliant speech.

The three representatives gathered around a large, wooden table on the front stage. Over the table, a paper. The Argentine, the Brazilian, and the Uruguayan made quick pen strokes and then held hands.

What followed was a round of applause mixed with cheering voices. Where is Tamandaré? Joana turned to Artur, sitting beside her. "Where is the Admiral?"

"To not show Brazilian dominance in the alliance ceremony, he preferred to stay in the upper galleys, leaving the central stage to only one delegate from each country."

"But what about his—"

"Signature? It was not easy, but he signed before heading up the stairs. You both owe me one now."

Artur nudged Joana with his elbow and pointed with his head toward a rostrum. There, the *gaúcho*, commander of the Brazilian navy, watched the ceremony with little excitement.

"Is there something still missing?" Joana asked.

"On the bureaucratic part, nothing. The other signatories also signed in advance."

"Other signatories?" Joana stared with uneasy eyes.

"Yes, Flores, Mitre, and Osório. What a pity! I thought I would finally meet such legendary figures." Artur shrugged.

"So, do we have an alliance then, Lieutenant Artur?"

"That's what the paper says, Miss Secretary."

***

Two weeks on standby at the Rio Pardo camp had a negative impact on Luis and his men. The lieutenant used the days for military exercises with Lieutenant Gabriel—the educated and disciplined young officer he shared a tent with—and his soldiers. Gabriel's platoon was numerous compared to Luis' four-men unit, made of Nopitena, Primo, Martin, and himself.

But after so many days, there wasn't much to train. Shooting drills were rare as they sought to conserve ammunition, so the men got sharp in other activities such as preparing pits and building trenches.

During the morning of May 9, scouts interrupted the camp's routine with an announcement. General Caldwell arrived, and with him, the prospect of breaking camp and marching into battle.

All officers received an invitation for a welcome dinner with the general. In the afternoon, the soldiers pitched a large tent near the camp's headquarters, and for the joy of those invited, cooks prepared fresh meat instead of the usual salted beef. The chilly autumn winds could bother a poorly dressed man, but the officer's heavy blue jackets were warm enough.

Luis and Gabriel walked through the camp to the dining tent. On the way, they passed through rows of soldiers' barracks, where men gambled and drank, forgetting about any war. The long wait had eroded the volunteers' enthusiasm, discipline, and combative spirit during the last two weeks. Many were just counting the days, already thinking that the battle cry would never come and that the money and prizes at the end of enlistment would be a reward for doing nothing.

"Did they assign your unit for the battery, Luis?" Gabriel asked while running his hands through his hair, as if checking for a millimeter of imperfection in the hairstyle, done with martial precision.

"It was the plan, but then they realized there are no cannons ready yet. What a joke!" Luis snorted. "What about you? Is your cavalry platoon ready?"

"Not really. We are still lacking a few horses. And nobody knows who will be our battalion commander." Gabriel shrugged.

"No cannons, no horses, and no colonel. I doubt we will march from here soon." Luis raised his right hand and pointed the indicator to the soldiers, playing and chatting in the barracks. "See, Gabriel? They summon flocks of volunteers and gather everyone in the middle of the prairies with nothing to do, just waiting for some general miles away. We are like children with no father," grumbled Luis.

"What?" Gabriel twisted his neck and looked at his friend. For a young officer from a rich and stable family, an analogy with orphans was difficult to grasp.

"I mean the lack of command here. Not even a colonel our battalion has!" Luis waved his hands as if his anger and disappointment could be better expressed by convulsive gestures. "Nobody knows where to go, what to do. Just wait and wait."

"My friend!" Gabriel smiled, touching Luis' shoulder. "The art of war is about rushing to get somewhere, and once there, sit and wait until you die of boredom or dysentery."

"Did you hear this somewhere?"

"I think so, just don't know where."

Luis laughed at the plagiarized wisdom as they took places at the table. General Frederico Caldwell finally arrived. His sleepy eyes, slow movements, slender body, and white mustache made him look like a strict grandfather mixed with a tired southern farmer.

"How old do you think he is, Gabriel?" Luis asked.

"Only God knows, but I heard he was already a captain when Brazil was still a colony."

"We have been independent for over forty years." Luis did some quick math. "If he's been a captain back then, it means around fifty years of service."

"Likely. He served King João VI, Emperor Pedro the First, and now he is at his third monarch. He fought at Cisplatina at the side of Bento Gonçalves, then later against Bento Gonçalves, then he fought against Argentina and now..."

Luis shook his head. "The man already gave half a century of his life for the Empire. Why doesn't he retire?"

"Because it's convenient for many people," Gabriel said, "And also because there are not many generals around here. The two Mena Barreto and Osório are all in Uruguay."

Luis heard about Osório. His former captain, Benedito de Faria, served under the legendary general during his youth and made frequent remarks about the hero of the forty-two battles. But he did not know who the two "Mena Barreto" were.

The dinner started. Lieutenants and captains filled the tables, The senior officers present were only a few majors, colonels, and general Caldwell. The inevitable effect was a banquet where lieutenants spoke with lieutenants, captains with captains, and the majors or colonels with the general.

The exception was lieutenant Gabriel, who had some high-ranking acquaintances.

Caldwell tapped his glass with a piece of silverware, attracting the eyes of all guests.

"Gentlemen, noble servants of the Brazilian army. It is with great pleasure that I join you today to form the first fatherland volunteer battalions. The first *Voluntários da Pátria!* Once General Canabarro's reinforcements arrive, which I hope won't be late, we march!"

What does he mean? The battalions are already here! thought Luis. Caldwell's words and the few other speeches that the elderly general made implied only one thing: they would still wait for a long time in Rio Pardo.

Luis remained quiet, with lips curled downwards in a bitter semblant, thinking about what to do. Gabriel chatted with the other lieutenants, captains, and Major Docca—a colonel's nephew—until he realized that something bothered his tent mate.

"What's wrong?" Martinez asked.

"Me and my men. We need to depart." Luis was one of the few guests drinking coffee after the feast. The majority drank mate from their typical calabash gourds—including Gabriel.

"Depart? The general just told us we need to wait for reinforcements," whispered Gabriel, careful to nobody hear the comment that bordered on insubordination, "and Canabarro will take time before sending anyone to reinforce us, for he is as lethargic as the General."

"If it was only me, I would stay here counting the hours for my promotion. But this is not the purpose to which my men volunteered. They trusted me to lead them into battle, not to an eternal standby." Luis withheld part of the truth, for even he had enough of the camp's doldrums and wanted to move ahead.

"All right. I have a suggestion." Gabriel sipped his mate and extended his arm, offering the hot infusion to his tent mate, who refused politely. "Major Docca commented about Colonel Tristao sending a detachment to Sao Borja. Maybe you can volunteer for that, so you depart with no risk of desertion."

"Sao Borja? What's there?"

"The border with Uruguay. From what I've heard, an entire Paraguayan column is approaching." Gabriel laid his mate gourd, now empty, at the table. "I can give him positive references about you, as the Colonel is a friend of my family."

"Hum...Could you?"

"Come here!" Gabriel stood up, gesturing for Luis to accompany him to the colonel's place at the feast. Both approached Tristao, who listened to Martinez's proposition and recommendation.

"So you want to go to the border?" The colonel asked, turning to Luis. "Do you have battle experience, Lieutenant Gomes?"

"I fought at the Siege of Coimbra, sir."

"Coimbra?" The colonel widened his eyes, pausing for a few seconds. "Did you fight alongside Portocarrero and Benedito de Faria?"

"They were my commanding officers, sir."

"It is impressive that you came so far. Do you have any men under your command here?" Tristao stood up, showing greater interest in the lieutenant who traveled from the distant lands of Mato Grosso to the very south of Brazil.

"Yes, sir."

"A company?" The colonel asked while lighting his pipe. A company meant about eighty men.

"No, a little less."

"A platoon?"

"A little less, sir colonel."

"What?" The colonel was about to smoke his pipe, but Luis' surprising response interrupted him. "You're a lieutenant, and you don't even have a platoon. I guess you command a squad, at least?"

Luis just shook his head from side to side.

"How many men do you have, Lieutenant Luis?"

"Two recruits and a well-trained anspeçada, sir. And three horses."

Colonel Tristao guffawed. Gabriel grinned at the embarrassing situation while Luis stared at his tent mate. *This was your dumb idea, Martinez. You will pay me back for that.*

"So you want to ride to the border with only three men?" Colonel Tristao recovered his seriousness. "You're brave. I give you that."

"Thank you, sir. Do I have your authorization?"

"Uh, my authorization?" The colonel turned to one of the cooks. "Soldier, bring us more meat!"

"Sir?" Luis asked, still unsure if he had just embarrassed himself that night.

"You have it. But as you know, we don't have enough horses and by my accounts, your....squad?" Tristão had one more laugh burst. "Alright, let's call it a squad. Your squad is also missing a horse. If you arrange an animal by Thursday, I nominate you and your men to the expedition to São Borja."

It was Tuesday. Luis had two days to find another horse. He thanked the colonel and turned to go back to his place, but Tristao called him over.

"Lieutenant, I forgot to tell you. If you go to São Borja, you will join the battalion of a colonel friend of mine. A gaucho with unrestrained bravery. You will be a suitable officer under his command. So go get that horse."

"Yes, sir." Luis tapped the brim of his cap, saluting Colonel Tristao, and returned to his table. The renewed scent of roasted meat made his mouth salivate. The dinner gave him a reason to celebrate.

Chapter XXVI

May in the southern plains was a month of drastic temperature changes happening in a matter of hours. While noons were still hot, dawn had single-digit temperatures. The dew formed on the shallow grass often froze overnight, covering the fields with a white veil that endured a few minutes after the first sunlight.

Luis filled his tin cup with hot coffee from the officer's kitchen. He held the mug with both hands, using the heat from the steaming liquid to warm his palms. The sun was still absent, but the sky gradually changed to lighter shades of blue.

He walked to the soldiers' barracks, toward the tent where Primo Francisco, Nopitena, and Martin lived. Or, as he called them at that point, "my men." The soldiers shared four-man tents, and the fourth was a *furriel* from Gabriel's company named Carlos. That's because that tent was supposed to be for the soldiers of Lieutenant Martinez, who agreed to accommodate the three volunteers commanded by Luis.

They are lucky I met Gabriel. Luis' thoughts contrasted with his doubts about Martinez on the officers' dinner the previous night. When Colonel Tristao laughed at his face, Luis suspected that Gabriel settled the situation to make him a joke. But he couldn't be more wrong, and the encounter provided a unique chance to depart on an expedition to Sao Borja. He only needed one extra horse.

Nopitena, Primo, and Martin were eating pieces of dry bread during their breakfast.

"Good Morning, chief. Served?" Nopitena pointed to a basket with hard bread.

"No, thanks, Anspeçada. I have good news: our wait is finishing. We may depart to the border soon. All we need is an extra horse."

"That is good, chief. We heard rumors about Guaranis crossing Argentina to invade us." Nopitena nodded. Martin also had an excited smile at the lieutenant's message.

Primo was the only one with a serious, frowned expression. "How we will go to the border? I've had enough of riding with this German scarecrow rubbing his bony thighs on me."

Luis stifled a laugh at hearing another insult masked as a nickname that Primo created for poor Martin. Before losing the thread, he addressed Nopitena.

"Anspeçada, do you think Eka is in good condition for.." Luis rolled his eyes, looking for a proper word. "For a race?"

"A race? Eka is well fed and rested boss, but slower after staying in one place for so long."

"What about you?"

"Me what, chief?"

"Are you also out of shape? Can you beat a cavalry officer in the gallop?"

Nopitena squinted. "I don't get it."

And neither did Martin.

"Oh, come on, chaps." Primo smirked. "That is how Louy Lieutenant plans to get a horse. A good old bet."

"Primo, you gossip better than an old widow. Spread to Carlos and to the rest of Gabriel's soldiers a rumor that he is no longer the Ginete because there is an Indian who is a better horse-rider than him." Luis sat on a wooden crate used as a bench during breakfast. "In the afternoon, Martinez will meet his soldiers for drills, so you have three hours to make a fuss about his new rival."

Primo nodded, swallowed the rest of his hard bread, and strolled toward the stable. There, Furriel Carlos was combing Gabriel's horse, and the mulatto distilled the tales about the Kadiweu Indian that became the new *Ginete*—the most skilled horseman in the Rio Pardo camp.

"Nopitena, whoever asks if you're that good at riding, just confirm. But tell that you can only prove it with a horse. No one will agree because almost none of Gabriel's men have their mounts ready yet."

"And then, chief?" Nopitena ate slower, so he still held an entire piece of bread.

"In the evening, Gabriel will return to our tent with his ego hurt. I'll suggest a bet to him. A horse race between you both. If he wins, I give him Nickel. But you will win, Anspeçada, and we get one of his stallions."

Nopitena's jaws dropped. "Chief, are you going to put Nickel at stake? What if I lose?"

Martin, whose despite the slender body, ate more than everyone, froze his movements, letting a piece of half-chewed bread rest in his mouth.

It was unbelievable for them that Luis could risk such a splendid horse as Nickel. Its silvery mane already made an unmistakable pair with the lieutenant's wavy black hair and husky body. Even the animal's balanced temperament complemented the Lieutenant's audacious personality.

"What if you lose? Hum...Then don't lose. It is an order."

Luis walked to the officers' stable and spent the rest of the day riding Nickel. He was well aware of Nopitena's abilities from his years of service at Coimbra and the long journey out of Mato Grosso. The fact, however, that an entire camp, including captains and colonels, called Gabriel as *the Ginete*, meant the Kadiweu had a serious rival.

Alternating gallops and trots, Luis dashed across the grass-covered prairies. Nickel's steel-colored coat gleamed under the radiant sky. The horse seemed to enjoy the ride, accelerating with ease at his owner's commands, not showing any sign of exhaustion. *I think you know that this might be a farewell*, the lieutenant thought.

Nickel, as if reading the thoughts from Luis, nickered.

Dom Caetano once explained to his son that every horseman should pay attention to three sounds in his animal. The first was the neighing, a high-pitched sound made with a closed mouth when the horse demanded something, including the company. The second was the squealing, another high-pitched sound, but made with the mouth close, made by a stallion either when he is in danger or during intercourse. The third was the nickering, a low-pitched sound that came from the animal's guts, indicating satisfaction and joy for the moment. Later on in the afternoon, Luis returned to the stable. At the same time, Nopitena arrived with Eka.

"Went for a ride?"

"Yes, chief. Some exercise to wake up the muscles."

As usual, Luis didn't know if Nopitena was talking about himself or his animal.

The Lieutenant dismounted from Nickel, running his hand over the animal's sweaty face. *Goodbye, my friend.* When Luis turned his back to him, the horse let out a long neigh.

He turned to Eka and stroked the brown fur of the skittish and mighty horse. "Now it depends on you..." Luis said in a smooth tone to the animal, grinning. "No pressure."

He returned to his tent, and just after raising the entrance canvas flap, a figure jumped from a bunk.

"You had told me that an Indian of yours is good at riding, right?" It was the sparkling voice of Gabriel Martinez, contrasting with the tired look of Luis. "At first, I thought it was a joke, but men seem to believe in this delusion."

"Sooner or later, people would recognize the Kadiweu skills." Luis sat on his bunk, and under the dim light of a candle, unlaced his boots.

"Skills? Luis, my dear friend! Maybe the cannon bursts in Coimbra clouded your judgment." He snorted. "The worst is that the soldiers believe in this nonsense."

Gabriel sat on his bunk, pulling off his gleaming boots.

Luis scanned his tent mate. In front of his soldiers, Gabriel always had a flawless presentation, as if every day was a parade. The impeccable look was an attempt to compensate for his soft, inexperienced—and, a woman would

say, even handsome—appearance. Soldiers may not like
flamboyant leaders, but shining boots and sabers help to look
authoritative.

"Why not end the doubts through a race between you
two?" Luis suggested in a trivial tone, "It will be enough to
prove that *El Ginete* lives up to the fame."

"For what? If I prevail, it just confirms what everyone
expects. If by a miracle, I lose, it is his glory. I have nothing
to win in this arrangement."

"Well, I would bet my horse against yours."

"Whoa...Wait...What?" Lieutenant Martinez stood up
and walked in circles, ignoring that he was barefoot on the
dirty floor—something Luis had never seen before. "Are you
saying you would risk your horse on a bet against me?"

"Yes. Don't take it personally."

Gabriel frowned and approached Lieutenant Gomes,
putting a hand over his shoulder. "Are you sober?"

Luis laughed. "Are you in or not, Gabriel?"

"Tomorrow, 08:00, on the Jacuí bank. If the Indian
wins, you take one of my horses. Will you inform him or
prefer me to send a messenger?"

"I will tell him."

Luis jumped up from his bunk and laced his boots. After a brisk walk to the soldier's barracks, he found Nopitena dining with the rest of the men.

"Anspeçada, tomorrow you have a race to win!"

The Indian gritted his teeth and continued to drink his soup.

***

When Luis opened his eyes the next day, Gabriel's bunk was empty. He filled his tin mug with coffee at the officers' mess, saddled Nickel, and left for the stable.

He arrived on time to intercept Nopitena, Martin, and Primo already on their way to the venue. Nopitena's mount, Eka, looked well-rested, unlike Nickel, who had taken a long, perhaps last ride with the lieutenant the day before.

The Kadiweu rode in absolute silence, something that reminded Nopitena's posture during the battle of Coimbra. Luis decided not to bother him with small talk while they went to the race site: the Jacuí riverbank.

More than a hundred soldiers waited for the competition at the place, many of them still eating the breakfast bread. In such a long and tedious camp, any contest became an attraction by itself. But a race with a celebrity rider like Lieutenant Gabriel "The Ginete" Martinez meant a must-see event. A morning show that even high-ranking officers like Colonel Tristao came to watch.

Next to the camp, the north bank of the Jacúi River had a flat corridor of over four hundred meters long by five meters wide. Nature, in its perfection, created the ideal place for a gallop. If not a military camp, it would be the supreme yard for aristocratic kids to exercise their equestrian abilities. On one side, the river, on the other, a gentle slope where the eager audience gathered.

Lieutenant Martinez stood in a dark uniform adorned with golden buttons and boots brilliant as onyx, with a gleam only comparable to his horse's dark coat. His eyes focused on the course, examining every inch of ground. The Ginete didn't accept the challenge as a friendly bet but as a serious competition.

Near Luis and his men, some local girls, likely peasants from neighboring villages, made excited remarks about Gabriel that could make an educated man blush.

Nopitena pulled on the harness, leading Eka to the beginning of the corridor.

"Anspeçada!" Luis shouted before Nopitena rode away.

"Yes, chief?"

"It's not just speed that wins a race. Watch out for Gabriel's strategy. Good luck, Kadiwéu."

Nopitena nodded. "Eka!" the Indian shouted, putting his horse into a trot. On the way, he took off his shirt, attracting the eyes of the crowd by revealing the white tribal tattoos on his upper body, and took a position at the side of Martinez.

Gabriel turned to the rival, scanning the wild-looking native, mounting a stallion that one could swear untamed.

Lieutenant Gabriel opened a wide, friendly smile. "Cheers, Kadiwéu rider!"

"Good Morning, sir." Nopitena, already used to the soldiers' derogatory comments, expected an officer like Martinez to say something at least offensive.

"It is a pleasure to know the soldier Luis talked so much about." The young Lieutenant Martinez offered a handshake, to Nopitena's surprise.
They greeted each other from the back of their horses. Nopitena and Eka on the right, closer to the crowd. Gabriel and his black steed on the left, near the river, and above both the morning sun and clear skies of the pampas.

Three minutes to go.

"He offered a handshake to Nopitena. Looks like a nice fellow this Martinez." Primo commented from the slope.

"Gabriel is a decent person. But this is a mind trick."
Luis said. "An affront from him would motivate Nopitena.
But if he is friendly—"

"Nobody enjoys defeating a friend." Primo completed,
and Luis nodded.

Down on the stripe, Carlos, the furriel from Gabriel's
company, positioned himself in front of the two riders,
holding a pocket watch.

"The course goes until that barrel, just over four
hundred yards from here." Carlos pointed to a metal drum at
the end of the race track. "You must turn around there and
return. The finish line is right where you start."

Luis, from the slope, listened to Carlos' explanation,
which filled him with optimism. He knew that more than
speed, Nopitena excelled in agility. The Indian could turn a
horse in the tightest alleys. That the course had a half lap in
such a narrow space favored the Kadiweu.

Less than a minute to go. Carlos looked at the watch,
and with his right hand, he took a pistol from the holster.

In the audience, at Luis' left side, an illustrious
presence: Colonel Tristao.

"An enjoyable way to get the horse you need,
Lieutenant. Congratulations."

"Thank you, sir, but how do you know this has a horse involved?
"An event of this sort could only mean a wager," the Colonel said.

On the race track, Furriel Carlos yelled. "Silence everyone! Riders, prepare!"

The pistol fired.

Gabriel's powerfully muscled black horse leaped forward, responding promptly to the slap of the boots and stirrups on its haunches. The lieutenant leaned, almost hidden by the animal's flowing mane.

Nopitena and Eka followed close behind.

The two horsemen had similar postures. Although the Kadiwéus had their own riding style, during sprints they adopted the same classic European posture: hips raised, floating over the animal, and backs hunched.

Their gallop raised dust from the dry soil covered by thin grass. Only Gabriel's black horse could be seen, and behind it, a yellowish sand cloud.

"They're at the same pace!" said Luis.

"Geh schneller, Scheißkerl!" Martin shouted, later berating himself in shame for cursing in a language that no one understood.

The riders approached the metal barrel, and the excitement soared. As Gabriel advanced first to make the turn, the crowd saw apprehension on his face. He looked back, just in time to see Nopitena and Eka squeeze into the narrow gap between Martinez's horse and the barrel.

Nopitena made an inside pass, with Eka and Gabriel's black steed almost touching. The Kadiweu's angle was so low that he almost brushed the ground with his knees.

The crowd's mouths were open in apprehension at the extraordinary maneuver they witnessed. A fraction of a second later, at the end of the curve, the Kadiweu darted in the lead.

"Eka, Eka, Eka!" Nopitena shouted wildly with a hoarse voice. He sprinted along the corridor, now closer to the river.

The Kadiweu looked back. Gabriel's mighty horse was not reducing the distance, but instead, the Ginete made a strange maneuver to move away from the river, toward the crowded slope. A sideways move like this cost Gabriel precious yards, and now there was nearly five arms' distance between them.

A sublime feeling flowed inside Nopitena's chest as he left the rival behind. His vision, blurred at the sides, saw only the finish line and the glory of, among all those strangers, a Kadiweu victory against The Ginete. As a stallion releasing his power through a snort, Nopitena yelled loudly to

accelerate the animal "Eka!"
Suddenly, Eka slowed down, and the back of the bronze sorrel trembled. Its legs faltered on the wet ground.

Nopitena was too close to the river. On the first half of the race, as Eka galloped on the dry soil of the opposite side, the Indian never noticed the muddy section of the corridor.

The Indian pulled the horse's harness to make the same maneuver as Gabriel had done seconds before, toward dry land. His eyes widened in despair.

"No! Oh, No No No." The Indian repeated.

Trying to escape from the viscous terrain, the beast turned his head to the owner with watery eyes and desperate neighs. Time slowed down, and all Nopitena could see was the suffering of his friend.

In the audience, interjections echoed, and hands covered astonished lips. After the risky barrel maneuver, many spectators rooted for the brave Indian who dared to challenge the Ginete.

Nopitena, with a herculean effort, brought Eka back to the dry surface just in time to hear hoofs rumbling at his side. The dashing shadow of Gabriel's dark horse passed him to cross the finish line just twenty yards away.

The Indian bent down, hugging his mount's neck. Eka did everything possible. Nobody ever saw a sharp turn as sharp as this one. But Nopitena led him into a muddy trap.

Gabriel dismounted under exultant shouts from his soldiers, while Nopitena remained in his horse after crossing the line, crestfallen, as if blaming himself for letting his friends down—be it human or not.

Martinez and his black stallion, still receiving applause for the victory, approached Nopitena. "What a splendid equestrian you are, soldier." He offered another handshake. "If for any reason Lieutenant Gomes disbands your unit, you have a place in my cavalry squadron."

"Thank you, sir. Congratulations on the victory."

Luis, Martin, and Primo watched the scene silently, each of them bearing part of the Indian's pain. None of them noticed Furriel Carlos arriving from behind, carrying a gelding colt.

"Lieutenant Gomes de Carvalho?"

"Hum? Ah, Furriel Carlos, right?"

"Lieutenant Martinez asked me to hand over this mount to you."

"Furriel, I don't know if you saw it, but we lost."

"I know, and Lieutenant Martinez told me to bring the horse here just after he beats your Indian, not before, so you wouldn't give up on the race."

Luis raised his eyebrows and peered the makeshift racetrack. Gabriel waved to him. He then looked at Tristao. The colonel chuckled, amused.

"Martinez was going to give you the horse anyway. Even more so after your willingness to go to São Borja," the colonel said. "Gabriel is still green, but he considers you a good friend. Besides, he is also a patriot."

"So why did he still wanted to race?"

"Because patriotism is no remedy for wounded pride," replied the Colonel. "Send my greetings to your Indian for the wonderful race. I've never seen anyone galloping so long ahead of Martinez. Now prepare yourself. You and your men will have a long road ahead."

Chapter XXVII

The smuggler Gaspar Picagua sat, resting on the bank of the Uruguay River. His stomach roared in hunger. The opaque whites of his eyes, sunk into the sockets due to thinness and malnutrition, contrasted with his skin reddened by days wandering under the sun.

It had been more than a month since he escaped from Corrientes, after Paraguayan invaders murdered his brother, torched Amarú's warehouse, and kidnapped Arami.

During the first days of his exodus, he went up the Paraná River, sailing at night and sleeping during the day to avoid the enemy's sight. Sail during the night was a treacherous task—a floating log or a hidden sandbank could destroy the barge. But at least the river provided some food.

Things turned to worse when he passed Apipe Island and faced another flotilla of Paraguayan ships blocking the river preparing to invade the Argentine province of Misiones. It was impossible to continue his escape by water. He abandoned his barge on a river beach and started walking.

For days, he crossed the meadows and marshes of the Iberá wetlands, saved from starvation by a group of travelers who accepted to exchange some of the last pieces of leather he carried for corn cobs. An expensive price, but it was that or death. The travelers knew Gaspar needed them more than the opposite, so there was no bargain. At other times, Gaspar did

the same—as when he ripped off the fleeing inhabitants of
Corumba by charging extortionate prices for goods and
transport until the pier. *Destiny is taking its revenge,* he
thought.

After losing count of how many days he wandered,
Gaspar saw a large body of water, almost as large as the
Parana. *The Uruguay River! The Pampas, with fertile fields,
dry land, and food, are on the other side. I just need to go
there.*

The smuggler ran, leaving behind the marshes and
putrid waters from the swamps. He found a tiny pier, where a
fisherman—more like a fisher-boy—prepared his nets and
canoe. The skinny youngster had a shaved head and was
barefoot.

"Boy!" the smuggler shouted.

The youngster, seeing the decrepit figure of the half-
naked vagabond with ripped clothes, took a penknife from his
sack and pointed to Gaspar. "Get out, robber!"

"I am no robber. My name is Gaspar Picagua. I need
your help, and I can pay for it." The smuggler unrolled the last
piece of leather he had, showing it to the fisher-boy. Despite
the long travel, the good was in a fine condition, with its
square, one-arm diameter shape.

"It is not bad, but if you want my canoe, you will need
to pay more than that."

"I don't want it. I just need you to take me to the other side of the river."

"You only want me to take you to the other side, and you will give me that, right?" The boy pointed to the leather roll.

Gaspar confirmed.

"I could use this leather for new shoes," the fisher-boy said. "Come, let's go."

After arriving at the opposite margin, Gaspar handled the rolled leather to the canoeist. "What is your name?"

"Nicolas, but everyone calls me Pelado, although I think on this side of the river this means another thing."

In Argentina, *Pelado* meant bald, but Gaspar did not know what the word meant in Brazil.

"Why did you shave your head so young?"

"Lice. It is common here. Everyone with hair will have it sooner or later. So I decided to not have any hair anymore." The boy reached for his sack and took out a shiny piece of metal. "I have an extra blade, just in case. Take it."

Gaspar accepted the gift, thanked Nicolas, and left to the shore.

The Correntine peddler made his first steps on Brazilian soil, far from the Paraguayans who would kill him for betraying the *Guarani nation*, as they did with Amarú. As they also did with his brother on a Good Friday.

Safe from bullets and bayonets, hunger became the next deadly threat on his path. The Pampa was a legendary land for cattle grazing and crops. But far from farms, the game was scarce. He needed to find a ranch, settlement, or homestead and pray that kind owners would share their food in exchange for his work.

Gaspar, however, was no Friar Pedro. Praying was not among the things he used to do. So he walked along the banks until he saw smoke on the horizon. Either it was a fire or a bonfire.

If it was the first, perhaps the flames would spare him from suffering a slow, hungry death. If it was the latter, it meant people cooking. Either way, he would benefit from it.

Dragging his feet and clearing the throat, he scratched his battered eyes that insisted on blurring his vision. His only companion was the pain from his burned skin and the wounds opened by thorns from the swamps. Gaspar attracted a swarm of flies, whose buzz no longer bothered him.

Less than two hundred steps from the smoke, his eyes watered with what he saw, and a tear leaked from his dry eyes, streaking the grimy cheek of the Correntino.

It was a clothesline with meat hanging, smoked by burning wood on the floor.

The Indian ran toward the treat, tripping twice in the short bushes that separated him from salvation. Like a savage moved by instinct, Gaspar saw nothing, heard nothing.

He reached for the meat, threw his filthy hands on a piece of sausage, and devoured it. The need to satiate his hunger put him in a trancelike state. He was no longer a merchant, smuggler, or the brother of a late priest.

He was an animal. An animal with grease and dirt and blood smeared on its face.

A dull, short-sighted beast that couldn't notice a group of approaching men.

"Enjoying the meat? It's your last meal, putrid Indian," were the last words the decrepit vagrant heard before blacking out.

A carbine butt hit his scruff. Everything turned black.

Moments later, the Correntino woke up trapped in a tree, leaning against the trunk. Close to him, two barefoot soldiers in blue uniforms talked.

"Must be a spy. He looks like a Guarani," said the shorter of the two men while standing with his back to the prisoner.

"If the Paraguayan spies are in these conditions, I'm more afraid of their illnesses than of their weapons." The second soldier had a gun hanging from his shoulder while he chopped tobacco with a knife.

Gaspar tried to say something, but he had little strength. His effort, however, caught the attention of the second soldier.

"Look, the Indian woke up."

The soldier spoke in Portuguese, reminding Gaspar that he was in Brazil. He tried to babble something. Drool fell from his mouth, as he had no vigor to control his jaws.

"Corren...Corren..."

The smaller soldier kicked him in the ribs. "Want to get unchained, Scoundrel? The Paraguayan scums didn't even teach Portuguese to their spies. First, tell us who you are."

"What a useless piece of man. What are we supposed to do with him?" the guard slicing tobacco said with a contemptuous tone.

"No idea. I sent Jânio to tell the Captain we caught a strange vagrant, looking like an Indian." He snorted. "Maybe we will lash him for stealing food, but in this state there, I don't know if he can stand it."

Gaspar tried to move his head, hurting from the heat, thirst, and blows.

A galloping noise resounded on his right, and another man approached the two guards.

"Take the spy to jail. Give him some water, and later we interrogate him," the horseman said. The two soldiers untied Gaspar from the tree. Using the same ropes, they dragged the Indian to a cage a ten-minute walk from there.

Chapter XXVIII

Joana worked in the anteroom of a large apartment in the Hotel de Lax Paix, where the Brazilian diplomatic mission established its office. As the minister's secretary, she ensured no conflicts in the busy schedule of Otaviano.

"Allow only the Vice-Admiral to enter my office today. When he arrives, you come together with him to take notes." These were the orders of her boss that morning.

An hour later, someone knocked on the door. It was an elegantly uniformed navy officer, similar to Tamandaré in age and rank, as signaled by his shoulder's insignia. Instead of a bald head like the Admiral, he had white, thin hair and a leaner face. His expression was friendlier too, something eccentric for high-level navy officers.

"Good morning, Miss. The minister is waiting for me." His accent revealed European origins.

"My apologies, sir. The minister informed me he is waiting only for the Admiral today."

"Admiral or Vice Admiral?" replied the uniformed gentleman, with no irritation or haste. Instead, Joana's refusal to let him enter amused him.

Admiral or Vice Admiral? What does this question mean? Oh, I remember now! Joana recalled Otaviano's orders: he, in fact, waits for a *Vice-Admiral*. She backed off, realizing her mistake.

"Are you the Vice—"

"Vice-Admiral Barroso. How can I call you, miss?"

Joana gave a nervous smile, although the guest didn't show any irritation with the now obvious confusion. "Joana Augusta, mister Vice-Admiral."

"Augusta, that is a lovely second-name! Is your father also keen on Roman history?"

"My father does like history, especially military tales." Joana stood up. If she allowed herself to be distracted by the friendly officer's small talk, he would be late for the meeting. "Please accompany me, the minister is waiting for you."

Barroso came in, and Otaviano stood up to greet him.

"Mr. Minister, what a pleasure!" The Vice-Admiral shook Otaviano's hand. "See, I was talking to your secretary, Miss Augusta, secretary to Minister Otaviano. If we put both names together, we have an emperor in the room! How splendid!"

"It's a pleasure to see you too, Mr. Vice Admiral." Otaviano grinned.

Joana sat on the side sofa to take notes. Otaviano and Barroso occupied the central chairs of the room. As in the other parts of the Hotel de La Paix, the mahogany wooden scent dominated the space. Otaviano, however, preferred to leave the windows open, and a chilly wind came from the outside, carrying the odor of horse manure. The smell couldn't be different since Buenos Aires was a large city, full of elegant carriages and merchant wagons.

"And how are things in these parts, Otaviano?"

"The war is profitable for Buenos Aires, mister Barroso. But upstream, the Paraguayans devastated all the resistance. They already took Corrientes, invaded Misiones, and are heading to our southern borders."

"My Good Lord..." The Vice-Admiral stiffened his back in the chair, rubbing the left hand over his wrinkled forehead.

"General Paunero recovered Corrientes for a while, but he had to withdraw because of the enemy's enormous numerical advantage."

"But Viana Filho told us that...that—" Barroso spluttered.

"Viana Filho underestimated the Paraguayans at least three times, sir." Otaviano adjusted his glasses.

The minister's words caused a momentaneous silence, allowing Joana to interrupt her note-taking and think for a second on the whereabouts of her brother, Luis. If the Paraguayans had already invaded Misiones with such a powerful force, they would reach the Rio Grande do Sul in weeks. Her younger brother again would face an overwhelming force.

"That is the reason for this meeting, Mr. Vice Admiral." Otaviano resumed the conversation. "President Mitre, knowing about Paunero's defeat, requested the Brazilian Navy to come to his rescue in Corrientes."

"What Tamandaré thinks about it?"

"He is well aware of it. But we must remember that the commander of the alliance between Brazil, Argentina, and Uruguay is not Tamandaré but President Mitre."

Barroso nodded. Besides being a trusted vice-admiral for Tamandaré, he was also his friend since they were just lieutenants. Unlike Tamandaré, however, Barroso didn't have so many reserves with the Argentinians.

"To which port should I take our squadron?"

Otaviano stood up from his armchair and walked toward a gigantic map of the Platine region hanging on the room's left wall. With his right index finger, he pointed to a spot.

"Corrientes. Our navy needs to reach the surroundings of the Riachuelo stream."

Chapter XIX

The four horsemen neared their destination at the Brazilian border. The sand-colored gelding colt Gabriel gifted Luis was given to Martin. A gentle animal and in good shape, as every horse trained and tamed by the *Ginete*.

Still, the German suffered. He was not used to mounting for so long. It took twelve days to travel across the Pampas, from Rio Pardo to São Borja, including a day to rest the animals—and the riders.

The bony immigrant panted after an entire day trying to adjust his legs on the saddle during the jagged road. They cooled off by swimming in a stream before entering the camp to take away the stench of so many traveling days. When Martin lowered his underwear to jump into the water, Luis and Nopitena noticed that the boy's inner thighs had crimson red bruises.

"His skin is too thin to ride that long. I am sure it is burning." Luis said to Nopitena while they bathed in the river. The lieutenant's hair grew to the point of almost reaching his shoulders.

"If it is burning, he is hiding well. I don't remember a single complaint from his mouth." said the Indian "a good motive builds the courage in our chest to endure physical pain."

"Courage in the chest? I think you mean heart," Luis grinned, suspecting that Nopitena confused the Portuguese words.

"*Aalegena*. In Kadiwéu, the two things are the same, chief."

"Makes sense." Luis pondered about the motives that moved his men. Martin and Nopitena were there for their own reasons. The first, for the memory of his father. The second, to get revenge on the Guaranis who destroyed his village and enslaved his people.

And me? What am I doing here besides seeking a higher rank and an easier life? Luis asked himself. He shook off his lethargy and returned to reality. It brings no good to doubt his own motives while leading men against a more prepared and numerous enemy.

He took a dip and left the water, walking in his bowlegged swagger.

After another half a day, they arrived at the road fork pointing to the camp, two leagues from São Borja. The first tents were visible, and the quartet rode toward one of them. A group of recruits, maybe younger than Martin and looking too inexperienced to be called soldiers, played cards and chatted.

Without getting down from his horse, Luis greeted them, asking where the officers' tents were.

"It is dispersed around. That one belongs to Captain Teixeira," one of them said.

"Dispersed around?" Luis frowned. The camp seemed to accommodate fewer than a thousand soldiers and did so in such a disorganized way that it looked amateurish.

Luis rode to the tent the recruits pointed.

In front of it, two men, one with a captain's insignia and the other of a lieutenant, were drinking coffee. Surely not southern officers, he thought. There was no better way to guess if someone was from the south or not than the sight of them drinking coffee or mate.

"Sir Captain Teixeira?" Luis got off his horse, while Martin, Nopitena and Primo waited a few yards from there.

"Yes? I don't remember seeing you around here. Are you part of the reinforcements?" Teixeira asked. Like most officers, he had his chin covered by a thick beard—in his case, with the same nutmeg color as his hair and mustache. He wore a wrinkled and unkempt uniform and clearly had no haircut for at least several weeks.

"No, sir. We are an expedition from Rio Pardo camp. I have a message to the colonel of the 1st Volunteer Corps."

"Understood. The Colonel left on a reconnaissance mission. He returns tomorrow before noon. But you can pass me the message, and I'll deliver it."

Luis Caetano raised his eyebrows. Reconnaissance missions were tiresome and risky. Officers sent for these tasks were often the greenest lieutenants or, at most, captains. But a colonel?

The lack of words caused a momentaneous silence, and Luis decided to not inquire why a high-ranking official ran such a puny errand. Instead, he delivered the message.

"Colonel Tristão sent me to tell that Caldwell's men will remain in Rio Pardo, but if the garrison of Sao Borja needs, they can send reinforcements."

"If we need?" The captain stood up, leaving behind the other lieutenant with whom he had breakfast, and walked toward Luis, his nostrils flared with each angry breath. With an abrupt movement, he pointed his finger and entire arm to the west. "There...There are over five, maybe even ten thousand Paraguayans on the other side of the river, under the command of Estigarribia. And how many are we? Less than a thousand, almost all green recruits. Only youngsters!"

Luis looked to the west, but the terrain didn't allow him to see the river. The captain's pale face and lips twitching in nervousness asked for a miracle.

"Sir, if you prefer, I can send one of my horsemen to plead reinforcements to General Caldwell." Luis tried to find a solution. "Perhaps knowing the gravity, they send a good number of men."

Teixeira fell silent, pacing back and forth on the dry, beaten soil of the São Borja camp. Luis, anticipating the captain's decision to send a messenger to Rio Pardo, shouted, "Nopitena! Come here!"

"No," the captain said, "we will not send a messenger today. Our colonel returns tomorrow morning, and perhaps he wants to send other requests to Rio Pardo. We wait."

"Yes, sir. I am also here to join your ranks, so which unit can I get in?"

"What is your experience, Lieutenant..." Teixeira's eyes scanned Luis's uniform, trying to find a tag with his name, but there was none.

"Gomes de Carvalho. 2nd Lieutenant Luis Caetano Gomes de Carvalho, former artillery officer at the Coimbra fort."

"Coimbra? Were you there?"

"Yes, sir."

"Bloody hell...It is a miracle how they could resist for so long. How many of our soldiers were there? Five or six hundred?"

"One hundred fifty-five men, sir," Luis recalled the truce caused by the image of Our Lady and beamed. "Indeed, it was a miracle."

"One hundred fifty-five men who held thousands of Paraguayans for days, and one of them is right here!" Teixeira's face muscles relaxed, and he patted Luis' shoulder. "Finally, they sent us an experienced officer!"

The officer that had breakfast with Teixeira before Luis's arrival made a disgusted expression. He had light-brown skin and a thin face with no beard but a large, dark mustache and a half-bald head. From all his characteristics, the most unnerving were his eyes, resting deep in their sockets, so that the shadow of his brow gave him a grim expression. One could even say that he was jealous because the captain overjoyed receiving a battle-tested officer like Luis.

"Unfortunately, Lieutenant Gomes de Carvalho, we already have an artillery officer. Lieutenant Peixoto, over there." Captain Teixeira pointed to the half-bald lieutenant, still sitting at the breakfast table. "But of course there is a place for a veteran from Coimbra. You and your men can join the 3rd Cavalry Company, under my command. Barracks are at the end of the row."

Luis nodded and extended his hand to greet the other Lieutenant, who hadn't said a word so far. "A pleasure to meet a brother-in-arms from artillery."

"It's my pleasure." The dark complexed man stood and greeted back.

"Peixoto, right? I had never heard such a name before. Where are you from?"

"I am from Alagoas. Peixoto is a surname. My name is Floriano."

***

At dawn, a soldier woke up Gaspar with a vigorous kick in his groin. The Guarani's legs hit the wall with the impact, and he groaned.

"Get up, vermin. The captain wants to talk to you."

The Correntine did not sleep well in the filthy cage. But at least the guards gave him water and hard bread, so he regained strength enough to stand up.

Until the day before, the smuggler was a rag, starving for days and convinced that the price to fill his stomach was the refusal of his own dignity. A dignity that vanished when he stole food and ended up in jail.

The guards took Gaspar to a tent, with a bunk at one side and a desk at the other. Behind the desk, an officer with short hair and a pair of glasses was writing numbers and letters on a notebook. The guards clicked their boots, announcing their arrival.

The officer raised his eyes. The stench coming from the squalid prisoner disgraced the entire room, forcing him to cover his nose.

"Mister...what name can I call you?" the officer asked, holding his hand over the nose.

"Gaspar, Gaspar Picagua," said the crestfallen smuggler.

"Mr. Gaspar, I am Captain Raimundo. The men told me you were stealing food and spying."

"I'm not a spy, captain. But it is true that I stole food."

"That was the answer I would expect from a spy, Gaspar." The captain smirked.

The Correntine opened his eyes and looked into the captain's face. Any wrong word at that moment could cost him his life. *What can I say? What can I...* The blows, the wounds, the long journey fleeing death, everything clouded his mind.

Gaspar said nothing.

"Picagua...This is a Guarani surname."

Of course it is! Gaspar wanted to explain that he was a Guarani, but not all Guaranis were Paraguayans. But were the Correntines on good terms with the Brazilians? Or were they enemies too?

"I'm a Correntino, Captain."

"Are you Urquiza's spy then?"

But what a disgrace! No matter what I say, they want to cut my throat. The smuggler grew desperate. Urquiza, the caudillo of Corrientes, had many enemies in the region. Gaspar decided that if he was going to die, it would be telling the truth, as his brother once advised him.

"I'm just a smuggler who sells goods along the Paraguay River."

"A smuggler from the Paraguay River that ended up so far away? As if every other day we didn't catch an Estigarribia's spy around here." The captain took a watch from his coat pocket, looked at it, and turned around to leave the room.

"Give him the lashes for food theft," Captain Raimundo told the two guards, "then interrogate about Estigarribia's numbers. If he refuses to cooperate, put him with the other spies." The captain closed the makeshift courtroom.

One man turned to Gaspar, and grimacing, he made a gesture passing his index finger across his throat. The other dragged the handcuffed prisoner toward a tree.

Minutes later, a mulatto servant recounted bland stories to Gaspar while tying him to the trunk. *Perhaps a slave, happy to see someone else suffer greater misfortune*, he thought. Once he was tied, a soldier with bulging eyes and a shrieking voice came with a lash, prepared to bleed Picagua's back with whipping blows.

Chapter XXX

An illustrious figure returned to the camp that morning. As he walked around the tents on his way to breakfast, rumbles and cheers from the eight hundred soldiers echoed.

The colonel was back.

He returned from a mission to investigate rumors of Paraguayan soldiers near São Tome, the Argentinian city on the opposite bank of the Uruguay River. Everything they found, however, was half a dozen merchants. One of them revealed that Estigarribia, the Paraguayan general sent by Solano Lopez to invade the Brazilian south, had over ten thousand men. Still, they were not ready to cross the river. Yet.

On the Brazilian side, the disorganized band of inexperienced soldiers and brats that called themselves *Volunteers of the Fatherland* curbed the optimism Luis once had. Upon hearing that a horde of Paraguayans crossed Argentina, bringing destruction and death, the Brazilians shouted: *Let them come! With Colonel João leading, each of us is worth five of them!*

They lacked a sense of reality, as if an entity beyond human reason seeded on those young souls the bravery of Ulysses with the irresponsibility of Icarus.

That alarmed Luis. After Coimbra, he knew what happened when an overwhelming number of soldiers advanced with far superior forces over daring young fighters. The result was scenes of indescribable suffering but also the cradle of heroic stories.

He gazed around for a few seconds trying to find the colonel, then left to have breakfast with his men—a decision that confused the other officers since every lieutenant wanted to eat with the camp's commanding officer.

Close to the soldier's tents, recruits sat around Martin and Nopitena, asking the Kadiwéu to tell them stories from the Coimbra siege. Even in such a distant place, the tales from the fort's resistance became part of the soldiery folklore.

"Anspeçada, Martin. Good morning. Where is Primo?"

"Someone asked him to help with prisoners, chief." The Kadiweu, although sitting nearby a bonfire, still used a long jacket that covered his tattoos and protected him from the chilly winds that were unusual for his body. Nopitena pointed to the west. "He went in that direction."

"I wonder what he will ask in return," Luis smirked. He sat, joining the chatting circle. Over the fire, a pot hung from a rope suspended by two twigs. Boiled water for the soldiers' mate.

A recruit no more than eighteen years old turned to the Lieutenant.

"Were you also in Mato Grosso?"

Luis wrinkled his forehead at the soldier's question. "Nopitena, didn't you tell them about me?"

"I told, chief." The Kadiweu turned to the recruits of the circle and, pointing his left hand to Luis, said, "men, here is Lieutenant Gomes."

All faces turned to the Lieutenant. The pot on the fire whistled, steam coming out of it. While they filled their mate gourds, questions poured in about Coimbra, Miranda, Dourados...For a moment, Luis felt like a celebrity. In his mind, however, a voice told him to not portray war as pure glory. *Otherwise, these boys will rush to their deaths.*

What battles were made of? Gunpowder smoke blinding the eyesight, the smell of feces invading noses, and feet sinking into a sludge of urine, gore, and blood. Sensations that Luis recalled from Coimbra. It would be cruel to deceive those young fellows into thinking that war was much better than that.

Several minutes passed before Captain Teixeira's aide-de-camp informed the Lieutenant about an officer's meeting at the colonel's tent.

The last days of May brought the first nuances of southern cold. At the meeting tent, the steaming coffee from the Lieutenant's mug denounced his roots from São Paulo, differently to the officers from Rio Grande do Sul who were drinking mate. Apart from Luís, the only non-southerner was Lieutenant Floriano Peixoto.

Inside the tent, Teixeira and another unknown captain stood behind a table covered by a map. Between the two, an officer around his forties, in a neat uniform with a colonel insignia. He had neatly combed hair from front to back, beard trimmed, and no sideburns. He looked more like a European nobleman than a soldier, reminding Luis of his friend from the Rio Pardo camp, Gabriel Martinez.

The colonel took the center of the tent. His steps were smooth as a jaguar. His dark brown eyes wandered over the presents like the warm breeze of late summer. There was a flame in his spirit, as if he occupied every space in the room at once.

He started to talk. The firm but lilting tone of his voice sounded like someone who could say elephants fly, and yet every man would believe it. Yes, he looked like a nobleman more than a common officer.

The colonel described what he had seen on his reconnaissance mission: nothing but more rumors about the many enemy soldiers of Estigarribia approaching from Argentina. But so far, no sign of them crossing the river to invade Brazil.

The firmness of his speech and his assuring words brought to light generations of military training and discipline—someone that was a commander before even leaving the womb.

Word after word, it became clear to Luis why so many volunteers would be glad to face an enemy wave under that man's leadership.

"At last, gentleman, we need to send an emissary to Corrientes, to link with the Allied fleet and inform the Argentinians about the land invasion from Estigarribia's soldiers." The colonel's eyes passed through Luis, fixing on him as if trying to remember if they ever met. Then he continued, "If we succeed in that, our ships will cut their reinforcement and supply lines. Questions?"

Seconds of silence followed the speech until one lieutenant raised his hand.

"How are we going to send an emissary to Corrientes if the Paraguayans are in the middle of the way between here and there?"

"By dodging them through the swamps of Iberá. All of you, ask your men if anyone knows that damned terrain."

"Sir, crossing the Iberá is perhaps even more dangerous than crossing the Paraguayan camp," said Captain Teixeira, a local with vast knowledge of the neighboring terrains. "The soldier who volunteers to do this is either suicidal, or he's not right in his head."

"It's time to find the freaks among us then." The colonel grinned. "Gentleman, I never said it was easy. We need a communication channel with the Navy in Corrientes, even though the Paraguayans are in the way."

"We also have a messenger from Caldwell, sir." Captain Teixeira gave Luis a gentle shove on the back, pushing him to greet the Colonel and give the message.

"Sir, I came under the orders of Colonel Tristao, himself under the command of General Caldwell in Rio Pardo, to inform that they are waiting for weapons and artillery from General Canabarro." Luis began to deliver the message with an open chest and in a firm tone. "Therefore, you should not expect them during the coming weeks." Many lips twitched and brows furrowed among the officers. The colonel, however, only asked him to continue.

"So my task is to ask if the 1st Volunteer Corps under your command, sir colonel, needs immediate reinforcement. If that is the case, they can send a detachment." After his last word, Luis exhaled, and his shoulders sagged, relaxed after delivering the message.

"In case we need it...aha." The Colonel smirked, shaking his head to left and right as if Luis' message bordered absurdity. "Lieutenant, please send an emissary to Rio Pardo informing that we gladly accept the reinforcement offered, because in a given horse you don't look at the teeth."

The colonel's good-humored words caused giggles among the present, easing the atmosphere.

"Anything else?"

Captain Raimundo raised his arm. "Sir, today we will execute a spy. I believe you have no objection to having it done publicly, right?"

"Are you sure he is a spy?" the colonel asked with his eyebrow raised.

Raimundo hesitated for a moment but confirmed.

"So be it."

***

"It is enough." The sergeant told his soldier, who stopped lashing the prisoner's back.
He waited until the condemned wretch recovered his consciousness and walked in his direction.

"You still have a chance to confess what Estigarribia is planning on the other side of the river, Guarani."

"But I don't know!" Gaspar, still tied to the trunk, replied. His back dripped blood after the scourge. The whipping was the punishment for stealing supplies. For espionage, the penalty was death.

"Bastard! Crook!" The sergeant shouted, kicking the smuggler's legs. Under the mild blue sky, over fifty soldiers watched, entertained by the thief's torture.

"Get this bum out of his misery!" yelled one spectator. "Put a bullet in the slacker's head! It's not worth a sword strike!" shouted another.

The blue-uniformed sarge took two steps back.

"You really aren't worth a sword slash. I leave mine to your *Mariscal Solanito* and to his Irish whore," the sergeant said. "Corporal Alvarado, bring my pistol!"

In the middle of the crowd, a mulatto attended the spectacle while eating a cooked corn ear. From his right side, two men approached, an officer and an Indian.

"Primo, what's so interesting here?"

"A little show, Louy. They're going to kill that Paraguayan spy over there." Primo pointed the corn ear toward the wooden trunk and the chained man. "I helped to tie him in exchange for an extra blanket from a soldier with an indisposed gut."

"Every day someone gets diarrhea from drinking this filthy wa..." Luis squinted his eyes, focusing the sight on the tied man. "Wait... Nopitena, isn't that man—"

"The smuggler who sold cachaça in Coimbra? He looks like him, chief."

Near the wooden trunk, a corporal handed a pistol to the sergeant.

"Primo, why are they going to kill that guy?"

"Because he is a Paraguayan spy. Why else?"

"Paraguayan?" Luis said in an inquiring tone. "He's a Correntino!"

"Well, I guess the sergeant over there doesn't know that." Primo shrugged.

Meters away from the prisoner, the sergeant loaded two bullets into the pistol.

Luis pushed Primo aside and, forcing passage among the crowd, went toward the trunk.

The sergeant raised his arm, pointing the gun at Gaspar.

"Say your last words, Guarani, because now it's too late to confess," the Sargeant said, aiming the gun at the prisoner's scruff.

"Oh, screw you!" replied Gaspar. "At least I join my brother, that is if I'm going to the same place as him."

"Sergeant, stop!" Luis shouted to the executioner, who was already cocking the pistol.

"What do you want, soldier..." the sergeant turned his head to the voice and realized it was from a lieutenant. "Sorry, sir. Do you want the pleasure of executing the spy in my place?"

"He's not a spy!"

The Sergeant put a puzzled expression. "Sorry, sir, but he is a Guarani."

"Correntine Guarani," Luis told the sergeant, then unsheathed his saber, and with a slash, cut the rope binding Gaspar. "As far as I know, the Correntines are not our enemies."

"Sir, this man was convicted and his execution allowed by the colonel." The sergeant still held the pistol.

"I know that. The colonel never spoke to the prisoner, and Captain Raimundo judged him wrong." Luis offered his hand so Gaspar could stand up. "Sergeant, put that pistol back to the holster before I think you're aiming at an officer."

"The Colonel will know about this," the sergeant stared at Luis.

"He certainly will. I'm going to him now."

Luis, along with Martin, helped Gaspar walk to the colonel's tent. Nopitena stayed behind. Although Gaspar was not Paraguayan, he was still a Guarani, like those who enslaved the Kadiwéus for decades.

"Thank you. I forgive the 200 reis for the last bottle that you never paid," Gaspar said to Louis with a wry smile. "We are even now."

"Even? No...you owe me now." Luis replied, still not knowing if his action would have any greater consequences. After all, the Lieutenant was also a newcomer to São Borja, and with that gesture, he gained some enemies.

Primo approached Luis, Gaspar, and Nopitena. The Correntine, seeing the mulatto who tied him to the whipping pole, gyrated and tried to utter some insult.

"Calm down." Primo snorted. "I just did that for an extra blanket."

Gaspar spat at Primo but missed the target.

"Soldier, I'm coming to talk to the Colonel," Luis told the guard in front of the headquarter's tent.

"The colonel is in a meeting."

Seconds later, the camp's quartermaster arrived, and the guard allowed his entrance right in front of Luis.

The lieutenant sneered. "Soldier, what I must tell him is more important than deciding about boots or uniforms."

"I just follow orders."

The tent flaps opened again, and a familiar face emerged. Captain Teixeira.

"Lieutenant Gomes? What is happening? And who is this?" The captain wrinkled his nose at the nauseating reek of the prisoner.

"I need to talk to the Colonel, sir. I believe we solved the problem discussed this morning."

"Oh...right, come in."

Luis told his men to wait outside and led Gaspar into the headquarter.

Inside the canvas pavilion, the map table and half a dozen wooden crates used as benches occupied the center. On the left corner was the desk used by the commanding officer for dispatches, some shelves, and an entrance to the private quarters. In the right corner, the colonel was lighting a pipe.

"Sir, with your permission?"

"Yes, Lieutenant." The colonel turned his head, looking at Luis and the prisoner. "Who is this ragged fellow?"

"The prisoner from this morning's execution."

"I'm still not on the terms of seeing ghosts, so I think we have called the execution off. Did he confess?"

"I'm innoce..." Gaspar muttered something, but Luis shoved him to stay quiet.

"He's a Guarani from Corrientes, sir. They thought he was a Paraguayan Guarani."

"The Correntinos are not our enemies." The colonel puffed on his pipe and looked at the bloodied prisoner. "But I am sure we didn't lash him for nothing. What was the reason?"

"Caught stealing food."

The colonel smirked. Stealing supplies was reason enough for a scourge but not execution.

"I see he has already paid for the crime." The Colonel turned his back, looking for the shelves. "Where did I leave my Chimarrão?"

Chimarrão was another name the southerners used for the yerba mate infusion. It became apparent that the brief meeting was concluded.

Luis, however, remained in the tent.

"Sir, he can be of use to us." The Lieutenant regained the colonel's attention. "During the time I served in Coimbra, this man smuggled goods from Corrientes to the fort. He is well acquainted with the region's rivers and terrain."

"Did you say Corrientes?" The Colonel got up and walked closer to the crestfallen Gaspar, all disheveled by the lashes and kicks. The prisoner's stench stung his nose. "You came from far away. How did you get here?"

"I sailed through the Paraná River until Apipé and then crossed the outskirts of the Iberá swamps."

An enormous grin dominated the colonel's bearded face. "Do you think you could make the way back?"

The idea of repeating the terrible journey that brought him there made Gaspar clench his teeth, close his eyes and take a deep breath. But he had no choice. Either he made himself useful, or he would be let to the flies.

"Yes, sir."

The colonel nodded and turned to Luis, tapping firmly on his shoulder. "Congratulations, Lieutenant Gomes. You pulled over the first madman we needed to link with the Navy in Corrientes. We must celebrate that with a chimarrão, but first, I need to find my gourd."

To add surprise, the noble-like high-ranking officer offered a handshake to the smuggler, who reeked like a beast. "What's your name?"

"Gaspar, sir, Gaspar Picagua. And you?"

Luis raised his eyebrows at the smuggler's audacity. Minutes before, he was a prisoner sentenced to death, but now asked for the colonel's name, who for his part did not take offense, kept the informal posture, and shook Gaspar's hand.

Perhaps that was why so many recruits there had for the Colonel the admiration reserved only for archetypes of military virtue. A leader whose aristocratic appearance hid the bravery and simplicity of the most heroic soldiers.

"From now on, you are Private Picagua. Welcome to the 1st Corps of the Fatherland Volunteers, fighting for His Majesty and the Brazilian Empire under my command, Colonel João Manuel Mena Barreto."

Chapter XXXI

Overlooking the bay of Asuncion, the striking neoclassical palace gleamed in its ivory color. Guarded by two stone lions, the entrance door led to a large hall adorned with mirrors and bronze ornaments. In the center, a luxurious marble staircase, designed and built by the Italian architect Andrés Antonini. He traveled all the way from Europe only for this purpose.

The stairs led to several rooms, but none of them was more breath-taking than the presidential chamber.

Parisian furniture, statues, and paintings of English and Italian artists, windows and doors made from the finest woods of Ñeembucú.

The palace, however, was still unfinished, lacking mere details. Inspecting the work, a well-fed man strolled through the vast mansion where he planned to live. He had a sparse beard and wore a blue-green uniform, with scarlet lapels and golden epaulettes like those used by field-marshalls.

The sound of steps echoed from the entrance, disturbing his contemplation. An officer with the insignia of captain approached and, clicking his boots, saluted. "Good morning, *Mariscal*!"

"Meza, any news from Barrios and Resquin in Mato Grosso?" the palace-owner said.

"Absolute success, sir. We took all the Brazilian garrisons from the border until Coxim," said Captain Pedro Meza. He just returned to the capital after months leading the Paraguayan steamships during the invasion.

"Excellent. Barrios again proved his worth. I was right to choose this man as a husband for Inocência."

"Yes, sir, wonderful choice of brother-in-law," replied the captain.

"Now Meza, we both will travel to Humaitá with the entire fleet."

Captain Meza widened his eyes. "The entire fleet, sir? Maybe we can sail only with the Tacuari, using the Salto Oriental and the Jejuy as escort ships."
The Marshall closed his eyes for a second, his veins pulsing. He then took a deep breath, and said, in a paced tone. "The Tacuari, the Salto Oriental, the Jejuy, the Yporá, the Paraguarí, the Ygurey, the Jejuí, the Yporá, the Paraná, even the Rio Blanco. I want the entire fleet moving."

"I will carry out orders immediately, sir," Meza said, calming the explosive Marshall. "What are the plans for Corrientes?"

Before the Marshall could respond, a woman entered the room. The only human being that didn't need to apologize for interrupting. Her rosy cheekbones, cotton-colored skin, and red hair—waving with each voluptuous movement from her legs—looked like an authentic version of Botticelli's Venus. A figure that contrasted with the two men in the room in the same way as a fairy tale queen contrast with dragons. To the Marshal, she was no less than a queen. One that he brought from another faraway world.

"Mi amor, Juanito is sick," she said.

The Marshal lost his sense of time every time he gazed at her ember hair. His eyes lit up, no matter what news she brought. He embraced the woman, kissing her forehead.

"I will send my best doctors to take care of the boy. Please tell my sister that her husband was victorious in Mato Grosso. I'll promote him to general."

"Vicente Barrios never disappoints us! *Gracias, mi Mariscal.*" the woman kissed the Marshal's cheek and greeted Captain Meza before leaving the gigantic hall.

"Where were we, Meza?" said the Marshal, regaining his sobriety.

"Sir, you said that we were going to sail to Humaitá. But what do we want there? The Fortress can stop the Brazilians."

"What do we want? What I want, Captain, is the Brazilian Navy."

Historical Notes

It is common in history that men underestimate the long-lasting, deadly power of war. There is a name for this kind of self-deception: the short-war illusion. It is a term used to describe the optimistic hopes of British and German soldiers before World War I. They expected to return home in a matter of weeks, but it took four years.

The same took effect with the Brazilians in the war against Paraguay.

One could think that a smaller nation like Paraguay could offer no threat to such a huge country. That was indeed the view of many Brazilian politicians and military leaders at the start of the conflict.

Paraguay, however, prepared for this advance for years. By 1860, four years before the war, they had 77000 permanent soldiers, while Brazil had 18320 men, Argentina gathered 6000, and Uruguay 3163.

With these numbers, Solano Lopez had three times more men than the triple alliance combined. Besides, he also counted with strong fortifications designed by European and Brazilian engineers and an uncharted territory with splendid defensive advantages.

Through the Prata River, Solano imported modern guns with rifled barrels and conical bullets. Only in November

1864 alone, Paraguay received from England 106 crates with rifles and bullets. He also hired British doctors and engineers to help in the war effort. To reinforce his navy, he ordered four ironclads to European shipyards.

In December 1864, the young empire was still recovering from internal revolts and a large continental conflict when Solano's massive army invaded it on two fronts. The first move was the invasion of Mato Grosso by a vast force of almost four thousand soldiers divided into two columns.

Over three thousand Paraguayans besieged the Coimbra fort and the 115 soldiers inside it. The great numerical superiority intended to destroy the Brazilian morale, force surrender, and wipe out any resistance.

But Coimbra resisted, in an effort akin to the most heroic struggles - equal to the Spartans in Thermopylae or to the Poles in Westerplatte. Like for the Spartans and the Poles, victory was not the outcome, but the heroes of Coimbra delayed the enemy and gave time for civilians to escape.

But unlike Leonidas and his hoplites, the defenders of Coimbra fell into oblivion. Men like Hermenegildo Portocarrero, Benedito de Faria, Lieutenants Simas, Balduino, and Melo "Bravo", as well as civilians like lady Ludovina and the musician Verdeixas, were actual people that deserve recognition.

Many other names cited are real characters. Vicente Barrios, Captain Meza, Luiz Gonzales were officers leading the invasion of Mato Grosso. On the Brazilian side, Pakalala, Minister Paranhos, Almeida Rosa, the Viscountess, most military leaders like Caldwell or Von Gilsa, and even the little Franz Schmidt are all true figures.

The family Gomes de Carvalho, as well as the Werthers, Nopitena, and the Picagua brothers, are fictitious in their names, but represent the average citizens afflicted by the bloodiest war in South-American history.

The events described are historical marks. From the siege of Coimbra and the river battle of Corumba—when the murdered Brazilian sailors had their ears hanged in the sails—to the assault of Corrientes. While Amaru and Arami are fictitious, indeed Paraguayans killed civilians who refused to accept their money in Corrientes.

The bibliographical references are in the next pages. I spent over a year reading documents and contacting historians in multiple countries to give the plot a decent factual basis. I took, although, a fair share of liberties—the Kadiweu body painting, for example, was not permanent as a tattoo, and needed to be retouched often.

In the middle of 1865, Solano Lopez, excited by his incredible streak of victories, ordered his entire fleet to sail south, to the Argentinian province of Corrientes.

Meantime, thirty-seven thousand soldiers (more than the armies of Brazil, Argentina, and Uruguay combined) occupied Corrientes. Of those, twelve thousand marched towards Sao Borja under the command of General Estigarribia.

Sao Borja, the same city where our friends Luis, Martin, Nopitena, Primo, and Gaspar Picagua camped, together with less than 700 fatherland volunteers under the command of Joao Manuel Menna Barreto.

For the second time, destiny reserves to Lieutenant Luis a clash against overwhelming odds.

Not only his military skills, but the spirit of him and his men will be tested. Will Nopitena avenge the destruction of his village? Will Gaspar fight at the side of those who tortured and almost executed him? Will Primo fulfill the promise made to Joana? Will Martin and his Dreyse do what his father couldn't?

Will Luis Caetano Gomes de Carvalho lead his men to glory or death?

The Platine Region is Burning

The next volume of the series *Frontiers of Fire* is coming soon, in 2022.

To get an invitation for an exclusive pre-sale (with a 50% discount), and also have access to side stories from Melo Bravo, Taunay and Almeida Rosa, join our list on the link below:

https://borbadesouza.ck.page/

See you again in the middle of 2022.

Borba de Souza

Bibliography

Some people consider a bibliography at the end of a novel to be a pompous and inconvenient thing. It may be a fair point.

But I still added it because of a personal philosophy: give credit where credit is due.

ARAÚJO, Maria Lucília Viveiros. As práticas testamentárias paulistanas da primeira metade do século XIX. Simpósio Nacional de História, 2005.

BENTO, Claudio Moreira. Forte de Coimbra - MS, Dois Séculos de História, Fé e Glórias. Biblioteca do Exército.

BRAZIL, Maria do Carmo. O Rio Paraguai e a Guerra. Anais do XXVI Simpósio Nacional de História – ANPUH, 2011

Canhoneira Anhambai (1858-1869), Histórico de Navios. Diretoria do Patrimônio Histórico e Documentação da Marinha.

DAMASCENO, Filadelfo Reis. O Ataque ao Forte de Coimbra. Revista A Defesa Nacional v. 52 n. 606, 1966

DIAS, Satyro de Oliveira. Duque de Caxias e a Guerra do Paraguay. Typographia do Diario, 1870

DORATIOTO, Francisco. Maldita guerra: nova história da Guerra do Paraguai. Companhia das Letras, 2002,

GAY, Cônego João Pedro. Invasao Paraguaia na Fronteira com o Uruguai. Edições do Senado Federal – Vol. 177, 2014

GRIFFITHS, Glyn. Dicionário Da Língua Kadiwéu. SIL International, 2002

JACEGUAI, Artur. Reminiscências da Guerra do Paraguai. Edições do Senado Federal – Vol. 152, 2011

KELLER, Hector. Juegos Y Deportes de Los Guaraníes de Misiones, Argentina. Bonplandia, 2011

MEIRELLES, Victor. Croquis de diversas Embarcações Brasileiras 1832-1903. Biblioteca Nacional

PARREIRA, Luiz Eduardo Silva. Mello Bravo! Report to Brazilian Army Historic Bureau, 2019

SEIDLER, Carl. Dez Anos no Brasil: Dez anos no Brasil, 1835 - Durante o governo de Dom Pedro e após seu destronamento - Com atenção especial ao destino de tropas estrangeiras e colonos alemães. Editora Ruta, 2020

SILVA, Adilson. Caxias, o estrategista: Análise da vida do Duque de Caxias. 2018

SILVA, Alfredo P. M. Silva. Os Generaes do Exercito Brasileiro 1822 a 1899. M. Orosco & C, 1906

TUOHY, John. Biographical Sketches from the Paraguayan War - 1864-1870. 2011

YGUA, Ruben. A Guerra Do Paraguai: Cronologia 1865-1870. 2019

Printed in Great Britain
by Amazon